*L*ifting a hand, Kian touched one of the curls that had fallen loose from the simple arrangement which she wore each day.

"You're going to cause such a stir in Town, Loris. You must be careful not to let any gentleman do anything foolish. I should hate to have to harm anyone."

It took Loris a moment to realize what he meant.

"You can't be serious, Kian." She slapped his hand away.

His amusement died, and he took her chin in a firm, but careful, grasp, keeping her gaze steadily on his.

"I believe I could even kill a man if he harmed you, Loris. You know how I feel, and regardless of your own emotions, you accept that I'm speaking the truth. I love you. You're mine. I won't tolerate another man forcing his attentions on you."

Loris twisted away, furious as only Kian could make her.

"You'd best make up your mind, my lord. And when you do finally decide what you want of me, be so kind as to let me know. Until then, I'd prefer not to speak on the matter."

"What I want of you?" Kian repeated, his own angry expression mirroring hers. "Damn you, Loris! I dread the days and nights that are to come, being parted from you. But you don't wish to speak of that, either, do you? Or of what's between us?"

"There is *nothing* between us," she countered. "Save a seemingly never-ending conflict. Why can we never have five minutes of peace between us, Kian? God above." She set a hand to her head, where an ache was beginning to throb. "Perhaps a trip to London will be welcome, after all. I shall have a little peace while I'm there, at least."

"No, my love, that you won't," Kian said, and before she could move away, he gathered her up in his arms. "And neither will I."

He set his lips over hers, kissing her in the manner that always made her lose her senses . . .

St. Martin's Paperbacks Titles
by Susan Spencer Paul

Touch of Night

Touch of Passion

Touch of

Passion

Susan Spencer Paul

St. Martin's Paperbacks

TOUCH OF PASSION

Copyright © 2005 by Susan Spencer Paul.

Excerpt from *Touch of Desire* copyright © 2005 by Susan Spencer Paul.

On front cover:
Photo of man © Phil Heffernan
Photo of landscape © Superstock
Photo of sky © PHOTODISC

ISBN: 0-312-93388-6
EAN: 9780312-93388-3

Printed in the United States of America

St. Martin's Paperbacks edition / December 2005

St. Martin's Paperbacks are published by St. Martin's Press, 175 Fifth Avenue, New York, NY 10010.

10 9 8 7 6 5 4 3 2 1

Prologue

Not the Red Fox again. We've gone there almost every night this past month and I'm sore weary of it. Dyfed threw a card onto the table and looked with consternation at his brother, who sat idly across from him. *And you've already had all the women there at least once, and most of them twice and three times. I don't know why you want to go to that filthy pit again.*

Kian regarded the cards he held with a smile. "Speak aloud, if you please, *fy gefell*," he said. "You're not to use the silent speech while we're in London, remember, lest you make a mistake while we're in company with mere mortals." With care, he placed three cards down, one next to the other. "As to the Red Fox," he continued pleasantly, "I happen to like it. And since you *haven't* had all the women there, I should think you'd want to go. You hate unfinished business." He glanced up at his brother with a knowing look, grinning.

Dyfed's cheeks pinked with a mixture of anger and embarrassment. "You've kept them all too occupied for anyone else to have a share. I can scarce be blamed for the outcome of your"—he cast about for the right word—"extravagance," then regretted the choice when Kian laughed with clear amusement.

"What's that you're saying, lad?" a gravelly voice demanded from the high-backed chair set near the fire. The next moment their father's well-lined face, framed by both a crown of shaggy, unkempt hair and an equally disheveled beard, peered around at them. "Kian's taking two at a time again, is he? I've warned you against such behavior, my boy. You're far too young for such nonsense, and will do yourself an injury. No more of that, now, or it's back to Wales for the both of you."

"It isn't two at a time, Father," Kian assured his parent. "It's just Dyfed being slow. His usual thorough self. He can't keep up, as ever."

"That's all right then," Baron Tylluan replied before Dyfed could make an angry rejoinder. "But I want you being careful. If your cousin the earl, may God bless and keep him, hears that I've let you loose in London again, he'll be at our door before we can think of any good excuse. You'll remember what he thought of your last visit to Town."

Even Kian lost his usual smirk. "Could we ever forget?" he asked. "I've never seen Malachi so angry."

"Have you not?" said his father. "Then I fear you've a short memory, my lad, for you've forgotten his fury after that fire you started on the docks. That was but three years past. And the riot that the two of you sparked in that gaming hell two years past. God help us, but that was a bad time. It wasn't only the earl who was obliged to keep you from the law, then, but your cousin Niclas, as well."

"Don't speak of it," Dyfed murmured pleadingly. "There's nothing so awful as having both the *Dewin Mawr* and Cousin Niclas furious at us."

"I should be glad never to speak of any of those unpleasant times again," their father replied sternly, "and far more glad if you'll give no cause for a repeat of such occasions. No fires," he commanded. "No burning *anything*. No riots. And above all, *no* magic."

• • •

The inn was busier than usual for a midweek night, for which Loris was grateful. The keeper and his wife were both in a foul mood, and having more customers to clean up after kept Loris from having to work either behind the bar or in the kitchen quite so much, where their hard, callused hands so often found cause to strike her cheeks.

And there was much cleaning to do, for the crowd was already unruly, spilling drinks and tobacco ashes on tables and chairs and on Loris, too, when she made the mistake of passing too close by. But she had learned to be quick and careful at the inn, especially on nights like this. Some of the rougher customers were given to touching any passing female if they had the chance, and she couldn't bear to feel their hands slapping, pinching, or roaming over her. The girls who worked above the inn called her foolish, but Loris could never accustom herself to the thought of letting any man grope her. Not even for money. The girls assured her that one day it would be otherwise, for she'd have little choice if she wished to keep eating, but the very thought made Loris ill.

And so she scrubbed the floors and tables and worked very hard, hoping that it would be enough to make the Goodbodys keep her as a servant. Her labor for them was free, excepting food and keep, but, of late, the Goodbodys had complained even about that small expense.

Two men sitting at one of the far tables rose to join a card game taking place at another, and Loris snatched up her tray and a cloth and moved quickly to clear it before anyone else sat there. Mrs. Goodbody didn't care so much about the comfort of the customers, but she kept close count of her tankards and glasses, and if one should go missing, Loris would find herself the worse for it.

She made her way through the smoke and noise, squeezing past the rough horde and striving to keep from being knocked aside.

Shifting the heavy wooden tray comfortably against her hip, Loris began to clear the table of mugs and glasses. The battered top was wet with ale and sour-smelling wine, and it was a difficult task to wipe it clean while balancing the tray. She did so quickly, though, for she still had bruises from the slaps Mrs. Goodbody had given her that morning for being too slow in sweeping the floors.

"Where's the serving wench?" A rough hand tugged at her sleeve, nearly sending the tray to the floor.

Loris purposefully kept her eyes on the table before her. It never did to look into the faces of the patrons. They were rough and lewd, on the main, and she had discovered that paying them any attention at all could lead to trouble.

"I'll go and find her, sir," she said loudly over the tavern's raucous din, and reached to wipe away the last few wet spots from the tabletop.

"Find her now!" he demanded, grabbing Loris by the elbow and forcibly swinging her about.

The tray slipped; Loris struggled to free herself in time to grab it, but it was impossible. She shut her eyes against the impending crash . . . only to find that it didn't happen.

"Let her go."

She recognized the voice, and her eyes flew open. It was one of the young gentlemen who'd been causing such a stir in the Red Fox these past few weeks. Twins, they were, handsome, rich young lordlings, slender and tall, with remarkable white-blond hair and chilling blue eyes. She had never seen anyone like them before.

They seemed hardly to be much older than Loris, and yet they had proved to be equal to the most dangerous rogues who frequented the tavern. The girls above stairs fought over the twins' favors, while the men below sought their company for gambling and fighting. One night Loris had seen the one who'd just spoken take on a much older, stronger man in a contest of swords and win. Another night he had gambled thousands of pounds against a notorious pirate merely for the company of one of the upstairs girls—a girl who would eagerly greet him at any time of day or night—and had come away with both the money and the desired companionship.

The pirate had protested, a brawl had ensued, and the young lordling had still come out on his feet, laughing merrily once all the fighting was done and the pirate and his crew vanquished.

His brother, who stood on Loris's other side, was as different as he could possibly be. He was far gentler and quieter in manner and, according to the girls who had lain with him, exceedingly kind and considerate. He gambled but little and only fought if his wild brother needed aid. But that, as Loris had seen, was seldom the case, for the first appeared to be fully capable of defending himself. More often than not it was left to the gentler brother to stop brawls before they began and to make peace when his sibling had angered a rival.

"I said," the first repeated in a soft, menacing tone, "let her go. Now."

The grip on her elbow tightened until Loris nearly buckled from the pain, and her angry captor rose, pulling her up with him until she stood on her toes. He was a big, tall man and very strong. With a single jerk of his wrist he brought her hard up against his side.

"And I suppose you'll make me, boy?"

The noise in the tavern began to die away. With a sinking heart, Loris could see Mr. Goodbody frantically pushing his way out from behind the bar, an angry expression on his florid face.

The handsome young gentleman smiled and lifted a slender, long-fingered hand. "Yes," he murmured, "I shall."

With a swiftness that seemed inhuman, he had placed his outstretched fingers upon the hand that gripped Loris, and the next thing she knew, she was released. The man cried out and fell to the floor, writhing beneath the fingers that still touched him as if their simple pressure alone were somehow imparting great pain to his entire body.

It was impossible that such a big, brawny man could be harmed merely by a touch, yet he knelt on the floor before her very eyes, crying out and begging for mercy.

The young gentleman scarce paid his captive any mind and

instead glanced at his twin. "I remember precisely what Father said, Dyfed," he commented, as if in answer to some silent question. "I'm not burning anything, and this could hardly qualify as a riot. As to the other, I'm only using a very little, and only for the noble cause of rescuing a helpless female. Malachi would scarcely be alarmed. And if you're so concerned about spectacle, you might recall that we're in public."

"I forgot," his brother replied with a flush of obvious aggravation. "You made me forget with your wild . . . your wild . . ." He seemed not to be able to find the right word and, when his brother laughed, finished angrily, saying, "*Why* must you always go straight into every trouble that presents itself? For pity's sake, let the man go!"

"In a moment," said the other, calmly returning his gaze to the pleading man who knelt before him. "I want to make certain he's learned his lesson."

His brother set aside the tray he'd yet been holding and, with a gentle hand on Loris's arm, pulled her back from the shocking sight. All around them the crowd pressed in, as amazed by the spectacle as Loris.

"Malachi *will* be furious," he shouted above the keen cries of pain. "Regardless of the circumstances. Do you really want to have another audience of that sort with the *Dewin Mawr*?"

"Oh, very well," the other replied, reluctantly releasing his victim.

The big man fell to the ground, whimpering with relief, and was at once dragged away by his friends, some of whom glanced back at the young lordling with fear and disbelief.

"Aye, take him away," he advised, "and teach him some manners. Ah, Mr. Goodbody"—his tone cheered as the innkeeper reached them—"well met, sir."

The Goodbodys found the custom of these particular young gentlemen to be most welcome, for they always had money and spent it freely. Mr. Goodbody, at the moment, looked very nervous about the thought of losing such desirable patrons.

"I'm sorry, sir," he said at once, his breathing labored from his hurry to reach them. "We do get that kind in from time to time. I apologize if you were bothered. He'll not be let in again, nor his friends. Loris! Stupid girl!" Grabbing her by the shoulder, he gave her a rough push toward the bar. "Get out of here and stop causing trouble. Leave these gentlemen be and fetch Tilda to serve them."

"Stop," the gentleman who'd rescued Loris said, in a tone of voice that even Mr. Goodbody was forced to obey. "The young miss did nothing wrong. She must not be scolded." Moving nearer, he handed Loris her tray. "Indeed, she was merely clearing a table for us when she was so rudely assaulted." He gazed at her for a long moment before turning back to Mr. Goodbody and saying, "Don't ever touch her in such a manner again. She is never to be harmed."

Loris's eyes widened, and she glanced at the innkeeper. If any other man had said such a thing to Mr. Goodbody, no matter how rich, he would have been barred from the Red Fox forever. But the way this young lord had spoken seemed to have stunned Mr. Goodbody into submission, for he merely nodded, bowed, and moved away.

"Are you all right now, miss?"

He was gazing at her with genuine concern, she saw when she dared to glance at him, the usually mocking expression absent from his handsome face.

"Yes, sir," she murmured, clutching the tray against her chest. "Thank you, sir."

"Leave the poor girl be, Kian," his brother said. "Can't you see that she's afraid of you?"

Without another word Loris curtsied and turned about, heading through the smoke toward the kitchen.

Five minutes later she stood in the damp alleyway, shivering in the cold, foggy night air, her ears yet ringing with Mrs. Goodbody's angry voice and her cheek stinging from the sharp slap she'd been given for being the cause of so much trouble. It occurred to her that the young gentleman had perhaps given his command to the wrong person.

Loris was grateful for a brief respite, though it was likely to earn her another slap, for she had sneaked outside without permission. And she was glad, too, for the cold air, despite her shivering, because the very sharpness of it helped to clear the remnants of noise and bitter smoke out of her ears and eyes.

With a sigh, Loris leaned against the clammy brick wall and relaxed. The shouts and laughter coming from the tavern's side door were dimmed here, sounding far more pleasant and cheerful. They were among the earliest sounds she could remember from her childhood: men and women laughing, drinking, and shouting with merriment or sudden anger. There were variations, depending upon the place and time and mood of the customers, but the sounds were always the same.

She often wondered what life beyond London's docks was like. Her parents had told her stories of other places, of the beautiful countryside where they had both grown up, but these had seemed like nothing more than unreal fairy tales to Loris. Her father had promised to take her out of London someday, to show her that he and her mother were speaking the truth about flowers and trees and unending valleys carpeted with green, but, like most of his hopes, it had never come to pass. His love of gaming had made all three of them captives to the docks and rookeries. When her mother died, Loris had felt, along with the loss and grief, a measure of envy. Heaven, she believed, would be welcome to all those who had lived in London's cold, dark, filthy alleyways.

There had just been the two of them after that, Loris and her father. Somewhere, she knew, there were other relatives, for once she'd overheard her mother speak wistfully of going home to repair matters with her parents, but Loris's father had quickly hushed her and insisted that there was no going back. And he had forbidden her to speak of such things in front of Loris again. Even as her mother neared death and had pleaded with him to at least let their families know about Loris, her father had remained unmoved. It was the only thing Loris could remember him denying his wife and, realizing how strongly he felt about their families, she'd never found the courage to question him about them. Not a day went by now that she didn't regret that reticence. Even if her parents' families had been cruel and horrid, throwing herself on their mercies surely wouldn't have been worse than being dependent on the Goodbodys. At the very least she would have been among her own people.

Perhaps her father had not been the best or wisest of parents, spending so much of his time and their modest funds in taverns and gaming hells, but he'd done his best to keep her safe and clothed and fed. More than that, he'd called upon the formal education he'd received in his youth and taught Loris to read, write, and do simple sums.

Those had been happy times, when Loris and her father had talked of so many better dreams, when he had foolishly thought that his daughter might somehow find her way out of the docks. Perhaps if he'd realized that his gaming and drinking would one day leave Loris without any hope at all, he would have stopped.

But it was foolish to recall such things now. She had been born in a tavern, would live all her life in and among them, and would die either in or because of one, just as both her parents had done.

"Aren't you cold?"

The voice startled her, but she knew at once who it was and turned her head to look at him.

He stood but a few steps away, near the open kitchen door, the tavern's dim light and smoke drifting out behind him, both illuminating and obscuring his tall, slender figure.

"No," she said without thought, stupidly, then, realizing how foolish that sounded, especially as she stood there shivering, amended, "Yes."

He took a step nearer; Loris pushed away from the wall and stood upright, watching him warily. He had been kind to her, but she had learned in her childhood to be careful with all men, even those who seemed kind.

"I mean you no harm," he said soothingly as he came near, his face and figure growing clearer in the mist. "I could not harm you, Loris, even if I had some wrong wish to do so." He stopped and gazed at her very directly. "But that moment will never come."

She was still wary, despite the gentleness of his words. He was a shockingly handsome youth, and that, coupled with his obvious wealth, probably meant that he'd been spoiled beyond all reason. Why else would so young a gentleman frequent a tavern like the Red Fox? In such places he was treated like a full-grown man, especially by the whores. He had no cause to treat her with anything other than guile in order to gain what he wished.

Everything about him bespoke wealth and high birth, from his tailored clothes to his finely formed features. His long, unusually light-colored hair was neatly tied back upon his neck. His blue eyes were disarmingly clear, so that they made her think of sparkling crystal, and yet were as penetrating as a hot sun. And his face was, simply, alarmingly beautiful. She'd never seen the like. He looked otherworldly, like one of the characters in the fairy stories that her father had told her at bedtime, slender and regal, almost delicate in form, yet undeniably powerful.

Loris knew which twin he was. From the very first night they'd come, from the very first moment she'd seen him, she had known who he was. Probably, she told herself, because of his expression, which was far more cunning than that of his brother. She wasn't truly afraid of him but recognized the look of a fearless, dangerous man when she saw one.

"She struck you," he said, and lifted a hand to touch her still-stinging cheek.

Loris stepped away. "How do you know that? You can't see that well in this darkness. Or did you hear what she said to me in the kitchen?"

"I didn't hear it," he told her, moving forward with purposeful care, clearly striving to not frighten her. "But I know she hurt you. I can make it better. Let me." Slowly, he stretched his hand out, and his fingers stroked her cheek with a gentle, tender touch. "You see?"

The stinging began to fade and within but moments had gone altogether, so that she could feel nothing but the pleasurable caress of his fingertips.

He had drawn even closer, so near that Loris could feel the warmth of his body. She stood, transfixed by the intense blue eyes, so light that they were visible even in the darkness, and wondered if he possessed some kind of hypnotizing magic. She felt captive, as if she couldn't move while he stood there, his hand resting now upon her cheek, warm and strong.

Loris had felt this way with him once before, on that first night when he and his brother had come to the Red Fox, well over a month ago. There had been a moment during the night when she had passed near his table and their eyes met . . . and he had stared at her almost as he was doing now. She had felt captive then, too, and drawn to him in an irresistible way. But the moment had passed, and Loris told herself that it had only been a trick of her mind. The fine young lord couldn't have truly taken notice of her. It had simply been a mistake. A dream.

But this wasn't. He was very real, standing before her. And he was gazing at her in the same compelling manner as he had then.

"Loris," he murmured, and smiled, seeming pleased by the sound of the word. "How did you come to be given such a name? I have never heard it before."

"My father named me," she replied, her voice small and thin to her ears.

"It's beautiful," he said, still smiling. "As you are. You have such lovely hair, like gold"—his fingers slid upward, touching one of the unruly curls that had come loose from the ribbon she'd tied it up with earlier—"and such dark, pretty eyes. It wouldn't have mattered what you look like, but I confess to being glad that you're so pleasant to gaze upon."

She opened her mouth to protest the compliments, as she knew she should do, but couldn't. The words were far too sweet, and he said them in such a wonderful manner. No one but her parents had ever spoken so kindly to her before.

"Where is your father?" he asked. "And your mother? How did you come to be at the Red Fox?"

"My parents are dead," she told him. "My father often gambled here, before he fell ill. When he died, the Goodbodys were kind enough to take me in." She left out the fact that they had demanded her service in payment for the money her father had owed them.

Sympathy filled his gaze, and he murmured, "I'm sorry. If I'd only known earlier that you were here, alone, I would have found a way to come to you. But of course that would have been impossible," he added, a touch of sudden amusement in his tone, "for I didn't truly believe you existed until I set sight on you. And even after that it took some weeks before I at last believed the truth."

Loris reached up to the hand that yet cradled her face with the intention of pushing it away, but before she could do so his fingers folded over her own in a movement so quick that she couldn't comprehend how it was that their hands were suddenly clasped.

"Sir—"

"I'll not harm you," he said again, and lowered her captive hand to gaze at it. "I realize that you have no cause to think well of me. I've done nothing to gain your goodwill these past several days"—he glanced up, looking suddenly embarrassed—"though I have wished for it. You see, I am not always kind, as my brother is, and when I first saw you and felt such strange magic, I fought hard against it." He sounded nervous, as if he were making a confession of grave wrongdoing. Clearing his throat, he pressed on. "My behavior when you've been present has been . . . well, perhaps we shouldn't speak of it in detail." He gave a small shake of his head. "I wish I'd not been so free with the other women in front of you, but it can't be helped now. I thought, at the time, it might somehow change things, but that was a foolish wish. You've no need to fear that the behavior will continue." He lifted his other hand so that hers was completely enveloped in a warming clasp and smiled at her reassuringly. "Now that I'm certain of what's happened, I'll be different. Everything will be different, Loris. You need never worry. I shall be faithful, even if I have not been before."

Loris began to feel rather alarmed at this incoherent speech, and at his strange behavior. "There's no need to say such things to me, sir. I must go back in now, if you please."

He didn't release her. Instead, he continued speaking. "The trouble was," he said, as if she should already understand, "that I didn't truly believe what my family had told me about such things. But it happened all the same, just as they said it would. I was so taken aback." He laughed softly. "It was like being run down by a post coach. I scarce knew who I was. And what a strange place to find one's destiny." He cast a glance back at the light that spilled out of the tavern's open doorway. "I always thought it would be in Wales, if it was going to happen at all, at some party or ball or family gathering. But, except for what you've suffered here, I don't mind this being the place." He smiled at her warmly and lightly squeezed her hand. "I'm just glad it's happened."

"Please, sir," she pleaded, "I only came out for a moment, and must go back in. Mrs. Goodbody will be very angry if she finds me gone."

"Oh, you needn't worry about her any longer, for I shall take care of you now. You must come to live with us until you've grown old enough for marriage. What are you? Thirteen? Fourteen?" He laughed again. "So young—I'm still amazed to think of it. But it is just as well, for you'll have time to get to know me. I'm just turned seventeen, so we're well matched. I don't think I could have borne a very great difference in ages, could you?"

He was mad, she decided. Completely crazed. Or drunk. Or, more likely, both. Loris began to tug at her hand.

"Sir . . . my lord . . ."

"Kian," he corrected. "I should have told you that before, but I fear my wits have gone begging." He released her at last and stepped back to make her a formal bow. "Kian Seymour, of Castle Tylluan in Montgomeryshire, North Wales." He straightened. "You'll love Tylluan, for there is scarce more beautiful land on God's earth. My father is Baron Tylluan. You'll like him, too, once you've had a chance to get used to him. He is rather mad much of the time, but harmlessly so. And he'll love you—he's always longed for a daughter." He turned his head slightly, toward the open kitchen door. "And here is my brother coming to find me. Dyfed!" he shouted. "I'm here, in the alley, and I'm in company, so mind how you speak."

His brother's blond head appeared from around the door, illuminated by the light. He stared at them for a silent moment until he was able to make out their figures in the foggy darkness.

"Kian, for God's sake, what are you doing out here?"

"Speaking to beautiful Loris," Kian said happily, moving quickly to pull Dyfed out of the tavern complete and in Loris's direction. "You've both already met in a way, though perhaps you are not aware of each other's names. Dyfed, this is Loris. Loris, this is my brother, Dyfed Seymour. He's the younger, if you were worried about that. I am the inheritor of the lands and title."

Loris stared from one to the other, wondering whether she should start screaming for help. But the look on the face of the second twin stopped her. He was clearly as bewildered and concerned as she was, and that gave her a small measure of comfort.

"Kian, how could you?" he asked in a low tone, sounding utterly disgusted. "She's but a child."

His elder brother frowned at him. "It isn't like that. Not at all."

"I know *just* what it's like," the other said. "You've gone too far this time, Kian. It's worse than two or even three at a time. I'm sickened to think of what you intended. And if you've done this child any harm I shall make you pay for it dearly. Come, girl, and I'll take you safe inside." He reached out a hand, and Loris took it gladly.

Kian stepped in their way. "You'll not take her anywhere," he said. "You misunderstand everything, Dyfed, and give both Loris and me great insult."

Loris began to tremble and felt the younger brother's comforting arm come about her.

"Do I?" he countered angrily. "I suppose you were discussing British history with the young miss, or perhaps your favorite passages from *The Mabinogion*? Don't take me for a fool. I know you too well to believe such lies. I shall tell Father of this, and perhaps even Malachi."

Kian took a step nearer, his expression one of fury, and began to speak harshly in a strange language that Loris didn't understand. His brother countered in kind, and soon they were shouting at each other in the indecipherable tongue.

She'd had more than enough and broke away, running too quickly for the elder brother to catch her, though he certainly tried. He might have had better luck if his twin hadn't grabbed his arm and forcibly held him back.

"Loris!" she heard him cry, but she pushed her way into the kitchen, not looking back.

"Damn you, Dyfed! Let me go!"

Kian tried to shake his brother off, but Dyfed held him fast.

"What's the matter with you?" Dyfed demanded. "From the first time you lay with a female you preferred full-grown women, and there are plenty of them here to satisfy you. Leave that young girl be."

"Idiot!" Kian shouted furiously. "It has nothing to do with that!"

Dyfed's grasp only grew stronger. "What does it have to do with, then?" he demanded. "Tell me and I'll let you go."

"Let me go *now*," Kian said in a warning tone, "or I'll make you do so. Your powers are nothing to mine."

"Aye, your powers are stronger," Dyfed agreed, "but I've strength enough to hold you until I can make you see sense."

Kian made a sound of complete exasperation. "There's nothing to make sense of. I can't tell you anything yet. Not until I've talked to Father. And Malachi."

"What do they have to do with it?"

"I have to explain something to them. That's all. Dyfed, let me go!"

"Tell me what you have to explain," Dyfed insisted, "and why the girl matters."

"Because," Kian said with impatience, "I want her to come and live with us at Castle Tylluan. That's *all* I'm telling you now."

Dyfed pulled his brother closer, looking carefully into his face. "You want to take her to Tylluan?" he repeated with disbelief. "A young girl, among so many rude men? A stranger to us, who knows nothing of our ways, nothing of magic?"

"I know it's odd," Kian admitted. "I felt the same way only days ago. But I'm telling you that it *must* be."

"And I'm telling you that it cannot be," said Dyfed, releasing him at last, slowly. "I've just learned that she's being sold to Gregor Foss. He's to take her this very night. Mrs. Goodbody told me so when she saw you follow the girl out here."

Kian was stunned. Gregor Foss was overlord to one of London's most dangerous rookeries and counted among the deadliest men in the city. Kian had gambled with the fellow once before at the Red Fox and had decided never to do so again, even though Kian had come out the winner. Foss wasn't a man who took losing lightly, and Kian wasn't so foolish as to press his luck with a man who'd as soon kill him for a half crown as win it.

A chilly wind riffled his hair and sent shivers coursing down the length of his spine. "That's not possible," he said, shaking his head. "He'd have no interest in a mere girl like . . ." Then realization struck. "He wants her for one of his whores," he said, anger rapidly taking the place of incredulity.

Gregor Foss was one of those who liked starting his whores young so that he might make the most profit from them. Women who plied their trade on the docks tended to die at an early age; a girl of thirteen would last a good ten years, at least, before falling ill. And Foss would be more than willing to pay a goodly sum for a beauty like Loris, for whose company he could demand a higher price.

Kian's anger soared. The very idea of another man so much as touching the one who had been destined as his filled him with an uncontrollable wrath.

"He'll *not* have Loris," he vowed harshly. *"Ever."*

Dyfed reached out to grasp Kian's arm again. "You can't stop him without using magic," he said firmly. "He's too big and has too many of his men with him. He'll try to shoot you the moment you say a word against him, or attempt to stick a knife in you. You'll be forced to use magic to stop him. Either way it's going to be a terrible mistake. If you must rescue the girl, at least let me call for Malachi or Niclas. They'll take care of it without any trouble."

"There's not enough time," Kian said curtly, shrugging free. "We don't even know whether Lord Graymar is in London. And Cousin Niclas will be at some party or ball, as he ever is. It might take hours for you to get in touch with either of them."

"Give me ten minutes," said Dyfed. "Just let me try."

"I don't need their help," Kian retorted. "I can manage Foss on my own."

"Not without using magic," Dyfed said insistently. "And if you use more than you already have this night, we'll be banished from London forever. I don't *want* to be banished."

Kian gave him a look filled with scorn. "Your concern for Loris is astonishing, Brother. What happened to the champion of moments ago?"

"He's standing here being sensible, as usual," Dyfed shot back with matching contempt. "Please, Kian, just stop for once and *think* before you do something rash. Even if Foss takes the girl, Malachi can get her back before any harm comes to her. No one denies the Earl of Graymar anything that he demands, certainly not a knave like Foss. There's no need for you to be a fool and risk so much for the both of us."

"Oh yes, there is," Kian said softly, holding his brother's gaze. "Loris will be filled with fear if Foss takes her, and I'll not let her suffer even a moment if I can stop it. Now make your choice, Dyfed. You may come back inside, or send for help, or go home. It matters not to me what you decide, but I am going into the tavern *now*."

Gregor Foss was a big man. *Very* big. And powerfully built. He towered over more normal men and seemed to fill any room that he entered with his dark, hairy person.

Loris had always been terrified of him, knowing his reputation for violence, but never more than at this moment, when she realized that none of her pleading was going to change the Goodbodys' minds. Foss had offered them a sizable sum for her, and they'd be unlikely to turn it aside for the sake of a mere serving girl. Even if they'd wanted to do so, they would be far too afraid to anger so powerful a man by refusing him what he wanted.

His hands were in accord with his size; Loris could feel the strength in them as he ran his large palms over her arms and waist, examining his new purchase with a satisfied smile.

"There's a good, healthy girl you are. Pretty as a flower, and just as sweet I'd wager, eh?" He laughed and gave her a squeeze, then slid his meaty hands down to her hips, which he patted with more care. "What do you think, then, lads?" he asked the men who'd accompanied him, all of whom were sitting behind him, drinking ale and eyeing her with interest. "Is she worth what I paid?"

"Pretty," one of them agreed. "But she's a skinny little bit, ain't she?"

"Aye, that she is," Foss agreed. "Look how small her waist is. I can almost wrap a single hand full around it." He laughed again.

Another of the half-drunken men sat forward, a tankard wavering in his grip. "She's still growin'." He leered at Loris, his appreciative gaze wandering over her young figure. "Looks like she'll have what she needs in a year or two."

"I'll make a fortune off her long before then," Foss declared. "Only think what she'll bring after."

Loris stood captive, stunned beyond speech or movement. Mr. Goodbody's pronouncement that she'd been sold to Foss had caused a desperate, almost involuntary pleading on Loris's part, but the following realization of her situation had silenced her. From the moment Gregor Foss set his hands on her body, fear and shock had left her as chilled and immobile as stone. She knew she was present but felt far, far away. So far that when Kian Seymour reentered the tavern and began to push his way toward her with forceful purpose, she could scarce make her mind think of anything more useful than what a fine figure he made against the rough crowd filling the Red Fox.

He held her gaze as he approached, and she felt a dim hope—so faint that she could scarce hold on to it—that the young gentleman might be able to save her again. He might be half-mad, as evidenced by his behavior in the alley, but she would far rather go with him, anywhere, than spend another moment in Gregor Foss's unpleasant grip.

The tavern, already muted because of Foss's presence, grew more silent. Gregor Foss and his men took note and turned to watch as Kian Seymour made his way.

Despite the focus of his course, he looked, Loris thought, as relaxed and swaggering as any of the dissolute nobles who found their way to such dismal places. He smiled at Foss and his men as he neared Loris and greeted them easily.

"Good evening, Foss. I heard you'd come. I hope you're in a gaming mood. I thought we might try cards this time."

Foss's smile wasn't quite as friendly. He clearly hadn't forgotten the memorable night when the young gentleman had won a large sum from him in a game of dice. Though he'd attempted to engage Kian Seymour on other nights, he'd been rebuffed. But tonight the lordling appeared willing.

And that made Gregor Foss suspicious.

"Not tonight, Master Seymour," Foss replied in civil, if not particularly friendly, tones. "I'm busy just now. How d'you like this girl I've bought?" He grinned into Loris's pale face, revealing an unpleasant set of tilted, blackened teeth. "Ain't she a pretty little one?"

"Remarkably so," Kian replied without so much as a glance toward her. "I congratulate you. But women are readily available at all times and in all places, while money is not." Reaching inside his expensively tailored dark blue coat, he withdrew a small leather pouch, giving it a shake to show how full it was. "I've often wondered whether I might have the same luck against you as I once did, Foss. It was so simple a thing to take your money that I almost can't believe I didn't dream it."

Kian won the first game and lost the second. The third, almost finished, was falling his way, but nothing could be taken for granted. By some small grace he'd not been driven to use magic yet, which, despite Dyfed's belief, Kian was loath to do. The magic he'd used earlier to rescue Loris from her rude captor had been so minor as to be laughable, but this was entirely different, and far more serious. Gregor Foss's penchant for violence made it serious. Even if Kian could be discreet in using it, magic, just now, could ruin everything.

Loris stood to one side, watching the game with glazed eyes. She was clearly in shock, and Kian wanted nothing more than to finish this farce and get her out of the Red Fox and back to his father's town house, where she would be perfectly safe. And where Kian might do better in explaining himself than he had in the alley.

She must think him quite mad. He could scarce blame her; Kian had thought himself mad for the past month and more, since he'd first set sight on Loris. He could remember the moment vividly, could recall every thought, every feeling, on that fateful night when he and Dyfed had so casually entered the Red Fox, thinking only to entertain themselves, first with drink and games of chance, then with some of the women.

It had been the merest chance that they'd come—a thought that later gave Kian pause, considering how momentous the occasion had been—having been sent in the direction of the tavern by acquaintances they'd met earlier at a more respectable gaming hell. The women at the Red Fox, they'd been assured, weren't shy about performing certain tricks for well-paying customers. That had been sufficiently interesting to send Kian on his way, dragging an only partly unwilling Dyfed along.

Their entrance had made a stir, but they were used to such an initial reaction from the types of patrons who frequented dangerous places. The brothers' outward appearance, bespeaking wealth and gentility, roused the interest of the thieves and pickpockets present, but their demeanor, confident and completely unafraid, had given those same would-be assailants pause. Kian and Dyfed were well used to handling themselves among rough crowds. Indeed, Kian favored such company, finding it far more amusing than that of his peers. He liked a good fight, and they were far easier to come across in taverns like the Red Fox.

A good half hour passed before it happened—the single most significant experience he'd yet undergone in his seventeen years. A bolt of lightning coming through the tavern roof and striking him between the eyes couldn't have been more profound.

He had been sitting at a table—he remembered the precise location and exactly which chair—surrounded by a friendly group of fellows, a half-emptied tankard of ale at his elbow and a pair of dice clutched loosely in one hand. The other hand had been employed in keeping the plump, lively young woman he'd decided upon for the evening's amusement safely moored upon one knee—not an easy task, considering how delightfully and enthusiastically she wiggled whenever she became excited. Which was often, and for any and every reason. She had been writhing with particular energy—anticipating his toss of the dice—at the very moment Loris appeared.

She had only come to clear and wipe down a nearby table, bearing the rag and tray that he ever after saw her with. She looked weary and hot and with an impatient movement swiped a few stray curls back from her face. Normally, Kian never would have paid her more than a moment's notice, despite the fact that she was disarmingly pretty. But she was a mere girl, and he didn't care for females who were closer to his own age. He preferred older women, both within the *ton* and out of it. Even his first lover had been older than he—fifteen years older, in fact—and sufficiently enchanting that he'd thereafter developed an intense appreciation for the charms of grown women.

But something about Loris had captured his attention. There was a clarity, a sharpness, as if his eyes had never truly seen clearly and she alone was in focus. Everything else around him—sound, noise, sensation—dimmed, while she grew clearer and clearer. He almost thought he could divine her emotions, see through her eyes, know her feelings, both physical and mental. A sharp pain suddenly gripped him, deep within—so intense that the dice fell from his fingers, forgotten. He lifted his hand and pressed it against his chest, wondering if he was dying, and then . . . then Loris had turned and looked at him.

His companions were shouting at him to toss the dice; the girl on his lap was wriggling about and asking what was wrong. He knew it was so, but he wasn't truly aware of any of it or of them. There was only the girl—for he didn't know her name yet—and her eyes, beautiful dark eyes, glowing amber and gold, and that feeling of death. And life. Everything that had mattered to him before slid away, meaningless, and at the same moment something wonderful and new was being born.

He'd stood, pushing the girl who'd been on his lap slowly aside, and opened his mouth to say something. Loris must

have felt something, too, for her gaze softened, grew curious, and she took a step nearer. Kian's only desire in life at
that moment was to touch her, hear her voice, and she came
even nearer, her gaze fixed on his . . . and then Dyfed had set
a hand on Kian's shoulder and pulled him back down into
his chair and Mr. Goodbody appeared, shouting at Loris and
dragging her away.

Sound and sense returned, and Kian gave himself a firm
mental shake, telling himself that whatever had happened
had merely been an aberration, brought on, most likely, by
too much drink. But he couldn't put the girl from his mind
and found himself seeking her out with his eyes throughout
the remainder of the evening.

Days passed, but still he couldn't forget her or what
he'd felt. He certainly tried hard enough, bedding as many
females as his body could manage, drinking as much and
as frequently as he could, gaming at every opportunity—
recklessly, too—and starting numerous fights. All he managed
to do was exhaust himself, worry his father, and aggravate
Dyfed—especially when he forced him to continue returning
to the Red Fox, night after night.

Kian couldn't stay away from her, and he couldn't stop
thinking of her. And every time he walked through the tavern's doors and knew he was near her, he couldn't control
either his excitement or the pounding of his heart. He questioned the Goodbodys about Loris in as casual a manner as
possible, trying to discover who her people were, where her
parents were, and how she had come to be at the Red Fox.
He had learned very little. The Goodbodys assured him that
their serving girl was far beneath the notice of so fine a young
gentleman and were frustratingly vague.

A full month passed before Kian had at last begun to accept what had happened. He had never really cared much
about the prophecies that had been made regarding him at his
birth; he'd certainly never considered what they meant to his
future. The fact that a *unoliaeth*, or oneness, with a particular
female had been foretold as being part of his destiny hadn't

bothered him in the least. Many among their kind were destined for such unions, and Kian had supposed he'd be happy enough with whoever had been chosen for him. But he'd certainly not expected that she would be a mere mortal or that he'd find her in a place like the Red Fox, laboring as a common servant.

But none of that mattered. Kian knew she was the one. He would lie awake at night, hungry for the sight of her. Always the next day he would wait impatiently until he and Dyfed could at last begin their way toward the docks. Toward her.

Kian had expected that Loris would have the same intensity of feeling for him, even if she didn't understand it. But, clearly, she'd not yet been struck by lightning, as he had. Whatever interest she'd had in him that first night had long since been tempered by his wild and foolish behavior. He had acted terribly, especially with the women at the Red Fox, before at last coming to terms with what she meant to him. His energetic efforts to push Loris from his thoughts must have given her a very poor impression of him. One that would likely take a great deal of time to correct.

And then there had been his behavior toward her tonight. His own exuberance at finally deciding to claim her as his *unoliaeth* had clearly overridden all his senses. He had been clumsy and stupid and had frightened her. The knowledge made him even more determined to save her from Gregor Foss. Once Kian had Loris safely away, she would never again have to be afraid. Of anything or anyone. He would make certain of it.

Kian laid down his last card and saw, with immense relief, that he had won both the game and a great deal of Foss's money. He prayed it was the lion's share of what that man had on him tonight, else magic might become necessary, after all.

"That's it, then," Kian said with a smile, forcing a lightness into his tone that he was far from feeling. Casually, he began to pick up the various bills and coins on the table.

"Thank you, sir, for the sport. I'm glad to know I wasn't dreaming."

Foss's large hand fell upon the pile of money. "You'll not be quitting now," he said angrily. "Not until I've had a chance to win my money back."

There were moments when being wellborn had a certain value; this was one of them. Kian lifted one brow and gazed at Foss's hand in silence until Foss, breathing harshly, withdrew it. Only then did Kian look up at him.

"As a gentleman I shall, of course, be pleased to oblige any request you make of me, Mr. Foss."

It was gratifying to see Gregor Foss's face redden beneath the veiled contempt in the comment, but Kian wasn't sure it was enough to set the man off balance and keep him there. A clearheaded Foss was the last thing Kian wanted just now.

"We'll have a toss of the dice, then, if't pleases you," Foss said, reaching into his filthy shirt to pull out a small pouch.

"Perfectly," Kian acquiesced with a leisurely nod, though inwardly he filled with unease. Unlike the cards they had just gamed with, the dice Foss tended to use were cheats, a fact well known among those who dwelled in London's slums. Kian could counter that and had often done so before when the outcome hadn't been so important, but he would be required to use magic. "What wager shall we begin with?"

"You have all my money," Foss told him angrily. "Will you take my note? I'm good for it, as all here will attest to."

Those surrounding them, intently watching, murmured and nodded.

"I'm certain you are," Kian replied pleasantly, "and if I thought I should be in London long enough to collect, I would be more than happy to oblige. Unfortunately, I'm to leave for Wales at week's end, and must insist upon something more substantial. It needn't be anything of particular value." He glanced at Loris with feigned disinterest. "You could even use this girl you've just acquired."

Foss shook his head. "Not the girl. I want her."

"And there's no reason why you shouldn't have her," Kian replied with growing impatience. "I certainly have no need for such a female. I merely assumed Mr. Goodbody would buy her from me, *if* I win, after which he could again sell her to you. And as Mr. Goodbody is not, I believe, leaving for Wales at week's end, there is some likelihood that he'll have no difficulty in accepting your note."

Mr. Goodbody responded to this with a vigorous nod.

It didn't take long for Foss to agree. The man was unabashedly certain of winning.

"One roll t'decide the final winner," Foss said. "Highest score takes all." He handed Kian a worn pair of honest dice, keeping the fixed pair for himself. "We'll roll together, eh?"

"Certainly," Kian replied. "Who'll give the signal?"

One of Foss's men did, and the dice were rolled. Kian rolled a six and a five; Foss rolled two threes.

"Very well, that's settled." Kian began to rise.

Foss stopped him. "Wait!" He stared at the dice in disbelief. "That's not right. Someone must've jostled the table."

Kian sat down once more. "If you feel that is so, then we must try again."

"Aye, that we must," Foss said gruffly, picking up his pair.

They rolled six times more, and each, with the help of magic, landed in Kian's favor. Foss demanded that they switch dice and still he lost. After ten minutes, Kian was beginning to grow weary.

"I fear the night grows long, sir, and I must be on my way. I thank you once more for the sport." He stood with finality and stepped from the table, gazing at the avid crowd surrounding them. Loris, he saw, was now sitting in a nearby chair, her hands clasped tightly upon her lap, her head lowered. He wished she would look at him so that he might reassure her that all would be well.

"Mr. Goodbody, may I speak to you regarding the girl?"

Mr. Goodbody approached at once, all obsequiousness, saying, "I shall be more than happy to pay what Mr. Foss gave for her, sir. More than happy. I shall go and fetch the money direct."

"Let me have a better look at her, first, to make certain of her worth," Kian said. "Her name is Loris, is it not?"

"Aye, sir, it is. Loris! Get up, girl, and let Mr. Seymour have a look at you."

She rose from her chair and moved slowly, her head yet lowered, and came to a stop before him.

Kian set a finger beneath her chin to lift her gaze to his and was dismayed at what he found. Her eyes were damp with tears and filled with fear. But there was also a spark of hope, and a plea for help. Kian excelled at deception, but it was nearly impossible for him to maintain his composure. He longed to draw her into his arms and make her know that he would always keep her safe.

Holding her gaze, he spoke his next words carefully, striving not to let the effect her reaction had on him show.

"Do you know, she is rather pretty. And healthy, to all appearances." He set his hands on her shoulders and turned Loris from side to side, examining her. "I believe I'll keep her, after all."

"No!" Gregor Foss roared, shoving away the table at which he sat while the rest of the tavern broke into loud, confused noise. "You'll not have her!"

Two things happened as Kian turned to face him. Foss stood and pulled a pistol from his belt, and Dyfed burst into the tavern, followed by their cousin, the Earl of Graymar, whose fury as he entered was evinced by a blast of wind that blew all the doors and shutters open and made the windows rattle.

It was precisely the distraction Kian needed. Shoving Loris in Dyfed's direction, Kian lunged at Foss with supernatural speed, an arm outstretched to grasp the hand holding the pistol. If Kian could but touch Foss, he could overpower him without endangering anyone else.

But it was too late. The pistol rang out, striking Kian's shoulder and sending him flying. He landed on his back with a grunt of pain. Loris screamed and Dyfed shouted Kian's name. Malachi swore as only Malachi could, with a sharpness that made all those who heard it recoil as if they'd been physically struck.

Blackness and pain washed over Kian, and he struggled to keep from losing his senses. The room spun wildly with color and sound, and yet somehow he saw Foss, his face set with rage, coming straight at him, a knife in his fist.

With every ounce of strength he possessed, Kian lifted the arm from his uninjured shoulder and focused on Foss. He pushed at the air with his hand and saw, with dim vision, Foss flying into the nearest wall. Some of his men were caught in the powerful magic and flew with their master, each, like Foss, impacting with a loud *thud* and then sliding to the floor, insensate.

There was a brief, stunned silence, and then the tavern exploded again with sound and activity. Feet thundered past Kian as he slumped back to the filthy floor, blurring his already troubled vision.

Kian!

Dyfed's alarm flooded Kian's mind, and he reached out to grasp his brother's arm as Dyfed knelt beside him. Fear made Dyfed forget to speak aloud.

Are you all right? Oh, God, you're bleeding.

"Where's Loris?"

She's safe. Don't worry over her. But you . . .

Kian gripped Dyfed more tightly. "Swear to me that you'll bring her with us. Take her to Father. Don't leave her behind. Swear it!"

Before Dyfed could reply, he was physically lifted off the floor and set aside.

"Let me have a look at him."

The Earl of Graymar's angry, formidable face appeared, and, markedly different from all the other times when he'd caused trouble, Kian was incredibly glad to see it. "Malachi," he murmured, and with an overwhelming sense of relief knew that all would be well. Lord Graymar was the most powerful wizard in Europe; he would make everything right.

"Don't speak," the earl commanded tautly, obliged to raise his voice over the frantic chaos. "I'm not in the mood to hear your excuses, you foolish, idiotic boy. *Why* must you always act without first taking a moment to think?" With an expression of annoyance he lifted his head and said, loudly, "Silence!"

All sound stopped at once, and every occupant of the tavern fell still, staring at Lord Graymar.

"Much better," said the earl. "You may all proceed, but quietly. Dyfed, find the keeper of this unsavory establishment and bring him to me. And do something about that weeping girl."

Weeping girl. Kian could hear her. Feel her, just as strongly as he'd felt her these many weeks.

"Loris," he said, straining his neck to find her. *"Loris."*

"Is that her name?" Malachi was kneeling beside Kian now. "Dyfed has her well in hand."

"She must come with us," Kian managed against the hot pain in his shoulder. "Malachi, listen to me—" He pushed away his cousin's hands as they sought to pull back his jacket. "Loris. The girl. You must bring her. She is my *unoliaeth.* My oneness. You told me I should find her one day, and I have. Even here, in this strange place." He suddenly found it difficult to draw in breath. "My . . . *unoliaeth.* Do you hear me, Malachi?"

"I hear you, but I don't believe you. You're delirious. Now be still." Lifting his head, Lord Graymar addressed someone standing nearby. "Are you the proprietor? Bring me clean towels and fresh water and have the goodness thereafter to fetch the night watch to deal with Mr. Foss and his companions."

Darkness threatened to overwhelm Kian, but he was too stubborn to give way. Reaching up, he took hold of Malachi's coat and shook it with what little strength remained, insisting, "She's mine! Just as you told me. It was for her that I came. Don't leave her behind. Swear to me." He shook Malachi once more before his hand fell away, slack. "Swear it." His eyes began to drift shut of their own accord.

"I give you my oath that she will come away with us," his cousin vowed. "Now be still, Kian, and be quiet. I'll take care of everything."

Aye, Kian thought dimly as the blackness overtook him. Malachi would take care of everything. Loris would be safe, and all would be well.

When Kian woke, it was to find himself in his own bed, his aching shoulder packed with what smelled like one of his cousin's remedies and securely wrapped in linen.

A fire glowed in the hearth, giving but little light to the dark, quiet room, but enough so that Kian could make out the tall figure standing before it. The blond hair, shorter than Kian's but nearly the same light shade as his own, gleamed in the firelight. Oddly, it had come undone and hung loosely about Malachi's shoulders. Kian had never seen it like that before, for his cousin tended to be temperamental about his appearance. Events at the Red Fox must have been rather trying to make the Earl of Graymar forget his usual perfection.

"How are you feeling?" Lord Graymar asked quietly. He was gazing into the fire, his back turned to Kian, but the earl scarcely needed to see a person to know whether he was sleeping or awake. Malachi Seymour wasn't merely a powerful wizard; he was the *Dewin Mawr,* or Great Sorcerer, whom the vast majority of magical beings in England gave their allegiance to. He was possessed of senses and gifts that even Kian, who at his birth had been foretold as the future *Dewin Mawr,* couldn't entirely understand.

"The wound has been cleaned and treated," the earl continued quietly. "I've given you something for the pain, but I fear you'll have a difficult night. Or day, rather, as the sun is shortly due to make its appearance."

Kian didn't doubt that, or that he'd be in far worse condition if his cousin weren't also a gifted healer.

"Where's Loris?"

"She's here," Malachi replied. "She's sleeping. The recent

events have been rather exhausting for her, poor girl. Your father and brother have assured her that she's to come to Tylluan and live there, safe from the Goodbodys. Your father was especially delighted, and she seemed relieved to be in his care. Ffinian may not be much of a wizard, but he certainly possesses a welcome gift for handling females."

"I knew he would love her at once, just as I do." Kian attempted to rise up on his good arm but quickly gave up the effort when it proved impossible without a great deal of pain. "Is she not the most beautiful creature you've ever seen, Malachi?" he asked, smiling despite his discomfort and weariness. "She's perfect. Beautiful and intelligent and . . . I never realized what it would be like to find her. My *unoliaeth*," he said happily. "My oneness. It's like nothing I've felt before. I've only known Loris for a few weeks, but I love her as dearly as if we've always been together. All of my happiness is dependent on her now. Nothing will ever mean more to me than she does."

"Aye, that is how a *unoliaeth* is, or so I've been given to understand," Malachi murmured, sounding strangely melancholy to Kian's ears. "She was destined for you, and you for her, as it was foretold at your birth. Neither can know true happiness or fulfillment apart from the other."

"She must be frightened by us," Kian said thoughtfully. "Did you explain to her? About the *unoliaeth*? About our kind? I had hoped to tell her in a far different manner, but everything went wrong. She'll be one of our sympathetics, of course, even if the idea of magic is strange to her at first. But her heart will reveal the truth to her, just as mine has to me."

Malachi was silent, making no reply. He was angry, Kian knew, and rightfully so. The wild Tylluan Seymours had wreaked their usual havoc. Or, rather, one wild Tylluan Seymour had.

"I know it won't do any good to tell you I'm sorry about what happened at the Red Fox," Kian offered contritely, "but upon my honor I vow that my only aim last night was to bring Loris out of the place. I had finally accepted the truth of who she was, and had decided to tell her and convince her to come away with me. Everything else that occurred with Foss and his men was completely unexpected, and I—"

"Foss is dead."

The words staggered Kian into silence. *Foss was dead?*

"His neck was broken when he struck the wall," Malachi went on. "If I hadn't been so distracted I would have felt the change when his soul departed. You have progressed far enough in your powers that I believe you would have noted it, too, though you were certainly in no condition to do so."

Lord Graymar turned from the fire and slowly approached the bed.

"He's dead?" Kian whispered. "I *killed* him?" His senses reeled at the knowledge.

"You acted in defense of your life," Malachi told him firmly, "and no man will lay blame for that at your door. There were witnesses who have already attested that Foss was the attacker. If they are not entirely able to remember how you managed to send Foss and some of his men into the wall, that isn't surprising. There was a great commotion at the time, and memories can so easily be blurred."

Kian understood what his cousin was telling him. Malachi had taken care of everything, just as he had promised, and all those who'd been present would remember only those facts that the Earl of Graymar wanted them to remember. But that was little comfort in the face of Foss's death.

"I killed a man," Kian murmured, filled with dismay. "And I used magic to do it." His voice shook slightly as realization took full hold. "I'm going to be cursed, aren't I? Or already have been. By the Guardians. Blood cursed. Isn't that so, Malachi?"

Slowly and carefully, Lord Graymar sat on the bed beside him.

"There are some who would argue, and I among them, that you did the world a great favor by ridding it of a man like Foss. He was a flesh peddler of the worst sort. A foul and evil murderer who had already taken a number of innocent lives and would have taken many more had he lived longer." He paused before going on. "Unfortunately, though we live in the world of mere mortals, we are not solely beneath their rule. If that were the case, Foss's death would be forgiven and you would escape punishment. But the Guardians who judge our kind tend to view such matters in a far different manner."

A shudder ran the length of Kian's body. "I didn't mean to kill him. And it was but a small measure of magic. A child's magic."

"Of a certainty it was," Malachi agreed. "Especially for a sorcerer possessed of your considerable powers. But that doesn't pardon what you did. You were arrogant and impatient, and took matters into your own hands when you should have sought the counsel and aid of someone older and wiser. More than that, you used magic for your own gain. Mere mortals could not realize that, but the Guardians would, and did. There is no one else to blame. You knew the risk you were taking."

"Yes." Kian closed his eyes tightly. "I knew." He drew in a deep breath and steeled himself for what was to come. A blood curse was the worst fate that could befall one of their kind, but nothing could stop one being placed once the Guardians had made their decision. It would be far better to face his punishment and immediately seek the remedy. There was always a way to break such a curse, if the cursed one could but discover what that way was.

Opening his eyes, he turned his head to gaze directly into Lord Graymar's dimly lit face. Kian had never seen his cousin looking so grim.

"Your youth might have softened the Guardians' judgment," Malachi said. "But this is far from the first purposeful misstep you've made, and the forbearance they have acted with before now has gone."

"What is it, then?" Kian asked. "Am I to go blind or deaf or be made speechless? Will my powers be taken from me, or in some way be lessened? Shall I be disfigured, made bald and hideous so that no one can gaze upon me without a sense of horror? The Guardians did that to Uncle Meurig after he shot that fellow in Hyde Park."

"Uncle Meurig was insufferably vain," the earl said. "The man he wounded pricked that vanity with a silly insult and Meurig reacted foolishly. He deserved his punishment and learned a great deal about humility before the curse was lifted and his beauty restored. But although I understand that women both young and old tend to swoon upon setting sight on you and your brother, neither of you is particularly vain. As to your powers, they must necessarily remain and continue to increase, for prophecy, unlike judgment, cannot be altered. One day, whether you find a way to lift the curse or not, you will take my place as *Dewin Mawr.*"

Kian began to relax a little. If none of those things that he had most dreaded weren't to be his punishment, perhaps the curse wouldn't be so daunting.

"Tell me, please, Malachi," he said.

The Earl of Graymar rose from the bed and moved back toward the fire. He contemplated the flames for a long moment before turning back, his tall, elegant figure illumined by the flickering light, to face Kian.

"Have you not already thought of what it must be?" Malachi murmured solemnly. "A blood curse almost always strikes at the heart. What is dearest to you, Kian? Or, rather, who is dearest to you?"

Weeks ago the question would have taken some thought for him to answer, for Kian would have to choose between his father and brother. But now the answer was immediate.

Loris.

For a moment Kian forgot how to breathe. When he finally did draw in air, it came as a desperate gasp. He began to shake his head, but Malachi only continued to gaze at him.

"They can't curse her," Kian said at last. "She's not one of us. And they can't take her away from me because our union was destined. Prophecy—you only just said it—prophecy cannot be altered."

"It cannot and will not be," Malachi told him. "Loris will remain your oneness, and you hers, and both will never find true happiness apart from each other, but the *unoliaeth* will not affect her as powerfully as it already does you. She will not even believe in its existence, unless you can find the way to convince her of it. But more than that, from this moment your touch will only give Loris pain, Kian, not pleasure. The Guardians have made it thus. You are cursed to need her as deeply and passionately as you now do, and that need will drive you to be close to her. But your touch will be as a stinging fire to Loris. She may desire you, she may even come to love you, but she'll not be able to endure the pain of your embrace."

"*No*," Kian said hotly, throwing off the covers with his uninjured arm. With a grimace of pain, he forced himself into a sitting position. "I'll speak to the Guardians. Plead with them. Make them change it. I'll accept any other punishment they like. *Anything* but this."

"Lie down," Malachi ordered sharply, "before you open the wound again."

Kian, unlike Dyfed, had a reputation for being difficult and disobedient and for ignoring orders unless he wished to comply. With one exception. He had never disobeyed the *Dewin Mawr*. Until now.

Looking very directly at His Lordship, Kian said, "Take me into the spirit realm," and, wincing again, he bent to pick up one of his boots.

He expected Malachi to rail at him, but to his great surprise, his powerful cousin only looked mildly relieved.

"It may be an unfortunate moment for your manhood to assert itself," Malachi said, moving forward, "but the timing couldn't be more propitious."

If Kian did possess any vanity, it was in the knowledge that he was, like the *Dewin Mawr*, an extraordinary wizard. Kian's powers sometimes astonished even himself, and those powers would increase as he aged, but despite that, somehow, Malachi managed to get him back into the bed, lying down and tightly covered, before Kian even knew what had happened.

"I'm deeply sorry for you, my cousin," Malachi said with all sincerity. "But it is a blood curse, and cannot be changed. There's no sense in doing anything but accepting the truth of that."

"I can fight it," Kian said wrathfully. "I can find the remedy, and *that* is exactly what I'm going to do."

"Aye, you can and must fight it," Malachi agreed. "And I vow that I'll do everything possible to help you. But for now you must be calm and force yourself to think very clearly. You must prepare for what is to come, and determine that, regardless of what Loris may say or do, you will be patient."

"I love her," Kian said. "I would never hurt her, for any cause."

Lord Graymar sighed and gave a shake of his head. "I pray that it will be so, *cfender*, but I fear the truth is that you have a great deal to learn about love and pain. I do not envy you this journey. I can only hope that it is brief, and that both you and Loris survive it unbroken."

CASTLE TYLLUAN, WALES, THREE YEARS LATER

The visits began shortly after Loris's sixteenth birthday. On that first night, she had come awake to find a stranger standing beside her bed, gazing down at her and speaking her name. It had been such a dim, unreal moment that at first Loris thought herself dreaming. But he had been real enough. When he'd lowered himself to sit beside her on the mattress, Loris had opened her mouth to scream. His hand had pressed over her lips, not hard, but enough to stop the sound.

"Shhh," he said, his voice low, gentle. "I've not come to harm you. There's no need to call for help."

He'd released her, and Loris had scrambled away to the far side of the bed.

"Who are you?" she demanded, her voice shaking badly. "How did you get in here?"

"Through the balcony doors," he said, nodding toward the doors. They had been locked before she'd gone to bed but now stood open, swinging gently in the night's cool breeze.

"The balcony doors?" she repeated in disbelief, gripping the blankets and pulling them up to her chin. "That's impossible, unless you're a wizard. Are you?"

"I can't tell you," he replied. "But I'm not here to harm you, Loris."

He was a complete stranger to her, tall and muscular, with long black hair that fell to his shoulders and black eyes that gazed at Loris with disturbing intensity. He was very handsome, though not in any refined or elegant manner, as Kian and Dyfed were, but rugged and fully masculine. She wondered for a fleeting moment if he was a gypsy or pirate, then discarded the notion almost at once. His simple clothes bespoke the faerie folk who lived near Tylluan.

She stumbled out of the bed, taking the covers with her. "You'd better go," she told him, her knees wobbling. "A powerful wizard lives in this castle. An extraordinary wizard, and he's but three doors away. I don't care how powerful you may be. You won't be able to stand against him."

"Do you mean Kian Seymour?" he asked, standing and slowly moving around the bed toward her. "Would you truly call him to come to your aid? I thought you hated the very sight of him."

"What I feel doesn't matter," she said, backing away as he advanced. "And I'm not going to discuss such things with you. Kian will come if I call, and he'll deal with you." She pointed a shaking finger at the balcony doors. "Now go, or I'll scream. I mean what I say."

"Please don't scream," he said. "I promise you there's no need. I'll sit here, by the fire." He waved a hand toward one of the two chairs set before the glowing flames. "And if you'll only speak with me for a few minutes, I'll leave."

He sat while Loris stayed on the other side of the room, protecting herself with the blankets and feeling unutterably foolish. She should scream for Kian. She knew she should. But the stranger was sitting there, smiling at her in a beguiling manner, and, somehow, she couldn't bring herself to do what was wise.

"Who are you?" she asked again. "Why have you come here? I have nothing of value to give you."

"But you do," he said. "The most valuable thing possible. Your time. Your smile. The sound of your voice."

"What?" she asked, bewildered by his words. "I don't understand." No one wanted such simple things from her. Not without something more. Ffinian wanted her to run his household, and Dyfed wanted her to make his life easy so that he might spend his days reading and hunting. Kian wanted her heart, which she couldn't seem to give him even in those moments when she wished she might.

"I only wish to be near you, Loris. Just to speak with you."

She shook her head. "I don't even know you. I've never seen you before."

"But I know you," he replied. "I've looked for you since the first day when you came to Tylluan. I've seen you growing more beautiful with each passing day and watched you with the lord and his sons. I simply . . . wished to be closer to you. To know you better."

"You're one of the faerie folk, then?" she asked. "Those who live in the woods near the castle? What's your name?"

"I can tell you nothing of myself," he said, his expression somber. "I paid the *consuriwr* of Llangoren for the enchantment that would let me come to you, but that enchantment will be broken the moment you learn my true name. And I don't wish to stop coming to you, Loris. If I cannot be near you, even for a few moments, I'll go mad. I love you, you see."

"Oh no," she said, alarmed anew. He *loved* her? He was a stranger—a complete stranger. He couldn't know anything about her, certainly not enough to make such a bold statement. He must be crazed. Or worse. "No. You can't. You must leave now and never come back. *Now.*"

"I will," he promised, his black eyes gleaming in the firelight. "If you'll but sit here beside me for a few moments. I give you my word of honor that I'll not touch you. I simply wish to speak to you. That's all."

Loris was unconvinced. But curious as well. No one had ever spoken to her in such a manner as this before. But that wasn't quite true, she told herself. Kian had often spoken gently, sweetly. Then his words led to touches, and his touches to misery.

The stranger had promised not to touch her.

"Only a few moments," Loris said. "And then you'll go?"

"Yes."

Slowly, dragging the blankets along, she moved to the chair, watching him the whole while, and sat.

He smiled, and she was struck by how painfully handsome he was, and how different from other magic folk she'd known.

"You *are* one of the faerie folk, are you not?" she asked. "You're not a wizard or . . . something else? Kian will know if you've come to bring ill to Tylluan."

"I know who he is, and what his powers are," her visitor said. "I have no intention of making so powerful a wizard angry, nor of bringing harm to anyone at Tylluan."

"Very well, then," she said, pulling the blankets all about her like a soft fortress. "I'm here. What do you wish to speak of?"

"Of you," he replied simply. "Tell me of yourself, Loris. I want to know everything."

"There isn't much to tell," she replied honestly. "And what there is, isn't very interesting."

"I'm sure that's not so," he said. "Do you like living at Tylluan? Are the baron and his sons kind to you?"

She told him, haltingly at first, of how greatly she loved Tylluan and the people there, of how Ffinian had become a father to her and his sons like brothers. He asked more questions, gently prodding her along, and Loris found herself telling him what was in her heart. She was not used to speaking of herself, nor of probing her memories and feelings, but the stranger made it easy. He seemed to know her already, using questions like keys to unlock doors that he knew led to a certain destination.

Before Loris knew what had happened, an hour or more had passed as they'd talked, and she'd not only relaxed but also had a pleasant time.

The stranger had done nothing to frighten her, and, true to his word, when she asked him to leave, he rose, escorted her back to the bed, bowed over her hand in a gentlemanly fashion, and departed, locking the balcony doors behind him.

In the morning, Loris had convinced herself that it truly had been a dream and said nothing of it to anyone. But that night the stranger came again. And the night after that, and the night after that, until Loris had to accept that he was real.

Each visit was like the first. He woke her, and they would sit by the fire and simply talk. As time passed, Loris began to look forward to his coming and tried to stay awake to greet him. And, some days, she found herself longing for night to fall, simply so that she could see him again.

He had become her friend, someone, the only one, really, whom she could talk to. He would ask her about her day when he came, about her relationships with Ffinian, Kian, and Dyfed. And he would listen quietly while she tried to explain, sorting through her thoughts and sometimes making sense of them even to herself.

She loved Ffinian as she had loved her own father. There was nothing complicated about her feelings for him. He had brought her to Tylluan and given her charge of the castle. She had been grateful for the responsibility, for it had made her feel secure and needed and trusted and she was good at it. He was openly affectionate and called her his darling and his dearest, making Loris feel just as if she truly were his own beloved daughter.

She adored Dyfed, because he was so gentle and kind, and his own love for her was never demanding or unsettling. It was a safe affection, steady and sure and, best of all, passionless.

Loris didn't like passion. Passions, she explained to her new friend, could only ruin one's life. Her father had let his passions rule him and had made her mother and herself captive to his whims. Perhaps that was why she felt so secure living beneath Ffinian's hand. He was wild and reckless, too, but unlike every other man she'd known, he gave Loris the power to control her surroundings, to make decisions for herself and for the entire castle. He never forced her to do what she did not wish, and he seemed to know when she wanted to be left in peace.

But that was precisely why her relationship with Kian was so . . . complicated. Unlike Dyfed, Kian was deeply passionate, about almost everything. And unlike Ffinian, Kian wanted Loris to feel those passions, too. Indeed, he seemed determined that she do so.

Kian thought they had a special relationship. A *unoliaeth*. He believed he loved her; he'd told her so numerous times since she'd come to live at Tylluan and valiantly tried to woo her, in so many ways that it secretly made her heart ache for him. Loris knew how painful it could be to want something and have no hope of attaining it. But though her heart was often disobedient in its reaction to Kian, it had never yet felt an emotion to match the love he spoke of. Loris wouldn't let it do so.

And yet despite that, Loris found herself physically aware of Kian. Even drawn to him, though she would never tell him so. Sometimes, she admitted, the mere sound of his voice could capture all her senses and send shivers tingling down the length of her body.

And then there had been the kisses, which Loris could only describe with a measure of embarrassment. Why she told her friend at all she wasn't entirely sure, save that she'd held the feelings inside for so long and felt a measure of relief in confessing them aloud.

She had enjoyed the kisses, she told him. At least while they had lasted.

Kian had taken her into his arms numerous times since she'd come to live at Tylluan; some of the embraces had been tempestuous, driven by a determination to prove something to her, while others had been achingly tender and gentle.

But no matter how well the encounters started, they always ended badly.

The first few moments made Loris senseless, almost dizzy with pleasure, but then it all changed. Pleasure became pain; her lips burned and her skin prickled wherever he touched her, as if she were being tormented by sharp needles.

Loris always came away from the embraces shaken, and Kian always came away angry. And frustrated, though it had taken Loris some time to appreciate that part of it.

"We seem to always be angry at each other these days," she told her friend. "I don't want to fight with Kian, but he purposefully does what he can to bait me, and I simply can't control my temper with him. He tells me that he can't bear my coldness, that he would rather have my anger than nothing at all. But if he finds my manner so unpleasant he should strive to keep from being in company with me so often, and spare us both a good deal of grief."

Her friend listened and murmured sympathetically. He didn't lecture Loris or tell her that she was wrong or argue with or embarrass her. He offered thoughtful advice and encouraged her when she'd had a hard day. Or when Kian had been particularly unpleasant.

She never told anyone about her nighttime visitor, though Loris felt certain Kian must know. He was far too powerful a wizard, far too aware of what took place at Tylluan, not to know. Yet he said nothing, apart from occasionally mocking her with comments regarding her dreams. He certainly never attempted to stop the stranger from coming.

After several months, Loris began to wonder what she would have done without her friend. She asked him time and again who he was and what his name was, and he always gave her the same answer, that when she knew the truth he would no longer be able to come to her. And since she didn't want him to stop coming but needed to be able to call him something, they came to a compromise. He told her to decide upon a name that she liked and he would answer to it. After a great deal of consideration, Loris had chosen Liw Nos, because it meant "by night." And that was who he became.

Then, on the night of her eighteenth birthday, everything changed. Liw Nos came to her, as usual, but he was different. He didn't wish to talk but drew her into his arms and slowly, very slowly, kissed her.

And then he pulled away and looked at her, as if waiting for something to occur.

Loris had been stunned. The kiss hadn't been unpleasant, but it was strange to be touched in such an intimate manner by someone other than Kian. And, though she knew it wasn't, it felt wrong, too.

But there was no pain with Liw Nos. He kissed her again, longer this time, and then again. His hands moved over Loris gently, encouraging her to move even closer, so that she could feel the strength and warmth of his body.

Again he pulled away, breathing a little more harshly, and gazed at her.

"Liw," she murmured. "We shouldn't . . ."

"I love you," he said. "I must be near you, Loris. Please. I'll not hurt you. I would never hurt you."

He kissed her again, more fervently, and Loris became lost in the sensual discovery of what an uninterrupted kiss could be.

She didn't know his real name, wasn't even precisely certain what he was, whether angel or demon, and yet, as he kissed her, she felt as if they were connected in some unfathomable way. There was a feeling of wholeness, of rightness . . . and of intense pleasure. If he hadn't brought the embrace to an end, she never would have done so.

"God forgive me," Loris whispered when he'd at last gone, her hand moving to cover her heated cheek. She was ashamed to think of her response to him. And a little frightened, too.

He couldn't come again. That was clear. It was one thing when they had only spent the nights talking, but if he came again and began to kiss her . . .

"You mustn't let it happen, Loris," she instructed herself firmly, gazing at her reflection in the mirror. "Liw is still so much a stranger to you, after all. It's terribly wrong."

She believed herself and vowed to resist him if he came the next night. But in her heart she knew she wouldn't.

Moonlight streamed through the open window, giving enough light for Kian to see himself in the full-length mirror. As many times as he'd made the transformation, he hadn't yet grown bored of watching the changes that came over his face and coloring and clothes. It was so odd, becoming someone who didn't exist. But it was necessary.

For years he had done everything he could possibly think of to lift the curse, to no avail. He had tried to do something to make recompense for killing Gregor Foss but hadn't been able to find anyone to make recompense to. Gregor Foss had no family to aid. Nor did he have any friends. He had left behind only enemies and victims. Kian had done what he could for the victims, with some help from Malachi and Niclas, quietly using his own measure of the Seymour fortune to better their lives. But the curse hadn't been lifted.

Next, Kian had applied himself studiously to doing whatever the Guardians and his family asked of him in the way of preparing to become the next *Dewin Mawr.* He had practiced the various magical arts, learned of mysticism and astronomy and healing. He had made visits to the spirit realm under the guidance of his cousin Steffan, the most powerful mystic among the Seymours. And he had avoided getting into any trouble, especially while in London.

But none of this had been sufficient to move the Guardians to lift the curse. Kian would simply have to keep striving and seeking. Unfortunately, he also had to continue living at Tylluan, with Loris, and find a way to keep from going mad.

He had to be near her. No, not just near, for he was close enough each day to feel the coolness toward him that the curse had placed in her heart. But she was his *unoliaeth*. His oneness. *His,* no matter how often or soundly she rejected the fact. If the curse kept her from recognizing him as her true mate while he was Kian, it didn't seem to stop her from at least liking him in another guise. For more than that he didn't hope.

She'd let him kiss her last night and, better still, had kissed him in return. Kian had thought he might reel from the sheer wonder of it. That was how it would have been between them if the curse had never been placed. Loris was his by right, and if it wasn't precisely noble of him to take her affection by deception, then nobility would have to go by the wayside. His need for her smile, her touch, her companionship, was akin to obsession.

The change took but moments. His already lengthy blond hair grew slightly longer and darkened until it was almost black. The lightness of his blue eyes faded until they were the same color as his hair. His finer features grew bolder, his nose lengthened, and his shoulders widened a fraction. He looked a little like one of his dark-haired Seymour cousins. Kian's garments took a few moments longer to complete the transition, taking on a mien similar to that of the fair folk who dwelled in the woods. It had seemed a good choice when he'd first decided to make these secret visits to Loris. It wasn't unusual for faeries to sneak into the dwellings of mortals at night, either to take something they desired or to lay blessings or curses upon the family within. Or even to simply cause mischief.

Fortunately, Loris had immediately made the assumption he'd hoped for and hadn't pressed too long or hard about him being a wizard. He'd told her the truth when he'd explained that once she realized who he really was he would no longer be able to come to her. The transformation enchantment that he'd bought from the *consuriwr* of Llangoren came with certain conditions. The moment Loris discovered who truly came to her, Kian's ability to transform into Liw Nos would come to an end.

Kian thought of the embrace they'd shared the night before and imagined what the coming hours would bring. The conjurer had told Kian that it might be thus, that his transformed self might be free from the effects of the curse, but he'd not believed that the Guardians would allow such a powerful magic to be so easily deceived. Desire had finally driven Kian to test the matter, and it had been true. As Liw Nos he could touch her for as long as he wished without giving her pain. The knowledge made him giddy, and expectation made his breathing quicken.

The night was dark and cold as he made his way to the small balcony outside his window. A fitful wind lifted his hair at the ends and fluttered the edges of his tunic. Kian took a deep breath and let the anticipation within him rise.

She was waiting for him. He could feel it.

She had locked the windows and bolted the doors, but Loris knew it wouldn't do any good. He would come, and, apart from running away, all she could do was wait. Minutes passed, and then an hour. She was weary from a day filled with keeping the castle and longed to lie down upon her soft bed. But she couldn't bring herself to do so. It would make her feel too . . . vulnerable.

Weariness at last won out, and she settled into one of the large chairs near the fire. Leaning her head against the cushions, she closed her eyes and let her thoughts drift. Sleep beckoned, but she was too wary to follow.

"When will he come?" she murmured aloud.

"I'm here, Loris."

She opened her eyes and saw him standing there, having

suddenly and silently appeared, as he was sometimes given to doing. The balcony doors were closed; she'd neither heard him open them nor felt the cold night air that surely would have entered the room had he done so. He was already at the mantle, leaning against it in a relaxed pose, gazing down at her.

The fact came to Loris once more that she knew almost nothing about him or what powers he possessed.

"It isn't good for you to come here anymore, Liw," she said, looking fully into his dark eyes. "It isn't safe."

"Why?"

"Because I don't know you. Because I don't know what you want, to be my friend or . . . or something else."

He smiled. "You know what I want." He pushed from the mantle and straightened. "You're tired, Loris." Slowly, he moved to kneel before the chair and took her hands in his own. "You've had a difficult day?"

She ignored the question.

"I *don't* know what you want," she repeated, searching his face by the dim light of the fire. "I don't even know who you truly are. Or what you are."

"Is it Kian Seymour who wearies you so?" he asked. "He's cruel and unkind. I know how greatly you hate him."

"I don't hate Kian," she told him firmly. "He can be difficult and obstinate, but I have never hated him."

"Then perhaps it's his brother, Dyfed. Or Lord Tylluan. They're too demanding in what they want of you."

"It isn't any of them," she said impatiently. "But if it were, at least I would have an honest name to accuse them by."

"I'm not your enemy, Loris," he said, lifting one hand to stroke the backs of his fingers gently down her cheek. "I mean no harm to anyone at Tylluan. Most especially not you."

With a sigh she pushed his hand away and stood, pulling her dressing gown more tightly about her waist and stepping around Liw's kneeling form.

"You should go," she said. "And never come back."

He didn't move. Didn't rise to his feet. Didn't even look at her. Loris bit her lip and turned away, toward the fire, and prayed that she wouldn't start crying.

"Do you want me to go?" he asked in a low voice.

She didn't answer. Silence stretched out for a long moment, and then she heard him rising to his feet. His hands, warm and strong, fell upon her shoulders and gently turned her to face him. Searching her face, he asked once more, "Do you want me to go, Loris?"

"I want to know who you are, Liw. Who you truly are."

He lowered his head and softly kissed her lips, a brief and tender caress. "In your heart, you already know who I am," he murmured.

Loris shook her head in denial, but he kissed her again, more deeply, and she felt once more the rightness between them. It was so very like what she fleetingly felt with Kian before their embraces came to an end, not as powerful or compelling, but similar enough to be a shadow. She pressed closer to the solid warmth of his body, sliding her arms up about his neck.

When it ended they were quiet again, holding each other, swaying slightly back and forth. His cheek was pressed against the top of her head, and she could feel his breath against her hair.

"Won't you tell me something about yourself?" she whispered. "Please."

He pulled away to look into her eyes and stroked the hair back from her face.

"I am one who wants to be near you always, Loris, just as I have always been," he said softly. "I will never harm or dishonor you. I want to come to you freely, without fear, without shame, and give you pleasure and respite. I want to go on being the one you tell your secrets to, your dreams, all of the things that you can tell no one else. I want to hear of your days and be part of your nights, to hold and touch you, to be touched by you in turn. I want to hear your voice and carry the memory of it away with me until I'm with you once more." He kissed her again, slowly, deeply. "This is who I am, Loris." His hand cradled her face. "Is it enough?"

"Yes, Liw," she whispered, drawing him back down to her. "It's enough."

One

NORTHERN WALES, 1821

"They're all dead, my lord," Horas said, standing up from the body he'd been inspecting and looking at the field strewn with others. "Some half-eaten. Some just killed for sport. But either way, they're all dead."

Kian surveyed the sight before him in silence, his gaze moving from one mutilated sheep to the next. He'd spent the five previous mornings surveying the exact same scene, save with varying players. Sheep were the main victims, but there had been cattle and goats and pigs as well. All had been his tenants' livestock, and all the attacks had occurred on his lands.

Something evil had come to Tylluan.

"Are there no prints again, Horas?"

"No, m'lord. None that I can find. There might be some under all the water, though. Kind of hard to tell."

"Damnation," Kian muttered. It was always the same. There was never any sign of who or what the predator was— no prints, either human or animal, no tufts of fur—yet there was always a tremendous amount of water muddying the field where the destruction had taken place. It was as if rain had fallen heavily in only one place, leaving behind a watery swamp littered with dead carcasses.

"I'm sorry, Allan," he said to the tenant, who stood beside him. "Is it the entire flock, then?"

"Aye, m'lord," said Allan. Behind him, a group of his fellow tenants murmured and nodded and cast glances at their new lord. Kian felt their appraisals keenly, knowing full well what they were thinking. He had only been master of Tylluan for seven months, and scarce a week had gone by that some misfortune or other hadn't befallen either someone or something on the vast estate. Illness, injury, fire, dry wells, inexplicable destruction—just when Kian thought he had everything under control, something else occurred to get Tylluan's inhabitants into an uproar.

His tenants were beginning to whisper that Tylluan had been cursed, and Kian was starting to wonder precisely the same thing. Unfortunately, they were also starting to wonder whether Kian was capable of being a true lord to them, protecting them and their children, their homes and livestock. His father, the previous baron, had managed well enough, though in a somewhat uninvolved manner. Whenever trouble occurred, Ffinian Seymour was content to call upon the *Dewin Mawr,* rather than tend to the matter himself. Lord Graymar had always come, if not entirely happily, and fixed the problem, which both the tenants and Kian's father had found very welcome. The *Dewin Mawr* worked quickly and powerfully; even the most tenacious spirits had been readily vanquished with ease.

When Kian had taken Ffinian's place as baron at Tylluan, however, he had vowed that he would only call upon his cousin in the direst need and only if Kian himself couldn't find the solution first. This was partly due to pride, he knew, because he was, like Malachi, an extraordinary wizard and ought to be powerful enough to handle difficult problems. But more than that, Kian felt the need to prove himself. If he couldn't manage a single estate like Tylluan with some semblance of success, he'd certainly never be able to oversee all the magical Families who gave the *Dewin Mawr* their allegiance.

At the moment, he'd simply like to gain the allegiance of his tenants. They were not all of magical descent, but they were all, from generations past, sympathetic to those who were and understood the responsibilities that came with giving their loyalty to a lord possessed of great powers. The people of Tylluan, like many Welsh, kept the mysteries of magic secret from the outside world. In return, however, they rightfully expected some manner of recompense. Especially in the way of safety and security.

"Might've been something wild," Horas said contemplatively, rubbing his chin. "Boars, maybe. Or wolves."

Kian appreciated his steward's loyal attempt to find a more normal solution to the problem, but after spending six mornings looking at fields of dead animals, they were well beyond pretending.

"Something wild, aye," Kian agreed. "But it wasn't any creature known to mortal men."

His tenants murmured quietly in agreement.

Horas glanced at Kian and gave a single nod. "Is it Cadmaran, then, do you think?"

The question was asked so casually that anyone who didn't know the history between the Cadmaran and Seymour families might not understand the meaning behind it. But that wasn't the case with all those who were present. They fell silent and waited to hear whether Kian would make a public declaration of his belief in his distant neighbor's guilt.

Morcar Cadmaran, the Earl of Llew, was, like Lord Graymar, both an extraordinary wizard and the powerful head of an ancient magical family. Unlike Lord Graymar, Cadmaran practiced dark magic. Evil magic. Magic like the kind that had caused the mayhem and death strewn out on the field before Kian. It wouldn't be the first time that a Cadmaran had visited such destruction on a Seymour.

The two families had been at odds for centuries, contending over which should wield the greater authority over the other magical clans. Thus far the Seymours had maintained the place of most power, but only, the Cadmarans claimed, by cheating at every given opportunity. The charge had enraged past generations of Seymours, who found it to be entirely unjust, and a mutual enmity had been birthed between the two families. There had been arguments, volatile encounters, even battles fought over which family had suffered the greater insult. In time, the Seymours had simply begun to ignore the ridiculous feud, but the Cadmarans found it impossible to set aside. Indeed, the current Earl of Llew seemed determined to carry on the unpleasantness at all costs.

Morcar Cadmaran believed that the Seymours had done everything possible to ruin him. They had even denied him the woman whom he had chosen for his wife, Ceridwen Seymour, a gifted sorceress with whom Morcar believed he would be able to produce wildly powerful offspring. He had been thwarted in his attempts to secure her hand by Malachi, who had allowed her to marry the man of her choice, a mere mortal. It had been the final straw in what the Earl of Llew saw as an endless string of misdeeds. He wanted to topple the Seymours from their place of power; and the best way to do that was to destroy their head, the Earl of Graymar.

There was only one acceptable way among their kind to bring down one who had been recognized as the *Dewin Mawr,* and that was through a duel of powers, properly challenged and properly accepted, according to the rules laid down ages past by the Guardians. But Morcar hadn't been able to force such a duel, because Malachi continuously found ways to avoid meeting him face-to-face, a fact the Earl of Llew found endlessly frustrating. Yet he determinedly kept trying to lure Malachi out into the open. The troubles that had been plaguing Tylluan of late were, Kian believed, evidence of such efforts. Cadmaran knew that if Kian couldn't find a way to stop the attacks on his lands, he would eventually have to send for the *Dewin Mawr*'s aid. And then the Earl of Graymar would be in North Wales and that much closer to the Earl of Llew's lair.

Unfortunately, Kian had no proof that Cadmaran was behind the attacks, and he wasn't going to make his suspicions public. Such an open assertion of blame was, among their kind, akin to a declaration of war. He would have to tread carefully until he knew better what was going on and whether Lord Llew was truly involved.

In the meantime, Kian had to pacify his tenants' desire for action.

"What I think," he said clearly, "is that someone from Tylluan should visit *Fynnon Elian* as soon as possible to see whether a curse has been set upon us and, if so, pay the fine to have it lifted."

This suggestion met with loud approval among those present, for they were, like most Welsh, deeply superstitious. It had likely crossed their minds before now that some evildoer had gone to Elian's Well and thrown a curse into the water, bringing all this misery upon them. Although Kian certainly didn't deny that such curses were true, he didn't believe for a moment that paying the well keeper a few coins to lift a curse would solve the troubles at Tylluan. But it would buy him a little time and soothe his tenants for a few days.

"I should be glad to go, m'lord," Allan offered, nodding toward the field. "Once this has been cleared and the carcasses burned."

"Aye, and me with him," said another, followed by a chorus of volunteers.

"It is good of each of you to offer," Kian told them, "but I shall ask my brother to go." He understood what it would mean to the people of Tylluan to have someone so close to their baron perform the task. "Dyfed will leave tomorrow morning and, God willing, be home before the week is out. Let us all pray God that whatever has been bedeviling us will be gone by then."

"Not those, Elen." Loris waved a hand to keep the girl from picking any more thyme. "We've enough for tonight's stew and I want to save plenty for drying. What a glorious day this is." A crisp, cool breeze caressed her cheek and she lifted her head to smile at the white clouds above. "I can scarce remember a spring here with so little rain and so much sun."

"The rain will come, miss," the younger girl said gloomily. "It always does. And the fog with it."

"Aye, that they will, praise be to God," Loris agreed. "We'd be in sore misery if it were not so, especially here on Tylluan's high hill. Look, Elen." Standing, Loris strode nearer to the edge of the garden, where a sheer drop gave way to the valley below. "I never weary of seeing it, do you?" She glanced back at the girl, who trudged unhappily over to join her, dragging her mostly empty basket along as if it were a great burden.

"It's the same as it was yesterday," Elen replied, "and the day before that and the day before that. Nothing ever changes here."

"No," Loris murmured with pleasure. "I pray it never will."

It had been ten years since Ffinian Seymour had taken her into his heart as an adopted daughter and brought her to live at Tylluan. Ten glorious years out of London's dark alleys and filthy dens. And all of them spent here, in this wild and beautiful land. There had been a great deal of work for her to do in the beginning, for the castle had been in a disastrous condition and Ffinian and his sons and their men were given to living like animals, but Loris had gladly applied herself to the challenge of putting everything and everyone into order. And somehow, in the process, Tylluan had become her home. Her own beloved home, made clean and comfortable and lovely by her own hand. She was safe here, and happy as she had never dreamed she might be.

"I know you can't see Tylluan as I do, Elen," she told the girl. "You've never known anything else. But you're very young, yet, and might one day have the chance to see something more of England. And then, perhaps, you'll realize just how beautiful Tylluan is by comparison."

Elen sighed aloud. "I hope so, miss," she said. "There must be so many wonderful things in other places. Shops and carriages and beautiful things. And something exciting to do once in a while. Nothing ever happens here." She sighed again. "Nothing good, anywise."

"We did, too, have something good happen," Loris reminded her. "And only a few months past. Can you have forgotten the wedding so soon?"

"That's true, miss," Elen agreed unhappily. "But that wasn't really a good happening, was it? I never thought the baron would leave us, just because he wanted to take a wife."

"It was a difficult change," Loris agreed sympathetically, remembering the sadness among the people of Tylluan when Ffinian, who had been their beloved lord for so many years, stepped down from the title. "But it *was* good, whether you realize it or not, and it certainly wasn't unexpected. The title has always belonged to Master Kian. He inherited it from his mother at her death. Master Ffinian was merely running the estate until the time came for the current baron to take his rightful place."

Elen shook her head and set the basket in her arm on her hip. "I miss the old baron, though. Why couldn't he have married Lady Alice and stayed at Tylluan? She could've come here and been his baroness."

"Lady Alice's estate is almost as large as Tylluan," Loris said. "It needs someone to look after it, and now that she and Master Ffinian have wed, she'll have a very capable husband to lend her his aid."

"But they're not even *at* Glen Aur," Elen countered.

"Well, no, not at the present time," Loris said. "But once their honeymoon is over they'll return to Glen Aur and very likely remain there much of each year, as Lady Alice was given to doing before she married Master Ffinian. And just as soon as they return from the Continent I'm certain they'll come to visit us. The former baron could never stay away from Tylluan for long. He loves it as much as the new baron does." Loris hoped that would be so, for she missed Ffinian terribly. Tylluan seemed empty without his loud, booming voice and raucous laughter. And meals were almost dull without his outrageous storytelling and jests.

Elen made a sound of disbelief and said, "I hope Master Ffinian returns soon. He'll put everything to right in a shake, just as he always used to do. Allan Jones lost his whole flock today, so I heard."

"I heard the same," Loris said sadly. It was a shadow marring the beautiful day, just as so many days had so recently been shadowed. "But don't despair yet, Elen. You and the others must give Lord Tylluan some time to discover what's causing so much destruction. He's trying very hard to find the source and what the cure may be."

Despite their difficult relationship, Loris knew how deeply Kian loved Tylluan, and had seen him spend night after night poring over ancient texts, striving to find answers to the troubles that had been plaguing the estate these many months. He ate little, of late, and slept even less. Many a morning the upstairs maid had reported that his bed had not been slept in, and Loris could see for herself the weariness and strain that had begun to creep into Kian's face. It seemed unfair to her that his tenants should have so little faith in their lord and lack so much patience in giving him a chance.

"But how many more sheep must die, or worse, before he at last calls for the *Dewin Mawr* to come and save us?" Elen asked.

"That's enough, Elen," Loris said, her temper beginning to rise. "You'll not speak of the baron in such a manner again. Regardless of what you or the others may think, he deserves your respect and loyalty."

The serving girl made a sour face but curtsied and obediently answered, "Yes, miss."

"Take the basket into the kitchen, then, and tell Cook to get started. I'll be in presently."

As Elen made her way slowly back to the castle, Loris watched, glad to have a few moments to herself before it became necessary to go back indoors and supervise the daily work.

The garden was already in bloom this year, thanks to an early spring and numerous days of sunshine. Bright daffodils grew in the midst of the rows of vegetables and herbs, breaking the monotony of orderly green. Loris took out her scissors and cut several stalks to grace the tables in the great hall. Although the current baron didn't appear to care much for the beauty of fresh flowers during his evening meal, she continued to put them out. Ffinian had loved flowers in the castle, and it made Loris happy to think of how pleased he would be if he could see them.

"Loris!"

She looked up to see Dyfed coming through the garden gate, two of his favorite hunting dogs loping alongside, his hand aloft in greeting. In his other hand he carried a bow, and over his shoulder were slung a quiver half-filled with arrows and a number of limp birds tied together by the legs. *Excellent,* Loris thought. There would be fowl on the table tonight, along with the mutton.

"It looks as if you've had a good morning," she said as he neared her. The two dogs hurried up to have their heads scratched.

"Aye, and that I have. Look at these fat partridges I brought down. And these grouse. We're going to have a fine season this year, I vow."

"At least we've that to be thankful for," Loris said as Dyfed divested himself of his burdens, laying them on a nearby bench. "Did you hear about Allan Jones's flock?"

Dyfed gave a grim nod. "It's the same as the others. Six mornings in a row, now," he said. "Kian's going half-mad trying to find out what's behind it, poor devil." With a wave of his hand, Dyfed sent the dogs away. Then he bent and gave Loris a quick, affectionate kiss before sitting on the bench to admire his catch.

Watching him, Loris thought of how deeply she loved him and of how very different that love was from the conflicting emotions she felt for Kian. Dyfed was like a brother to her, or what she had always thought a brother might be like. He had been unfailingly gentle and kind to her from Loris's very first day beneath Ffinian's care, and had almost always taken her side against Kian during their frequent arguments. There had been a time when she had hoped that something more might come of her and Dyfed's relationship, and had even gone so far as to let others believe that she and Dyfed were betrothed. It was something Ffinian had desired, having given up hope that she would ever come to love Kian, despite the *unoliaeth* they all believed in, and wanting her to marry at least one of his sons. But that had all been foolishness and had long since been forgotten. There could never be any romantic passion between Dyfed and herself. Only a deep and abiding affection.

Dyfed was a lesser wizard, possessed only of the single gift of silent speech, which he used, thankfully, only when absolutely necessary. When Loris had first come to live at Tylluan, Dyfed had been in the habit of forgetting himself and speaking only with his thoughts—an experience Loris had found oddly unsettling. It had been for her sake, in part, that he had considerately forced himself to speak aloud.

Though he was a man full-grown, Loris still saw vestiges of the boy he'd once been, for his days were filled with ease. Kian, however, had left every hint of boyishness behind the moment he took up the duties of the estate. Loris had found it a welcome change; they had at last found a common ground upon which to build a tentative peace after all their years of constant fighting.

Loris had been afraid, at first, that Kian might find a way to wrest the management of the castle away from her, but he'd let her go on precisely as his father had. Better yet, Kian had a far greater interest in Tylluan's prosperity and security than Ffinian and spent a great deal more time managing the estate than he had done. Between the two of them,

Loris managing the day-to-day chores of the castle and Kian managing the rest, Tylluan was, for the first time since she'd come to live there, actually heading in a forward direction. Or had been, until the troubles had begun to take their toll.

"Dyfed," she said, coming to sit beside him. "What do you think is causing the destruction of the cattle? It can't simply be wild beasts, for there would have to be a great number to kill so many animals in one night, and surely someone would have seen other signs of them."

"No, it has to be something supernatural," Dyfed agreed. "Kian suspects that one of the ancient creatures has been unleashed, somehow, and I believe he must be right. If I had to wager a guess, I'd say Cadmaran was behind it. That would appeal to him, bringing a forbidden dark magic back to life."

"An ancient creature?" Loris murmured. "Do you mean like the ones that Ffinian was always telling stories of? The giant beasts and evil spirits?"

"The very same. They all truly existed, though he made them sound far more fantastic than they were. Many roamed these very lands. It would be against all our laws to bring such a creature back to life, but Cadmaran has nothing to lose by doing so. The Guardians have already blinded him for trying to kill Cousin Niclas three years past, and he knows they won't take his life. The Guardians never pronounce a judgment of outright death, even though they've sometimes put a cursed one's life in the hands of another. But that only happens in the direst circumstances—not simply because some sheep have been slaughtered. Cadmaran knows what the limits are."

Dyfed sounded perfectly at ease, but Loris felt a stab of fear at the idea. Morcar Cadmaran was a fearsome, evil wizard, and he hated the Seymours. He was also, unfortunately, lord of an estate that lay not far from Tylluan, which made them particularly vulnerable to his scheming.

"But it required many great wizards to overcome such creatures so long ago. How can Kian possibly manage on his own?"

"He can't," Dyfed replied distractedly, examining his bow with a frown and running his finger along a scrape in the wood. "He should have called for Malachi to come long ago."

"Not you, too!" Loris cried, rising to her feet. "Is there no one in Tylluan who has any faith in their lord? Not even his own brother?"

Dyfed looked up at her, surprised. "Don't be angry, Loris," he said. "Of course I have faith in Kian. But it's simply a fact that he hasn't the power or knowledge to overcome Cadmaran's wiles. Only the *Dewin Mawr* can. Don't you remember how many times Malachi was obliged to come and remedy the troubles Lord Llew caused while my father was the baron of Tylluan?"

"But Ffinian isn't an extraordinary wizard," Loris countered. "Or even a greater wizard, for that matter."

"He isn't even truly a lesser wizard," Dyfed put in. "He doesn't possess any powers at all, apart from the ability to charm women."

"But that's what I mean," Loris said. "He *had* to call for help, because he couldn't do anything himself. But Kian isn't so helpless. One day he'll be just as powerful as Lord Graymar."

"Aye, one day," Dyfed said. "But not now. Kian's powers are great, but they're still limited. He can't take to the air, yet, or make himself invisible. His senses regarding the presence and powers of other magic mortals are yet being developed, and he hasn't mastered half of what Malachi knows in the way of potions and spells, to say nothing of fast traveling, which he's only just begun to learn. If Kian truly wants to do what's best for Tylluan, then he'll put away his pride and admit that he needs help. One would think he'd have learned his lesson after what happened ten years ago, at the Red Fox." Dyfed went back to examining his bow.

Loris gazed at him for a silent moment, considering his words. On the one hand, she agreed completely that Kian possessed an enormous ego, but on the other, she wasn't insensible to the fact that Kian's pride had driven him to save her from Gregor Foss and, ultimately, her miserable life in London.

"You could help him," she suggested gently. "Above lending your aid in keeping watch at nights, which of course is your duty to both Tylluan and Kian. Some of the tenants have magic, and perhaps if you all combined your powers, you might—"

"It wouldn't be enough," Dyfed told her. "Trust me in this, Loris, and leave the matter be."

"I can't," she said, shaking her head. "And you shouldn't, either."

He glanced at her. "It's curious that you should care so much. Not about Tylluan, of course."

It took Loris a moment to understand what he meant. "About Kian?" she asked. "He's the master of Tylluan. Why would it be odd if I were to worry over him?"

"Because you hate him," Dyfed replied simply.

Loris threw her hands up into the air with exasperation. "I do *not* hate Kian. We disagree a great deal, but that has nothing to do with hatred. How many times must I tell you so?"

Dyfed looked at her with patience. "You've been cursed, and no matter how you deny it, I know what your feelings for Kian must be. At least until the curse is lifted and the magic of the *unoliaeth* fills your heart."

The curse again. And the *unoliaeth*. God help her, but she was sore weary of hearing about both of them. Loris had learned a great deal about magic since coming to live at Tylluan. She knew and believed that both blood curses and *unoliaeths* existed, for she had known magic mortals who had existed beneath them. One of Ffinian's great-nephews, Niclas Seymour, had been blood cursed after inadvertently causing the death of a friend who was a mere mortal. In the years that had followed, until the curse was lifted, Niclas had been unable to sleep and had suffered terribly.

She accepted that she and Kian had been cursed—there

was no other way to explain the odd burning pain she felt when he touched her for longer than a few moments—but she could not and would not accept that she had been cursed to hate him as well. Her feelings for him were confusing, often angry and distressing and always deeply felt, but none of these had to do with hatred.

"I don't hate Kian," she said again. "And there is nothing odd in my being worried about him. Tylluan—all of us here—depend upon him. We should all be worried. You most of all."

Dyfed uttered a laugh. "Are we speaking of my brother, dearest Loris? Kian doesn't want anyone worrying over him. In truth, it would make him quite irate to know of your concerns. Now leave the matter be, I beg you. Kian will come to his senses soon enough."

"Will I?" The garden gate closed with a loud snap. "That's reassuring to know, *fy gefell*."

Dyfed stood as Kian approached.

"It might be," Dyfed said, his tone filled with displeasure at the knowledge of being overheard, "if we had any hope of the event happening sooner than later. There was another slaughter last night. Are you at last going to send for Malachi?"

"No," Kian replied simply. "I'm not. I'm going to send you to *Fynnon Elian*, instead, to pay for the lifting of any curses that have been sent into the cursing well."

"*Fynnon Elian*?" Dyfed repeated with disbelief. "That's a full day's ride. You're jesting, surely."

"Not in the least," his brother replied pleasantly. "You're to leave in the morning. If the weather holds, it should be an agreeable journey."

From the expression on Dyfed's face Loris could tell that the brothers were about to have a serious disagreement. Sighing, she turned to fetch her basket.

"You can't actually believe that everything that's happened has to do with a mere well curse?" Dyfed demanded.

"Perhaps not," said Kian, "but you'll go, nonetheless, and pay the well keeper a goodly sum for a blessing."

"It's a fool's errand," Dyfed insisted. "And it's not going to buy you much time."

"Don't argue, Dyfed," Loris said sternly, walking past them with the basket in hand. "Do it for the sake of the people of Tylluan, if you find that you can't do it for any other cause. I shall have your bag packed and made ready for you first thing in the morn."

"Loris!"

It was Kian who called her. She turned about and gazed at him inquiringly.

"Yes, my lord?"

"Another letter has arrived for you. From London."

She almost dropped the basket.

"Another . . ." She felt chilled all over and drew in a shaking breath.

Kian looked for a moment as if he might come toward her. One of his hands clenched and unclenched.

"It's in my study," he said more gently. "Come when you have a moment and I'll give it to you."

"Is it from—?"

"Come to my study," he repeated. "We'll discuss the matter then."

Loris swallowed and nodded and, turning about, made her way back toward the castle. Behind her, the battle between the two brothers began again, the sound accompanying Loris all the way to the kitchen door.

Two

$\mathcal{K}$ian stood by the window in his study, gazing at the deepening afternoon sky. The view looked over the gardens to the valley beyond and, farther, to blue mountains rising in the distance. The beauty of the land never failed to give him pause, to fill him with appreciation and awe. He loved Tylluan with a fierceness that dimmed only when compared to the love he felt for Loris, and had always done so. He'd often dreamed of the time when he would take his rightful place as lord of the estate and put to right all that his wild father had let go. But the reality was turning out to be far different from those grand dreams. Everything seemed to be going wrong.

Well, perhaps not everything.

The tenants had been glad of the improvements that Kian had begun, the new fences and better ditches and leveled roads. He had plans for building new dwellings and cattle sheds as well, as soon as the land began to return a profit, but with every flock and herd that was slain, that hope was becoming increasingly dim.

He wished, not for the first time in his life, that he had the gift of personal levitation. It would be remarkably handy just now to be able to fly over all his lands during the coming night to see where the evil would strike next and perhaps

stop it. He would even be glad for the ability to immediately
and accurately feel a stranger's presence within the borders
of his land; at least then he'd have some idea of which direction to go in order to hunt the intruder down.

Malachi possessed both of those gifts, of course, and Kian
supposed that he would, too, one day. Extraordinary wizards,
unlike greater and lesser ones, continued to increase in powers until they departed for the spirit realm. But though Kian
was glad to know that he'd eventually gain such abilities, it
did little to help him now. And so, tonight, just as they'd done
for the past five nights, he and his men would do what mere
mortals were required to do when hunting a predator. They
would mount their horses and frantically ride about, hoping
to catch the killer before he or, more likely, it struck again.

He was so weary. If he got within ten feet of a bed he
would be asleep before he could close the distance. And he
missed Loris with growing intensity. He'd not been able to
visit her as Liw Nos since the troubles began, and he longed
to hold her in his arms again, to kiss her. To lie upon her bed
and simply talk, as they often did, and then to do all those
other things that had nothing at all to do with talking. His
body hardened simply thinking on it.

Loris must wonder, too, why Liw hadn't come to her
chamber for so many nights, though there had been other
times in the past when Kian hadn't been able to do so. When
he and his brother and father had gone to London each year,
for instance, and Loris had so stubbornly remained behind,
refusing to accompany them. Surely she must have become
suspicious that Liw stopped coming to her until Kian returned, but she had never said anything of it when he at last
crawled over her balcony and into her bedchamber.

It was proof, he believed, that she suspected who Liw
Nos really was and didn't want to risk losing him by speaking the truth aloud. The idea made Kian a little jealous, for
he realized that she preferred his other self to his true self.
The trouble was, he often felt the same way. After so many
years, Liw Nos had become a part of him, and if Kian were

asked, it would be difficult for him to say which of his two selves he preferred.

He should stop deceiving her. It had always been terribly wrong, and when Loris at last knew the full truth she would likely never forgive him. Time and again he'd told himself that he'd not go to her, and time and again only a few short days had passed before he'd given way to desire.

Just as he wished to give way to it now, despite all the dangers at Tylluan that demanded his attention. He had become addicted to being with Loris in the night hours, and it was impossible for him to force his mind into obedience when it was most necessary and to think on what must be done, rather than on when he would be alone with her again.

And so, as he couldn't master his unruly mind and his unwilling body, he would have to take the next wisest step and send Loris away. Not simply to remove her from his reach but to keep her safe as well. He knew little thus far about what was happening at Tylluan, save that it was very bad. He wanted Loris to be as far away from it as possible. Only then would he be able to fully concentrate on ridding his lands of the evil that had come to them.

And more than simply her safety or his sanity was involved now. There was the matter of the letters that had been coming to Tylluan, addressed to Loris, for the past few months. She had refused to read any of them, and Kian had been content to quietly verify the truth of the claims that the missives made. Proof had at last come, sent by his cousin Niclas, whose word could certainly be trusted, and had arrived at almost the same time as the latest letter.

Matters in London could wait no longer for Loris to attend to them, else the man who was seeking her might take it into his mind to come to Tylluan himself, and the last thing Kian needed just now was a visit from a wealthy, powerful nobleman who was both a mere mortal and not sympathetic to those possessed of magic.

Dyfed would have to go with her, of course. There was no one else, and she certainly couldn't go alone. Kian had always hoped that he would be the one to reintroduce Loris to London, to replace all her unhappy memories with good ones, and to make certain that she enjoyed a proper Season. Indeed, shortly after the letters first started arriving, he'd begun making plans for a possible visit. Unfortunately, just as word had come from Niclas, the killing of the cattle had begun. After six mornings like the one that had just passed, there was little hope that the matter was going to be quickly remedied. And so Dyfed would be the one to escort Loris to her first ball, perhaps to partner her in her very first dance, to see her smiling delight as she experienced the sights and sounds of a London that she'd not experienced in her youth. The thought only made Kian feel even more desolate.

He looked down at the letter in his hand, rubbing a thumb across the thick, waxy seal, and willed Loris to come to him. Closing his eyes, he concentrated. Her image came clearly into his mind's eye, happy, smiling, jesting with someone nearby.

Loris had been a beautiful girl and had grown into an even more beautiful woman. She was taller than most of the females Kian had known, slender and regal in her bearing. Her thick, curling hair had grown so long that, unbound, it fell like a shining dark gold waterfall to her hips. Her face could, without prejudice, only be called beautiful. Not pretty or comely or lovely, but strikingly beautiful. Her features were in perfect proportion to one another, neither too large nor too small, save perhaps for her cinnamon-colored eyes, which were prominently set beneath delicately arching eyebrows.

She was in the great hall, putting flowers on one of the tables, directing some of the servants in the placement of cups and bowls and plates. Kian could feel her contentment and pleasure as if it were his own and knew that familiar stab of pain at the knowledge that she seldom felt such things when he was near.

Kian had no idea how long Loris would have to remain in London. Weeks, perhaps even months, might pass before they would see each other again. It would be an awful time. He wasn't quite sure how he would survive such a separation.

"Come to me," he whispered softly. "Come, my *unoliaeth.*"

She would come, whether she wished to or not, whether she thought it was her own idea or not, because even the curse couldn't change what they were to each other. She had the power to call him to her side as well, though when she did he always came to her as Liw.

He could see her straightening. The flowers were set aside, and she said something to one of the nearest servants. Wiping her hands on her apron and running her hands over her loosely bound hair, Loris turned and walked out of the great hall. She was coming.

Loris hesitated before knocking lightly on the study door. It still seemed strange not to see Ffinian in the room but to walk in and see Kian sitting behind the desk that had fit his father so well.

But Kian wasn't sitting there now. He was standing by the window, gazing out at the view beyond. She saw the letter in his hand even before she spoke.

"I'm sorry if this isn't a good time," she said. "I've come about my letter."

He turned to her, and Loris was struck by how terribly tired he was. His handsome face was drawn and pale, and his blue eyes were heavy with weariness.

"When did you last sleep?" she asked, and quickly wished that she hadn't. She'd learned long ago that it never did any good to worry about Kian. He would only mock her for being concerned.

But, to her surprise, he simply replied, "I can't remember," and held the letter out to her.

And that made her even more concerned. If Kian didn't have the energy to say something tart and unpleasant, then he was clearly far more exhausted than she'd realized.

She moved closer and took the letter, but continued to look up into his face.

"Why don't you lie down for a few hours? There's enough time before night falls and I can prepare a tray for your room so that you needn't rise for the evening meal."

A certain look came into his eye and he tilted his head slightly. "Are you worried for me, *darling* Loris?" he asked, sarcastically emphasizing one of the endearments that his father had called her by. "How sweet, and how very odd. Perhaps you're sickening with something that's made you lose your senses."

The familiar anger that rose up in her when she was with him finally came to life, and out of habit Loris tensed, straightening full-height. If she had been cursed to dislike him, which she still doubted was true, then he had been cursed as well—to make her feel that way. No one else could aggravate her so quickly and thoroughly. But that was what he wanted to do, of course. As he so often reminded her, Kian preferred her anger to her kindness—or her coldness, as he called it.

"Yes, I forgot myself, of course," she said tightly. "For a moment I mistook you for someone else. Dyfed, perhaps." That did it, as she knew it would. Nothing made him angrier than being compared to Dyfed. The taunting smile on Kian's face thinned into a straight line. "Forgive me for being so foolish."

"That's better," he said, his tone filled with scarcely suppressed amusement. "Absent your waspish tongue, I might have mistaken you for someone else, as well. And then here we'd be, two strangers discussing a letter meant for you."

The letter. Loris immediately forgot their sparring and gazed down at the object in her hands.

"Is it from the Goodbodys again?"

"Yes."

"Why can't they leave me in peace?" she said unhappily, beginning to feel sick, as she did whenever she remembered her days at the Red Fox. "It can't be so very important, can it? They probably want money."

"Sit down and open it," Kian said, his tone gentler now. "You need to read it this time, Loris."

She looked up at him and saw the emotion in his blue eyes before he could hide it. "You know what it is, don't you?" When he began to look away she reached out and touched his arm, stilling him. "And all those other letters. The ones I threw away. You knew what was in them as well."

He stared at her hand, then nodded. When he looked up at her, his expression made her tremble with fear.

"Come and sit," he said, taking her hand and guiding her to the nearest chair. "You look as if you're about to faint." He pulled up another chair and sat beside her, leaning to set a strong, reassuring hand over her trembling ones. "I swore to you long ago that no one would ever harm you again, most especially not the Goodbodys, and regardless what you may feel for me, you know that I hold to my promises."

That was true, Loris thought. Kian Seymour was an irritating wretch, but he was an honorable man. And he cared for her. He still believed that she was his *unoliaeth,* regardless of every proof otherwise. He would feel duty-bound to keep her safe.

"Open the letter," he murmured, sitting back. "And then we'll discuss what's to be done."

It took some doing, for her fingers still trembled, but at last she had it opened and unfolded. The handwriting within was difficult to read at best and completely indecipherable at worst.

"It seems to be from Mr. Goodbody. Or perhaps his wife. I believe she knew how to write. I can't quite make it out. . . . Is this about my mother?"

Loris held the missive out to Kian, but he didn't look at it. He gazed directly at her and answered, "It seems to be."

Loris frowned and gave her attention back to the letter. "It says . . . I believe . . . my mother's . . . What is this word?"

She held the letter up to him once more. This time he looked, squinted at the word, and replied, *"Family."*

"Family?" Loris repeated faintly, and looked at the letter. "My mother's family is . . . is searching for me?" She lowered the missive to her lap and turned to the man sitting beside her.

Kian was still regarding her steadily, not in the least surprised. But of course he wouldn't be. He didn't need to read the letter to divine by magic what the Goodbodys had written.

"Tell me what it means," she said. "Can this be true?"

"It is, in a way," he replied calmly. "A certain gentleman has been seeking his runaway daughter for some years. He had gotten as far as discovering the existence of a woman—your mother—who closely resembled this daughter, though he could not be certain that it was she, as she had long since died. He learned that the woman had left behind a husband and child. Following their trail—which you will understand was not easy, being many years old—at last led the gentleman to the Goodbodys, who were able to tell him of both you and your father. Their description of your departed father accurately fits the appearance of the fellow who ran off with this gentleman's daughter. Apparently the Goodbodys had never met your mother, and thus could not give the gentleman any information regarding her."

Loris nodded. "She died when I was seven. We lived in a different part of London then, and only came nearer to the Red Fox when I was ten."

"That may be, in part, why it's been so difficult for you to be found," Kian said. "The gentleman—Lord Perham—had reason to believe that his daughter was with child when she disappeared, and that child, if living, would now be approximately your age. Unfortunately, Lord Perham has had several false turns with fortune hunters pretending to be this unknown grandchild, and is understandably wary of believing the claims made by the Goodbodys. He is determined, however, to meet you himself before giving up hope entirely."

A grandfather, Loris thought in amazement. *A blood relative.*

"If this man, Lord Perham, believes he's my grandfather," she asked, "then why hasn't he simply come to Tylluan to find me? Or at least written to me himself? Why would he contact me through the Goodbodys?"

"He doesn't have any alternative," Kian told her. "Have you forgotten the kind of people the Goodbodys are?"

No, Loris thought grimly. She hadn't. She looked at the letter once again, scanning it more carefully. "And there's no mention of how I might find this gentleman, either—they wisely didn't supply his name or title—if he is indeed my grandfather. If a meeting is to take place, it must be arranged by them. For a price. Aye, that's why they've written so insistently, for they cannot make so much as a ha'penny until I've replied. What horrid people." She looked at Kian, a new thought occurring to her. "And you knew, from the first letter that arrived those many weeks ago, what their purpose was? You divined its contents just as you did this one."

"I did," he confessed.

Anger began to rise again, but this time Loris didn't bother to calm herself.

"You *knew* that my grandfather might be looking for me and never saw fit to tell me?" She shook the letter at him.

He only continued to gaze at her calmly. "I knew that the Goodbodys claimed your grandfather was looking for you. I also knew that they were liars and cheats and not to be trusted. And you can scarce lay the blame at my feet for your ignorance," he added. "You made it abundantly clear that you didn't want to know. You threw every letter away, and would have done the same with this one had I not made you open it."

"But you should have told me!"

"The time wasn't yet right."

"Then why now?" she pressed. "Why did you choose this particular missive to reveal the truth?"

"For one thing," he replied, "the Goodbodys were clearly going to keep sending them and oversetting you. And for another, I've at last had word from my cousin Niclas, who was kind enough to look into the matter for me. He is the one who managed to discover that the gentleman in question is the Earl of Perham and, having investigated further, reports

that His Lordship's claim to be your maternal grandfather
may have merit."

"The Earl of Perham?" she repeated faintly. "My mother's
father was an *earl*?"

"Perhaps," Kian said. "I do not say that he is your grandfather, only that he may be. We'll not know with certainty
until you've met face-to-face."

Loris stared at him. "Meet him . . . at the Red Fox?"

Kian made a sound of impatience.

"You will never be made to step into that establishment
again," he vowed. "The Goodbodys have been removed from
the situation entirely. They remembered that you came away
to Tylluan but must have forgotten that the young gentlemen
who used to frequent their tavern had powerful relatives in
London. Or perhaps Malachi made them forget, which is
entirely likely. I only wish I'd been present to see how my
cousin Niclas handled the Goodbodys when he went to visit
them regarding the matter. Suffice it to say they won't be
writing you any more letters. This is the last of them."

Loris could imagine how terrified the Goodbodys had
been of Niclas Seymour. He was a lesser wizard but a powerful man nonetheless. Niclas served as the *Dewin Mawr*'s
right hand and oversaw the many Seymour ventures and the
family's vast fortune. Apart from that, Niclas was physically
quite different from the blond Seymours, who, like Kian, had
inherited elfin features and tall, slender frames. Dark-haired
Seymours were far more powerfully built, and Niclas was no
exception. He possessed astonishing strength and could have
lifted both of the portly Goodbodys with but one hand.

"Is he to come here, then?" she asked hopefully. "Lord
Perham?"

"No, Loris." Kian sat forward and briefly rubbed at one
temple, as though he had an ache there. If it was possible, he
looked even more tired. "He's not. You're to go to London
and meet him there. I've decided that you'll be more comfortable staying with Niclas and Julia, rather than at the town

house, and, of course, they would much prefer to have you with them, as well. As to Lord Perham, Niclas will make arrangements for you to meet each other in a manner that will be comfortable for you both. Dyfed is to escort you to Town," he said with a slight stiffness in his tone, and stood to walk toward the desk. "He doesn't know about the visit yet, and I'd appreciate it if you'd not say anything to him until I've had a chance to tell him. You'll be leaving shortly after he returns from *Fynnon Elian*."

London, she thought with dismay, her senses whirling.

Loris didn't want to go back to London, ever, and Kian knew that full well. Ffinian had never been able to convince her to join them when he and his sons had made their brief visits to Town each year, and she'd actually begun to feel hysterical on the two occasions when he'd jokingly teased that he would tie her up and throw her into the carriage.

Just as she felt slightly hysterical now.

"I believe it would be better if Lord Perham came here," she told Kian, rising from her own chair. "It makes far more sense."

Kian had his back to her, and when he spoke it was in a dismissive tone.

"The arrangements have already been made, and I'll not change them. I intend that you and Dyfed should make this a proper visit, and remain in Town through the rest of the spring. You'll be arriving in time to enjoy the Season and be introduced into society, regardless of whether you're related to the Earl of Perham. And if you are his granddaughter," he said, casting a brief look back at her, "believe me, society is going to be desperate to be introduced to you. Your beauty is going to cause a stir, regardless, but being a long-lost granddaughter to a nobleman of Lord Perham's standing will make you an absolute sensation." He uttered a laugh. "Every unmarried man in England is going to be falling at your feet, and quite a few who are married, as well. Dyfed's going to have his hands full, poor fellow."

"I don't want to be a sensation," she whispered, struggling to push the panic down. "Kian, I don't want to go to London. I don't want to leave Tylluan."

"I've asked Niclas to appropriate sufficient funds from my account in Town to cover your expenses," he said, ignoring her. "You'll require an entirely new wardrobe. Julia will help you with all that, so you've nothing to worry about."

"I'm not going," Loris stated flatly. "I'm not. Lord Perham will simply have to come to Tylluan if he wishes to speak to me. I shall be very glad to welcome him, and I'm sure you won't mind if he desires to stay for any length of time." She neatly folded the letter and slipped it into her apron pocket. "I must go and make certain that Cook isn't putting too much pepper into the stew. You know how heavy a hand she has at times."

Resolute, Loris turned and strode to the door. She set her hand upon the handle and prayed that it would open. It didn't. Kian's magic had locked it.

"Open . . . this . . . door." She said each word slowly and distinctly so that he knew just how serious she was.

"Loris—"

"Open this door," she repeated more loudly. *"Now."*

He was silent, waiting, and Loris began to tremble. If there was anything she hated, it was showing weakness in front of Kian. He would either mock her or try to be kind, and she wanted neither from him.

"Kian," she said, her voice wavering badly. "Don't do this to me. Please."

"Loris," he said again, much closer now. She realized that he had used his magic to silently move up behind her, which was something she'd always felt was ungentlemanly. Under different circumstances she would have railed at him, perhaps even struck him, but at the moment she could only think of the awfulness of being so far away from Tylluan. Since she'd come to live there ten years past, she'd not been more than half a day's journey from the castle, and then only to buy goods in the nearby towns and make a quick return.

Even those brief journeys had been difficult, and she'd felt an urgency to be safely back within Tylluan's borders.

Everything that she loved, all that constituted her happiness, was here. A miracle had brought her to this perfect place. If she went away, especially so far as London, she might never find a way to come back.

Loris was shaking so hard now that she scarce felt Kian's fingers tentatively touch her shoulder. She instinctively jerked away, pressing closer to the door.

"No," she managed, furious with both him and herself. *"No!"*

"Let me help you," he murmured, slowly, so slowly, putting his arms about her. "I can make it better. Let me."

It was the same promise he'd given her on that night so long ago, in the alley outside the Red Fox, when he'd soothed the pain in her stinging cheek with but the touch of his hand. And it was the same promise he'd given any number of times since then, when she'd been troubled. It was one of his gifts, and no matter how they fought, he had never withheld it. Yet, somehow, Loris had never learned to willingly accept any kindness that Kian offered, even when she needed it.

"I can't leave," she said as he turned her stiff, unyielding body toward him. She was horrified to hear tears in her voice. If she began to weep in front of him she'd never be able to live with herself. "I won't go. You told me . . . you *promised* me . . ."

His chest was warm and comfortingly solid as he folded her tightly into his embrace. Her legs, which had been trembling so badly that she thought they might give way, were suddenly relieved of the burden of carrying her weight.

"There is no need to be so overset," he told her. "I gave you my promise that I would always keep you safe, and I will keep that promise, just as I've kept the others. Tylluan is your home. You'd not be made to give it up, even if you wished to."

"Wishing means very little to a woman," she said haltingly against the cloth of his coat. "I have no means of leaving

London on my own, of finding my way back to Tylluan. I do not possess a carriage, or horses, or have a driver. I don't even have enough funds to buy a ticket on the post coach. I would walk, if I had to, but I"—she swallowed back a sob—"I wouldn't know which road to take."

"Don't let fear take you," Kian whispered near her ear. "Close your eyes, Loris," he commanded gently, evidently not aware that she'd already done so. "Let me calm your shaking. We've only a few moments before the pain begins."

He began to speak in a language she'd heard many times before at Tylluan but had never after been able to replicate. It was soft and melodious, flowing over her raw senses like a warm caress. When Kian spoke like this he made her think of Liw, who knew how to give her peace, as well, though without imparting pain.

Liw Nos. If she went to London she'd not see him for weeks, perhaps months. Or ever.

Kian must have felt her tense again, for he said, "Is it the pain?"

"Not yet," she whispered.

Then he began to chant again in the same low, soothing tone.

Whether Loris wished to let go of it or not, the fear was drawn out of her, inexorably, like the drawing of a wound, as Kian continued his incantation. The fear stopped, her mind and body relaxed, and her thoughts calmed.

"What is it that you fear most?" he asked. "Being kept in London against your will? Being taken away by force to Lord Perham's estate in Cumberland and made to wed some nice, safe gentleman with a large fortune and many properties?"

The very idea made her shudder.

What is it that you fear? The words tumbled through her mind. It was difficult to put into words, and she didn't know if he would understand. Kian and Dyfed had always had so much freedom. Too much, really.

"I fear losing what I've gained," she told him at last. "And of becoming unnecessary to . . ." She nearly said "you" but stopped herself. That wasn't at all what she'd meant. "To Tylluan," she finished. "Once I've gone, you'll realize just how little you need me here."

"That day will never come," Kian said softly. "You are very necessary. You always will be."

"Not so much that you find it difficult sending me away."

She felt it then, a slight, tingling discomfort that prickled along her skin wherever their bodies touched. Kian recognized what her stiffening meant and quickly released her. Sighing, he turned and moved back toward the window.

"I knew you'd not be pleased, but it never occurred to me that you'd take such fright at the notion of going to London, especially not to meet a man who may be your own grandfather. But you must go, Loris," Kian said solemnly. "You and Dyfed both. For a short time, at least."

"Must go?" she repeated. "You make it sound very urgent, of a sudden, when you've been content to wait so many weeks to even tell me of it." She took a step nearer, staring at his profile as her suspicions grew. "This doesn't truly have anything to do with Lord Perham, does it?" she asked slowly. "Surely it's not because of the troubles?"

Kian didn't look at her and made no reply, and Loris knew she'd guessed right.

She moved to stand before him. "But that's foolish. You need us, both of us, most especially now. You depend upon Dyfed for so much, and you need me to run the castle and keep it and the grounds in order. Sending us away will only make your burdens more pressing."

He shook his head. "It can't be helped."

"It can," she pressed. "Perhaps Dyfed's right. Perhaps it's time for you to admit that you need help. Why don't you send for Malachi, rather than sending us away? Or at least ask him for advice?"

Kian turned his head slightly and looked at her, a thin, mocking smile on his lips. "Do you think, Loris, that the

Dewin Mawr is unaware of what's been occurring at Tylluan these past months? Of every disaster that's happened since I became baron?"

Surprise rolled over Loris at the words.

"But if Lord Graymar knows," she said, "why hasn't he come, or even contacted you?"

Kian's expression was troubled. "I believe it's a test of sorts."

Loris understood that. Considering the idea, it made perfect sense, and she could only wonder that it hadn't occurred to her before. Of course the Earl of Graymar would know what was happening in Tylluan. He was the *Dewin Mawr,* and it would have been nearly impossible for events with such dire consequences to take place without him either knowing or hearing about them. And using the circumstances as an assessment of Kian's nerves and skills made sense, too. Such tests were common among the magical Families, when wizards sometimes had to prove themselves worthy of particular honors. This, then, was Kian's test, and Loris knew that'd he'd not call for help unless there were absolutely no other options left to him.

"But that is only more reason why Dyfed and I should remain," she argued. "You need to concentrate on solving what's happening here, and you can't do that if you're distracted with having to run the estate and tend to the troubles as well."

"Loris," he said wearily, "*you* are my greatest distraction. I know from long experience that you dislike hearing me speak of what is between us, that you don't even believe in our *unoliaeth,* but it is very real to me. It's difficult enough worrying about the safety of my tenants with my thoughts so fixed on you, and if you should become endangered by the evil that's befallen us, I doubt that I would care about anything else."

He was right: she disliked hearing about the *unoliaeth* and was even more aggravated by the fact that he meant to send her away from Tylluan for such a nonsensical reason.

But what she thought didn't really matter. Kian believed that some mystical relationship existed between them, and it appeared to be impossible for him to think otherwise.

"I'll go to London for a short visit, then," she said, "but only on the condition that I'll be allowed to return to Tylluan when I wish."

"You would return even if you did not wish it," he said. "We cannot be apart from one another for long and know any real happiness. Your heart will bring you back to Tylluan, even if you don't understand why. Always, it will draw you back."

"I don't want to speak of your *unoliaeth*," Loris said impatiently. "I want your promise."

He looked away, out the window again.

"I give you my vow that nothing, and no one, will be able to keep you from returning to Tylluan."

"Not even Lord Perham, if he should truly be my grandfather?"

"Especially not Lord Perham," Kian said solemnly. "You alone will decide if you wish to visit his estate in Cumberland in order to establish a relationship, but Tylluan will always be your home, Loris. You do not need the permission of another to enter and remain, because it belongs to you and cannot be taken away. And no one could keep you from returning, because I would come for you and bring you safely back."

She believed him, but wanted to make certain they understood each other perfectly.

"And what of you, Kian?"

"What of me?"

"Will you stop me from returning to Tylluan?"

He looked at her, his clear blue eyes piercing, and said nothing.

"I must hear you say the words," she told him. "The Guardians must hear them, else they're not binding."

He was silent for a long moment, then at last said, "I will never keep you from returning to Tylluan, unless it would be dangerous to you to be here."

She shook her head and waited.

He made a sound of exasperation. "You're a stubborn female, Loris," he muttered.

"Say the words aloud," she said.

"Very well, then." He set a hand against the wall and leaned closer to her, speaking very deliberately. "I make my vow before the Guardians that I will not keep you from returning to Tylluan. For any cause."

Loris nodded and stepped back, away from their uncomfortable closeness. "I believe you, then," she said. "I will go to London to meet my grandfather, if Lord Perham is indeed that man. But I will not stay a moment longer than I must, regardless of whether the troubles at Tylluan have been resolved. Just as soon as I have matters sorted out with Lord Perham," she vowed, "I'll be coming home."

Three

"Another beautiful evening." Morcar Cadmaran lifted his sightless eyes toward the sky and smiled. "I can feel it. The fog grows heavier, does it not, my sweet? A perfect night for the hunt."

Desdemona Caslin pulled her cloak more tightly about her neck and cast an unpleasant glance at the tall, handsome man beside her. She disliked being called such silly endearments, even by the lord she had been brought here to wed. She was not sweet and never had been, as Morcar Cadmaran knew very well. And that was precisely why he'd paid her father so much for her hand in marriage. Lord Llew wanted a wife as dark in nature as he was, and equal in powers. Desdemona was both of these things, perhaps even more so. And that gave her pause. Lord Llew might believe that she was his ideal mate, but Desdemona wasn't entirely certain that she agreed.

Not that it mattered. Her father had abandoned her here and gone back to the Americas, leaving Desdemona without a way to get home. She knew no other magical beings in this foreign land, apart from Lord Llew, and was completely dependent upon him until she could either discover some way of escape or make contact with another wizard or sorceress who would lend her aid.

But the Earl of Llew was no fool, and his blindness did little to alter his powers. In some ways it made him an even more fearsome wizard, for it gave him the gift of complete concentration. Desdemona would find it a challenge to leave England without his knowledge—she couldn't even depart the castle while he was in it, unless she had his permission, for it was heavily enchanted—and as he'd paid such a large sum of money to get her, it was unlikely he'd let her go without a fight.

But Lord Llew would discover, if he didn't already realize it, that any contest between them would result with her as the winner. Only one wizard existed who knew the secret that could force Desdemona into complete submission, and her father was now too far away to perform the enchantment. When she at last found another haven for those of her kind—and surely there must be one, even in this awful land—she would leave Llew and its blind lord behind forever. And then, she thought with dark anticipation, she would repay her father for the treachery he'd practiced in abandoning her to Morcar Cadmaran's care. It wouldn't be a simple matter to best Draceous Caslin—no one had ever managed to do it before—but Desdemona would find the way, no matter how long it took or the price she had to pay.

"The beast should rest," she told Lord Llew. "It's hunted for the past six nights. It will have no interest in food for some time."

"It need not eat," Lord Llew said. "Simply wandering will be enough. I don't want the Baron of Tylluan sleeping peacefully for another week, at the very least. Desperation will drive him to call the *Dewin Mawr* to his rescue. We need only keep pushing to break his stubborn pride." Turning to Desdemona, Cadmaran reached out with seeking fingers, touching her arm and then sliding down to clasp her hands in his. "You don't mind terribly, do you, my love?"

"Of course not," she replied, and meant it. She loved wandering the land at night, free from Cadmaran's—from anyone's—attentions. The few precious hours until daylight gave her the only peace she'd known since she'd been brought to Wales. "How else will the beast be called to rouse itself? But I warn you, it will do little damage before it returns to its resting place." Pulling her hands free, she moved a few steps away, gazing out over the terrace wall to the darkened valley beyond. It would soon be shrouded in fog.

"Even an hour will be enough," Lord Llew told her, his voice slightly cooler. Using the staff that helped him find his way, he moved toward her, tapping the smooth stone beneath his feet with each step he took. Desdemona often thought he did it as a guise; he could sense well enough where she stood.

Reaching her, the Earl of Llew slid a hand about her waist and drew Desdemona near, up against the solid length of his body. His sightless eyes were turned toward her face, as if he could see her, and both his touch and voice were gentle.

"I realize that we have not known each other long, Desdemona," he said, "and that you have little cause to trust or even like me, but I give you my vow that, when you are my wife, all that you wish, all that you desire, will be yours. No one else will be able to understand you as I shall, my sweet, for we are two of the same kind. We crave power, and are not afraid of that which we already possess. Together we will become the most feared of our kind, and our children will inherit unimaginable gifts. I shall worship you, Desdemona, as you deserve to be worshipped, and you shall be as a queen among our people. No one, and nothing, will dare naysay or deny you. I shall make certain of that."

He bent from his great height and sought her lips, kissing them with a lover's care. Desdemona stood still beneath the caress, waiting for something to spark within her, but nothing came. Her heart was cold, as it always had been, and despite his pretty words, Lord Llew knew how immovable she was. But when he lifted his head he smiled, not in the least displeased.

"You are my perfect mate," he murmured, and caressed her cheek with his fingers. "A hundred mortals might die beneath your hand and you'd shed nary a tear. I vow I have

never loved another woman as I shall love you. Go, then, my
darling, and rouse your slumbering beast. Enjoy your wandering through the night and return to Llew come dawn.
Your chamber will be ready to receive you."

Why hadn't he come?

Loris opened her balcony doors and stepped into the
cold, foggy night, straining to hear whether there was any
sound of Liw's approach. She had never been quite certain
about how it was that he came to her, except that it was always by way of the balcony. Whether he was able to fly or
simply scaled the castle walls she neither knew nor cared, so
long as he arrived safely.

But when would he come? And what had been keeping
him away so many days? She needed him desperately, especially tonight. There were so many things to tell him—about
Lord Perham and London. And there were questions she
wanted to ask, as well, about what was happening at Tylluan.
She'd never thought to ask him before, but surely Liw knew
something that might help Kian put an end to the troubles.
The faeries were powerful beings, and if they could but lend
Kian their aid, matters might be made right far more quickly.

But more than any of that, she wanted to be in Liw's
arms, to hold him and be held by him, to touch and kiss for
perhaps the last time in many months. She wanted memories
to take away with her, and to tell him that she was going so
that he'd not worry and wonder if he should come one night
and not find her there.

"Please come," she whispered aloud. "You must come,
Liw. I need you."

Kian brought his mount, Seren, to a halt and cursed aloud,
long and fulsomely. Horas reined in beside his master, waiting until he finished before saying, simply, "Aye."

"Damn this night!" Kian said fiercely. "And damn this
fog! We can scarce see our hands before our faces, let alone
anyone bent on destruction."

"Or thing, m'lord," Horas added calmly.

"Aye, thing," Kian agreed hotly. *"Damn!"*

Frustrated, he tossed a leg over the saddle and slid to the damp earth. Kneeling, he placed one hand upon the ground and closed his eyes in concentration.

"The faeries have gone deep into the trees and streams," he muttered irately. "They'll be of no help to us until the trouble has gone." A long, silent minute passed, and then he said, more softly, "Something moves a few miles from here. I can't tell where. It's distant. Faint. But it shakes the ground with each step, and disturbs the water."

"The same as the other nights," Horas said. "Is it a giant, do you think?"

"Perhaps," Kian murmured, his eyes still closed. "It's slower tonight, expending far less energy. Its powers are dimmed."

"Is the other still with it? The darker power?"

"Aye," Kian said, frowning as he felt that power moving so close to his lands. It had to be Morcar Cadmaran; Kian could think of no other wizard who emanated a darkness so intense that it could be readily divined, even from a distance. "But where are they? *Where?*"

Why hadn't the Guardians gifted him with the ability to sense strangers on his lands with greater accuracy? It would have been a tremendously wise thing to do upon the occasion of his becoming Baron Tylluan. Instead, they'd given Kian the power to revive dying plants and increase the mating abilities of various livestock. They were both wonderfully valuable and useful gifts, of course, and would be extremely helpful once the troubles had gone and the herds and land needed replenishing, but at the moment they weren't any help at all.

"The others may find them, m'lord," Horas said. "They're keeping watch on all Tylluan's borders. Tonight may be the last of it."

"I pray God it is," Kian said, rising full height. "I fear it's only the beginning." With fluid ease he remounted his patient horse. "We'll go to each lookout, starting at the lake.

Dyfed and his men are there, and—" He fell silent and turned in the saddle, listening.

"Did you hear something, m'lord?" Horas asked, turning to look toward where Kian was gazing into the thick fog.

Aye, he'd heard something. He'd heard Loris. She was calling him. Him, not Liw, though perhaps she believed otherwise. This beckoning came from her heart. She was summoning her *unoliaeth,* and Kian could do naught but respond.

"I must return to the castle," he said.

"To the—" Horas stopped himself and gave a curt, obedient nod. "Aye, m'lord."

"Go to each lookout and if any of the men have seen or heard anything, have Dyfed contact me at once. I'll be able to hear him even from the distance of the lake, and will meet you there as quickly as I can, one way or another."

Kian turned Seren about, spurring him in the direction of the castle, and made his way as rapidly as the fog would allow. Anticipation and desire made him a little reckless, and pleasure, too, for Loris had clearly missed him as much as he had missed her.

He was usually in his chamber when he transformed into his other self, but he hadn't the luxury of time for that just now. Standing in the castle shadows far below her balcony, Kian became the man Loris thought she wanted.

The change completed, Kian reached out to press both hands firmly against the castle wall. The stone was cold, wet, and hard against his palms, but after a moment's pressure the solid material softened. He dug his fingers into the wall as if it were made of damp clay and began to climb.

Her balcony doors were open, despite the cold, damp air, giving testament to her surety that he would come.

"Loris."

She was waiting by the fire and rose when he spoke. The smile she gave him, which he so seldom saw as Kian, sent his heart tumbling wildly.

"Liw!"

And then she was in his arms, soft and warm, enveloping all his senses, holding him as tightly as she possibly could. Kian buried his face in her silky hair and shut his eyes. This was what he longed for every moment of each day. Loris. With him. Her heart open to him, as it would have been if not for the curse.

"I'm sorry I've been absent so many nights," he murmured. "It was impossible for me to come."

"It's all right," she said, pulling away just enough to look up at him. "Terrible things have been happening at Tylluan. It's dangerous for you—for anyone—to be out in the dark. But I had to see you."

"I've missed you," he said. "So terribly. If you hadn't called me to you, I would have lost my senses altogether."

Lowering his head, he kissed her, gently at first, then, as she responded in kind, with deeper passion. His hands slid over the thin fabric of her dressing gown, finding the curves and valleys that his fingers knew so intimately. He had always taken the greatest of care with Loris, challenging though it had been, to never cross irredeemable boundaries, but that didn't mean he hadn't tested the limits as much as he possibly could.

She wasn't like any other woman he'd held in his arms. There was nothing fainting or frail about Loris; she was tall and splendidly formed—she'd slapped him so many times when he was himself that he knew very well how strong she was—yet she was entirely feminine just the same. Her waist was firm and slender, her hips delightfully curved, and her breasts soft and full beneath his palms. Her golden hair, tied in a thick braid that fell almost the length of her back, slid against the backs of his hands in a silky caress.

To touch her like this, to be close to her, made him want to weep with both joy and longing. Joy for the small measure that he had with her, but longing for so much more.

There was an urgency in her kiss tonight, in the way her hands clasped him, a fear and tenseness that emanated from her to him. With slow care, he brought the kiss to an

end and held her close, waiting until their breathing had
calmed and Loris had relaxed more fully against him before speaking.

"What's happened?"

"I pray that you'll be able to tell me," she said. "Something terrible has been happening at Tylluan, and the baron
has been unable to discover anything about it. But surely you
know what it is, Liw." She lifted her head to gaze up at him.
"You or one of your people. Don't you?"

He shook his head with regret. "I know what you speak of,
my love. Of the death and destruction that have been occurring. But I know nothing more. If Kian Seymour, being one of
the great *dewins,* hasn't yet divined what's at hand, it's unlikely that any lesser folk would know."

"Can you help him in some way, then?" She stepped back,
out of his embrace, and searched his face intently. "Not just
to discover the source of the troubles, but a remedy, as well?"

"Why should I do such a thing?" he asked curiously.
"Why do you want to help him?"

Loris's expression grew troubled. "Because he needs
someone . . . even though he'd never admit it or even ask,
because he's so terribly proud, you see . . . but despite that
he needs someone to stand with him once Dyfed and I have
gone."

Kian strove to look as surprised as he possibly could by
this statement. "Gone? You're leaving Tylluan?"

She nodded. "The baron is sending us away to London.
We'll be leaving in a few days."

"Because of what's happening here? He's afraid for you?"

Even in the dim fire glow he could see the blush that
suffused her cheeks.

"Yes," she replied. "In part because of that. I don't wish
to go, and he knows that full well, but Kian can be foolish
about such things. And stubborn."

"And will he let you return once the troubles have ended?"

"He will," she said, and with a sigh turned to move back
toward the fire. "And I intend to return very soon, whether

the danger is banished or not. I hate the thought of London, and have no desire to be there even for a few days."

"Loris," Kian said softly, moving to stand beside her. "You know that I have almost always been sympathetic to you in your feelings about Lord Tylluan, but in this matter I believe he may be right."

She looked at him with wide-eyed surprise. "Liw! You want me to go away, too? I would have thought that you . . ."

He gathered her into his arms and silenced her with a kiss.

"Of course I don't want you to leave," he murmured afterward. "I love you. The very thought of being parted from you is terrible to me. But this evil that has come to Tylluan may well be far more dangerous than anyone knows. Only consider again, Loris, what it means for a wizard of Kian Seymour's standing to be unable to readily deal with what's been taking place. For all we know the threat might reach the castle doors before it can be stopped."

"Nonsense," she said, pushing away once more, this time a little angrily. "Kian wouldn't let such a thing happen."

"He might not be able to help it."

"Don't say that!" she said with sudden and surprising anger. "You don't know him as I do! Kian would die before letting Tylluan fall to such destruction."

Well, that was interesting, he thought, watching as she began to pace agitatedly before the fire, the knuckles of her right hand pressed against her lips. Loris was offended on Kian's behalf. It was a strange, but perfectly welcome, occurrence.

"I believe you." He stepped forward quickly to grasp her hand before she could twirl about and pace away again. "But until Lord Tylluan has banished the evil here, I want you to be safe. And if London is the surety of that, then I want you to go."

She looked down and said nothing, and Kian had the dreadful intimation that she was about to start weeping. He knew that Loris couldn't bear to cry in front of others.

"My love," he said, gently tugging her back into his arms. "My sweet love. I know that you dislike London—"

"Hate," she corrected him, and he heard the despair in her voice. "I hate it as passionately as I love Tylluan." She struggled with herself for a moment, then said more steadily, "I'm sorry, Liw. That was childish. I shouldn't say such stupid things. Especially tonight, when I may not see you again for such a long time."

Sighing, Kian bent and swung her up into his arms. "You're weary," he said, carrying her to the bed. "And not particularly happy at the moment. Nothing you say is foolish or childish, but understandable."

He set her down, laying her head upon a mound of soft pillows, and followed suit, stretching out beside her. She rolled into him as he set his arm about her, falling into the comfortable position they'd spent hours in during the past years. Her cheek rested upon his shoulder, and his hand slid to her waist.

"You have terrible memories of your life in London," he said. "Perhaps this will be the chance for you to make new memories. Better memories."

"Perhaps." She drew in a shuddering breath and he felt her relaxing. "It would be good to visit with Niclas and Julia again, and Lord Graymar, as well. And I might meet my mother's father while I'm there. My grandfather."

"Ah," he said. "Does this thought not give you pleasure?"

She nodded against his chest. "I should like to know who my people are. I've often wondered about them and why my parents cut off all communication with them. But it's very strange, Liw. I always used to think that having the chance to meet my relatives would be the most wonderful thing in the world, yet now it frightens me a little."

"How so?"

"What if my grandfather asks me to live with him? What if he insists that I can't return to Tylluan? Kian has promised that no one will be able to stop me from coming back, but it would be difficult to naysay a blood relation. Oh, God." She pressed her face against his chest and fisted the cloth of his tunic in one hand. "I don't want to leave Tylluan. I have a terrible fear that I'll never see you again, or this blessed place."

"Of course you'll come home," he said, kissing the top of her head. "And have I not told you that I will only stop coming to you if you either banish me forever or discover my true name? I cannot live apart from you for long and know any happiness."

Lifting her head, she blinked up at him. "How strange it is to hear you say that," she murmured.

"Why?"

Her brows knit together slightly. "It's so very like what Kian has sometimes said to me."

God help him, Kian thought with a stab of panic. He was truly more weary than he'd imagined to have made such a misstep.

"Then he is a very wise man," he said, and rose up, pushing Loris down so that she lay upon her back. He needed to distract her. Quickly. "You're so beautiful, Loris," he said, leaning over her and smoothing a few stray strands of hair from her forehead. "So dear to me. I love you."

He kissed her, not giving her a chance to speak, already knowing that she'd not say the words back to him. She never had, not once in all the years that he'd come to her as Liw. He liked to believe it was because she couldn't, that Loris knew, in her heart, that it was Kian her love belonged to. And so he gave her pleasure, instead, which she readily took from him, and made both of them forget anything either of them had said.

His lips parted over her own, lightly tasting her sweet depths. When the tip of her soft tongue touched the line of his mouth he opened to her and responded in kind. She moaned when his fingertips found her breast, and slid her hands across his back. His body hardened painfully with need, as it always did, but he made certain that neither of their caresses grew too bold or too intimate.

It was the worst manner of torment, being with her like this, unable to satisfy the desire they both felt. But it was necessary. The first time they were joined as one he wanted to be Kian, not Liw, and hear her speaking his real name upon her lips. But more than that, he feared what the Guardians would do if he abused the gift they had given him in allowing these few hours with Loris, able to touch without her knowing pain. If he took her maidenhead as Liw, it would make a mockery of the *unoliaeth*.

The embrace came to an end as it always did, slowly, with both difficulty and regret. Their breathing was heightened and their hands clinging, reluctant to let go.

"I must leave soon," he said shakily, rolling to lie on his back. "I don't wish to, believe me. But there's something I must tend to before the sun rises."

"You'll not come again before I leave, will you?" She slid a hand across his chest, resting it upon the bare skin at the edge of his tunic.

"Not unless you call me," he said, reaching his own hand up to clasp her fingers. He closed his eyes and strove to slow his breathing. "But you mustn't call me, Loris. Not if you want me to try and help Lord Tylluan."

"Will you help him, Liw? You and your people, as well?"

His people, he thought. She meant the faerie folk who lived in and about Tylluan.

"No," he answered truthfully, staring at the firelight as it flickered on the canopy above. "They're too fearful."

"Faeries are never fearful," she said. "You're not."

"They can be, if something particularly evil is near. The *tylwyth teg* may be bold when an opportune moment arises, but they're not foolhardy."

Her fingers curled tightly around his. "I can't go to London, then," she whispered. "I can't leave him so alone."

She'd never before been so worried about him. The thought both intrigued and pleased Kian deeply. She did know, in some distant part of her heart, what he was to her.

"He'll not be alone, I promise you," he said, turning his head to smile into her worried eyes. "He'll have a good deal less to worry over once you've gone. And he'll be able to solve the trouble that much more quickly. But now you must sleep, Loris, for you're weary and need rest."

It always seemed a tad ironic to Kian that he had the power to cause Loris to fall into slumber. How many men, he wondered, were able to claim that they habitually put their lovers to sleep? It was necessary for him to use such powers, however, for it would be impossible for him to leave her otherwise. And Loris seemed never to realize that he'd done it. Apparently, when she woke the next morning, her memories of the night before were sufficiently blurred to keep her from remembering precisely how they'd taken their leave of each other.

"I won't be able to sleep," she said, smiling a little as well. "And if I do, you'll leave me."

"I'll stay a little while longer, my love. I'm going to miss you while you're away. All of the men in London who see you will fall in love with you, and I shall be so far away that you'll forget me."

"No, Liw. I'll think of you every moment. And long for you to come each night."

She began to close her eyes and yawned, cuddling closer to his warmth.

"I'm glad," he murmured, watching closely as she slid more deeply into slumber. "Because when you leave Tylluan, Loris, you'll be taking my heart with you, and all my happiness. I'm going to rid Tylluan of the evil that's come to us, I vow, and missing you is what will drive me to do it as quickly as I possibly can."

Four

"Where did all this water come from?"

Dyfed's booted feet sank into the mud as he measured the length of ground that was still partly covered in large puddles. It was as if a giant wave had somehow formed in the midst of the lake and rolled inland for half a mile before retreating.

"It's very odd, sir," one of the men said. "Is it the beast again, are you thinking?"

"We don't know that it's a beast yet," Dyfed replied, though privately he believed that everyone in Tylluan knew it must be. But Kian didn't want anyone to make any absolute determinations—not yet, leastwise—and Dyfed would do his brother's bidding. He shook his head at what little he could see in the dense fog. There was so much destruction. Every plant had been pulled out by the roots and left to die on the muddy ground, and every rock had been dragged out of place.

What could it possibly be, except a great beast? he wondered. Possibly some type of giant mortal, but there were no footprints to indicate such a being. Indeed, the most frustrating thing about the troubles that had befallen Tylluan was the lack of any clues to lead them in one direction or another.

"Will you call for His Lordship, Master Dyfed?"

"No, not yet. I want to see how far this goes first, and whether there's any sign of what caused this flooding. We'll discover what we can and tell Horas once he's returned from the last lookout and see what he advises. Bened," he said, nodding at one of his companions, "you ride to the south, and Lud, you go north. I'll head up into the tree line and find out whether the water managed to go up as far as the top of the hill. We'll meet back here in half an hour's time. Call out if you discover anything before then."

Mounting their horses, the men rode away into the fog.

With the exception of the faint wind ruffling the early spring leaves, Dyfed was aware of a strange silence as he entered the trees. There were none of the usual night sounds; the creatures who generally made them either had departed for a safer place or were simply too afraid to make a sound.

It grew darker, and the trees thicker, as he ascended the hill, but his horse, excellent animal that he was, readily picked his way through the foggy maze. Dyfed reached out a hand and felt of any trunk they passed near enough to, hoping to discover how damp they were. Instead, he felt something that had him bringing his mount to a sudden halt.

"What is this?" Dyfed murmured. He looped the horse's reins over a nearby branch and moved to more closely examine the tree that had brought them to a stop. Running his hands over the trunk, he felt what the darkness and fog made difficult to see. The tree had been struck by something large and tremendously powerful, for it was bent to one side, half out of the ground, some of the bark and a few low branches stripped away. He moved to the tree beyond it and felt the same, and then to the next with the same discovery. Kneeling, he set his hand to the earth and felt how wet it was. Not as soaked as the ground nearer to the lake, but far wetter than mere fog would make it.

The horse, which he could no longer see for the fog, whinnied nervously from where he was still tied, and Dyfed said reassuringly, "It's all right, Bachgen. Be easy. I only want to know how big this thing is, and then we'll go."

He felt a little foolish walking with his hands stretched out before him like a blind man, but he was a lesser wizard, possessed only of a single gift, and the fog made it necessary.

Each step he took without coming to the trees that should have been there, stumbling over broken branches strewn across the damp ground and tripping over ragged stumps, made his heart beat a little faster. The path that the beast, or whatever it was, had made was far wider than he'd expected.

It was definitely time to call for Kian.

Bachgen whinnied again, louder, more frantically. Dyfed heard the horse pulling at the branch he was tied to, rearing up and coming back down to the ground with a loud thud, and was suddenly seized by a stark premonition of grave danger.

Kian. Dyfed sent the thought across the distance that separated his brother and himself. *Come quickly. It's here.*

Bachgen's terror heightened. The beast emitted a terrifying sound that echoed across the valley, and Dyfed heard him struggling wildly to be free. A tree crashed to the ground and the earth shook. Dyfed shouted out and began running in the horse's direction, blinded by the fog, until the violent uproar ended with Bachgen's broken body being flung down nearly on top of him. Dyfed couldn't stop his forward motion; his legs struck the horse's twisted form, sending him tumbling forward, over still-warm blood and spiky bones. He landed on his back, the wind knocked out of him, and scrambled in a vain attempt to gain his feet.

There was a flash of brilliant light, revealing a blur of motion. For one brief moment he thought he saw the shape of a woman, and then, slipping in the wet mud, he lost his precarious balance and fell again. His head hit the ground and exploded with pain, and that was the last that he knew.

"Stop." Desdemona lifted a hand to keep the beast from crushing the man who lay upon the ground. Despite what Cadmaran believed, she was loath to take part in the killing of any mortal, magic or otherwise. She had no wish to have a curse laid upon her by the Guardians. Killing the animals and destroying the crops had brought her close enough to punishment; she had to take every care not to cross any unforgivable boundaries.

She had made the man insensible a moment too late; he had clearly seen her, though she wasn't certain of whether he'd seen the beast. But she would take no chances. Distant shouts warned her that his companions, who'd surely heard the violence that had occurred, were coming.

"Go," she told the beast. "Return to the lake and rest until I call you again. You must be quiet."

The scaly dragonlike beast obeyed at once, almost relieved to be let go. It shrank from its great height, thinning and spreading into a large puddle on the ground, and when it had finished transforming, it seeped into the earth, seeking an underground passage back to the safety of the lake.

The man's friends were coming closer, but the fog, thankfully, made their task more difficult. She might have disappeared as easily as the beast had done, but there had been something in the man's face when he'd seen her, something intriguing, that made Desdemona stay.

She whispered aloud into the cold, damp air and soon heard a great tumble of noises some quarter mile away. There was nothing particularly distinct about the sounds—they might have heralded an earthquake or an avalanche, both highly unlikely in this particular area—but they were more than enough to send the man's frantic companions in the wrong direction.

"Now," she murmured as their voices died away, "who are you?"

She knelt beside him and lifted one hand, palm up. A small flame appeared, illuminating a face that she found almost more beautiful than handsome. Not that he appeared to be in any way soft or feminine, but his features were so elegant and striking that they might have been crafted by a tremendously skilled artist. Desdemona recognized at once that he had been blessed with elvish blood. Even a very small and distant amount could do wondrous things to the forms and faces of magic beings. It had certainly done wonderful things to him.

He was a wizard. She had felt the presence of her own kind at once, but his powers, she sensed, were limited. Which meant that he couldn't possibly be the great Kian Seymour, the Baron of Tylluan, of whom Cadmaran had so often spoken. Perhaps he was the twin brother? Cadmaran had mentioned with intense hatred the physical beauty of certain Seymours, their *Dewin Mawr* and his heir, Lord Tylluan, among them. Seeing this man, Desdemona understood full well why Cadmaran's words had always held a tinge of jealousy.

She touched his pale cheek with her other hand, gently stroking along the line of his jaw, feeling the slight stubble growing there, then slid her fingers into the long, silky blond hair that had come undone at some point during the night. It was so fair as to almost be white—something else his faint elvish blood had gifted him with.

There was power in this man . . . not magical power, but something quite different. She could feel it beneath her touch. Bravery. Honor. She understood all those things at once, and more. He was a quiet man, but in his heart . . . there was much left unsaid.

Her hand slid down to his neck, paused to feel the strong pulse beating there, and then lower to test the muscles of his shoulder and chest and arm. Then lower still, across his taut stomach, where she lingered.

He was young and healthy and beautiful, and Desdemona wanted him. She'd not had a man since coming to this foreign place, had not particularly felt the need for one. Certainly not for Cadmaran, despite his handsomeness and obvious experience with women. She couldn't fault Lord Llew for making the attempt, nor for leaving her in peace when she expressed no similar interest. But not until this moment, with so enticing a lover before her, helpless to do anything save her bidding, had she felt that powerful surge of desire that sometimes drove her to be incautious. Desdemona wanted him, needed him, and she would have him. Her hand began to move once more, her long fingers sliding over the flap of his breeches, exploring, caressing . . .

It had not been Desdemona's experience in life to be very often surprised. Her father had managed to do it a number of times, but he was the greatest sorcerer known to their kind in the States. Cadmaran had tried, probably to see if he could do it, but to no avail.

But this man surprised her. His arm shot up from its formerly motionless position upon the ground and his fingers closed over her wrist, yanking her hand firmly from his body.

Desdemona's gaze slid calmly back to his face, discovering that his eyes—intensely blue, even in the darkness—were open and perfectly aware. And extremely angry.

What do you think you're doing?

She heard his chilly voice in her head and realized at once that he possessed the gift of silent speech.

As disconcerting as being surprised was, Desdemona didn't panic or even experience a rise in her heartbeat. He was a lesser wizard, after all, and she his superior by far. He could wield no power over her, nor could he resist whatever commands she gave. She would make a pet of him. A slave, as she had done with other men she had taken as lovers. He would be deeply in love with her in but moments, suffering for want of her. And then he would do her bidding, all that Desdemona wished, and would come to her, day or night, whenever she desired him to do so.

"Release me," she said softly, tugging lightly at her hand in expectation of instant freedom.

But then something inexplicable happened. He didn't do what she'd told him to do. And not only did he not release her, but his grip on her wrist actually tightened.

"Release you?" He had found his physical voice at last, and it was filled with fury. "You'll be fortunate to come away from our meeting intact. Who the devil are you, and where have you come from?"

Desdemona frowned and stared at her captive wrist, which was beginning to ache from the tight grasp he held on it.

"Release me," she said again, more firmly. *"Now."*

"Not until I have some answers." Wincing, he rose to his feet, dragging her up with him. He was a good deal taller than Desdemona, and she was obliged to look up to see his face. "First," he said, "I want your name."

Panic, like surprise, was a rare experience for her, but Desdemona distinctly felt it welling up inside of her. Something was amiss, and she had to gain control of this situation. Quickly.

It was time to make a display of her powers, in order to give her captor a better understanding of who she was and why he should be far more afraid than angry.

Lifting her free hand, she sent the flame that was still on her palm flying into the haze above their heads. It took but a thought to cause the flame to multiply until there were dozens, then a hundred, circling overhead, filling the place where they stood with light. With another wave of her hand Desdemona made the fog fade in the area immediately surrounding them, so that they could see not only each other, but the fallen trees and Bachgen's mutilated body as well. A couple of trees hadn't yet completely fallen, but with a mere pushing motion Desdemona sent them slamming to the still-muddy ground.

The sound was loud enough to draw her captor's companions back in their direction. She heard their shouts and saw him lift his head slightly, communicating with them through his silent speech. Looking at him, seeing even more clearly just how striking he was, Desdemona felt a renewed surge of desire. Somehow, his foolish determination to overpower her only made the thought of possessing him more desirable.

"Release me," she said once more, "and I won't hold this against you once we've come together. If you do not, I shall have to punish you."

He looked at her as if she was mad and said, "Let's try this again. I'm Dyfed Seymour. My brother is Lord Tylluan, and these are his lands upon which you're trespassing. You don't have to tell me who you are, if you don't wish to, but I can promise that you'll tell him. He'll be here very shortly."

The idea made her smile. "I shall look forward to meeting Kian Seymour," she told him. "I have heard much of him. And I will gladly tell him my name. It is one he will not hereafter forget."

Dyfed's eyes narrowed. "You're not Welsh. Or English. Your speech is—"

"No, I'm not English," she said coldly, "for which I thank God. I'm American. Your companions are coming." Desdemona nodded toward the trees. "I grow weary of asking, Dyfed Seymour. I don't wish to harm your friends, but I will, if you don't let me go."

"I see that what I've heard of Americans is true, then," he replied tightly. "They have no manners. Not even their women. If you harm my men, you may well drive me to do something that I've never done before. Strike a female."

She laughed at that. How amusing that he should think he could best her in any way. She was going to enjoy taming him into submission.

"Then before they arrive and you discover what you can—and cannot—do to me, perhaps we should make good use of our time. Now you will kiss me."

She rose up on her toes and lifted her free hand to pull him down to her, but again was surprised.

Dyfed reared back. *"Kiss you?"* he repeated with disbelief. "Are you witless? You killed my horse!"

Desdemona was beginning to grow rather angry, too. "You *must* obey me," she stated tautly. She was clearly his superior. Why hadn't he realized it yet?

Now it was his turn to laugh. "Must I? Americans are not only ill-mannered, I see, but arrogant."

"No one disobeys me," she informed him, striving to impress upon him that she meant what she said, "save for the most powerful among our kind, which you assuredly are not. I am Desdemona Caslin, daughter to Draceous Caslin." She waited for an appropriate reaction to her words, but Dyfed only continued to gaze at her as if she was slightly mad. "Does that mean nothing to you?" she demanded.

He gave a single shake of his head. "Not really. I perceive that you are a gifted sorceress, and that those gifts are dark, but your name and your father's are unfamiliar to me."

"A gifted sorceress?" she repeated as insult grew within her breast. "I am no mere sorceress. I am the daughter of *Draceous Caslin*. My powers are beyond what you could ever hope to possess, beyond your imagining."

Dyfed Seymour appeared to disbelieve her. He said nothing but lowered his gaze to her wrist, still captive in his grasp, then looked up at her again with a mocking smile.

Desdemona clenched her teeth and made a fist of her free hand. "Don't you dare to laugh at me!" she warned him wrathfully. "I don't know why I can't make you obey me. I certainly had no trouble making you insensible before."

"Do you mean when I fell?" he asked. "You had nothing to do with that. I hit my head on a rock. It's aching like the very devil"—he gingerly touched the back of his head—"and I imagine I'll have a rather large lump in the morning."

She was taken aback. Why would he say such a ridiculous thing? How could he make up a tale so utterly false? And why on earth was her attraction to him growing more intense by the moment? She should hate Dyfed Seymour, and the fact that she didn't only made her that much angrier.

"That's not so! You're a liar and a fool!" Desdemona struck him on the shoulder and, when he only laughed, struck him again. She *couldn't* be helpless. It was impossible. Certainly not because of *him*. Panic began to overwhelm all her better senses, and she struggled to be set free. "Let me go! Let me—"

His companions came suddenly crashing through the trees and into the clearing. Her captor turned to look at them, momentarily diverted, and the men themselves were taken aback by the sight before them. They fell still, panting from the exertion of running, their eyes drawn upward to the sight of so many flames floating above their heads.

It was all the distraction Desdemona needed. With one violent twist she freed herself, shouting, "Sleep!" at the two men and then whirling away, out of Dyfed Seymour's reach, before he leaped forward to grab her.

She was quick, but Dyfed's anger made him quicker. The little fiend had somehow been involved in the destruction surrounding them, which meant she knew what had been happening at Tylluan. And she had killed his horse, or let him be killed, which was just as bad. But this was the last straw. Bened and Lud crumpled to the ground beneath the force of her curse, and Dyfed had had enough.

She moved with the speed that their kind could call upon in times of need, but so did he. Well before she reached the other side of the flame-lit clearing, he had her.

She screamed and struggled and threw every curse she could think of at him, from *"sleep,"* to *"be still,"* to *"fall down,"* and everything in between, but nothing happened. He appeared to be protected from her powers, great though he believed them to be. She certainly believed them to be far above average, if her frustration and fury at the moment were anything to go by.

Dragging her diminutive, resisting form along, Dyfed sat upon the nearest felled tree, threw Miss Desdemona Caslin across his knee, tossed her heavy black skirt up over her head to expose her undergarments, and, with the flat of his palm across her small and attractively rounded bottom, gave her the thrashing she deserved.

From the screaming outrage that accompanied the task, it was clear that she'd never been subjected to such punishment before. Which explained a good deal, Dyfed thought.

"This is for Lud," Dyfed told her, landing a solid blow. "And this is for Bened. This is for the trees and plants you destroyed. This is for behaving in such a spoiled and reckless manner. And this," he said, giving her an especially hard whack, "is for my horse!"

She was weeping by the time Dyfed was finished, more out of mortification than hurt, he supposed. If the little wretch thought this was bad, however, only wait until Kian got through with her. He would be here soon. Dyfed could feel it.

"There," he said, pulling her up into a sitting position and settling her on his lap. "That's done, and no less than you deserve for being so ill-mannered a brat. Calm yourself and gather your wits. I want you to release Lud and Bened from your curse as quickly as possible."

"I don't understand," she managed between sobs, shaking her head. "Something's wrong. Why are my powers useless against you? It's n-not possible."

She had given up fighting him, at least for the time being. The shock of not being able to curse him had evidently stunned her into a temporary surrender. Temporary, he knew, because magical beings of great power generally made wily prey. He'd spent his life with just such a person and knew very well how quickly Kian could regain his composure, even after a tremendous blow. To be safe, Dyfed set one arm firmly about Desdemona's waist. With his other hand he tilted her chin up to have a better look at her.

Americans, he decided, might not be civilized, but they were certainly very attractive. Or, rather, this particular one was.

Her hair was as black and sleek as a raven's wing and quite long, if the several strands that had come loose from her arrangement were proof to go by. Her face was as delicate as the rest of her, heart shaped and deceptively sweet, with a small nose and softly rounded cheeks. Her dark brows were high, slender, and arching, and beneath were eyes the color of amethyst, framed by long black lashes. Her lips were slightly bowed, curving into an almost childish pout, especially now, when she was so unhappy. Gazing at it, he felt a disarming urge to give her the kiss she had asked for earlier.

Aye, she was a rare beauty, as so many of their kind were. Unfortunately, also as with many of their kind, it was a beauty that belied the heart that lay beneath. Hers was a dark, cold magic, and nothing other than that about her could be believed.

She gazed up at him, forlorn and unhappy, her face streaked with mud and tears. She was some years younger than he was, he thought, perhaps twenty, no older, and Dyfed felt an unwanted stirring of pity for her.

"I don't know what to do," she whispered. "This has never happened before. You're not even a great wizard."

"No, I'm not," Dyfed agreed, and with one finger pushed a few stray strands of hair from her face. "I'm a lesser wizard, and perfectly happy to be so. What I should like to know now is more precisely who you are and why you're here from the States, and what you're doing at Tylluan in the dead of night. And, of course, what you have to do with the troubles we've been experiencing here these past many months."

She sniffled and wiped her wet face with both hands. "My powers may have gone astray, but I'm not a fool." She looked up at him, her eyes filled with misery. "Why wouldn't you kiss me? I thought at least you'd *want* to obey that command."

"Why do you want me to kiss you?" he asked. "You came to Tylluan to bring destruction, not to claim kisses."

"Why?" The question seemed to bewilder her greatly. "Does there have to be a reason? I want you to, that's all. But you won't, and I . . . I don't understand how that can be."

He took her chin in one hand and sighed. "You've clearly been terribly spoiled, Desdemona Caslin, if you've been able to command strong men to do whatever you bid. You'll think me an antiquated boor, I fear, but I'm not in the habit of kissing strange young women who trespass on my brother's lands, kill my horse, and put spells on my companions."

"I'm sorry about the horse," she said tearfully, her arms going about his neck. "I'll give you a new one."

"Will you?" He gave her a disbelieving look. "And where will you get it? Do you intend to create one from out of thin air, or did you happen to bring your stable over from America?"

"No," she said, "but I'll get one, I promise you."

"I'll believe that when I see it. For now, however, I shall be satisfied for you to release my men from their slumber."

She drew in a shaking breath and calmed a little. "I will, if you'll kiss me first."

"I'm not a whore," he replied with renewed anger. "I don't dole out kisses as bribes."

"Please," she begged. "Lord Tylluan is coming. I can feel his approach. Please."

Dyfed regarded her for a silent moment before at last giving way. It was all foolishness, as far as he was concerned, but if it would cause Lud and Bened to be wakened more quickly, it would be worthwhile.

Dyfed meant it only to be a momentary caress, as chaste as the kisses he always shared with Loris, but as he bent nearer, Desdemona's arms tightened about his neck, and tighter still as he brushed his lips against her own.

What happened then was ever after something of a mystery to him. Dyfed knew what powerful magic was and had from birth been surrounded by wizards and sorceresses who both wielded and experienced powerful magic. But being a lesser wizard, he'd always been a spectator and never before been directly involved in anything more amazing than his gift of silent speech. He wasn't even able to levitate small objects, which was considered an almost childish achievement among his peers.

But the moment he touched Desdemona Caslin's lips, Dyfed knew that he'd been cast headlong into a magic that far surpassed the ordinary. It felt as if violent explosions were going off in his head, not giving pain, but instead imparting an intense clarity. He had read a good deal about passion in books and had, he believed, experienced the same emotion with some of the numerous females he'd bedded in his life. But he'd been wrong. For the first time he truly *knew* what passion was, for it had come to life in him through nothing more than an innocent kiss with this strange woman from America.

Lifting his head, Dyfed gazed at her and saw that she had felt it, too. Her eyes were wide, filled with the same astonishment he was experiencing.

He lowered his mouth to hers again and they came together with a sudden eagerness, their arms holding each other tightly, their fingers grasping fistfuls of clothing and hair. Dyfed's brain spun from the exertion of it—he had never kissed anyone with so much energy before. Or been kissed in that manner, either. He had the alarming feeling that they were both going to faint from lack of air in a few more moments.

But it didn't come to that. She tore away, panting, and frantically pushed to make him sit upright.

"He's almost here!" she said. "Please, I cannot let him see me. I must go." Casting her glance back at Lud and Bened, who still lay insensible upon the ground, she cried, "Awake!"

"I can't let you go," Dyfed said as she turned back to him. "I'm sorry, but—"

She silenced him with a hard kiss. "I'll find you again, very soon," she told him. "Forgive me for your horse. I vow I'll make the loss up to you."

Bened and Lud began to stir, just as they heard Kian's shout, not far away.

Desdemona shivered. "I can feel his powers," she whispered. "Cadmaran didn't tell me the full of it."

"Cadmaran?" Dyfed repeated.

Kian shouted once more, much closer, and Dyfed could hear the sound of horse hooves approaching through the trees. Desdemona reached up and kissed him again, a brief, sorrowful parting, and then she pushed free and, in a blur of motion, was gone.

Kian rode into the clearing with Horas behind him, taking the scene in with what Dyfed thought to be an admirable lack of shock.

"Where is he?" Kian demanded.

Dyfed's arms were still in the place they'd been moments before, as if she were still in his embrace. Dropping them, he looked dazedly at his elder brother and repeated, stupidly, "He?"

"I felt the power of an extraordinary wizard," Kian said sharply, turning Seren about. "Was it Cadmaran? Where has he gone?"

Dyfed shook his head, disoriented. How had she gotten out of his arms so quickly? Where had she disappeared to?

"It was a girl. A young woman," he amended. "She's an American. I don't know which direction she took, but at the last she mentioned Cadmaran. She may be heading for Llew."

Kian and Horas spurred their horses across the clearing and back into the trees, aiming in the direction of Llew. Once Desdemona crossed Tylluan's borders, she'd be free of danger, for the magic that gave the lord of the land an advantage would be gone, but if Kian could catch her before then . . .

But he won't, Dyfed thought grimly, watching as Lud and Bened carefully gained their feet. Desdemona Caslin was clearly more than a match for Kian, perhaps even for Malachi. Dyfed had a feeling that she would only be caught if she wished to be and only held captive by a man against whom she was powerless. And that, strangely enough, seemed to be him.

Five

$\mathcal{B}$y the time they returned to the castle, it was almost dawn. Kian and Dyfed made their weary way inside while the others stabled the horses.

With a wave of one hand Kian set flames dancing in the fireplace in his study, then poured each of them a drink. Dyfed tumbled into a chair near the fire, rubbing his face with both hands in a futile effort to stave off exhaustion.

"I'm sorry that you won't have a chance for much rest before you leave for *Fynnon Elian,*" Kian said, handing his brother a glass before sitting in the chair opposite him. The warmth of the fire was most welcome after so many hours in the fog. "I never imagined we'd be out so late this time."

"It's all right, *fy gefell,*" Dyfed said, sitting back and sipping from his glass. "That a woman has been involved with what's been happening was something you couldn't possibly have divined. I'm sorry you weren't able to catch her."

Kian uttered a weary laugh. "Horas and I never had a chance of doing so. She was—I almost can't believe it, Dyfed—she was flying. Or so it seemed. Perhaps the fog played tricks with my eyes, but all I could see was a moment's flash of color well above the earth. This woman is a sorceress of immense powers. You must tell me everything you learned about her."

"It's not very much," Dyfed replied, setting his drink aside on a nearby low table. "Her name is Desdemona Caslin. She's from America. She said she would replace my horse." He wasn't about to tell his brother about the kisses he and Desdemona had shared. Not until he'd sorted them out in his own mind.

Kian was looking at Dyfed with interest. "She said she would replace Bachgen? She must not be aware of how difficult—almost impossible—that would be. And that's an odd thing for someone bent on destroying Tylluan to say."

"Aye," Dyfed agreed somberly. "I know that, but she said it, nonetheless. Several times. Oh, and she told me her father's name, as if I should recognize it. Draceous Caslin. Does it mean anything to you?"

Kian shook his head slowly. "No. I've never heard the name before. But we are not in much communication with those of our kind who adopted the Americas as their place of refuge after the exile. Perhaps he's their idea of a *Dewin Mawr*." Kian was thoughtful for a moment, gazing at the fire and fingering the glass in his hands. "But Cadmaran must know something of them, since the girl mentioned his name. I wonder how, though?" Looking at Dyfed, he said, "Tell me all that you remember of your encounter, and quickly, so that you can have at least a couple hours of sleep before you must go."

Dyfed did as his brother asked, telling him everything except for those parts that had to do with her touching him or demanding a kiss or those actual kisses that came after.

"But how is it that you were able to hold her?" Kian asked. "Her powers must necessarily make her a difficult prisoner."

"I find it as bewildering as you, Brother, but have no explanation for it. But there is something far more curious to me. Though her powers are great, I don't believe she alone has caused the destruction at Tylluan. There was something with her. A creature, or even perhaps one of the ancient monsters, as you've suspected. I didn't see it, but I know it was there."

Kian sat forward, sighing. "I thought there must be, for the signs of destruction were the same as before. The water and the haphazard damage to the trees and plants—those are not the earmarks of our kind. We are almost peculiarly neat and tidy when we wreak havoc." Standing, he moved toward the fire, gazing into the dancing flames. "But what is this thing? And where does it disappear to so quickly? It must be tremendous in size and strength, yet it leaves behind almost no mark, no trail."

"It leaves a water trail," Dyfed countered. "Can you not seek the advice of the water faeries? Surely they know something useful."

"All those that once lived within Tylluan's borders have gone. But I've thought of going elsewhere, perhaps to Glen Aur, to ask of the beings there." He took another sip from his glass, then turned to look at Dyfed. "When you're in London, you might do me the favor of visiting Professor Seabolt and getting his opinion on the matter."

Dyfed was taken by surprise. "Surely you still don't expect me to go to London after this?"

"Of course I do," Kian replied. "I need you to escort Loris and introduce her about Town. And keep her safe."

Dyfed smiled wearily. "She'll hardly need me to act as guard with Malachi and Niclas keeping an eye on her. And Julia will see that she's properly introduced into society."

"I'll rest easier knowing that you're with her," Kian told him a bit more tersely, and Dyfed couldn't decide whether his brother was growing irritable because he was weary or truly becoming angry. "I don't want her being bothered by hordes of men when she attends parties and balls. I expect you to stay by her side and keep the wolves at bay. Apart from that, you seemed eager to go when I told you of the trip this afternoon. You've always loved to be in Town."

"I do," Dyfed said, "but you need me here more. I can help you find Desdemona Caslin."

Kian's eyebrows rose, and Dyfed knew he had stepped wrong. He had to be careful how much he revealed to his cunning brother.

"Can you?" Kian asked, eyeing him curiously. "How?"

Again, Dyfed hesitated to reveal everything that had transpired. He should have told Kian that Desdemona had said she would find him again, but he couldn't. Or, more truthfully, didn't want to. What he wanted was to see Desdemona once more, alone, and he couldn't do that if he was in London or if Kian knew of it.

"Because I'll recognize her," Dyfed answered at last. "Even if she changes her appearance, I'll know the sound of her voice."

"Or you might not," Kian said. "A very powerful sorceress can change everything about herself, even the sound of her voice. No"—he watched Dyfed closely—"I believe it would be best if you and Loris proceed to London as planned. I appreciate your desire to lend me your most excellent aid in solving the troubles here, but the arrangements for your journey have already been made. I have no intention of altering them for my sake alone."

Dyfed rose from his chair, ready to argue further, but Kian lifted one hand to silence him.

"I'll do very well on my own, *fy gefell*. All I ask of you is to keep Loris safe and enjoy your time in London. And don't forget that you must always speak aloud while there. *And,*" he added with a slight smile, "try not to get into trouble. The last thing I need just now is Cousin Niclas or Malachi complaining to me about any havoc."

"I'm not the one who always gets into trouble when we visit Town," Dyfed told him.

"That's true enough," Kian admitted. "I won't be there to get you into any scrapes, but I also won't be there to get you out of trouble, should any arise." He grew more serious. "Swear to me, Brother, that you'll keep a close eye on Loris. Don't let anyone upset her or . . . make her unhappy."

Dyfed understood what his brother was asking of him.

Kian always fretted when he and Loris were parted, which, during the past few years, had been seldom and for two or three weeks at most. He'd not enjoyed their yearly jaunts to London because Loris refused to go, and had always left Dyfed and their father there long before their planned visit was done in order to return to Tylluan, where he and Loris had doubtless badgered each other without ceasing until Ffinian had come home and made them stop. Dyfed imagined that those had been happy times for Kian, happy because he had Loris to himself for a few weeks, despite their fighting, and because she had no one else to turn to when she needed company.

"I give you my word that Loris will be kept safe and happy," Dyfed promised. "But you must promise me something, as well. If you cannot find Desdemona Caslin within a few days' time, you must send for me and let me help you. And if you do find her, swear to me on your honor that you'll not harm her."

Kian gave him that curious, searching look once more, then nodded. "If I can avoid doing so, of course. I cannot know what she may attempt, but I should not wish to harm her, or any woman."

"Thank you."

"Go to bed, Dyfed," his brother said. "Loris will be having you wakened as soon as the sun has brightened and the fog cleared. Sleep as much as you may until then."

"What about you?" Dyfed asked. "You're as weary as I am."

"Don't worry over me," Kian replied. "I'm going to ride over the tenant lands and make certain no destruction came to them during the night. It was bad enough losing a rare horse like Bachgen, but for the tenants to continue losing livestock . . ." He sighed and drank deeply from his glass, wiping his mouth with the backs of his fingers after. "I'll be here to see you off to Elian's Well, and then, I promise you, I shall seek my bed and sleep like one of the dead."

Dyfed thought the same thing as he made his way to his chamber. He was so weary that it would be a miracle if Loris could rouse him come the morning. But that wasn't the case. He had barely laid his head upon his soft pillow when he heard a voice, calling his name.

Weariness made him confused at first, and then, as he sat up and peered into the darkness, he recognized that it was her. Desdemona. Calling him.

Sliding out of the bed, he went to his balcony doors, flinging them open. The fog was still thick, but the intense blackness of night was giving way to a softer, lighter darkness. In a few hours the mist would fade altogether, leaving behind another bright, warm, beautiful spring day.

Somewhere, she was calling Dyfed's name, yet he knew that he alone could hear it. This must be what it was like for others to hear his voice in their heads, rather than with their ears. He heard her so clearly that it was more a feeling than simple knowledge. Her voice poured over and through him, sweet and caressing, filled with a longing that his own emotions suddenly matched.

He tested the sensation, closing his eyes and thinking her name, wondering if she could hear him as well. Part of his gift let him communicate with certain individuals despite a great distance, but those individuals had always only been close relatives or those who lived at Tylluan.

Desdemona heard him and answered with a pleasure that made him smile. Dyfed stood in the cold, damp air, shivering, and wondered what he was feeling. It was new and strange and a little frightening. He didn't even know her, had only been in company with her for a few brief, somewhat frantic moments, yet there was such an intensity of desire, even in this delicate connection of thoughts. It made his heart ache.

I must see you, he heard, and answered that he would be leaving Tylluan soon.

She paused; then it came again more firmly. *I'll find you.*

He hesitated and then, not entirely certain that it was either right or wise, began to tell her about his journey to *Fynnon Elian.*

Six

Castle Llew was a massive, imposing structure. It had been constructed in the same century as Tylluan but had undergone few alterations since that time. There were a few modern touches: balconies, larger windows with glass panes, gravel roads. But apart from these Llew remained, in the main, a foreboding medieval fortress.

Kian slowly brought Seren to a standstill and gazed at the impressive edifice, considering what he was about to do. Loris had railed at him for a full hour this morning before he'd at last managed to escape, telling him in impressively fulsome terms that he was every kind of fool for facing Morcar Cadmaran both alone and uninvited. Kian had been encouraged at her fears for his life—any amount of concern from Loris was rare and welcome—but unwilling to follow any of her suggestions, such as waiting for Dyfed to return from *Fynnon Elian* in order to accompany him. Dyfed wouldn't return until tomorrow night at the earliest, but even if he were home, Kian still would have gone alone.

Kian tried to imagine what Malachi would have done, how he would have approached a wizard like Cadmaran, but it did little to encourage him. Malachi had always moved with such power and natural confidence, even when he'd been a youth, that it seemed impossible to emulate.

From his earliest childhood, Kian had watched his older cousin with care, filled with awe and admiration for all that he said and did. Malachi never seemed to step wrong or be at a loss for what to do in any situation. How it was that Kian had been declared to be the future *Dewin Mawr* was a great bewilderment. Worse, it was a fearful thought, knowing that one day not only the Seymour family but also other families like theirs would look to Kian for guidance and security.

And that wasn't going to happen if he couldn't at least muster up the nerve to confront Morcar Cadmaran. Alone.

The road to the castle seemed long enough when Kian first spurred Seren onward, but in a surprisingly short amount of time he found himself at the castle gates, which swung open for him without the help of human hands. Guards stood on either side of the entryway, silent, not moving even as Kian dismounted and walked into the outer bailey, leading Seren along.

Cadmaran, evidently, was waiting for him.

Kian had been at the castle only once before, when Cadmaran had taken his cousin Niclas's future wife, Julia, captive. They—Kian, Dyfed, their father, and their men—had waited outside the castle, ready to attack if need be, while Niclas had gone alone into Cadmaran's lair to free Julia. It had been one of the bravest and most foolhardy acts Kian had ever witnessed, for Niclas was a lesser wizard and possessed no powers to match the Earl of Llew. Instead, Niclas had taken only an ancient magic necklace to bargain with, as well as his love for Julia. Those two simple things had proved sufficient to bring both him and Julia safely back out, victorious.

Cadmaran had fared rather worse after their confrontation, for he had used magic to try to kill Niclas and the Guardians had placed a blood curse on him, making him blind. That had been three years past, and, until today, Kian hadn't seen Cadmaran, not even in London, which the Earl of Llew had used to frequent.

An eerie quiet greeted Kian as he made his way across the bailey. The few servants who went about their various duties were silent, save for the sound their footsteps made in the gravel as they walked past. No one looked at or spoke to Kian, not even the boy who approached to take Seren's reins. Not meeting Kian's eye, he led the horse away toward the stables.

Another set of gates silently opened across the way, leading Kian into an inner bailey and a courtyard graced with a beautiful, if ruthlessly perfect, garden. Every leaf, every blade of grass, was cut to astonishing precision, so that for a moment Kian wondered whether it wasn't merely a vision that Cadmaran had conjured. But as he followed the path that led to the massive castle doors, he realized that it was real enough, if far from natural.

It was an impressive display of magic. Clearly Castle Llew, and all those in it, was beneath a powerful enchantment. The knowledge made Kian slightly more tense; he'd never even known such magic as this existed, let alone seen it firsthand.

The castle doors opened when he reached them, as the gates had, allowing Kian entrance. He stopped on the wide steps, gazing into the dark depths of Castle Llew, seeing before him a long hallway lit only by flickering torches mounted at intervals upon the bare stone walls.

He hesitated, sensing the strength of the dark magic that lived within. It was the lion's den, and he was very likely a fool to go in willingly. Reaching up, he pulled the hat from his head, smoothed his other hand over his hair, then pushed forward into the elegance and grandeur that belonged to Morcar Cadmaran.

The doors shut and Kian waited to see if anyone would appear to lead him on, but no one did. Somewhere down the length of the hall he heard another set of doors opening, and accordingly followed the sound. They led to another hallway, which led to another, with walls lined on either side by elaborate, shining suits of armor. Still there were no oil lamps or even candles to be found, but torches lit the way. It was like stepping back in time hundreds of years, and Kian could feel the spirits of those who had come before watching and listening.

At last he came to two tall, beautifully carved wood doors and knew that he had arrived at the entry to the great hall. Silently, the doors swung open.

The great hall of Castle Llew was as remarkable as the rest of the immense structure. It was a room built on a grand scale, constructed with the original intention of housing a very large number of people. Now the cavernous hall served as the intimidating seat of the Earl of Llew, and as Kian made his way, he had to admit that he was impressed.

The room was richly decorated with both furniture and ornamentation that maintained Cadmaran's preference for the medieval. Ancient weapons graced the walls, and more suits of armor kept silent vigil near the several huge fireplaces that were currently putting both light and heat into the room, along with dozens of torches. Beneath Kian's feet were a series of expensively crafted carpets, all of which looked to be as antique as the weapons and suits of armor, somewhat faded but as beautiful as they had been hundreds of years ago.

At the end of the hall was a dais, and upon the dais were what appeared to be two thrones, the larger one set in the center and the smaller one just off to the right. Kian could see at once that Morcar Cadmaran's large, muscular frame filled the first, but the young woman who sat to his right was a stranger to him.

The Earl of Llew, as usual, was dressed predominantly in black, his clothing expensive and beautifully cut, presenting the perfect figure of a fashionable gentleman. The woman was clothed in a gown made from a silken deep green fabric that shimmered in the flickering torchlight. It was a charming creation, cut low at the bodice to expose an alluring amount of white flesh and tied high at the waist to make the most of her slender, feminine figure. She sat ramrod straight, as elegant and noble in bearing as a queen.

This, then, must be Desdemona Caslin.

Dyfed had described her as dark and delicate and lovely, but the words hadn't done her justice. She possessed the kind of beauty that was so striking it was difficult to keep from staring at her. Even before he reached the bottom of the stairs that led to the dais Kian could see the unusual color and clarity of her catlike eyes. They were like crystalline violets and were gazing very directly at Kian, as unwelcoming and cold as arctic ice. Morcar Cadmaran's blind expression, by comparison, was almost friendly, and it was well known how much the man hated all Seymours.

"It took you long enough to make this visit, Lord Tylluan. I expected that you would come months ago, but Seymours have always been foolishly stubborn, and you do not appear to be an exception. My congratulations, by the by, on at last taking your rightful place as baron. That was long past due, as well."

"Yes, it was," Kian replied, glancing from Lord Llew to Desdemona Caslin, who was still gazing at him in that piercing manner. "I realized that almost immediately after I took the title. If I'd done so years ago, the troubles that have plagued Tylluan would have long since been dealt with. Though you were always diligent to bother us when my father was baron, too."

Lord Llew smiled with unveiled dislike. His unseeing gaze turned more accurately in Kian's direction. "Do you wish to accuse me of something in particular, Tylluan? I'm eager to hear the words."

Kian's eyebrows rose. "Accuse you aloud, my lord? You must think me a complete imbecile to readily do something that the Guardians would consider a challenge. But, then, we do not know each other well, do we? And I do not know this young lady at all."

"How remiss of me," Cadmaran said lightly. "Allow me to make known to you my betrothed, Miss Desdemona Caslin, of America." He swept a hand toward where she sat. "Desdemona, my love, this is one of our neighbors, Kian Seymour, the Baron of Tylluan."

Kian bowed. "I'm glad to meet you, Miss Caslin, having heard something of you. I believe you've already met my brother, Dyfed."

Her eyes narrowed and her mouth thinned; Cadmaran turned toward her with a touch of honest surprise in his face, saying, "Is that so, my dear? You neglected to tell me."

"I killed his horse," she stated without emotion. "Last night. It was in my way."

"Oh dear," Cadmaran murmured, pleasure glinting in his dark, blind eyes as he turned back toward Kian. "What a pity. I'm certain my beloved regrets the incident. Have you come to ask me to replace the animal? I should be more than happy to do so. I keep an excellent stable, as I'm sure you know."

Desdemona Caslin was still gazing at Kian in that hard, penetrating manner, and he found it impossible to look away. He felt the tremendous power leashed within her—power such as he had rarely encountered before. He wondered if he would be able to match her, should such a thing become necessary. How had Dyfed managed to detain the woman even for a moment?

"You're from the States, Miss Caslin?" Kian asked, keeping his voice low.

"From Boston, sir," she replied with frigid politeness.

"Your father would be Draceous Caslin, I assume?"

Cadmaran frowned, but Desdemona's expression remained unchanged.

"Do you know of him?" Lord Llew asked.

"Of a certainty," Kian lied. "He is one of the great wizards in America, is he not?"

"He is *the* great wizard," Desdemona stated tightly, the first rise in emotion Kian had seen since he'd entered the hall.

"The Caslins are the most prominent and powerful family of our kind in the States," Lord Llew said. "Just as the Cadmarans are in Europe." He paused briefly to see if Kian would argue the point. "This will be the first of many unions between the two families. I hope you will wish Miss Caslin and me happy?"

It was all Kian could do to keep from uttering a laugh, but he reminded himself of where he was and that Cadmaran's powers were increased within Llew's borders, just as his were within Tylluan's.

"Certainly," he said pleasantly. "I'm sure that you and Miss Caslin will be . . . well matched." He couldn't quite bring himself to say "happy," for he'd never yet known a Cadmaran who was.

Something flashed through Desdemona Caslin's violet eyes, a fleeting look of disgust, but it was so quickly gone that Kian couldn't be quite certain.

"As to my brother's horse," he went on, "I don't require that you replace him. Bachgen was descended of that ancient breed which has served the *dewins* among our kind for many generations. He was given to my brother as a gift by the *Dewin Mawr,* and was trained to accept a lesser wizard as his master. He cannot be replaced by animals bred by mere mortals, which, unless I'm mistaken," he said, tilting his head consideringly, "are all that the Cadmarans possess. Though I'm certain your stable is perfectly presentable, otherwise."

A faint smile tilted Desdemona's lips, but the Earl of Llew was far from amused. Hundreds of years ago the Cadmarans had managed to kill off the enchanted horses that had been allotted them, mainly from maltreatment and neglect. It was a mistake that the current earl had tried to rectify, offering the other Families a good deal of money to part with some of their animals, but to no avail. The creatures were far too valuable, and the loss of Bachgen was a blow that couldn't be easily recovered from.

"However," Kian said, "if some manner of amends would be made, I should be pleased to have the destruction that my tenants and their livestock have suffered come to an end."

Cadmaran's sightless eyes glittered. "I thought you said that you weren't going to be so foolish as to accuse me of anything. That sounds very close to making a rash mistake, Kian Seymour. Are you intimating that I am behind such suffering?"

"Did I say as much?" Kian asked.

"Not yet," Lord Llew said. "But I believe that may change in time. You haven't yet told us why you've come to Llew. Uninvited."

"I wished to inform you that certain inhabitants of Tylluan will be traveling to London soon," Kian told him. "Over the next few days, in fact. One of those travelers will be my brother, Dyfed, and the other is one who is dearer to me than my own life. I do not want them to be disturbed in any manner, or waylaid upon the journey. So many unforeseen accidents have occurred of late that I thought it best to take no chances."

"Closer and closer, my lord," Cadmaran said, and laughed. "And how, pray, does telling me this most interesting news lend the journey greater protection? Surely you don't suggest that I should ever harm innocent travelers?"

"Certainly not," Kian replied. "I merely wanted to make it known that the woman is my *unoliaeth,* and that any harm that may come to her will be considered by the Guardians as having befallen me. I shall be granted like for like of the one who is at fault, whether that one's own hand was the means of harm or not. And if so much as a tear should fall upon her cheek because of another of my kind, I shall exact repayment in full. Thus I make my vow aloud, so that the Guardians know of it. That is all I came to say." He sketched a proper bow to Desdemona Caslin, whose gaze had grown thoughtful as it rested upon him, and, straightening, set his hat upon his head.

"Good day to you, Miss Caslin. Good day, Lord Llew."

Cadmaran and Desdemona sat in silence as their visitor walked away. With but a thought Cadmaran opened the great hall doors, then shut them as he heard Kian Seymour walking through.

When they were fully closed, Cadmaran said, "What did you think of him, my dear?"

"That I wish I had killed his horse, instead."

Cadmaran laughed and, turning toward her, sought her hand with his own. Desdemona did nothing to make the task easy for him.

"He intends to take us on alone, my love. That is why he sends away his beloved."

"And the brother?" she asked. "Is he of no help in the matter?"

"None at all. I believe the only gift he possesses is that of silent speech. He's clearly of better use squiring the girl about London. We shall go to Town one day soon, my dear." He at last found her hand and squeezed it tightly. "You must be introduced into society. I shall take you as soon as our business here is done."

Desdemona nodded. "Then we must be quick, my lord. I'll take the beast out again tonight. It's rested well these past two days, and will be hungry."

"Excellent," Cadmaran said, clearly pleased. "Perhaps you might come across another of the ancient breeds again, and be obliged to rid its rider of its excellent services. I understand Kian Seymour's own mount is descended of the same sire as his brother's was. How unfortunate it would be should he lose him."

She looked at Cadmaran, into his handsome face with its dark, unfocused, unseeing eyes.

"Aye," she said, and with a rush of displeasure realized how very alike their thoughts were. "It would."

Seven

"No, Elen, I'm quite sure I won't be needing my gardening clothes in London."

The girl obediently folded the worn, much-faded garment and put it back into Loris's clothing chest. "Won't it be lovely to have new clothes made, miss? His Lordship said you're to have the most beautiful gowns and hats and shoes." She sighed happily. "And he said I'm to have new things, too. He's so kind and good, isn't he, miss?"

"She isn't the right person to ask, Elen," came a voice from the doorway, and they both turned to see Kian standing there. "I feel quite certain she'd not agree."

"You're back!" Loris exclaimed, both surprised and relieved. She felt an unusual, and somewhat alarming, urge to rush at and hug him. "Thank God."

He sauntered into the room. "Why, Loris, darling, you almost sound glad to see me. Were you afraid Cadmaran would murder me outright or hold me captive, leaving you all alone to manage Tylluan?"

She gave a shake of her head, angry anew that he'd gone to Llew in the first place. He should have waited for Dyfed to return and accompany him or at least taken some of the men for added protection. She had never met Morcar Cadmaran, but she knew enough about him to understand that he wasn't a man to be trusted. It had been unutterably foolish for Kian, who had so many lives dependent upon him, to go right into his enemy's fortress, completely unarmed save for his enormous ego and various powers—powers that Cadmaran was, at least for now, more than equal to.

"You may leave, Elen," Loris said. "Go and tell Cook to prepare a plate with some bread and cold meats for His Lordship. I'm sure he's hungry, having missed the afternoon meal. Unless Lord Llew was kind enough to feed you?" She looked at Kian inquiringly.

"No," he said, grinning at her. "Cadmaran wasn't that pleased by my visit. Tell Cook to have it sent to my study, Elen. I'll be there just as soon as Miss Loris has finished venting her wrath upon me."

Giggling, Elen curtsied and departed.

"Now she's going to tell the others that we're fighting again," Loris chided, returning to the task at hand. "I believe you're already familiar with my feelings regarding your ridiculously foolish visit to Llew. What I want to know now is what transpired, and what you and Cadmaran said to each other. And the young woman—did you meet her? Is she just as Dyfed told us?"

"She was a statue of ice," Kian said, casting his gaze about Loris's chamber, taking in the various trunks being packed. "She said very little, but what she did confirmed to me that she's not a pleasant woman. Cadmaran was his usual uninspired self. Malachi has always said that Lord Llew isn't a particularly clever wizard, and I believe he must be right."

"Was she beautiful? And powerful?"

"Very, on both counts. And memorably frightening. Poor Dyfed, having to face such a dreadful female alone. You're a fearsome enough lot when you're merely trying to manage men's lives, but add the ability to wreak havoc and mayhem and women become impossible to live with."

Loris couldn't stop the laughter that escaped her lips. It wasn't in her nature to be easily amused, though Ffinian had always had the ability to make her smile, but Kian's mood, at the moment, was light and teasing, and Loris felt her own spirits rise. She knew, though he never would have admitted it, that Kian been worried about facing Morcar Cadmaran. Now that the deed had been successfully done, he was clearly buoyant.

"She's his betrothed," Kian went on, picking through the pile of unfolded clothing that Loris intended to pack.

"Cadmaran's betrothed?" Loris asked, much surprised by the news. "He intends to wed an American? Is it allowed?"

Kian shrugged. "I suppose it must be, especially as he hasn't been able to find a potential wife among the Families in Europe. Certainly not after my cousin Ceridwen was married before he could force her to the altar."

"But if she's very powerful, won't the Families be concerned about such a union?"

"Deeply concerned," Kian agreed. "Their coming together will likely produce magic mortals possessed of vast powers. I'm surprised that the Guardians would allow it. And Miss Caslin didn't appear to be fainting with joy at the idea, either."

Loris glanced at him as she bent to pick up one of her better dresses. "Perhaps the marriage wasn't of her choosing," she suggested.

"That may be," he replied. "I'm going to have to do some reading in the Seymour family history to discover if there's any mention of a clan named Caslin. From what I saw of Desdemona Caslin, they may very well be the American version of our Cadmarans. Which is a truly unpleasant idea." He picked up a tattered wrap with obvious revulsion. "Gad, you do need a new wardrobe, don't you? How old is this thing?"

Reaching out, Loris snatched it away. "I made that years ago. I made all of these clothes. You've never found them lacking before. And Tylluan is not precisely the center of fashionable society, is it?" she asked. "I need clothing that is practical and comfortable, not fine. And whatever you buy for me in London will be a waste of good money—which we happen to need just now. I can't imagine that any of it will be usable once I've come home."

Kian ignored this and picked up another garment, wrinkling his nose after closer examination. "I shall write Julia and instruct her to burn every last item once your new wardrobe has been delivered. Come to that, she'll probably consign them to the fire upon sight, so you may be required to remain indoors for a few days."

Dread twisted in Loris's stomach at the words, for she knew very well that it wasn't only her wardrobe that society in London would find lacking. She possessed none of the fine manners that both Kian and Dyfed could so easily call forth, nor the kind of education that would lend itself to good conversation. She was plain and simple and only knew about plain and simple things, and she felt quite certain that none of the people she was going to meet at grand balls and parties were going to be interested in either of her lives, current or former.

"I would far rather remain at Tylluan and spare you the expense. We could use the money to repair the fences along the southern border."

"There's no need for you to worry about having sufficient funds," Kian said, briefly playing tug-of-war with her over the garment he held, at last letting her win. "We have our share of the Seymour fortune, and there should be enough for both your Season and the repairs that will be needed at Tylluan once the troubles are gone. And as this is likely the only time in your life that you'll be in London again, considering your aversion to travel, I want you to enjoy your visit there as much as possible."

Loris abruptly dropped the garment she was folding and turned about, truly angry now. "Kian Deiniol Owain Seymour," she began, and he laughed.

"God's mercy, this is going to be unpleasant. She's said my full name in that fearsome manner."

Loris put her hands on her hips and glared at him. "Never tell me you've dipped into that money for this journey. Even

Ffinian never touched it, and you know how dearly he wanted to. That money is only to be used for Tyllwan, and we may well need it before long."

"Is that what has you so worried?" he asked, clearly amused. "Put your mind at ease, darling Loris. I should have said that *you* have a share of the Seymour fortune. Malachi made certain that money was put away years ago so that you could have a proper Season, and it's been growing by the day beneath Cousin Niclas's tender care. You and Elen may enjoy your new wardrobes with a clear conscience." Kian's gaze traveled slowly over her figure, and he moved nearer. "I only wish I could see you in the latest fashions, with your hair stylishly cut and arranged." Lifting a hand, he touched one of the curls that had fallen loose from the simple manner in which she wore her hair each day. "You're going to cause such a stir in Town, Loris. You must be careful not to let any gentleman do anything foolish. I should hate to have to harm anyone."

It took Loris a moment to realize what he meant. "You can't be serious, Kian." She slapped his hand away. "Do you mean to say that you'd actually fight a duel with some poor man because of me?"

Kian's amusement died away and he took her chin in a firm, but careful, grasp, keeping her gaze steadily on his. "I believe I could even kill a man if he harmed you, Loris. You know how I feel, and regardless of your own emotions, you accept that I'm speaking the truth. I love you. You're mine. I won't tolerate another man forcing his attentions on you. If I thought it would do any good I'd let you and Dyfed trot out that ridiculous betrothal that somehow came into being years ago, but your behavior toward each other is so much like brother and sister that no one would believe it was true."

Loris twisted away, furious as only Kian could make her. "You'd best make up your mind, my lord, whether you want me going to London or not, and whether I'm to enjoy myself or not, and whether I'm to dress in fine clothes and cause a sensation. Or not. And when you do finally decide what you want of me, be so kind as to let me know. Until then, I'd prefer not to speak on the matter."

"What I want of you?" he repeated, his own angry expression mirroring hers. "Damn you, Loris, have a care what you say to me. You think it a difficult thing to leave Tylluan, and perhaps it is, but I dread the days and nights that are to come, being parted from you. But you don't wish to speak of that, either, do you? Or of what's between us."

"There is *nothing* between us," she countered. "Save a seemingly never-ending conflict. Why can we never have five minutes of peace between us, Kian? God above." She set a hand to her head, where an ache was beginning to throb. "Perhaps a trip to London will be welcome, after all. I shall have a little peace while I'm there, at least."

"No, my love, that you won't," Kian said, and before she could move away had gathered her up in his arms. "And neither will I."

He set his lips over hers, ignoring her attempt to strike him, and held her still, kissing her in the manner that always made her lose her senses, not harshly, but with a gentleness and care that belied the hard arms lashed about her. It was impossible to fight him when he kissed her like this, and the trouble was that she never wanted to.

No one else could do this to her, not even Liw. Only Kian could make her forget everything but the feel of his lips caressing her own, the heat of his body warming her, his strength enveloping her. Her hands lifted of their own accord and grasped him, one digging into the hard muscles of his shoulder, the other sliding around the soft skin of his neck. He moaned at her touch, and with his tongue parted her lips, stroking gently inside.

Her body felt suddenly light, as if she might float if let go and was only kept from doing so by the arms about her. Some of her senses were dimmed, so that both sound and light faded away, while others were heightened, and her awareness of Kian grew almost painfully acute.

His grip on her lessened, and his hands slid upward, stroking her bare upper arms. The fingers of one hand journeyed farther upward, sliding into her hair, imparting a sweet caress that made her helplessly murmur with pleasure.

And then it happened, as it always happened, though this time it had taken longer to begin. The pleasure faded, to be replaced by a sharp, burning pain. Needles pricked her skin where his hands and lips touched, quickly becoming unbearable. Wincing, she pulled back, hearing Kian plead, breathlessly, "No. Loris, no."

"I can't," she managed, firmly pushing him away and turning aside.

"The curse," he muttered. "As always."

"Yes," she agreed, not looking at him. "As always." She busied herself with smoothing down the front of her skirt and waited for the odd feelings to pass. Drawing in a deep breath, she turned back to the task of packing, folding clothes with but the slightest trembling in her hands. Kian stood nearby, fuming.

"You shouldn't kiss me," she told him. "It always ends badly."

"Aye, that it does," he agreed, "but it's a journey well worth making. One you enjoy as much as I do."

"Believe that if you wish," she replied. "Pass me that heavy skirt, please. I'm not entirely certain, having only packed clothes for men before now, but I believe the heavier items should go on the bottom."

"God's mercy, how is it that women can recover their wits so quickly?" he muttered, running both hands through his hair. "I find it incredibly difficult. And frustrating."

"So you've told me," Loris said, aware that he was still breathing rather harshly. "Perhaps you should make a visit to the village soon," she suggested, placing the skirt neatly on top of another garment. "While Dyfed and I are gone."

Kian was quiet for a long moment, and Loris could feel him gazing at her.

"To have a woman, do you mean?" His voice was low and

carefully measured, but Loris noted, with surprise, that there was a slight edge to his tone.

She glanced at him and saw that his expression matched his voice exactly. *Is he angry?* she wondered. *But why should he be? Surely he isn't embarrassed by the suggestion?* She found the idea vaguely amusing, considering how legendary his prowess with women was. The girls at the Red Fox had told Loris astonishing stories about both Kian and Dyfed.

"If it would be helpful to you," she replied, keeping her own voice level, unperturbed, though she allowed herself a little smile as she gave her attention again to the task at hand. "I doubt Neli Wynne's tavern has as much variety to offer as the places you frequent in London, but surely the outcome of your visits is much the same. And that's what truly matters to men, is it not?"

He touched Loris's arm, pulling her to face him. "You want me," he said slowly, "to go to the village and lie with one of the women available there? You *want* me to do that, Loris?"

"If you wish," she said. "I've never tried to stop you from doing so before, have I? I'm sure there's no need to do so now. It's really none of my business, after all. And you have to go somewhere to assuage your . . . needs," she said, slightly uncomfortable at having to find a word for what she meant. "I suppose I would be angered if you or Dyfed dallied with any of the castle maids, but if it's one of the women at Neli Wynne's—Kian, for pity's sake, I don't know why you should look so shocked. I used to live with such women, if you remember. Women, as it happens, who had all been in company with you and Dyfed—and more than once or twice. They weren't in the least shy about telling me about the both of you—in great detail—so there's no need for you to pretend surprise for my sake."

He didn't look surprised. Rather, he looked stricken, almost as if she had slapped him across the face rather than made a simple statement of fact.

"I remember far more than you do, apparently," he told her, the words taut with emotion. "Have you forgotten the vow I made that night at the Red Fox? That I would be faithful to you alone?"

She had forgotten it, Loris realized with a touch of chagrin. Or perhaps she simply hadn't believed him. She had always assumed that he visited women outside of Tylluan, either in the village or while he was in London. But now that she thought on the matter, Loris remembered that Kian had seldom, if ever, accompanied Dyfed during his visits to Neli Wynne's.

"I haven't had a woman since that night, Loris," Kian said. "And I'll not do so until the curse has been lifted and you come into my arms with the full knowledge of what we are to each other."

Now it was her turn to be surprised. He'd not lain with a woman in over ten years? Because of *her*?

"Oh, for heaven's sake, Kian," she said angrily, pulling free of his grasp and sitting down on the bed to stare at him. "Do you truly mean to say that you've denied yourself because of that imaginary *unoliaeth*?"

The words hurt him. He flinched, and his eyes filled with unmistakable pain. Loris hadn't expected that. She'd thought he would make his usual sarcastic retort, mocking her and what she said. For some reason, his reaction made her only angrier.

"That's the most foolish thing I've ever heard of," she snapped, wishing now that she'd never even made the suggestion. "And it's not fair to me, to make me the cause of any deprivation you suffer. There's no need for it. I don't want you to keep yourself pure for my sake, Kian," she said, and watched him pale. He took a step away; Loris had never seen such a strange look on his face. And still she couldn't stop her anger.

It *wasn't* her fault that he chose to go without female companionship. She'd never asked him to make such a sacrifice. "I'm not ignorant about what such fleeting unions signify," she said. "Or what they don't signify, rather. From what I've been told it's a perfectly common and natural thing for men to do, especially when they're not bound by marriage. And since you're not bound by marriage, there's no reason for you to suffer. If you feel frustration because of me, then, please, go and rid yourself of it."

He only continued to gaze at her. Then, slowly, he shook his head.

"Don't look at me like that!" she shouted, standing. Why didn't he say something? Something tart or cruel? What was the matter with him? "You'll *not* make me feel guilty, Kian Seymour. I don't even believe in the *unoliaeth*. You know I don't. I've never asked you to deny yourself in any way."

He looked away at last, still shaking his head as if he simply could not believe what she said. Silently, the chamber door opened, and Kian turned and walked out of the room.

"It's unfair to blame me!" Loris shouted after him, but he didn't stop walking. "*Kian!* It isn't fair!"

Her only reply was the chamber door swinging slowly back again, until it closed with an almost imperceptible click.

Eight

It had not been Kian's habit, since attaining his majority, to drink overmuch. He enjoyed a glass of whiskey when he was in the company of other men and drank his share of ale and wine with meals and on the rare occasions when he found himself in a tavern. Whenever a celebration was held at Tylluan, he would be the first to confess that he drank a good deal more than he should, but never enough to even approach being drunk. He knew about being drunk, of course, and had been in that condition a sufficient number of times during his reckless youth to last a lifetime. Following one particularly harrowing recovery, he had concluded that the suffering that occurred the day after wasn't worth the numb pleasure of the night before.

But he drank tonight, much to the surprise of his men when they rode out for their nightly surveillance, readily sharing the several flasks they'd brought along. And to the surprise of the footman who greeted him at the castle door, as well, when Kian told the man to bring a full bottle of his best whiskey—the kind Loris kept locked safely away in the cellar—to his bedchamber. Loris, who had wisely stayed away from him for the remainder of the day, even excusing herself from the evening meal, must have agreed to the footman's request for the key—Kian could just imagine how surprised *she* must have been—for the bottle was delivered to his chamber a few minutes later.

He'd been working on emptying it since, sitting morosely before the dimly glowing fireplace, and still hadn't come close to banishing her words from his memory.

Perhaps you should make a visit to the village soon. . . . You have to go somewhere to assuage your needs. . . . That's what truly matters to men, is it not?

A wave of fresh pain washed over him, and he closed his eyes in misery.

He was a *fool* and had been since he'd met her. He'd thought himself so noble all these years, saving himself for her—no, not saving, for there'd been nothing innocent in him left to save, except his heart, and she didn't even want that. But he'd tried to make up for his reckless past, for all the women who'd come before, and had kept himself from so much as lusting after another female. Even when he'd wanted to. Which he had, for he wasn't blind, after all, and there wasn't any sin in simply looking . . . but no, even that had been too awful a thing to do to *darling* Loris. Kian had firmly kept his eyes to himself, determined to prove how much he loved her. To show her that she could trust him.

She'd never even noticed.

I don't know why you should look so shocked. I used to live with such women . . . They weren't in the least shy about telling me about you . . .

Of course she hadn't noticed. She didn't care about him. Not even a little. She spurned his professions of love and denied the truth of the *unoliaeth*, despite accepting that a curse had made his touches painful. His touches . . . she liked them well enough while they lasted. But not enough to care about whether he bedded other women.

I don't want you to keep yourself pure for my sake, Kian. . . . From what I've been told it's a perfectly common and natural thing for men to do . . . If you feel frustration because of me, then go and rid yourself of it. . . .

That was just what he should do, Kian thought angrily. He should go to the village now, no matter how late it was— or early, rather, as midnight had surely come and gone—and wake up Neli and all her girls and enjoy each of them in turn. And when he'd gone through the lot he'd start over again until he'd driven all thoughts of Loris out of his brain.

But still it wouldn't be enough, he knew. He could never quench the need he felt for her. Never exorcise his soul of her.

"Because you're a fool," he told himself angrily, pushing the bottle into the air, where it floated, waiting until he wanted it again. "The *unoliaeth* doesn't force you to love her, but you do, anyway. And she doesn't love you at all."

But why would she? Loris only loved those people or things that made her feel safe. His father and Dyfed. Tylluan. And Liw Nos. He could understand it, in a way, knowing what he did of her past. She didn't want to find herself bound to someone wild, someone like him, no matter how hard he tried to prove himself trustworthy. But understanding didn't make the pain of rejection lessen any.

A soft knock fell on his door. So soft that Kian scarcely heard it. He ran a hand over his face and blinked, surprised that he'd not realized Loris had left her chamber and traversed the long hallway to come to him. He always felt her presence when they were both in the castle, and knew where she was. The whiskey must have dulled his senses, he thought. Or perhaps he'd just been too lost in self-pity to think of anything else.

"Kian?" The heavy, medieval latch slowly lifted, and the door pushed slightly open just as Kian turned to look at it. "Are you awake?"

He neither moved nor spoke, but waited, wondering why she'd come.

The door opened wider to reveal her standing in the dimly lit hall, dressed in her nightgown and dressing robe. Her long hair hadn't been braided, as it normally was each night, but left to fall like a curling, golden waterfall down the length of her back. Her feet, he noticed with a frown, were bare and probably freezing. What on earth had made her leave her room without her slippers? Surely the matter wasn't so pressing that she couldn't have taken a moment to put them on.

She saw him sitting by the fire and took a few steps into the room. Her hands were doing what they always did when she was nervous, twisting restlessly, one against the other.

"I'm sorry to bother you so late—so early, I mean," she said, her voice tellingly high-pitched. "I know I should have waited until later, but I was afraid that—perhaps—you were having as much trouble as I am sleeping." She released a shaking breath and took another step forward. "Because of what happened earlier," she clarified. "Because of the things I said. I wanted to come and tell you that I'm sorry. Truly sorry, Kian. I had no right to say such things to you and wish very much that I hadn't. I know you'll not want to forgive me. I don't expect you to, at least not for a long while. But perhaps you might be able to sleep now. Because you must sleep. You've been so weary of late, and I don't want to add to the cause of that. So, I—I'll just go." She backed away, toward the door. Her gaze fell away from his. "Good night, Kian," she said, and closed the door gently behind her.

His heart, Kian discovered, was beating wildly in his chest. He stared at the door and wondered if he'd just imagined what had happened. If Loris had truly been there at all or if it had been a vision wrought by a combination of desire and whiskey.

Slowly, he turned back to face the fire. God help him, but she made such a muddle of his emotions. Want had replaced anger, but that wasn't anything unusual. And she was lying awake . . . because of him? She'd been concerned about him. About his weariness. But he'd not be able to sleep now. And he doubted she would, either.

He'd not thought to go to her again as Liw Nos before she left for London. But they were both awake, and there was so little time left for them to be together. And she was feeling guilty about what had happened. Liw could make her feel better. He could give her peace. He always did.

• • •

Loris had tried lying down on her bed when she returned to
her own room, but sleep still evaded her. Had she done the
right thing in going to make her apology to Kian? He'd said
nothing, had given no sign that he accepted her regrets. He'd
only sat in his chair, unmoving, and stared at her, his face
completely without emotion.

She tossed the bedcovers aside and sat on the edge of the
bed, staring into the darkness. Would he forgive her? she wondered. But why should he, when she'd said such terrible
things to him earlier? Even if she didn't share his feelings of
love, she was certainly well aware that he felt them. Kian had
done something for her sake—something difficult—and had
denied himself a pleasure he had once enjoyed regularly, before she had come into his life. He had done it for her, because
of love, and she had thrown it in his face as if he'd been a fool.

"Oh, God," she whispered, setting a hand to her forehead
as she thought anew of how she'd hurt him. His expression . . . his eyes . . . she couldn't get the memory of them out
of her thoughts. Even if she didn't want Kian to deny himself
for her sake, there were dozens—hundreds—of better ways
that she could have let him know. Whatever he'd felt for her
before must surely now be dead. The fact that he'd said nothing to her when she'd apologized was proof of that, wasn't it?
Kian was never at a loss for words, especially not when he
could gain the advantage over her. But he'd said nothing, she
thought with despair. He must hate her now. He was probably
glad that she was going away to London.

A sudden chill filled the room, causing the fire in the
hearth to flicker violently, and Loris looked up to see the
balcony doors opening.

Glad hope filled her heart, and she leaped to her feet.

"Liw?"

The next moment his tall, muscular figure appeared, and
Loris uttered a cry of relief.

"Oh, Liw!" She hurried across the chamber and into his
open arms. "Oh, thank goodness. I'm so glad you've come."

And then she did what she hated doing and burst into tears.

"Darling!" He held her close with one hand and shut the balcony doors with the other, then scooped her up into his arms and crossed the room to sit in one of the comfortable chairs near the fire. "What's wrong, Loris? Don't cry, love."

"Oh, Liw," she said, pressing her face against the comforting solidness of his chest. "I've done such a terrible thing to Kian. I said such awful things to him, and he was hurt by them."

"Shhhh," he murmured, and kissed the top of her head. "You couldn't have done anything so dreadful. I'm sure he's forgiven you for whatever it may be."

She sniffed and shook her head. "I went to apologize and he just stared at me. He didn't say anything. Not a word. I don't blame him, but I thought . . . I thought he'd at least—" Tears made it impossible to finish the thought.

"I'm surprised that you care so much about what Kian Seymour thinks or feels," he said, stroking gentle fingers over her head, down her back. "He hasn't always been kind to you."

Loris drew in a shaking breath and strove to master herself. "No, he hasn't," she said at last. "But this was different, Liw. If only you could have seen his face. He's never . . . never looked at me like that before. It was as if I'd b–broken his heart." She uttered a sob. "I c–can't stop thinking of it."

"Hush, sweet," he whispered, and gathered her even more closely into his embrace. "If he suffered a little, then perhaps it was for his own good. And perhaps . . . perhaps it means that your own feelings for him aren't precisely what you think. Perhaps you love him a little, Loris. Could it be?"

Loris stilled at the idea.

"I don't know," she whispered.

"Don't you?" he asked. "But then why would you care so much about hurting him?"

She sniffled and wiped her cheeks, then, calmer, relaxed against him.

"I don't know," she said once more, and it was the truth. "He makes me crazed. Nothing is simple where Kian is concerned. But once, when we first met, I thought for a moment that I . . ."

"What?" he prompted.

She shook her head and sighed. "Nothing. It was so long ago that I often think my memory of it can't be trusted. But it doesn't matter now." She lifted her face to look up at him. "How did you know that I needed you so much tonight, Liw? I didn't have any hope of seeing you again before I left."

His fingers, warm and strong, cradled her face, and his dark eyes gazed into hers. "I had to come," he murmured. "I had to see you once more, Loris. I couldn't stay away, even when I knew I should."

He lowered his head to kiss her, gently at first and then more fully. Loris found his nearness deeply comforting and returned the embrace, sliding her arm up about his neck.

"I'm glad," she whispered when he pulled away. "I'm going to miss you so terribly, Liw."

"Do you love me, Loris?" he asked. "I know that you don't feel as I do—I've never expected you to. But do you love me—even a little?"

"Of course I love you," she said, touching his cheek with her fingertips. "Very much."

"Not only as a friend," he said, grasping her hand to still it. He gazed at her intently. "Do you love me enough to trust me completely? To let me give you peace and respite beyond what you've known before?"

Loris gazed at him for a long moment. Her heart seemed to beat faster as the seconds passed, and her breathing heightened. At last, she said faintly, "Yes, Liw."

His breathing quickened, too. He kissed her again and then rose from the chair, carrying Loris in his arms. He stopped just before they reached the bed, and set her on her feet.

"We have lain together here many times before now," he said, framing her face with his hands. "And we have given each other innocent pleasure. I've taken you to the edge of fulfillment, but never completely over to it, for I didn't believe that right was mine. But now I want to make you a gift of such pleasure, if you'll let me. If you'll trust me. I'll not take your maidenhead," he promised, "and if you tell me to stop at any time, I will." His thumbs stroked lightly over her high cheekbones. "You've often wondered what it would be like to finish the journey we've so often started, have you not, my love? Will you let me give you this gift?"

Loris swallowed hard against the nervousness that was rapidly rising within her and knew a strange, fleeting longing for Kian. But Kian wasn't here, and Liw was. Liw, who was so safe and certain, who had given her so much pleasure during his many visits. He was right. She had wondered what lay beyond the touches they had shared. Beyond innocent pleasure, as he'd called it.

"Yes, Liw," she murmured. "I trust you." And she did.

He smiled, and his hands fell from her face to slide about her shoulders and draw her near. He brought his mouth to her own, touching her lips with his tongue, then sliding beyond to caress the depths of her mouth. He hadn't been the one to teach her this manner of kissing; Kian had done that. But Liw had been the one to show her just how sensuous a pleasure it could be when done gently, without hurry or the fear of impending pain.

His fingers found the single lace at the neckline of her simple gown and pulled it free of the bowknot Loris had earlier looped it into. The garment loosened about her shoulders, and then he pushed it off altogether.

Loris felt the cloth pooling at her feet, felt air touching her bare skin, and pulled free of Liw's kiss. She had never been so naked as this before him; he had touched and kissed her breasts, but always through the opening of her gown. She felt suddenly embarrassed and looked away, feeling Liw's gaze on her.

"Loris," he said, and drew in a sharp breath. "I've dreamed of you so often, but you're far more lovely than any dream could be." His hands trembled as they coursed lightly over her arms, her waist and hips. "You're beautiful. So perfect and beautiful. Come and lie with me, love."

He picked her up and set her in the middle of the bed, her head upon the pillows. Then he sat beside her, pulling off his boots, never taking his gaze from her, and stood to pull his tunic off and toss it aside. He smiled as he moved toward her, clad only in his leggings, saying, "You look at me as if you've never seen me before."

She had seen his bare chest before—it was quite magnificent to look at—and had touched that same chest countless times. But somehow he seemed more handsome. More masculine and fine.

"I think you're far more beautiful than I am," she said as he came to lie beside her, setting a palm against his smooth, warm skin, feeling the muscles beneath.

"Then your judgment is seriously to be questioned," he said, sounding so much like Kian that Loris felt a slight sense of surprise. But he began to kiss her again, and his hands began to move over her, and sensation overwhelmed thought.

His mouth moved lower and his tongue touched the tip of one nipple, licking lightly, while his hand covered the other breast completely, kneading with gentle pressure. Loris closed her eyes, trying to hold back the moan of pleasure on her lips, but then his mouth closed over her nipple completely and she lost the battle. She lay beneath him, arching upward toward the wet heat of his tongue and lips as he took his pleasure of first one, then her other breast. She tried to say his name, but he rose up at the sound and stopped the word on her mouth, kissing her deeply.

She was trembling when he at last pulled away. His tongue laved a path down her neck again, past her shoulders and even past her breasts, down to her stomach, where the rapid kisses he pressed against her skin made her shiver.

"Oh no," she murmured breathlessly as he moved lower. She fisted both hands in his hair and made him stop.

He laughed, his breath pelting her skin. "All right," he said.

"We'll save that for another time. Darling, you're pulling my hair out by the roots."

"Oh, I'm sorry," she said, and forced her taut fingers to release their steely grip. "Sorry."

"Shhh." He moved to lie half beside her, half over her. "It's all right. Relax, love. I'll not do anything that you don't wish." His hands stroked over her legs, up her thighs, his fingers moving with gentle care. "Only let me give you pleasure." His fingers slid upward, drifting across her hips, then lightly—so lightly—feathering over the curls between her legs.

Loris shuddered and drew in a sharp breath. One of his hands moved to slip beneath her head, turning her to receive his kiss, while the other slid farther down, gently parting her legs. "Let me touch you, love. Open yourself for me. Yes, like that. Just like that."

His hand pressed closer, and she felt one of his fingers slipping gently inside the folds of her body.

"Liw," she moaned. It felt so very strange, and a little frightening. *"Liw."*

"I'm not Liw tonight," he whispered huskily, against her lips. "I'm the man who loves you, Loris. Your heart"—he drew in a sharp breath as his finger pushed all the way inside her—"your heart tells you the truth. Oh, Loris. You feel so—" But he could only make an inarticulate noise, which made him sound as if he were dying from the pleasure of touching her. His hips moved and she felt his manhood, fully aroused, pressing against her.

Loris kept her eyes tightly shut as sensation washed over her. He pulled his hand slowly out, then pressed in again, and she could hear the sound of wetness. He made the movement again, then again, and then she felt another finger joining the first, stretching her, filling her.

"Oh," she uttered foolishly, unable to think of anything coherent. She could only *feel,* and what she felt was unlike anything she'd known before. Pleasure began to build, growing stronger with each thrust of his fingers, and then his

thumb touched her in another place—far more sensitive, so
that the pleasure became a kind of pain.

Loris had no idea what she said or moaned or did. His
mouth moved over her face, kissing, and he spoke, but she
made no sense of any of it. It wasn't Liw's voice any longer.
It was Kian's. Kian's face that she saw, even when she
closed her eyes, and Kian's voice telling her he loved her . . .
loved her . . . loved her . . .

The pleasure in her exploded, then, and Loris clutched at
him, digging her nails into his scalp and shoulder, and cried
out his name. Her body lurched upward, seeking his touch
and the pleasure it gave. And all the while he murmured and
told her he loved her and said her name. Kian's voice.
Kian's words.

Sensation overpowered her completely, followed by a
sweet darkness and an intense feeling of relief. Her eyes
drifted shut, and she was only vaguely aware that his body
was yet moving with passion, thrusting against her, and only
dimly heard his hoarse cry of release. Then he fell still,
gasping for breath and lying heavily upon her. Loris didn't
mind in the least. His body felt wonderful. With what little
strength she had left, she slid her arms about him, pushing
one hand into his silken hair.

He made a groaning sound and shifted, nestling more comfortably against her. His own arm came about her waist, and
he murmured something soft and indistinguishable against the
bare skin of her shoulder before falling still.

Loris smiled and, holding him near, followed him into
slumber.

Kian came awake slowly, savoring the comfort of his bed
and the knowledge that he'd had a long, much-desired rest.
He couldn't remember the last time he'd felt this good upon
waking. This well rested.

He had no idea what time it was, whether it was morning
or afternoon. The heavy bed curtains were drawn, shutting
out all light.

Turning on the pillows, he stretched and began to feel the rumblings of an empty stomach. He hoped Loris had something ready for him to eat. Something hot and savory. But she would, of course. She always seemed to know exactly what he desired.

He sighed and slowly pushed up into a sitting position. God's mercy, but he felt good. His body felt as relaxed and replete as in the old days, when he'd been in the habit of . . .

"Oh, God."

He recalled everything all at once, in one brilliant flash of memory.

"Oh, *God above*."

He thrust the curtains apart and swung his legs to the side of the bed.

"Loris!" he called, momentarily blinded by the light filling the chamber. Blinking, shading his eyes, he rose and looked about. *"Loris!"*

She wasn't there. The room was in perfect order. Her traveling trunks had been packed and were sitting by the door, waiting to be taken out. And his clothes—*his* clothes, not Liw's, for they must have transformed back to their original state, as well—were neatly folded and lying on a chair near the bed. His boots sat on the floor, side by side.

"No," he murmured. "No. Oh, God."

He strode to the nearest mirror and looked at his reflection, hoping against all hope that Liw's dark eyes would be staring back at him. But it was his blue eyes—his own wide and horrified blue eyes—that greeted him.

But of course they were. She had said his name. She had known who he was last night and had said his name aloud, not Liw's, when the pleasure came over her. And he'd not thought anything save that it was right and wonderful, because . . . because they had been making love and he had forgotten that he was supposed to be someone else. He had loved her as Kian, and she had recognized him as her true mate.

The knowledge would have thrilled him to the core at any

other time, but just now the implications were settling over him like an ominous cloud.

He had transformed back into himself at some point during the night, and Loris had come awake to find Kian, not Liw, in her bed. And she had realized everything. All his lies. The trickery he had used to deceive her for so many years, to steal her confidences and her heart. To be near her.

It was all over now. He could never come to her as Liw again. All of his pretenses were forever gone.

Kian had to find her. He had to explain and beg her to understand and . . . forgive him. Please, God, let her forgive him.

He snatched up his clothes and began to put them on, stopping when he took a better look at himself. He had forgotten more than he knew, evidently, for a large, visible stain on his pants gave proof that he'd lost control of himself like an untried, callow youth with his first woman. Kian certainly hadn't meant that to happen; he'd wanted to concentrate solely on Loris. But her cries of pleasure had made his traitorous body forget his good intentions.

He would have to take the time to return to his chamber and dress in clean clothing. But perhaps that wasn't such a poor idea. He needed to compose himself, Kian thought, picking up his boots and moving toward the door. He needed to be prepared for Loris's wrath, or her coldness, or even her hatred. He deserved all of them and much more. And this time, there would be no Liw to go to her afterward and soothe her anger and hurt. Kian was completely on his own.

Loris didn't know how long she'd been sitting in the garden before she heard his voice. It seemed as if hours had passed since she'd felt the familiar burning sensation that had wakened her and risen to find Kian lying beside her, deeply asleep.

She'd sat there, gazing down at him in the early morning light that was streaming through the balcony doors—they had forgotten, being so occupied, to close the curtains—until realization had finally crept into her shocked brain.

And the moment it had she'd gone into immediate motion, jumping out of the bed and running to the basin to wash herself—everywhere. Then she'd simply stood there, utterly naked, towel in hand, shaking like a leaf, unable to think of what she should do. Even breathing seemed a difficult thing to accomplish; she was drawing in air in great gasps, yet somehow she felt as if she were suffocating.

Long minutes passed and she calmed by degrees. She had been through far worse things than this, Loris told herself. And if she wasn't precisely certain of what had happened, she would sort it out. And telling herself that, Loris at last got herself under control. Her body and mind settled down, and she could breathe normally once again.

She moved about the room in a purposeful manner, not looking at the bed, not even glancing at it until she at last had to go and draw the bed curtains. And even that was accomplished without letting her gaze drop to the mattress and the man lying on it.

She dressed and then brushed and arranged her hair in her usual simple style. And then she had calmly finished her packing and stacked her trunks by the door. Before she left the room, she picked up the garments that Kian had discarded and folded them, setting them and his boots near the bed where he could find them when he at last woke.

Then she had left the chamber, shutting the door quietly behind her, and made her way down to the kitchen, where Cook greeted her, exclaiming that Miss Loris was up even earlier than usual this morning.

She gave Cook her instructions for the day and then went out into the great hall to ask a footman to inform the other servants that Lord Tylluan had had a very late night and would likely sleep through the morning. He was not to be disturbed. *No one*—she emphasized the words—was to step foot on that particular floor of the castle until His Lordship had risen and presented himself downstairs. Kian had never required the services of a valet or personal manservant and had always shaved and dressed himself. None of the servants would think it odd to leave their master to his own devices.

Having seen to the day's first duties, Loris sought the comfort of her beloved garden. She sat on her favorite bench, which provided a beautiful view of the valley beyond, beneath the shade of a large, sheltering tree, and, then, at last, let herself think. She hadn't intended to remain for so long, but time had passed without her being aware of it, and as Kian now came near, Loris suddenly realized that the sun had moved a good distance in the sky and that morning had given way to afternoon.

"Loris." He was striding toward her in a purposeful manner, she saw when she glanced in his direction. His expression was set, grim, and his eyes filled with anxiety. Otherwise Kian looked as he ever had: handsome, elegant, powerful. She glanced up at his hair, which he had left undone so that it fell free to his shoulders, and remembered the feel of it beneath her fingers the night before. That was why it had felt so silken, rather than coarse, as Liw's thicker hair did.

His steps slowed as he neared her and came to a stop altogether when he reached the bench.

"Are you all right?" he asked, the words tense, clipped.

"Yes," she said, and turned to look out over the valley.

"You've been crying."

"A little," she replied. And it was true. She'd not been able to stop the tears. Her heart was filled with grief. "I can't seem to help it when I think of Liw. I'm going to miss him so terribly." The last two words came out in an embarrassingly strangled manner. Loris pressed her lips together and prayed she wouldn't weep again. Not in front of Kian.

Slowly, he sat on the bench beside her, wisely not attempting to touch her. Loris had a feeling that she would blacken both his eyes if he so much as laid a finger on her today.

"I know," he said, his voice low. "I know you won't believe me, but I'm going to miss him, too."

"Yes, I'm sure you will," she said tautly. "But he meant

something rather more to me than simply a way to get what I wanted."

"Did you never . . . Loris, did you never even consider who he truly was?"

Her lips trembled, then, and a hot tear spilled from her eye and slid the length of her cheek.

"Yes," she whispered. "I think I even knew the truth not long after he first started to come, for it didn't make sense to me that you'd not know he was there. You even know when a single mouse is running about in the cellar. It hardly seemed likely that you'd not realize one of the faerie folk was but a few rooms away from your own bedchamber. But he became so real to me as the years passed, and I came to need him so much, that I didn't let myself consider how strange it all was. He was my f-friend." She drew in a sobbing breath and, when she saw him lift a hand, warned, more angrily, "Don't touch me, Kian. I can't bear the thought of you touching me."

He lowered his hand and was silent.

Loris wrestled herself back into control and, when her voice was steady, asked, "How did you manage it without anyone else finding out? I can't think Ffinian would have let you come to me using such deceit."

"He never knew," Kian replied quietly. "Neither did Dyfed. I don't possess the gift of transformation, so they never suspected, and you know my father well enough to believe that, if he had found out, I would have been the worse for it. I sold a piece of jewelry that I had inherited upon my mother's death and with the money bought an enchantment from one of the *consuriwrs* who live near the border. That was why it was so fragile, having been bought and paid for rather than being a natural gift, and was able to be broken merely by calling me by my true name."

"But surely the Guardians knew," she said.

He nodded. "They must have. I don't know why they never stopped me, or why they let me touch you as Liw without imparting pain. Last night, when you said my name, you didn't seem to feel the effects of the curse, as you usually do."

Loris lowered her gaze to her lap. "I felt it later, as we were . . . lying so close together. That's what woke me."

"Oh," he said, sounding deeply disappointed.

They were silent again for a few moments.

"I realize it won't do any good for me to tell you how sorry I am," Kian said at last. "But I am, nonetheless. If there is something I can do to make up for what I've done, please tell me. I'll do as you ask."

"Would you?" she asked stonily, all feeling dead within her. "Would you leave me in peace in the matter of the *unoliaeth,* and never speak to me of it, or of love, again?"

"Yes," he murmured. "If that is what you wish. But I don't think you understand what a *unoliaeth* is, Loris, if you can say such a thing. Perhaps that's always been part of the trouble between us. The *unoliaeth* has never been properly explained to you. Being fated doesn't require love of the two who are chosen; they are simply two separate beings who cannot be whole apart from each other. Most who are destined do love, and very deeply, but it's not essential. That you don't love me isn't a sign that the *unoliaeth* between us doesn't exist. No matter what your feelings are, even if you can only feel hatred for me, you will never be whole apart from me. I could let you leave Tylluan forever, or I could go away, but in time your heart would seek me. Mine would be sick with want from the moment we were apart. Just as it will be when you leave for London."

"I don't believe you," she said. "You've been gone from Tylluan for weeks at a time and I've never felt the lack of your presence." It wasn't entirely true, for Tylluan had been terribly empty and lonely on those occasions, but that, she had convinced herself, was because all three of them, Ffinian, Dyfed, and Kian, had been gone. That Kian's early returns had made everything feel right wasn't something she wanted to consider at the moment. If ever.

"Is that what you want of me, Loris?" he asked. "To never

again speak of what I feel for you? To let you leave Tylluan forever?"

"No," she said, standing and moving to look out over the half wall. The valley beyond was so beautiful. So serene. It was part of what she loved, and would miss, about Tylluan. "I'm not certain yet what I want. Or what I wish to do. I need time to think and sort my feelings out. I'm going to London now not because you've told me to, but because I want to go."

"I understand," he said softly. "You wish to be away from me for a time."

"Yes," she replied, and wondered why she should feel like weeping again. "That's why. But I want you to remember the promise you gave me, that I can return to Tylluan whenever I wish, and that no one, not even you, will stop me from doing so. No matter what."

She heard him stand, as well. He moved nearer, still careful not to touch her.

"I gave you my promise," he said, his tone gentle. "I know you have no reason to believe this any longer, but I always keep my promises. Especially those I give you, Loris. Regardless of what you may think now of what happened last night, in time I hope that you'll remember it wasn't simply lust or some desire to punish you for the things you said yesterday afternoon that drove me to come to you. It has never been that. I came to you as Liw because I had to be near you without feeling your scorn. And I kept coming because I couldn't live without the smiles and caresses you gave him, or the friendship you gifted him with. If you believe you're going to miss him, then know that I'm going to miss him, as well. Through him I knew the greatest possible happiness these past many years, because he gave me time with you that the curse kept me from knowing as Kian. And I needed to have that time, because I love you, Loris."

She closed her eyes and lowered her head, struggling to keep the tears back.

Kian took a step closer, his voice near her ear. "What happened between us last night was love. Not merely desire or passion or anything simply physical. You called my name out because you recognized who I was—your fated one. Your *unoliaeth*."

"Don't!" she cried, turning away from him.

"I only want you to know one more thing, and then I'll leave you in peace. If you've been laboring under the idea that I only care for you because of the magic that binds us together—that I have no choice in the matter and therefore my love is worthless—then you're very wrong. I may have been infatuated with you because of the *unoliaeth* at the beginning, but I've fallen in love with you, with *Loris,* during the years since you came to live at Tylluan. If the *unoliaeth* somehow disappeared this very moment, it would make no difference to me. I love *you,* Loris, because of who you are. Because of everything you are, from your smile, to the way you order us all about, to the look you give me when you find me exasperating. I don't need magic to tell me what's between us. And neither do you."

He began to walk away but stopped after taking only two steps and turned back to her.

"There's no need for you to grieve for Liw," he said. "He's here, alive in me, and always will be. And for what it may be worth, though I grant you that it may not be much," he said more softly, "I'm here, too."

Nine

I can't think it a good idea for you to go off on your own, Master Dyfed," Horas said. "His Lordship wouldn't be pleased with me if anything were to happen to you. And considering the troubles, sir, and what happened just a few nights ago . . ."

"I'll be fine, Horas," Dyfed said. "I only want to stop in the village for an hour. There will still be plenty of light in the sky by the time I return to Tylluan, and you know full well that the troubles never begin while it's yet daylight."

Horas looked up at the sky consideringly. " 'Twon't be light for long, Master Dyfed. It's going to rain soon. The clouds are beginning to gather. The roads will be muddy for your journey on the morrow, I fear."

"Then I'd best hurry if I want to find a place at Neli's before too many other patrons seek shelter. I'll finish my business there and make my way home as quickly as possible. Truly, Horas, there's no need to be worried. It's been many a year since I was in need of a mother."

He smiled with all the charm he possessed and saw the older man wavering. Kian had given both Dyfed and Horas strict instructions to stay together both to and from *Fynnon Elian,* but they were well within Tylluan's borders once more and Dyfed knew that Horas was eager to get to his cottage, where his wife and children were waiting, and thereafter to the castle, where Kian awaited a report.

"I'd invite you to join me at Neli's," Dyfed said, "but your wife would have my head on a platter. I'm sure Marged is waiting impatiently for you to come home. Go on," he urged. "Go see your wife and I'll meet you at the castle in an hour or so."

A few minutes later, having promised faithfully that he'd take every care until reaching the castle, Dyfed watched with relief as Horas rode away. Then Dyfed turned his horse in the direction opposite the village and headed toward the lake.

There was no sign of the water that had swamped the area a few nights earlier, but the destruction that had been done remained. Kian hadn't seen the benefit of clearing it away until they were certain that the cause had been dealt with. If it had looked bad during the fog and darkness, it looked far worse in the light of day.

Dismounting and tying the horse to one of the few trees still standing, Dyfed walked over some of the ground that he'd covered three nights ago. Kian had probably already been over it several times, looking for signs of what, exactly, had taken place.

The lake was the most obvious clue, clearly being the source of the water that was found at each site of destruction. But if the beast or creature, or whatever it was, lived in the lake, then it certainly didn't leave any kind of trail when it came out. Farther into the trees, the path that the creature had forced was so wide that it looked as if a small herd of elephants had gone on rampage, but except for the remaining dampness, there was no disturbance on the ground around the lake. Even if there hadn't been footprints or paw prints, there should have been something—perhaps a path where a large beast had dragged itself along, out of the water, or impressions where it had leaped from spot to spot. Yet there was nothing.

It had been foolishness for him to go to *Fynnon Elian*. Whatever was happening at Tylluan was far more powerful and mysterious than a mere well curse. But attending to such rituals was important to the people of Tylluan, and so he and Horas had made the journey to the well and paid the keeper to remove from it any curses regarding Tylluan that might have been thrown into its depths. It had been three days spent for nothing more than a calming of the people's nerves—a calming that would be lost the moment the next attack came.

But Desdemona had promised Dyfed that she would let nothing happen until he returned, on the condition that he would meet her at the lake as soon as he was across Tylluan's border. She would know when he was home, she'd told him, and would come to him as quickly as she could.

Standing at the water's edge, Dyfed wondered how long that would be. The clouds were growing darker in the sky, and a chill took the place of the sun's warmth.

Desdemona.

What a strange, compelling young woman she was. She had been in Dyfed's thoughts constantly since that memorable night, and he felt a curiously strong desire to see her. He began to walk up toward the trees with the intention of biding his time by examining the damage in the light of day, but had scarce gotten into the tree line before he sensed her presence.

Dyfed turned just in time to see a flash of color moving over the water, and then she was there, standing on the shore, a vision dressed in shimmering green with a long velvet cape fluttering over her shoulders and down to the ground. Her shining black hair was undone, falling down to her hips, and she was breathing a little harshly, her cheeks pink with color. She looked unutterably beautiful.

She said his name and began to move toward him, and Dyfed found himself striding full-length to meet her. He wasn't entirely sure what it was he intended—perhaps to say something or even kiss her—but he certainly didn't expect what happened.

They went into each other's arms, found each other's mouths—and promptly lost their senses. There wasn't a slow building of desire or even a few moments to explore and discover; they went straight from physical contact to desperate need.

The impact of the sensation was like being flung against a brick wall. Dyfed felt as if someone had set his body on fire and inflated his head to the point of exploding, both at the same time. His hands pressed Desdemona's slight body against his own with all the strength he possessed and her hands did the same to him, but they couldn't get close enough. They had to be one, *now,* or perish from want.

He had never known anything like this before, and, frankly, it was terrifying.

With a strength he didn't know he possessed, Dyfed managed to push her to arm's length. Gasping for air, he said, "This is madness. And it's wrong."

She nodded, shuddering for breath. "I'm frightened by it, too."

And that was the end of all discussion.

He took her there, to his absolute shock, right on the muddy ground, with her velvet cloak spread out as her only cushion. They tumbled down, tearing at each other's clothes, and then, with her skirts tossed up about her waist and half his trouser buttons torn off, he was thrusting inside of her. She rose up to meet him, and their movements became one, forceful, powerful, blinding in pleasure.

Only one word swept through his chaotic thoughts as he surrendered to the desire that drove them both. *Bliss.* This was as close to heaven on earth as he was likely to get. No other woman had given him this feeling; he knew with honest clarity that no other woman would.

"Desdemona." Her name tumbled off his tongue unbidden, and the sound of it made her weep.

"Dyfed," she whispered urgently, as if it were a plea, holding him, moving with him. "Dyfed. Dyfed."

Over and over she said it as they rose together to fulfillment, until the sweet release swept over them. It was so powerful that Dyfed's mind swam dizzily and for a moment he was completely disoriented. He collapsed on top of her, unable to spare her small, delicate body from his full weight. But she didn't seem to mind. Her legs and arms wrapped about him, hugging tightly as if she never wanted him to rise again.

She was still weeping. The sound penetrated Dyfed's whirling brain and brought him to his senses. Lifting his head, he gazed into her violet eyes and with a gentle hand swept the hair from her face.

"What's the matter, darling?"

"I don't know," she answered, tears streaming down her cheeks. "I never cry. At least, not since I was a child. But you've done something to me. . . ."

He lowered his head and kissed her softly. "Something's happened to both of us," he murmured. "This has to do with magic, Desdemona Caslin. You know that, too, don't you?"

She nodded. "Yes. I know. Oh no, don't," she said when he began to rise, disengaging their bodies. "Stay."

He smiled and kissed her again. "Don't worry. I'm going to make love to you again before we part. Far more slowly, if that's possible, and if rain isn't pouring down upon us."

He sat up and did his best to rearrange their clothes, then drew Desdemona into a sitting position and set both his arms and cloak about her to keep her warm. "This is a damnable place to have had this happen. We're both covered in mud, and anyone riding by might see us. I think we've both lost our senses. Please don't cry anymore, Desdemona. Are you so unhappy to find yourself sharing an enchantment of some sort with me?"

"I don't know," she said, wiping her face. "It was never foretold that I should have one who was fated for me, but it's the only explanation. I just . . . it just seems impossible that it should be with you. You're not even a powerful wizard."

"Fated?" he repeated, ignoring the insulting tone regarding his lack of powers. "I'm sure it can't be. We call such ones *unoliaeth,* or oneness, and that kind of union wasn't foretold for me, either. My brother, Lord Tylluan, has one, but not me."

"I know," Desdemona replied, and he heard a touch of bitterness in her tone. "He came to Llew and warned Cadmaran of your journey to London with this woman. His *unoliaeth,* he called her, and made a vow before the Guardians of what he would do to anyone who might harm her."

"Kian went to Llew?" Dyfed was astonished by this news. "He spoke with Cadmaran? And with you?"

"He came alone, and for that I must admire him, but I hate him for all the rest."

"Why on earth should you hate Kian?" Dyfed asked. "He's done nothing to you."

"He's sending you away to guard his woman, and there's nothing I can do to stop him. Or you." She looked up at him, lifting one cold, ungloved hand to cradle his face. "I cannot bear the thought of being parted from you, now that I've found you. These past three days have been endless for me. Please don't go away to London. Let someone else take Lord Tylluan's fated one there."

"I would if it were possible," Dyfed told her honestly. "But Kian is my lord as well as my brother, and I cannot gainsay him. There is but one way for me to return to Tylluan, and you hold that power in your hands. Tell me about what you've been doing for Cadmaran, and how it is that you came to be with him."

"I cannot tell you everything," she said, lowering her gaze and leaning more closely against him. "Lord Llew asked a favor of my father, and offered him a great deal of money in return. My coming was part of their agreement. Please believe me when I tell you that I did not know I would be left behind when my father departed. I hate everything about England, excepting you, and wish I might make you my captive and take you back to America. But as I cannot compel you to do my bidding," she said sadly, "then I must stay here, where you are."

"Yes, you must." Dyfed smiled at the thought. He certainly had no intention of letting her go so far away. "But that doesn't solve our more immediate problem. I know that you're not the one who has directly caused the troubles here, but you have something to do with them. And until those troubles have stopped, Kian won't allow Loris to come back to Tylluan, and I'll be made to remain in London to chaperone her."

"But why?" Desdemona asked miserably, clinging to him. "Surely you can find someone else to take the woman. I *hate* her. And I hate your brother for sending you away."

Dyfed didn't know why he should find the childish, petulant statement so amusing. His relationship with Desdemona was clearly going to be a trying one. She had obviously been terribly spoiled and would require a very firm hand.

"Hating my brother isn't going to do us any good. If you don't want me to be gone for any great length of time, then you'll have to help him rid Tylluan of this evil."

She glanced up, troubled, even slightly regretful. "It won't do any good, Dyfed. I control the creature now and it does my bidding, but I cannot keep it from seeking food when it grows hungry. If I do not take it out and let it feed, it will go anyway, and do as it pleases."

"What is this creature?"

She hesitated. Overhead a rumble of thunder sounded. "It is one of the ancient creatures, held in slumber by enchantments performed long ago by your ancestors, but raised back to life by my father. Cadmaran knew, or discovered by some means, that long generations of Caslins have retained the knowledge of how to unlock certain enchantments."

"But I thought that was forbidden by the Guardians," Dyfed said.

"If it is, it hasn't stopped wizards like my father from carrying on the tradition. But the secrets are held very dear within my family, so that Cadmaran was obliged to have my father come to him to perform the spell that brought the *athanc* back to life."

"*Athanc*?" Dyfed had a dim memory of the word from one of his father's stories.

"It lives deep within the lake," she said, "and comes out only at night and only to feed. But it's a clumsy, stupid brute, and without guidance it won't discern animals from humans. In a way, I've done your brother a favor, for I've kept the creature from killing any mortals."

"It lives in the lake," Dyfed repeated thoughtfully. "That would explain the water. But how does it travel without leaving a trail? From the damage it wreaks it must be quite a large creature."

"It can be," she said. "But it can also make itself small. The beast can transform itself into liquid and travel underground, rising where it wishes. But it cannot go far from the lake, else it would weaken and perhaps fall back into darkness. But before it did, I believe it would cause a great deal of destruction, for it can grow angry at the least cause."

A cold breeze blew over them, riffling their hair and chilling their faces, though they were warm enough pressed together beneath his cloak. Dyfed glanced up and saw that the dark clouds were about to open.

"Can it be killed?" he asked.

Desdemona shook her head. "None of the ancient monsters can be destroyed. They can only be returned to slumber, and the only wizard I know who can perform such an enchantment is my father, who is back in America. And even if he wasn't, I doubt he'd agree to help your brother, except, perhaps, for a very great price."

"Your father may be the greatest wizard in America," Dyfed said, "but I believe our *Dewin Mawr* could match, and perhaps even best, him. And Kian isn't far behind in powers."

"I have felt his strength," she said, "but they will avail him nothing if he does not know the ancient incantations."

"Do you know them, Desdemona?" Dyfed demanded, touching her chin to lift her gaze to his own. "You must tell me truthfully if you do."

"My father has been careful to keep them to himself. It's the truth!" she said insistently when Dyfed looked at her askance. "Can you think that I would lie to you now if I possessed the knowledge to keep you from leaving me? I only know how to call the beast and manage it, and how to send it back to the depths for rest. Nothing more."

"And you do this for Cadmaran willingly?"

Another clap of thunder, louder this time, and the first few drops of rain began to softly fall. Dyfed ignored it and continued to gaze at her, waiting for an answer. Desdemona lifted a hand high up into the chilly breeze and placed some kind of invisible shield about them. The rain continued to fall, but not on them, and the wind could no longer touch them.

Dyfed was impressed. "You're a useful female to have about," he said, sliding a finger down her soft cheek in a gentle caress. "Now tell me about Cadmaran."

"He doesn't care about your brother," she said. "It's your cousin, the one you call *Dewin Mawr,* that he wants. He knows your brother doesn't possess the powers necessary to rid Tylluan of the *athanc,* and will be forced to call for your greatest sorcerer to come to his aid. Cadmaran wants to challenge him, and he can't do that unless Lord Graymar first comes to Llew."

"But why are you helping him?" Dyfed asked again. "Because your father sold your services to Lord Llew and you have no choice but to do his bidding? Because you want to?" His grip on her tightened. "Are you in love with him?"

"No!" Desdemona put her arms about Dyfed's neck and held him tightly. "I can't abide being near him. I stay at Llew only because there is nowhere else, and I do what he asks with the beast in order to get away from him for a few blessed hours. I cannot go home, for my father would only send me back, after he had punished me for disobedience. I have no family here, no acquaintances, save Cadmaran. My powers are great, yet I have no notion of how to live apart from my kind."

"You have me now," Dyfed said fiercely. "I'll take care of you."

"You're about to leave me," she murmured, and the rain around them began to fall harder. "Shall I follow you to London in order to be with you? It's what I wish, but I cannot think it's what you want of me."

"Can Cadmaran control the beast?"

"No. My father forbade me to share the secrets of managing the *athanc*, and I'd not tell Cadmaran even if I could. If you believe the damage it's done thus far has been terrible, only imagine what Cadmaran would do. He hates all Seymours and enjoys nothing better than to see your brother running hither and yon, hopelessly trying to find a solution."

Dyfed nodded soberly. "He has always taken pleasure from any troubles that befall us, most of them at his hands. You're right. He cannot have power over the creature."

"And left to its own devices, it would run wild, just as I've told you, driven by hunger. Your brother's tenants would begin to die, mere mortals and magic mortals alike. The beast wouldn't know the difference."

Dyfed knew she spoke the truth. He drew in a tight breath and considered the best course of action.

"There is little choice left to us, Desdemona," he said at last. "You must remain here and do whatever you can to keep the *athanc* from doing too much harm, and I must do what I can while in London to help my brother find the right enchantments for putting the creature back into slumber. Surely my cousin Lord Graymar will have something useful in his library. And there's a mere mortal there, Professor Seabolt, who might be of help. He's one of our sympathetics, and knows a great deal about the history of our kind."

"I'll do what I can," she said, "but Lord Tylluan must never try to contact me. If Cadmaran should become suspicious, he'd likely refuse to let me leave Llew, and within its borders his powers are heightened, while mine are dimmed."

"I'll make certain that Kian never approaches you," Dyfed promised. "And you must take every care to keep Lord Llew from learning about us." He gathered her closer.

"As soon as I return from London, I'll bring you home to Tylluan. Cadmaran won't be able to touch you there."

"Will your brother allow me to be with you there?" she asked anxiously. "After everything I've let the creature do to his lands?"

"If you can keep any of his people from dying," Dyfed said, "and if you'll do what you can to help him rid Tylluan of the *athanc,* he'll be in your debt. You'll be welcomed at Tylluan, Desdemona. I promise you that."

"For that," she whispered, "and to bring you home I'll do everything possible. Please come back as quickly as you can. I don't know how many days I can endure being apart from you, now that I've found you."

Dyfed understood what she meant. He'd longed to see her, touch her, every moment since they'd parted ways three nights ago. And though they'd only just sated their passion, that same desire flared again, even more heated than it had been before. This magic that bound them was intense and strong and urgent; Dyfed knew in his heart that it would always be thus, from now until death took them from the earth and back to that realm that was the destiny of all their kind. And even there they would be together. He and Desdemona Caslin had been fated, and once they had found each other, nothing could part them. Save distance, and this damnable journey to London.

"I won't be able to stay away long," he told her. "I'll go mad without you, Desdemona."

He lowered her to the ground once more. The rain poured about them and the wind howled, but they were safe and dry in their invisible shelter. It was oddly sensual, making love in the midst of the wild elements, protected from their force. Darkness enveloped the lovers now, as it had not done before, giving secrecy and making Dyfed bold to linger.

He would make love to her properly this time and take the time to fully appreciate her love in return. Kian would worry as the hour grew late, and Horas would most likely become frantic, but Dyfed was determined to create memories with Desdemona that he would take with him to London and that she could hold near on her long nocturnal vigils with the creature. Memories that would comfort him through the days and nights and keep her from despair as she lived beneath Cadmaran's hand.

It was much colder now; their shelter couldn't keep the chill at bay. But despite that, their hands found buttons and hooks and then warm skin lying beneath cloth. They touched and kissed and murmured, and when they came together at last there was none of the desperation that had quickened their first joining. They moved together slowly at first, learning each other's rhythm, taking as much pleasure from their deliberation as from the union of their bodies. And when the rhythm changed and quickened, words fell from their lips, incoherent to the ear but full of meaning that their hearts understood. Dyfed said her name, as he had done before, and as before, she wept at the sound.

Ten

The rain continued throughout the night and into the morning, giving no sign of stopping. The mood within Castle Tylluan was equal to the weather: dark and somber and uninviting.

Loris had made certain that her trunks and Dyfed's, as well as Elen's bags, were packed in time to be loaded onto the coach. She had overseen the task any number of times for Ffinian and his sons in past years, but she'd never thought the time would come when she'd have to stand and watch her own things being tied atop the vehicle. She wondered, dimly, whether she would arrive in London to find all her carefully folded garments soaked, and realized that she didn't particularly care.

Dyfed looked as miserable as Loris felt regarding their trip, which was somewhat troubling. And extremely unusual. Between himself, his father, and his brother, Dyfed had always been the one who had enjoyed the yearly visits to Town. He'd even told Loris on several occasions that he wished he might live in London for a year or two, simply to take pleasure in all that the city had to offer. But as they partook of breakfast in the dining parlor, Loris could see that he was anything but cheerful at the thought of leaving Tylluan.

He had returned late in the night from his journey to *Fynnon Elian*, just in time to stop Kian and Horas and the rest of the men from setting out in frantic search of him. Kian had looked somewhere between relief and fury and had railed at Dyfed with such anger that Loris knew he'd been truly afraid for his brother's life.

Loris had been a little irate with Dyfed herself, for he'd foolishly stayed too long in the village, worrying both her and his brother, and when he'd at last come home it had been in a completely disheveled condition. He was wet to the bone, and his clothes were thoroughly soiled with mud. She hadn't even wanted to contemplate how he'd gotten into such a state and preferred to tell herself that perhaps he'd simply tripped and fallen while walking through the village rather than that he'd come to such ruin at the hands of one of Neli's girls—all of whom Loris hoped to never think or speak of again, certainly not to Kian.

But poor Dyfed. He'd looked so pale and weary that Loris hadn't had the heart to let Kian keep shouting at him, especially as she suspected he did it because he was still overset more by what had transpired with her than by anything Dyfed had done. She told Kian in as many words to leave his brother in peace and then had taken Dyfed by the arm and escorted him up to his chamber, ordering that a hot bath and food be brought at once. She'd practically undressed him herself, then pushed him into a chair by the fire and covered him with a blanket. He'd insisted that he must speak to his brother, but Loris had countered that she would only allow it after Dyfed had some food and a warming drink in his stomach. Then she'd taken the clothes and left, wondering how she would ever get the stains out without ruining the fine cloth.

Kian had gone up to Dyfed's chamber an hour later, promising Loris that he'd not lose his temper again, and the brothers had spent most of the remaining night hours locked up together. Loris had twice sent food to them, and both times the trays had come back empty, with no word from either man.

At last she'd given up hope of discovering what was afoot and had gone to her own chamber. Not to sleep but to listen to the storm raging outside her window and to toss and turn and wish that she could forget everything that had happened the night before. She wondered if she would ever be able to lie in a bed again and not think of what it had been like . . . the feel of his hands and mouth on her body. Kian's hands. And Kian's mouth. Her body ached shamefully as Loris remembered it all in detail, and when she at last fell into a fitful slumber, she dreamed of him.

Now morning had arrived, and she couldn't decide who looked more grim among the three of them: her, Kian, or Dyfed. What a merry journey this was going to be.

"You'll want to get to Shrewsbury as quickly as possible," Kian said, showing little interest in the platters of egg tarts and sausages that the footman had offered. He was pale this morning and looked as if he hadn't slept. Loris wondered if he had gone out to guard Tylluan after he'd finished talking with Dyfed.

Dyfed nodded but said nothing. His gaze was fixed on the tablecloth, and he seemed to be thinking of something other than the journey. He sighed aloud, a sad and mournful sound.

"I've made all of the arrangements for your stay in Shrewsbury and Coventry," Kian went on. "You might possibly make London in less than three days, but if the rain continues, it will likely be necessary to stop more frequently. Loris isn't used to traveling. She won't wish to spend so many hours inside the coach. You must be certain to stop at every opportunity and let her have a cup of tea and a bit of a rest."

Loris was slightly insulted by the words. She was a fairly hearty female, used to a great deal of daily exertion in both the castle and the garden, as Kian very well knew. She doubted that sitting in his comfortable traveling coach would be very trying.

"Of course," Dyfed replied, pushing his plate away. "I shall take excellent care of our darling Loris. That's what you're sending me along for, isn't it?" He flashed a curiously bitter look at his elder brother and stood. "I'm going to my chamber to pack a few more books for the journey." Looking at Loris, he asked more gently, "Will you be ready to leave soon, sweeting?"

She nodded and said, "I suppose so. Everything has been packed, but I should like to have a last word with Cook and the upstairs maids."

"Will half an hour suffice?"

"Yes," she said, and watched as he walked away. As soon as he'd gone, she turned back to Kian. "What in heaven's name has happened? You both look as if a death in the family had occurred. Has there been another attack?"

"No, thank God," Kian said. "There's nothing to worry over, Loris. Save getting to London. I pray the rain won't follow you throughout the journey. I had hoped for you to enjoy seeing some of England. I doubt you remember much of the journey from ten years past, when we first brought you to Tylluan."

"I recall every moment," she countered. "Ffinian spent each mile making me laugh with his stories and telling me everything about Tylluan. I thought he must be making it all up, for it sounded so wonderful," she said wistfully, her voice softening, "but it was everything that he said it was. And much more."

"I'm pleased that you love Tylluan so well," Kian said, watching her closely. "I hope you'll come back to it."

Loris drew in a breath and released it slowly. She didn't look at him. She'd been considering all that had taken place in the past two days. Her feelings and memories were still raw, but she wasn't so foolish as to deny the truth. What had happened between them in her chamber had changed everything. She simply wasn't certain yet in what way.

"I can't imagine being away from Tylluan for long," she said at last. "I've told you so before."

His hand, which she saw out of the corner of her eye, relaxed the grip it had been holding on a cup of hot tea.

"I'm glad," he said. "Everything will be just as you wish when you come home."

"Thank you," she murmured, wishing that they wouldn't speak as if they were strangers. But that was partly her fault, she knew. He felt too badly about what had taken place to be comfortable so soon. It would be up to her to make him act like himself again. She considered trying to aggravate him into making one of his mocking statements but decided that the time wasn't right. Loris straightened in her chair, instead, and said, "Tell me what happened between you and Dyfed last night. What kept you in company so long after he came home?"

Kian sighed wearily. "I cannot tell you everything, and you must promise me that you'll not press Dyfed with questions, for he cannot speak of it yet, either. Will you give me your word, Loris? You know that I'd not ask it of you if it weren't important. And yes"—he held up a hand when she started to speak—"I will tell you everything as soon as it becomes possible for me to do so."

"Of course," she said, though her interest was only far more piqued. "I shouldn't wish to upset Dyfed. He looks so unhappy already."

"Aye," Kian said, and, sitting back in his chair, rubbed both hands over his face. "God, I'm so weary. When this is all over I'm going to sleep for a fortnight."

"You'll find a way to be rid of the troubles soon, Kian," she said. "Once Dyfed and I have gone, you'll be able to fix your mind on the matter, just as you wish to do."

He dropped his hands and gazed at her. "I don't know if I will," he said. "But I suppose I must, as the duty is mine alone. There is something else I must ask of you. A great favor. Not for my sake, but for Dyfed's."

Loris looked at him curiously. "What is it?"

"Yesterday—no, the day before that, when I went to Llew. The day we quarreled over—"

"Yes, I recall it very well," she snapped, irate that he should remind her of the foolish things she'd said.

"I mentioned to you—before we quarreled—that Desdemona Caslin is betrothed to the Earl of Llew."

"Yes."

Kian leaned forward, looking at her very directly. "You mustn't say anything to Dyfed about the betrothal. Or tell anyone of it once you reach London. Not even Niclas or Malachi, should they ask you what you know about Miss Caslin. And don't tell Julia, either, for she'd certainly tell Niclas and then Dyfed might hear of it."

"Dyfed can't know of the Earl of Llew's betrothal?" Loris asked slowly. "Don't you imagine that all of London knows of it already?"

Kian shook his head. "I don't believe so. Cadmaran has always embraced strictly formal methods in regard to such matters. Desdemona Caslin must be properly introduced into society before Lord Llew will make the betrothal known. The *ton* will first learn of it when they read the announcement in the papers."

"But I still don't quite understand why Dyfed can't know about it," Loris said.

Kian's expression grew particularly bleak. "He believes he's in love with her. No, it's worse than that. He believes they are *unoliaeth*—that she's his fated one."

Loris blinked at him, stunned. "Dyfed and . . . *Desdemona Caslin?*"

Kian nodded. "He didn't go to the village last night. He met Desdemona Caslin, instead. Evidently he didn't tell me everything that occurred between them during their first encounter several nights ago. They arranged to meet secretly upon his return from *Fynnon Elian,* and—well, in part, she told him those things that I've already said I can't tell you now. She also made Dyfed believe that she loves him. But from all that he told me last night, she said nothing of her betrothal to Cadmaran. Which was likely wise on her part, for Dyfed might attempt to challenge Lord Llew for her hand otherwise."

Loris still couldn't get beyond the idea of Dyfed being in love. Or at least thinking he was. He'd never even been infatuated with a woman before. "Dyfed's far too sensible to do such a foolish thing," she countered. "And he couldn't have fallen in love with her after only two meetings."

"It happens among our kind quite often," Kian told her, looking at her in a meaningful way. "We are easily susceptible to the forces of nature. From what Dyfed told me last night, and by the manner in which he said it, I am absolutely convinced that he has fixed his heart solely and completely upon Desdemona Caslin, and intends to have her as his wife. The only thing that's keeping him from going to Llew at once and demanding her hand is the trouble that's been taking place at Tylluan. She is, for the time being, inextricably bound to Cadmaran and the destruction that's been occurring, and she must remain at Llew until I've found a solution for the problem."

"But if she knows something of what's been taking place—" Loris began.

"Not only knows of it," Kian broke in, "but has been part of it. Dyfed assures me, however, that Miss Caslin will do what she can now—for his sake—to lend me her aid. But she must do so in secret, without letting Cadmaran know, else he'll stop her from helping at all, and possibly imprison her at Llew. I pray that Dyfed is right in trusting her. I'm not entirely certain that I do, yet."

"Oh, heavens," Loris murmured unhappily. "She's filled with dark magic, is she not? She must be, if she's been helping the Earl of Llew. And an American. Could it possibly be any worse? Are you quite sure Dyfed's in love with her? Perhaps he was only enchanted by her beauty. She is very beautiful, you said. Or perhaps she put some kind of spell on him."

Sighing, Kian rose from the table. "I argued much the same with him last night, but he was able to convince me that his feelings are quite real. But getting her away from Cadmaran is going to be a tricky business. Until I know exactly what transpired between Miss Caslin's father and the Earl of Llew, and what vows were made, I won't know whether she can easily be stolen away or not. If she and Dyfed are truly *unoliaeth*, then nothing can keep them apart, not even the most solemn vows given by those outside the union. The Guardians will hold the *unoliaeth* above any other claim. But if they were not fated and Cadmaran has obtained a promise from the father for the daughter's hand . . ." Kian shook his head. "I don't know what can be done, save to offer Lord Llew whatever price he desires in order to free her from obligation to him."

"But Dyfed won't care about any of that," Loris murmured. "If he's truly in love with her, he'll not accept defeat."

"No, he won't," Kian agreed. "And that's precisely why he mustn't know of the betrothal between Lord Llew and Miss Caslin. He's content to let her remain at Llew for now only because he thinks she'll be free to come away with him once the troubles have been dealt with. But if he discovers that she's bound to Cadmaran by a betrothal . . . I greatly fear what he would try to do."

Loris shivered at the thought. "If Dyfed challenges the Earl of Llew," she said, "he will give up all of the protections that keep wizards from killing one another."

Kian nodded grimly. "To issue a challenge is to leave yourself open to death," he said, "and to give the one to whom the challenge was issued an advantage. Which is why our kind has always been so careful about such things. Cadmaran could kill Dyfed and never be punished for it. At least not by the Guardians. And I doubt any prison made by mere mortals could hold so powerful a wizard."

"Dyfed is usually so calm and logical," Loris murmured, unable to keep the worry from her tone. "But there's no denying that when he's overset, he can be terribly foolish."

"Dyfed is a man in love," Kian stated. "And I can tell you from experience that there's no more foolish man on earth."

Loris looked at him in silence.

"You'll say nothing to Dyfed of the betrothal, then?" Kian asked. "Or to anyone else? I believe that you and I are the only two who know of it outside of the Cadmaran clan."

"I'll say nothing to anyone, Kian. Certainly not to Dyfed. I give you my promise."

"Thank you. I won't worry on the matter, then, for I know your word is always certain. I'll leave you to have your chat with the staff. I'm sure they're very well prepared for your absence, though I believe they'll miss your guiding hand almost as dearly as I will."

Again, she made no reply. They gazed at each other, and then Kian turned and left the room.

Half an hour later, they took their leave of Tylluan. Dyfed helped Elen into the carriage and prepared to hand Loris up, as well, but Kian stopped him.

"I'll help her," he said. "In a moment."

Dyfed looked from one to the other, then nodded and walked away to mount the horse being held for him by one of the servants.

Kian took Loris's hand and pulled her a few steps away from the carriage and all those who were watching them— the entire castle staff, who had come out to bid her farewell, and most of Kian's men, whose jobs were to guard Tylluan and keep it secure. When they were just out of earshot he stopped, released her hand, and turned to face her.

"I realize that you haven't yet forgiven me for what happened," he said in a low voice, gazing very directly into her face, "and that you're still very angry. It will likely take a great deal of time before you feel any charity with me at all—"

"Kian," she said, her heart constricting painfully at how deeply he was suffering for what had happened between them. "Please, don't."

He looked stricken. His handsome face was already so drawn and pale, and, gazing at him, Loris wondered whether Cook or any of the maids would be able to convince him to eat as he should or get the rest he needed. It hadn't been easy for Loris to make him take care of himself these past many months, but, then, she never minded bullying him when it was necessary.

"I don't wish to speak of Liw yet," she said. "I confess that's too painful. But as to the other"—she swallowed before going on—"you were not the only one who wished to . . . participate." Her face felt as if it were on fire, and Loris had no doubt it looked that way. "You asked me if I wanted to, ah, proceed, and promised that you would stop, and I never . . . ahem"—she cleared her throat and looked down at her gloved hands—"I didn't wish to. Stop, that is. And so I don't want to leave Tylluan . . . and you . . . without letting you know that I'm not s-sorry about . . . about that. Nor am I angry," she added quickly. "Nor, if I would be perfectly honest, do I, ah"—here her voice fell to a whisper—"regret what we . . . what I . . . that is to say, the knowledge that I . . . gained." Then, thoroughly embarrassed, she added, in a rapid tumble, "I only thought it right to let you know."

She looked up to find that he was staring at her hands, too, his face tautly set and the muscles of his cheeks and mouth working to keep some manner of emotion at bay. She thought for an awful moment that he might laugh at her— typical Kian, making light of her foolish words—but in an instant she realized that he was struggling to hold back tears.

"Thank you," he bit out at last, his voice husky and low. He appeared to want to say more but didn't.

Loris swallowed again, her own throat suddenly tight. Kian never wept. *Never.* He covered his feelings with mockery and sarcasm and laughter.

She reacted instinctively and took a step forward, lifting her hands to fuss with his wrinkled cravat, which looked as if he'd thrown it on while half-asleep. She hoped that the servant who put Kian's clothes away would make certain they had been properly pressed before he let the baron put them on, as Loris always did.

"I shall be receiving reports from Cook as to how you've been eating," Loris informed him sternly, looking into his face, though it was still lowered and she was obliged to bend a little to see his eyes. "And I shall write to find out whether you've been getting enough rest, as well. If I discover that you've been so foolish as to fall into a decline or make yourself sick, I shall return to Tylluan immediately, whether I've had the opportunity to meet Lord Perham or not."

Kian laughed then, just once, but it was enough. Loris could see that he'd regained his balance.

"That's scarcely an incentive to make me desire food or sleep," he said, lifting his head to meet her gaze at last. Then his smile died away. "I'm going to miss you, Loris."

She stepped away, managing a wry smile. "If I come back to Tylluan to find either you or the castle or my gardens in disorder, Kian Seymour, I promise that you'll very much wish that I was on the other end of the earth."

Eleven

$\mathcal{I}$ apologize for disagreeing with you, Loris, but I'm afraid my wife is right. You look stunning."

Niclas Seymour made a slow circle about Loris, taking in the elegant gown that she wore. His three-month-old daughter, Sian, was in his arms. His twin sons, Macsen and Elias, just past two years of age, had taken up following their father wherever he went and toddled behind, each with a hand on the tail of his coat.

"It's perfect," he declared, coming to a halt beside his beaming wife. "That color almost exactly matches your eyes. Not quite brown, not quite gold. It's more a cinnamon, with perhaps a bit more red. And with your hair arranged in that becoming manner, I doubt any other female could possibly outshine you. Don't you agree, Dyfed?"

Dyfed smiled from where he stood and replied, "Very much. Fashionable society in London is about to be turned on its head."

"It is a beautiful dress," Loris told them, gazing down at the lovely garment with a mixture of pleasure and alarm, "but are you quite sure I'm to wear it out-of-doors? In the daylight? It's so . . ." Feeling herself flush, she waved a hand at her upper body. "Thin." She certainly wasn't going to admit in front of men that her bosom felt indecently bare, though of course they could see that for themselves. The gown was cut so low that if she'd been home in Tylluan, she would surely have come down with an inflammation of the lungs. Or frozen to death. "It hardly seems suitable for the purpose of calling upon an elderly gentleman."

"The purpose," said Dyfed, coming nearer, "is to make you look enchanting, which you are." He took one of her hands and kissed it. "And among the *ton* this dress will be considered scandalously prim and proper. Only wait until you see what you're to wear to parties and balls. This is merely a day dress."

"I never thought to have something so beautiful," she said, and moved to hug Julia. "You've spent so much time making me presentable this past week. I don't know how to thank you."

Julia Seymour was one of the few women whom Loris had been able to call a friend. She had been brought to Castle Tylluan years earlier by Niclas, on a quest to stop Ffinian from forcing Julia's aunt, Lady Alice, into marriage.

Lady Alice's estate, Glen Aur, lay in the valley below Tylluan, and she and Ffinian had become lovers following the death of Lady Alice's husband. But Ffinian had wanted much more, not the least of which was Lady Alice's fortune, which he thought he would gain through marrying her. Lady Alice, however, was content to leave their relationship as it was and had no intention of taking another husband so soon. Her family, unfortunately, didn't believe that she would be able to resist Baron Tylluan's attentions and had sent Julia to Wales to rescue her elderly aunt from what they perceived as Ffinian's ruthless clutches.

Niclas, for reasons of his own, had agreed to safely escort Julia to Wales, presumably to manage his uncle while she rescued her aunt. Along the way, Niclas and Julia had fallen in love, and now, following three years of marriage and three children, were the happiest couple Loris had ever set sight on. Barring Ffinian and Lady Alice, of course, who had married just as soon as Ffinian had agreed to give the title and lands at Tylluan into Kian's care.

And Niclas and Julia made a striking couple, as well. Niclas was a tall, handsome, dark-haired man with the piercing blue eyes common to Seymours, while Julia was small and feminine, with soft chestnut-colored hair and eyes a lighter shade of blue than her husband's. They were very much in love and almost always in each other's company.

Niclas had the ability, or curse, as he sometimes called it, to feel the emotions of mere mortals. Except when he was touching Julia. She was able to give him peace and surcease simply by touching him, with the result that they were constantly holding hands, especially in public, where the emotions of mere mortals could so easily make Niclas's life a nightmare. Society, Julia told Loris, thought their constant display of affection vulgar, but neither she nor Niclas cared. Loris didn't think it vulgar in the least, but vastly romantic.

"It is a beautiful dress," Julia agreed, smiling. "But only because you're wearing it. You do look stunning, Loris. Lord Perham is going to be very pleased."

Lord Perham. Loris had been trying for days not to think of her coming meeting with him, but it was proving to be impossible. She had tried to imagine what he looked like, sounded like, and what he would think of her when he saw her.

Her appearance had undergone a dramatic change since she and Dyfed had arrived in London, following what proved to be a rainy, but uneventful, journey from Tylluan.

Julia and Niclas had welcomed Loris warmly into the comfort of their beautiful town house, while Dyfed had gone to stay at Mervaille, the London estate of the Earl of Graymar. The very next day, scarcely giving her a chance to catch her breath, Julia had taken Loris in hand and set to the task of turning her from a country dowd into a lady of fashion.

The first order of business had been dealing with Loris's thick, unruly hair. It had never been cut before, and the length had always made it something of a problem for Loris to manage. At Tylluan she generally rolled it up into a haphaz-ard pile atop her head or simply left it unbound. On those rare occasions when they had company for dinner, she went to the trouble of braiding and arranging it more carefully, but even then several strands managed to escape. Kian never grew weary of teasing her about her unkempt appearance, of-ten fingering the loose curls to make her angry. He'd not find it so easy to do now.

She had feared that it might be rather sad having so much of her hair sheared away, but the result had been much the opposite. By the time Julia and her maids set down their scissors and curlers, Loris felt as if ten pounds had been lifted from her head. It was the most wonderful, buoyant feeling, and the new curls that Julia had created framed Loris's face in a manner that she found very pretty.

For the first time in her life, as she gazed at her reflection in a mirror, Loris began to feel a longing to be feminine. And dainty, though she knew, given her height and the firmness wrought from years of hard work at Tylluan, that was asking too much. She would have to settle for what was possible, and with Julia's help that would be more than enough.

A hot bath with a long, hard scrubbing had come next, and after that Loris's nails had been carefully trimmed and polished with oil. All manner of lotions and powders had been applied to her face and body following this, and, fi-nally, Julia had sprayed Loris with the most wonderful per-fume. She had been gratified when Cousin Niclas had sniffed her and remarked that he liked the scent on her al-most as well as on his wife.

Lord Graymar, having arrived with Dyfed that evening to welcome Loris to London as well as to dine, had declared himself astonished by the change in her appearance.

Julia, smiling with pleasure at her success, promised that it was only the beginning.

The next day they'd made an early start, visiting dress-makers, milliners, cobblers, and a great many stores where they purchased the necessities required by a woman of fashion.

Stockings and gloves and undergarments trimmed in lace, reticules and rouges and more powders, handkerchiefs, and pretty combs—some decorated with glittering jewels—for Loris's hair. It had been an exhausting day and, worse, very expensive, but when Loris protested about the cost Julia had immediately hushed her. She wasn't to worry over the expense. The family considered Loris to be one of their own, and it was long past time for her to be treated as such. Julia thought it shameful that Ffinian hadn't brought Loris to London years ago for a proper Season and appeared to be determined to make up for what she viewed as the former Baron Tylluan's neglect of his ward.

Dyfed came each afternoon to visit and see the progress that Loris was making in her transformation. He himself, having already been in possession of a suitable wardrobe for his visits to London, always arrived looking like a properly dressed gentleman, handsome and fine. He'd had his hair cut, though it was still far too long to be considered fashionable, and she saw that the nails on his hands had been cleaned and trimmed.

Despite the perfection of his outward appearance, Dyfed looked unhappy. He tried not to let it show, but Loris knew him too well to miss the gloom that had settled over him even before they'd left Tylluan. It had been present all through their journey and remained as each day in London passed. He and Lord Graymar were busy trying to find some solution to the problems at Tylluan, though Loris wasn't precisely sure what it was they were looking for. She'd overheard Lord Graymar speaking of the matter to Cousin Niclas in passing, but Dyfed never mentioned it. He looked tired and tense, much as Kian had before they'd left Tylluan, and Loris knew that Dyfed longed to return to Wales and his newfound love.

Still, he was always reliably pleasant during his daily visits, assuring Loris that she looked beautiful and that she would make a great splash when they began to attend balls and parties. He kept her informed about the arrangements that were being made for her meeting with Lord Perham.

Lord Graymar would be with her during the interview and would make certain, should the outcome not be what was hoped for, that society would not hear of it. They were all determined that Loris's one and only Season in Town should not be marred by gossip.

Although how that could be managed Loris didn't know. Rumors regarding Ffinian Seymour's long-secret ward had already begun to circulate, Dyfed told her, and those who had caught glimpses of Loris in company with Julia had reported that she was a beauty, although not, by appearances, in any way refined. But that, as Dyfed said, was to be expected, for London society held newcomers from the country in low esteem to begin with, more certainly those who harkened from Wales, which was scarcely considered to be civilized. But Loris was going to surprise them all, he predicted, when she made her first real foray out among the *ton.*

Loris wasn't quite as convinced. She had been introduced to some of Julia's acquaintances, whom she and Julia had come across while making their daily visits to the various shops, and had found the experiences to be very awkward. Julia tried to help Loris, guiding her through the meetings and being a perfect example of ladylike decorum, but she had never learned the art of polite conversation and usually ended up saying—or doing—the wrong thing. She had decided that the *ton,* or what she'd met of it thus far, was a terribly impractical collection of individuals and wondered at how Kian and Dyfed and Ffinian—who lived exceedingly practical lives at Tylluan—could possibly find a visit to Town refreshing.

On the other hand, she couldn't deny that her impression of London itself was vastly improved from what it had once been. She hadn't really believed what various members of the Seymour clan had told her about the great city, for she'd only had her own memories to go by. But there was so much more, she had discovered. There were beautiful homes and glorious parks and elegant shops.

Dyfed had taken her driving several afternoons in a

curricle that he'd borrowed from Lord Graymar, and Loris had been so astonished at how quickly they'd found trees and grass and flowers—and not so very far from the docks! She couldn't understand why her parents had never taken her to one of the several parks in the city during her childhood, especially having promised to show her such beautiful things. But perhaps, if her mother had truly been the daughter of an earl, they were afraid she might be recognized in so public a place. Loris found it amazing now to realize just how small her world had once been.

She was equally astonished—and pleased—by the changes she saw in herself. As each day passed and as she grew more used to the new face that she saw in her mirror, a measure of excitement began to grow in her heart. And then today, just in time for her meeting with Lord Perham, the first few of her new dresses had arrived, and the transformation had been complete.

She had been quite sure, gazing at her reflection, that this couldn't possibly be the same Loris who had arrived from Tylluan two weeks ago. The same person who had once labored as a serving girl at the Red Fox and who had spent the last ten years of her life as housekeeper at Castle Tylluan.

But not all of Loris's time was spent in buying clothes or improving her appearance and manners or enjoying the parks in London. She managed to find a few hours alone each day to think of Kian. And Liw. And of what had happened to all three of them at Tylluan.

The worst part was forcing herself to remember the countless nights when Liw had come to her, when she'd opened her heart to him. And she did force herself to the task, for given her own natural inclination, Loris knew she would have pushed the memories out of her thoughts forever. Because it hurt to know that it had been Kian she'd been confiding to all the while, that he had used deceit to lure her most private secrets out into the open. Loris had told him things as Liw that she never would have wanted Kian to know—most especially all those things she'd thought about Kian himself. And then he had pretended to be so understanding and had even taken her side against Kian, time and again. Worst of all, he'd advised her on how to approach Kian, how to appease and understand him. Loris had always been so grateful and had loved Liw even more because he was such a wonderful, caring friend. She had trusted him as she had not dared to let herself trust anyone since her father's death. But Liw had turned out to be completely false.

Aye, it was painful to think upon, but Loris knew, from past experience, that the best way to cure a terrible wound was to drain and clean it, day after day after day, until the infection had cleared and healing could begin. And so she made herself remember, and consider, and think over each instance when she had confided to Liw, or at least as much as she could recall. She brought back to mind the things he'd said to her, his smile and the comforting feel of his arms about her. And when she had finished facing down one memory and had told herself that it wasn't so very terrible to recall and that she could certainly live with it, she went on to the next. She wept a great deal, sometimes with grief for Liw, sometimes with fury at Kian, and afterward felt as if she'd drained off a good deal of the poison.

At night, lying in her bed or sitting beside the window, gazing out at the damp London nights, she strove to make some kind of order out of the myriad confusing thoughts and emotions that she'd come away from Tylluan with.

She thought of what Kian had done in coming to her as Liw and tried to understand what had driven him to do such a thing. He loved her, he said. They were *unoliaeth*, he told her, and there was nothing she could do to change that. Loris had scoffed at his words because she hadn't sought his love and refused to be forced into union with any man without having a say in the matter. She'd already had more than enough of others deciding what her life would be; she didn't want more.

But she hadn't understood the *unoliaeth*, he had told her only days ago. And he didn't love her simply because he believed they were fated to be.

I don't need magic to tell me what's between us, he had said. *And neither do you.*

The words haunted her, waking and sleeping, almost as much as what he'd said to her just before walking away.

I'm here, too.

The memory made her heart ache, for Loris had said those same words, save that then there had been no one else to hear. She knew what it was to be invisible, unimportant, powerless, to hunger for someone to notice that she was there. That she mattered. Loris wondered if she had ever before considered what Kian had gone through in all those years since she'd come to Tylluan, loving and not being loved in turn. If she'd been in his place, perhaps she would have been driven to find a way to be near her loved one as well.

There was a stir in the air, and Niclas murmured, "I believe Malachi has arrived."

And he was right. Lord Graymar appeared at the parlor door a moment later, dressed to gentlemanly perfection not in the daunting black he usually preferred, but in beige breeches, a tight-fitting blue coat that matched the color of his eyes, and gleaming black Hessian boots. His light blond hair, which, in typical Seymour fashion, was overlong, was tied back in its customary tail at the back of his neck.

Like Kian and Dyfed, Malachi had inherited the sharp, fine features that blond Seymours usually possessed. In fact, he looked so much like his Tylluan relations that those who didn't know better often mistook them for brothers upon sight, rather than cousins.

But there was a difference between the three men that Loris always found striking. Dyfed and Kian could look angelic when they wished, while no one who saw Lord Graymar would ever use that word to define him. He exuded a natural grace and power that made her think of nobility, even kingliness, but never anything that even approached angelic.

He stood at the door, his gaze moving critically over Loris's figure, from head to toe and back again. At last he gave an approving nod and offered a slight smile. "Julia," he said, "you have worked the miracle that I fully expected you would. She's ravishing."

Moving into the room, he first greeted Macsen and Elias, who had abandoned their father at the sight of their favorite relative. Bending down to pet their soft dark curls, Lord Graymar said, "There you are, my rascals. What have you been doing this fine day? Making your father old before his time, I have no doubt."

"No, in point of fact, it's their music instructor who has begun to sprout gray hair," Niclas told him. "The boys happened to discover the piano this week. I suppose we'll have to saw the legs off to make it safer for them to practice."

"The piano?" Malachi said, rising full-height. "I thought they'd only just started with the flute."

"Oh no, that was last week," Julia said, taking a slumbering Sian from her father's arms. "They've long since grown bored with it. We're beginning to run out of instruments to keep them busy." She cast her husband a teasing glance. "And to think we were worried that the worst they'd do was levitate their nursery toys."

"You must leave that to Sian, I believe," Malachi said, stroking a gentle finger across the sleeping baby's cheek. "Look at that red hair. She's going to be one of our greatest mystics. Well, Cousin," he addressed Niclas, "are we ready for the day and whatever it may bring?"

"We are," Niclas replied, then motioned to where Loris stood, Dyfed's arm about her. "I'm not certain we can say the same for Loris, however."

Lord Graymar gave Loris another appraising look as he moved to take one of her hands and turn her about. "I don't see why she shouldn't be," he said. "She's a diamond of the first water. We shall have to take turns fending off her suitors, especially if Lord Perham recognizes her as his granddaughter. Because then she'll not only be incredibly beautiful," Malachi said, lifting her chin with the tip of one finger and smiling into her face, "but wealthy as well. Very few men can resist such a devastating combination in a female."

"They shall have to do so in my case, my lord," she replied. "My intention is to return to Tylluan as soon as possible."

"And leave behind dozens of broken hearts, no doubt," said His Lordship. "Now, turn about and let me see precisely how elegant this gown is. Ah, very good. Excellent. Julia, your taste in color and cut is without equal. But there is one touch missing, I believe."

Both Julia and Loris looked at him curiously.

"And what is that, my lord?" Julia asked.

Lord Graymar reached into his coat, pulling a slender box out of an inner pocket. He handed it to Loris.

"This," he said simply.

All those present, save the twins, moved closer to watch as the box was opened, and murmured with surprise when she withdrew a gleaming strand of pearls.

"Oh, Malachi, they're perfect," Julia declared approvingly.

Loris gazed at the beautiful necklace in speechless wonder. She'd never seen anything so lovely in all her life. The beads were cool and slick beneath her fingers and glowed as if they had an inner light.

"Oh, Lord Graymar," she murmured, "I'm quite sure I can't accept these. They must be very valuable."

"Nonsense," His Lordship said, lifting the necklace from her shaking hand and stepping behind her. "Every young woman about to enter society should have a proper set of pearls."

She shivered as he arranged the smooth white strand about her neck and fixed the clasp.

"Very pretty," Niclas said, and Julia declared, "You were right, Malachi. They finish the dress perfectly."

Loris gingerly lifted her hand to touch the necklace. "Thank you, my lord," she whispered, and began to feel, with alarm, that she was going to weep, though whether from pleasure or fear she didn't know. She wished, fervently, that she were back at Tylluan. Back where she was always confident and certain.

Lord Graymar stepped back and surveyed the result of his addition with satisfaction. "The pleasure is mine, Loris. You should have begun a collection of jewelry long before now, but we shall see whether we can't make up for lost time. I will consult with Julia in the coming days regarding the proper jewels to complement the evening gowns you'll be wearing."

"Oh dear," said Loris, wondering what she would do with such fine things back home. "Thank you, sir, but I really don't need anything more. Do I, Julia?"

But Julia's expression was filled with anticipation and approval, and Loris saw that she'd find no help in that quarter. She was about to appeal to Dyfed, but he was distracted in quiet conversation with Niclas and wasn't paying attention.

"Don't fret over the matter, my dear," Lord Graymar said dismissively. "Now, are you ready to go and meet Lord Perham? I imagine he's becoming rather desperate, having been put off for so many days."

"Yes, my lord," she said, though inwardly she was quaking with fear. "I'm ready."

Dyfed approached and took Loris gently by the elbow. "Will you give us a moment alone, Malachi?" he asked, guiding Loris in the direction of the parlor door. "I only want a word with her in private before you go."

Lord Graymar frowned slightly but said, "I suppose five minutes more or less won't matter to Lord Perham after weeks of waiting. But be quick, Dyfed."

He led her to the library, where they were alone, and shut the doors. Turning to face her, he said, "Are you all right, Loris?"

"Yes, of course," she said, her tone unnaturally high. She folded her shaking hands together tightly. "Why shouldn't I be?"

"Niclas said you were about to cry," Dyfed said.

"Well, that's . . . he's . . ." She blinked back the tears that were insistently forcing their way forward. "Do you know, Dyfed," she said, the words trembling badly, "it's most unpleasant to be the only person in this household who is not immune to your cousin's gift."

The last word came out half-strangled, and she promptly burst into tears.

"Oh, Loris," Dyfed murmured, gathering her into his arms. "Darling Loris. Don't cry, love. I know how hard this is for you." He stroked her back with one hand and with the other cradled her head, his fingers buried in her hair. "But it will be over soon, and then we'll go home to Tylluan."

"I feel so guilty," she said, sobbing. "Julia and Niclas and Lord Graymar, they've all been so kind, and I am grateful. I truly am."

"Shhh," Dyfed murmured. "I know."

"B-but I don't wish to be a lady, and I don't wish to go to parties and balls and make a splash. And Lord Perham is going to find me a dreadful creature with n-no manners, just as Julia's friends have. But what else can I do when everyone is so kind and Lord Graymar is giving me pearls?"

"Lord Perham isn't going to think you a dreadful creature, love. And Malachi doesn't want to do anything but make you happy by giving you the pearls. If you don't wish to go to parties and balls, you need only say so. We simply won't go. No one will force you, believe me. I won't let them."

She hugged him tightly. "I know, Dyfed. If it weren't for you, I should be so wretched. I'm sorry," she said, pulling away and wiping her face with her bare fingers. The weeping stopped almost as quickly as it had begun. "I'll be better now." She sniffed loudly.

"Here, let me." He took a handkerchief from a pocket and lifted her face to dab at her wet cheeks. "You'd better run upstairs and splash a little cold water on your face. Everyone's going to know you've been crying, but the signs should have faded by the time you reach Perham's home."

"I hate to cry," she said unhappily. "It's such a childish thing to do. I'd blame it on Kian, but he's not here." She drew in a breath, striving to calm herself. "How I wish he was."

Dyfed fell still and gazed down at her. "What did you say?"

She sniffed again. "I said that if Kian was here, I'd blame my foolish weeping on him."

"No, after that. Did you say that you wish Kian was here?"

Loris wondered if Dyfed wasn't more weary than she'd supposed. "No, of course not. Why would I say such a thing?"

"It doesn't signify," he said. "Are you feeling better now that you've shed a few tears?"

She did feel better, she realized, and reached up to kiss him lightly. "Much better, Dyfed. Thank you. I'll be fine now. I'm sorry for being so foolish."

He kissed her, too, and said, "You're not foolish, Loris. I love you dearly. You know that, don't you? I want you to be happy."

She smiled. "I love you, too. And I'm so glad you're here with me."

"I'm glad as well," he said, but she recognized the gallantry behind the word. It was obvious by the pain that lurked in the depths of his eyes that he wished he were elsewhere and with someone else entirely. "Hurry now. Run upstairs and wash your face. Malachi doesn't like to wait."

Twelve

Dyfed was right. Lord Graymar, and everyone else, knew that she'd been crying when she came back downstairs, ready to depart. But it was Lord Graymar who sat beside her in his elegant carriage, patting her hand and speaking reassuringly.

"You must believe me when I tell you that you've nothing to fear," he said. "You belong to the Seymours as surely as if you'd been born into the family, and we take care of those who are ours. You've been as a daughter to my uncle Ffinian and as a sister to Dyfed. I won't speak of what lies between you and Kian, for I know that the curse has made it difficult for you to hear."

"Lord Graymar," she began, but he held up a hand to stop her.

"We won't speak of it further. I only wish to make you understand that no matter what happens today, you have a family that loves and will protect and care for you. Always."

"Thank you, my lord. The words will seem trite, but I truly am more grateful than I can say."

"Loris," he said with a touch of impatience, "please do call me Malachi. You've known me long enough to assume that familiarity."

"Thank you," she said again. "Malachi."

"You're stiff as a poker," he said. "If you wish, I could perform a certain enchantment that would—"

"*No*," she said firmly. "I'm fine. Truly. Kian has done that to me before, and if it should be done again without my permission I cannot promise that you won't be terribly unhappy with my response, my lord, once I've regained my senses. I mean to say, Malachi."

He laughed, inexplicably amused by this. "Very well, then. I shall restrain from calming you by magic. We'll be arriving at Lord Perham's home shortly. Shall I tell you something of him before then?"

"Yes," she said eagerly. "Please."

"He's an elderly gentleman," His Lordship began, settling into the cushioned seat more comfortably. "Quite wealthy, descended of one of the older families. Well connected. His wife died five years ago, and his only child, a daughter, ran off with a neighbor's son eighteen years before. He believes that she was pregnant at that time, though he cannot be certain. He's been trying to find that daughter, or his grandchild, since his wife's death. Evidently she had prohibited such efforts while she was alive."

"But why?" Loris asked. "Didn't she wish to find her daughter?"

"From what I've been able to discover, Lady Perham wasn't possessed of the usual maternal nature found in most females. She never wished to have children and resented the one she believed Lord Perham forced her to bear. She also didn't wish to be made a grandmother at too early an age, being one of these women blessed with youthful looks. Apparently, when she believed her unmarried—and unbetrothed—daughter to be with child, there was an attempt at forcing the daughter to be rid of it. Some kind of poison was secreted into the girl's cup one night at dinner."

"God's mercy," Loris whispered, horrified.

"It came to naught, however, as the young woman recovered and did not miscarry. Which is why Lord Perham isn't certain that the girl was ever pregnant to begin with."

"What happened after she recovered?"

"She fled with the young man," Malachi said, "never to return. Which was unfortunate, as the young man in question was something of a wastrel and given to a good deal of gambling and drink."

Loris stiffened. "My father was *not* a wastrel," she said hotly. "And if he was given to gambling and drink, he certainly never let it bring us to ruin." At Malachi's patient look, she amended, reluctantly, "Entirely, anywise." Looking out the window, she asked, "What was his family like? The young man's?"

"Their name was McClendon," he said.

"Scottish?" she asked, looking back at him with quick interest.

"Possibly," Malachi replied, smiling. "It would explain a great deal about you."

Loris's eyebrows rose.

"Your thriftiness," he explained. "And your strict management of Castle Tylluan. It might interest you to know that the addition of Scottish blood has always been of particular benefit to the Seymours. One of our most well-loved forebears, Glenys Seymour, had a Scottish mother, and she is the one who wed Lord Eneinoig, a mere mortal who renewed the strength of our bloodline and brought us back to an understanding with the spirit world."

Loris felt a little swell of pride. "Of course. That makes perfect sense. Loris McClendon," she said, testing the sound of it. "I like it. What else do you know of them?"

"The father—your father's father—was the rector at Perham. He and his wife, both departed now, had three children. An elder son, who has died, leaving neither wife nor children behind, a daughter, who has married and borne children of her own—these would be your aunt and cousins—and a younger son, who Lord Perham believes is your father. The younger McClendon was the wild and undisciplined man of whom I spoke earlier. He and Perham's daughter ran away together, and neither has been heard of since."

Loris sat quietly, pondering the things Lord Graymar had said. After a moment she sighed and said quietly, "I never knew my last name, you know. My father changed it each time we moved. It was Smith or Andrews or Clay. He never told me what it really was."

"Which is precisely why Lord Perham isn't certain that you're his granddaughter. And you may not be, Loris. You must prepare your heart for both eventualities."

"Yes, I know," she agreed solemnly. "May I tell you something in confidence, my lord?" She gave herself a mental shake and said, "Malachi."

"If I were your lord, Loris," he said, "I would readily give you my oath of secrecy. But you know that I am not. Another is, of whom we have already agreed we will not speak. I will keep secret all that you tell me, save from him, if he should ask me for such knowledge."

"Kian Seymour is only my lord as master of Tylluan," she told him. "He certainly won't care to know what I wish to say. He sent me to London to meet Lord Perham."

"What is it, then?"

"It's difficult to say," she began, "for I've often wished to know who my parents' people were. But if Lord Perham is not my grandfather, I think what I'm going to feel more than anything else is relief." She hesitated. "Is that wrong of me?"

Malachi was thoughtful, then said, "I don't believe it is. You love Tylluan and wish to remain there, and a grandfather who is not of magic blood complicates matters. From my own experience of him, I do not believe that Lord Perham is one of our sympathetics. If that is true, and if he should prove implacable in not understanding our kind, then a relationship with him would prove difficult. You would have to make a choice, and as I know that it is impossible for you to part from Kian for any great length of time, I have no doubt of what that choice must be."

Out of respect for the earl, Loris refrained from arguing with him about his assertion regarding her relationship with Kian. It would have been churlish to naysay Malachi, and fruitless as well. The Earl of Graymar wasn't given to being corrected. She focused, instead, on what else he had said.

"Are you quite certain, sir?" she asked. "That Lord Perham couldn't one day become a sympathetic?"

A sympathetic was a mere mortal who understood and accepted magic mortals. Sympathetics sometimes married into magic Families and helped to keep them safe. Seymours were especially fond of uniting with such beings, for rather than diluting their powers, the mixing of bloods increased them.

"No, I'm not," he confessed. "I do not know the man well, and have only dealt with him in regard to meeting you. Perhaps you might discover something in him that will give us an answer."

"Perhaps," she said as the carriage came to a stop outside of a very large town house. Loris looked out at it, and her heart gave a leap of fear.

"Malachi." Her voice sounded thin even to her own ears. "Please stay with me."

He took her gloved hand and squeezed it lightly. "I will. Don't be afraid, Loris. You're in the care of the *Dewin Mawr*, and Lord Perham is but a mere mortal. Nothing so very terrible can happen, can it?"

"I don't know," she murmured as the carriage door was opened. "He may well be a grandparent, and I've heard that they are the most powerful beings alive."

Lord Perham's town house was built on a grand scale; in fact, it looked more like an imperial mansion than a mere dwelling. Malachi was clearly comfortable with such surroundings, but Loris found them to be daunting. Which struck her as odd, considering that she lived in a beautiful medieval castle.

A butler in elegant costume opened the door and led them into an impressive entryway with marble floors and fragile antiques lining the walls.

"His Lordship awaits you," said the butler, and motioned for them to follow him.

Malachi took Loris's hand and set it upon his arm, and she found that her feet moved forward whether she wished them to or not.

The large room they were taken to was at once imposing and inviting, with ornate furnishings and a fireplace burning merrily in the far wall. Lord Perham was sitting in a chair near that fire, a book resting on his lap and a glass filled with an amber liquid in one hand, halfway to his lips. The glass was put back on a nearby table when they entered the room, and Lord Perham stood, closing the book and putting it aside as well.

He was a tall, slender, distinguished-looking gentleman, with a thick crown of white hair and neatly trimmed mustache. He gazed at Loris very directly, and she gazed at him, both trying to find some resemblance to the woman they remembered, one as daughter, one as mother.

Loris had been seven when her mother had died and had nothing but the dimmest of memories to remember what she had looked like. This very fine gentleman stirred nothing within her, and yet she couldn't say that he wasn't her grandfather. From the forbidding expression on his face Loris wondered if he wasn't having the same trouble.

"Is this the girl then, Graymar?" Lord Perham's tone was calm and steady, nearly absent emotion.

Malachi's hand was warm and comforting on Loris's back, and as he prodded her forward he replied graciously, "This is she. We do not know her last name, and have always called her by the first, which is Loris."

He kept pushing until she stood directly in front of the older man, who hadn't moved an inch. Loris could see his eyes now and drew in a sharp breath. They were the same color as her own. The same as the dress she wore. Not quite brown, not quite gold. That was how Niclas had described them, and it was true.

"Loris," Lord Graymar said, "I make known to you Alexander Bissinger, Earl of Perham. Lord Perham, this is

Loris, ward to my uncle, Ffinian Seymour, former Baron of Tylluan."

Julia had taught Loris how to make a proper curtsy, and she performed it now, praying that her feet didn't twist beneath her and send her straight down onto the exquisite carpet.

"My lord," she murmured.

"Miss Loris," Lord Perham said in return, his voice still perfectly level, as if there were nothing at all remarkable about the occasion that brought them together. "Thank you for coming to meet with me. I hope that you will not regret the effort. Will you leave us to speak privately, Graymar?"

"I regret to say that I shall not," Malachi replied in such an easy and friendly manner that Loris couldn't imagine anyone taking exception to his refusal. "But I will be glad to sit here, on the other side of the fire, far enough away so that you may both converse in a more comfortable manner."

Lord Perham frowned at his peer but seemed to realize that to argue would be pointless. The door opened and a servant entered bearing a tea tray.

"Set it here," Lord Perham directed, pointing to a table near the chair he'd been seated in. "Will you do us the honor of pouring, Miss Loris?"

"I should be happy to do so, my lord," she replied, glad to have something to occupy her mind, even briefly. "Please don't stand on my account," she said, looking at both men. "Lord Graymar, do you still take cream in your tea?"

The men settled into chairs as Loris prepared their cups. She was aware that Lord Perham watched her closely, but he would be disappointed if he thought she would falter in this particular task. She might not have any of the finer skills that ladies of the *ton* possessed, but years of being hostess at Castle Tylluan had trained her well in such small matters as serving tea. It was an ability that had been self-taught, with a little help from Dyfed and Kian, and Loris had added touches that simply made sense to her. By the time she settled into her own chair, next to Lord Perham's, she saw the approval in his eyes.

"You are aware of what my interest in you is, I believe," Lord Perham stated, rather than asked.

"Yes, my lord. You believe I may be your granddaughter."

"May be," he repeated. "Yes, that's so. I've had dealings with individuals who own an establishment where I believe you once lived—"

"The Goodbodys," Loris said. "At the Red Fox."

"Just so," he said, his tone tinged with obvious distaste. For that Loris didn't blame him in the least.

"They knew nothing of who your mother was," he said. "But they knew your father and described him to me in detail. And you also, of course."

"They wouldn't have known my mother," Loris told him. "She died when I was seven, and my father began to frequent the Red Fox when I was ten. Shall I tell you what I remember of my parents? Would that be helpful?"

"If you wouldn't find it too difficult," he said, sitting up more straightly in his chair.

Lord Perham appeared to steel himself for what she was about to say, and it occurred to Loris that he was the one who might find such knowledge difficult. *And of course it would be,* she thought, feeling a great deal of sympathy for the elderly gentleman. He had been searching for his daughter for years now, with so much disappointment. He must be very weary of wrong turns and empty destinations.

"My mother's name was Nancy, but my father's pet name for her was Nan. My father's name was John. As I was telling Lord Graymar earlier, I don't know what his actual last name was, for he changed it wherever we went. The name he was using when he died was Whitford."

She paused to see if Lord Perham wished to make any comment, but he wasn't even looking at her. His hands were tented beneath his chin, and he was deep in thought. When he noticed her silence, he glanced up and said, "Please continue."

Loris tried to think of what else would interest him or be helpful.

"Let me see. Well, my parents often told me about the countryside where they had been raised, that it was exceedingly beautiful and green, and that there were many lakes and rivers. They promised that one day they would take me out of London to see countryside."

"Did they keep this promise?" he asked curiously.

"No." Loris gave a single shake of her head. "It wasn't until Ffinian Seymour took me away to Wales that I saw the beauties that my parents had spoken of." She glanced at Lord Graymar, who nodded encouragingly and sipped his tea. "Tylluan—my home in Wales—is the most beautiful place on earth. I hope that, regardless how matters end between us, sir, you might see it one day."

"I'm glad that you found refuge in a happy place," he said. "Especially after the life you were forced to endure in London. Did your parents ever speak of any relatives?"

"My mother sometimes spoke of her family," Loris said. "Not anything specific, of course, for it always angered my father terribly, but in a general way. She wished to return and make amends, but my father wouldn't allow it. He didn't like her to speak of it in front of me."

Lord Perham sat forward, gazing at her intently. "She wished to return to her family?" he asked. "Your mother? Did she?"

"Very much," Loris assured him. "It was the final request she made of my father before she died, that I should at least know her people. But he was absolutely set against it. If she was your daughter, sir, then I'm very sorry."

He had lowered his head into one hand, grieving, and Loris's heart clenched at the sight.

"Damn him," Lord Perham said, his voice filled with anguish. "Damn that man. He took her away and kept her away, even when she wished to come back."

Loris reached out to touch his hand, wishing that she might soothe his pain. "Lord Graymar has told me something of what happened to your daughter, sir, at her mother's hand. If that is so, and if my mother was your daughter, does it seem so unreasonable to you that my father would be afraid to return? Not just for his wife's safety, but for his child's, as well?"

Lord Perham lowered his hand and looked at her, his expression a mixture of fury and sorrow. "My wife was an ill woman. Ill in her mind, if not in her body. I didn't realize it before she tried to murder my grandchild, but once I did, I would have done everything possible to protect my daughter and her child."

Loris privately thought that he should have protected his daughter long beforehand, for surely he'd had some idea of his wife's sickness, but didn't speak the thought aloud. Instead, she said, "I'm sure you would have, sir. I'm terribly sorry for your loss."

"But not for your own?" he asked. "Do you believe yourself to be my granddaughter, Miss Loris?"

"I do not know, my lord," she replied honestly. "Do you believe it?"

"You say that your mother's name was Nancy. My daughter's name was Anna, but there were those who called her Nan. The scoundrel who dallied with her and stole her away was the youngest son of our rector. His name was not John, but Donald."

"Oh," Loris said, surprised to find that she felt a touch of sadness, rather than the relief she'd told Malachi she thought she would know. "Then I'm doubly sorry for you, sir, for it seems that I cannot be the grandchild you've been seeking."

"And why not?" he asked. "It would be expected that they would not use their real names, for fear of being discovered."

"Yes, I suppose that's true," she agreed. "But how can we know for certain, one way or the other, my lord?"

"I believe this will tell us," he said, and with slightly shaking hands withdrew something from a pocket within his coat. It was a small portrait, and with fingers still trembling he passed it to her.

Loris gazed down at the painting and was deeply surprised to see that it was of a young woman who was very much like . . . well, like herself. They might almost have been sisters. The color of the woman's hair was identical to Loris's, as were her facial features. She appeared to be younger than Loris in the depiction but far more refined, and was clearly a very grand and elegant young lady.

But as similar as they might be, Loris was obliged to tell him the truth.

"I'm sorry, my lord," she said once more. "This isn't my mother." Looking at him with all the sympathy she felt, she said, "I do wish I could tell you that she is, if only to give you peace."

His eyes filled with tears, and he reached out to take her hands in both of his, folding the portrait into her palms.

"Do you know, my dear," he said, sounding very close to weeping, "I have shown that portrait to dozens of young women and men in the search for my grandchild, and each one has eagerly asserted that this was their mother. You are the first to deny it, though the resemblance between you and this woman is so striking that you must in some way be related. But you see, Loris, this woman could not be mother to any of them, or to you, as you have so honestly stated. Because this is a portrait of my wife. Of your grandmother, my dear, of whom you are the very likeness." A tear rolled down one of his leathery cheeks. "You are my granddaughter, Loris. I'm convinced of it."

She came out of her chair to kneel before him and went into his arms. They hugged each other tightly as Lord Perham wept into her hair and shook with what she thought must be tremendous relief.

"I'm so glad," she murmured, an indefinable happiness filling her. She stroked his hair and felt tears on her own cheeks. "I'm so very glad, sir. I've always longed to have someone to call my own. Now we will have each other, and you may rest from your searching. My mother would have been very happy, I think. You must tell me everything about her, and I shall do my best to remember all that I can, as well."

From his chair in the corner Loris distinctly heard Lord Graymar blowing his nose. He stood and said, in a thick voice, "Well, now that matters have been so happily decided, I believe it might be best for me to leave you alone for a little while." He paused to clear his throat. "I shall just have a walk through your gardens, shall I, Perham? I've heard tell that they're exceptionally fine. I won't be gone long, Loris, my dear, and if you should need me, send one of the servants."

Lord Perham was still beyond the ability to speak, but Loris smiled gratefully at Lord Graymar and murmured, "Thank you."

He left the room, shutting the door behind him. Lord Perham, hearing his guest depart, at last lifted his head and began to fumble for a handkerchief.

"I'm sorry, my dear," he managed, wiping his face. "I fear this isn't a very good way for us to begin."

"I don't mean to disagree with you, my lord," she said, rising and fetching him a fresh cup of tea, "lest you think me ill-mannered, but I think it's a wonderful way to begin." She sat down in her chair and smiled at him. "Indeed, sir, I can scarce think of any better one."

Thirteen

"D'you think she'll come tonight, m'lord? It would be five in a row for the first time since we've started feeding the beast."

"That's so, Horas," Kian agreed, settling Seren when the horse moved impatiently. "But we'll take no chances. She may be forcing the creature to rest after four nights of wandering, but Dyfed told me that he normally feeds for five. After tonight, we'll have another respite for a few days." He sighed. "And then we start again."

"A respite, yes," Horas said, "but we're going to run out of sheep if the beast's appetite continues on like this. We've another two weeks at most before we'll have to look for something else to offer."

Kian had been worrying about the very same thing. He was going to have to start buying sheep and cattle from other estates soon if he didn't find a way to put the beast back into a deep and lasting slumber. Given enough time, the *athanc* would destroy all the local flocks and herds and would start searching for what it could find without going too far from the lake that was its home. It would destroy everything in its path, as it had done before Desdemona Caslin had begun to lead it into this particular pasture.

They had an unspoken agreement: She led the creature to this safe spot, and Kian made certain that it was filled with a goodly number of sheep. When the *athanc* had finished feasting, Desdemona Caslin ordered it back to the lake, and it disappeared by draining away into the earth.

They'd been playing this scene out for over a month now, and Kian still hadn't gotten used to seeing the creature transform from its solid form into its fluid one. It was an astonishing magic that he never would have believed possible if he'd not seen it, and Kian had seen numerous astonishing things in his life.

Nothing appeared to touch the creature. Kian had attempted to put an invisible trap about the area once the creature was in it, but the barriers melted away at the *athanc*'s approach, unable to hold it captive. He'd tried various spells, even daring to get as close as he possibly could to make them more effective, but they bounced back with such force that he'd been obliged to protect himself from his own powers. He'd requested aid from the elements, but neither the wind nor rain had been able to halt the beast's progress or affect it in any discernible way.

Clearly, Kian needed an incantation, one that would draw forth the might of those spirits, both heavenly and earthly, to lend him the strength he needed to force the monster back into its watery bower.

The *athanc* gave him a new appreciation for the dangers that his ancestors had been obliged to face in centuries past. More than that, it caused him to realize that he had a great deal more to learn before he would be able to take on the duties of the *Dewin Mawr*. Though Kian supposed that even Malachi would be at something of a loss regarding how to deal with the beast. Thus far neither he nor Dyfed nor Professor Seabolt had been able to find the enchantments for overcoming an *athanc*. It was very frustrating, and incredibly surprising, since, according to Dyfed's reports, they'd found well-documented spells and enchantments for just about every other ancient trouble that Europe had suffered. But for some inexplicable reason, no one had bothered to jot down the remedy for dealing with monstrous creatures, although, according to the professor, such beasts—sea serpents, dragons, and *athancs* among them—had been numerous in ancient days.

Desdemona Caslin had proved herself a formidable ally in this conflict, and although Kian wasn't precisely happy that Dyfed had given his heart to a dark sorceress, he was exceedingly glad that she was now on his side, even if only for Dyfed's sake.

They never spoke when she brought the beast; in truth, they purposefully remained on opposite sides of the clearing. But they communicated nonetheless. They were very similar in powers and could sense each other's thoughts. Dyfed had told Kian that he'd been able to hear Desdemona Caslin, but this, Kian had told him, was not because she had the gift of silent speech but very likely because she was, in truth, his fated one.

Kian couldn't communicate with her that closely—nor did he want to, for that matter, for she remained as icy and forbidding as she'd been on the day when he'd met her at Llew. But he wasn't unaware of what he owed her. It was a perilous undertaking for her, controlling the *athanc* in order to keep Tylluan from harm, rather than doing as Cadmaran desired and letting it wreak havoc and destruction. She was still beneath the Earl of Llew's hand, and if he should discover her deception, Desdemona would be in grave danger.

An hour passed, and then another. The fog grew thick and the night colder.

"I believe she's managed once more to convince Cadmaran that the creature is sated after so few days," Kian said at last. "He's not going to be pleased, but Miss Caslin seems to be made of stern stuff. Apparently, she's more than a match for him."

"Hope it stays that way," Horas murmured, pulling his hat down about his ears. "Hell's mittens, it's cold tonight."

"It's going to rain on the morrow," Kian told him. "I can feel the storm approaching. This chill wind brings it to us."

"Rain," Horas muttered. "That's another thing we don't need any more of just now. Beasts and rain. God help us, what will be next?"

Kian understood how his steward felt. Weeks of struggling with the accursed creature were beginning to exhaust everyone who remained at Tylluan. Kian's tenants had suffered a great deal of damage before Desdemona Caslin had limited the *athanc* to this one pasture. Crops had been destroyed, and the sheep were still dying. Worse even than that, rumors were beginning to spread to the nearby villages that a fearsome beast was living at Tylluan. If Kian didn't get rid of it soon, people were going to start to wonder if he wasn't, in fact, the one to blame for the creature's appearance. He didn't even want to think of what would happen if the news spread beyond the border of Wales, to the ears of the English, who weren't as close to understanding or believing in magic as the Welsh were.

"Has there been any word from Master Dyfed, m'lord?" Horas asked hopefully. "Has he discovered anything of help, yet?"

"There's been word, aye," Kian told him. Indeed, a week hadn't yet gone by since they'd left Tylluan that Kian didn't hear from Dyfed and, more happily, from Loris as well. "But nothing particularly helpful yet. We shall simply have to be patient, Horas. There is nothing else we can do."

They waited another hour, sitting atop their obedient mounts until the fog and breeze had chilled them through to the bone. A few wolves attempted to sneak into the clearing, but Kian readily dealt with them, sending several rocks flying sharply in their direction so that they scattered and ran.

"Nothing is moving within Tylluan's borders," Kian said at last, "save those beings and creatures that would naturally be here. She'll not bring the beast tonight. Let's be on our way."

They lingered only long enough for Kian to place an enchantment on the area that would both protect the sheep from any more of the usual predators and keep them from wandering.

Horas rode with Kian as far as the gates to the castle's outer bailey, then bid him good eve and moved on toward his cottage a short distance farther down the mountain, where his wife and children lay sleeping.

Kian held Seren still and, with a measure of envy, watched his steward depart. How good it was to enter a dwelling where there were hearts and arms to welcome one. Kian hadn't realized just how much he had taken for granted in having his own loved ones with him at Tylluan.

He missed Loris so fully that it was a physical pain, but he wasn't the only one. The servants dutifully fulfilled the chores she'd set for them to do, and Cook prepared the menus that Loris had written out to fill several weeks. But the castle was somber and quiet, lonely.

Kian took his meals in the great hall with his men, all of them young and single and without hearth or home of their own. They drank and laughed and told tales and, common to the Welsh, burst into song without warning.

And yet Kian felt a stark, unfathomable loneliness. Especially during the long night hours, whether he was out because of the beast or sitting in his study. Or restlessly tossing in his bed, thinking of Loris and recalling every single moment of making love to her.

Guilt was his constant companion, but just now he'd gladly put all guilt and shame aside simply to hold her for five precious minutes. To feel her arms about his waist and her cheek against his shoulder. She would lift her face to receive his kiss, as she had done that night, and would meet him with that same sweet eagerness that sent all his senses reeling. Five minutes, aye. It would never be enough, but it would ease his longing for her, even just a little.

He stabled Seren himself, sending the half-asleep stable boy back to his slumbers, and afterward made his way into the castle to find that Cook had kindly left a tray of food for him and a ready tankard of ale. One of the footmen brought it to Kian in his study and then remained only long enough to help his master discard his gloves, hat, and heavy outer garments before he bade him good night.

With a sigh of relief, Kian settled into the chair behind his desk and, taking a long drink of ale, began to sort through the mail that had been delivered in the late afternoon. The warmth of the fire, kept burning for his return, began to seep into his skin and relax his weary, aching body. He would sleep tonight. Perhaps not well, but he would sleep. It would please Loris to know that he was following her instructions, at least when he could.

Taking another long drink from his tankard, he stood, picking up a tied packet that contained personal letters. Several always came at once, despite the fact that Loris and Dyfed wrote them nearly every day, for correspondence was collected in the village and ridden up the mountain three times a week, with the exception of those that were marked as urgent or sent by express. But nothing as yet had been that pressing, thank a merciful God. And if something so truly dire had occurred, Malachi would have found a much quicker way than the written word to get the news to Kian.

Moving to sit before the fire, Kian settled into his favorite chair and untied the string that held the various letters together. They fell apart, separating into his lap. There was a letter from Malachi this time—that was unusual—two from Dyfed, and three from Loris. Kian tried not to smile, knowing that his reluctant *unoliaeth* had written to him more often than even his twin—especially considering the unhappiness he had given her—but he couldn't help himself.

There were other differences in their missives as well.

Dyfed's letters were far less conversational than Loris's and always straight to the point. He reported his findings, or lack of them, regarding the *athanc* and kept Kian apprised of all those little details that Loris failed to mention, such as the rather large number of would-be suitors attempting to attach themselves to Lord Perham's granddaughter, who, despite her advanced age of three and twenty, had been declared a diamond of the first water by all those who saw her. Loris seemed not to understand that these gentlemen were casting lures in her direction, but the Seymour men were more than able to handle such nuisances in a thorough, quiet manner. That these dealings had given rise to rumors that Loris had already been spoken for by one of those same Seymours—either Malachi, Kian, or even Dyfed himself—was unavoidable, and certainly preferable to rumors that might link her name to another man.

Dyfed asked for news of Desdemona, and when he had the opportunity and time to do so, Kian sent back as many details as he felt he might safely relate. She appeared to be very much the same to him, but, then, he did not know the young woman well and his general impression was that she was a somewhat morose individual even at the best of times. If she was experiencing some greater sadness because of Dyfed's absence, Kian wasn't able to discern it. But this he did not tell Dyfed, and took great care to neither alarm nor depress his love-sickened twin.

Loris's letters were far more detailed. Kian didn't ascribe this to having been forgiven but to the fact that, whether she realized it or not, he was the person she'd grown accustomed to being in company with during the past ten years. No one else, not his father or brother or even Liw, had spent as much time with Loris as Kian had. They generally engaged in arguing during those hours, admittedly, but they had been together nonetheless. Loris had simply grown so used to their dealings that she had taken them for granted. Her letters were borne out of the habit she'd formed of telling Kian of her days, save now she told him of London, rather than Tylluan.

She was careful not to write of what had happened between them, only of what was taking place, day to day, and of her new and happy relationship with Lord Perham. She clearly didn't realize how intimate her tone truly was when she wrote to Kian or perhaps it was simply that she'd never learned how to write *ton*nish letters, but her missives were always so frank and open that he could imagine her standing right in front of him, speaking the words aloud.

She told him of how wonderful it was to have a grandfather, especially one like Lord Perham, who, according to Loris, was everything that a grandfather should be. She had accepted the earl's invitation to move into his grand London town house so that they could spend more time together and was trying to get used to being surrounded by such wealth and elegance. She worried about what Lord Perham would think of Tylluan by comparison but longed to bring him there, regardless, just as soon as she possibly could.

But she was discovering, as Kian had known she would, that it wasn't quite so easy to get out of a Season as into one. Now that she was Perham's granddaughter and heir, she had to have a proper come-out—a grand ball that was going to be given by both Lord Perham and Lord Graymar. And she had to be introduced to a great many people, many of them very high-ranking members of the nobility. Loris was finding it to be a rather exhausting and somewhat terrifying process, but she didn't wish to dismay or disappoint Lord Perham so soon. And so she did as she was told and made herself be patient. She had been assured, and hoped it was true, that the Season wouldn't last forever.

Her letters didn't dwell entirely on her new relationship with her grandfather. Kian had also learned about the fine new wardrobe that Julia had helped Loris to amass and of Dyfed patiently teaching her how to dance. She told Kian of her first few forays into society, such as her first dinner party and the obligatory visit to Almack's, where both Malachi and Lord Perham had caused something of a fuss by insisting that they be the first to partner her in a dance. Dyfed had evidently grown impatient with the two men and simply taken Loris by the hand and drawn her out onto the floor.

Some kind of contest had seemingly sprung up between Lord Perham and the Earl of Graymar, and this troubled Loris a good deal. Lord Perham wished to take precedence over decisions regarding her Season, but Malachi firmly refused to give way, probably, Kian thought, because of the unbreakable bond Loris had with the Seymours through the *unoliaeth*.

The result was that both men had begun to present Loris with a great deal of jewelry to mark the occasion of every event she attended. And each gift was more expensive and grand than the last, so that she was now in possession of so many bracelets, necklaces, ear bobs, and bejeweled hair combs that she didn't believe she would ever be able to wear them all. What would she do with such pretty things at Tylluan? she asked Kian in one of her most recent letters.

She reported that the balls and parties that followed these initial events were very nice, but wearisome, and that she didn't understand why members of the *ton* insisted upon keeping such horrid hours. In all truth, there was very little she understood about the ways of society, and her observations, always amusing, never failed to make him smile and wish that he might be there to see London through her eyes.

She enjoyed dancing, she said, though she favored being partnered by his brother or cousins or Lord Perham. She found the other gentleman she'd met thus far to be wonderfully elegant and fine but somewhat daunting for a girl who'd lived all her life among much simpler folk. She didn't mind it when Lord Graymar was being clever, for he reminded her so much of Kian that his dry remarks never bewildered her. But, she confessed in a particularly candid remark, whenever one of the Corinthians who'd taken a fancy to her began to tell her how lovely she was or that her eyes were like fine amber and her hair like the purest gold, Loris found it difficult not to giggle. Which was truly lowering, for as Kian knew very well, she didn't and never had giggled and had always thought women who did so quite foolish. It was proof, she said, that being in Town was starting to affect her nerves.

At some point, she always got around to asking Kian whether he'd made any progress with the troubles at Tylluan. She did a poor job of trying to discover, in a roundabout way, anything of what he'd learned from Dyfed about what was truly happening. Dyfed, evidently, hadn't revealed more than Kian had, so that Loris was near to tearing her hair out with curiosity. Why, she demanded, should everyone but her know what they had discovered from Desdemona Caslin? The insult Loris felt came through quite clearly, but Kian didn't yet want her to know of the *athanc*. She already worried too much over his lack of sleep and sustenance; if she knew that his struggle was with an enormous beast that was part dragon, part water demon, she'd be frantic.

As to his twin, Loris related that Dyfed was very busy both day and night, either in company with Professor Seabolt, searching through ancient manuscripts for special enchantments to solve Tylluan's troubles, or escorting her to various functions. She hadn't been surprised to discover how popular he was in London among the *ton* or how many young women had set their caps for him, for he was very handsome and personable. But she had been rather amazed at Dyfed's reaction to such adoration. He appeared not to care for it in the least and often found it wearying and distasteful. He was desperately eager to return to Tylluan, and as each day passed she thought he looked more withdrawn and unhappy. But he faithfully fulfilled his duties as chaperone and was ever vigilant to ensure Loris's comfort and pleasure, especially when they were in company. Loris assured Kian that she'd said nothing yet to anyone of the betrothal and heard no whispers regarding either Morcar Cadmaran or Desdemona Caslin when she was out in society.

She usually concluded her missives with additional instructions for the servants that she feared she had forgotten and asked repeatedly that Kian make certain her garden was being tended to daily, as she didn't wish to come home and find it all a shambles. The words comforted Kian deeply. Being Loris and exceedingly practical, she didn't waste her time as some females did in making coy or affected statements. If she spoke of coming home to Tylluan, then that was precisely what Loris intended to do.

Picking up the first of her letters from his lap, Kian sent up a silent prayer that those intentions would come true just as soon as they possibly could.

Fourteen

$\mathcal{L}$oris surveyed the letter she'd just finished with a careful eye. She hadn't been in the habit of writing much before coming to London, for at Tylluan she'd never had anyone to write to, save Julia these past three years, but Loris believed her skill was improving. The single page wasn't as terribly blotched with ink as her first few letters to Kian had been, and her handwriting was almost becoming legible.

She had surprised herself by writing to him so frequently, for she certainly would have found it difficult to speak to him as much if she had remained at Tylluan. At least until her feelings regarding his deception had lessened. But she found herself looking forward each afternoon to the time that she spent laboring at the little writing desk that her grandfather had had placed in her bedchamber and to telling Kian of all that had happened the night before at whatever ball or party they had attended. Though Kian understood the ways of the *ton*, Loris knew that no one else among her acquaintances would find society's odd behavior as amusing as she did.

Even their conversations were, she found, terribly funny. The *ton* had a dozen different ways of saying what they wished without ever actually saying it. Just last night she had stood among a group of Julia's friends and heard a certain unfortunate young man called a cake, a beetle-head, a rattle-pate, and a noddy. It had taken Loris a good five minutes of this sort of talk before she'd at last asked, "Do you mean to say he's a fool?"

They had all stared at Loris as if she had been terribly rude, but Julia, bless her, had laughed with delight and smoothed the matter over—just as she and Malachi and Dyfed and Niclas had been obliged to smooth so many matters over. Still, Loris couldn't recall the moment without a smile, and she knew that Kian would laugh over it as well.

He didn't write to her in turn very often, but Loris hadn't expected that he would write at all. Being the master of Tylluan wasn't like being a wealthy landowner of leisure possessed of many valuable estates, as Lord Graymar and her grandfather were. Kian was obliged to personally oversee the management of Tylluan's crops and livestock, to support his tenants with both his presence and decisions. She knew firsthand how little time he had to himself each day, and with the troubles to manage as well she was amazed that he found a few spare moments to pick up a pen and set it to paper.

It was strange to have his letters, to see how elegantly he wrote and to read over his carefully chosen words, to hear his voice in her mind as she read them. She had never read anything that he had composed before—apart from lists or instructions regarding Tylluan—and found the experience to be . . . well, she couldn't really think of the right word, though *romantic* had crossed her mind. There wasn't any arguing in his letters, or sarcasm or mockery. He didn't mention the *unoliaeth* or Liw or the experience they had shared, but he didn't pretend that all was perfectly well, either.

He told her of Tylluan and the things that he knew she wanted to hear of, assuring her that all was well with the servants and castle and gardens. He promised that he was both resting and taking proper nourishment and that the hunt for a solution to the troubles was going forward. He even managed to make his nightly outings with the men sound humorous, describing the jokes they played on one another and how they had a wager over who would be the first to successfully play one on Kian. No one, as yet, had come close, but that, Loris thought, was to be expected when one attempted to outwit an extraordinary wizard.

He brought Tylluan to life for her, describing the weather, the flowers that bloomed, and the way the valley was changing as spring progressed, the grass growing even greener and the streams widening as snow melted from the mountains. The days were growing longer, as well, and warmer, but still there was the rain, and the thick fog that crept in at night.

Loris realized how valuable the gift was that Kian gave her, telling her of such mundane matters. Anyone else would have found it dull, reading the same things in every letter. It was something entirely different to Loris. She was grateful. More even than that, she had realized, perhaps for the first time, just how well Kian knew and understood her. As no one else save Liw had ever done.

There's no need for you to grieve for Liw. He's here, alive in me, and always will be. . . . I'm here, too.

"Yes," Loris murmured, running a finger over the page before her. "I know you are, Kian."

She missed him. He'd tried to tell her that she would, and she'd not wanted to believe him, because it only made the *unoliaeth* seem more real. But he'd been right. Whatever she had enjoyed in London, whatever pleasure she'd felt, had only made the sense that something was missing worse. It had been food without seasoning, a painting without color. Wherever she went she was achingly aware that he wasn't with her, that she'd not be seeing him later in the day or hearing his voice. Even his mocking smile and sarcasm would have been welcome to her now. And as each day passed, the longing she felt for Kian was slowly but certainly overwhelming the sense of loss she felt for Liw.

A soft knock fell on the door, and Loris turned in time to see Elen's fair head peering in. The serving girl had come to stay at Lord Perham's town house with Loris, though Julia and Niclas had invited her to remain with them. But Elen, as it happened, hadn't been as impressed by city life as she had thought she'd be. The crowds and noise and busy roads frightened her. She had even begun to hint that it would be nice to go home to Tylluan soon, where everything was so peaceful and quiet.

"Beg pardon, miss. His Lordship has a visitor and asks you to come to the blue parlor to meet him as quick as it's convenient, please."

Loris smiled. Since she'd come to live with him her grandfather had busily been introducing her to all of his friends and acquaintances. It seemed that he wanted the whole world to know that he had found his granddaughter at last, and Loris was more than happy to do his bidding. And she had enjoyed meeting all his friends, especially those whom he'd known for so long that they were able to tell Loris about her mother.

"Please have Fuller inform the earl that I'll come at once. Oh, Elen, wait a moment and you may take this for me as well." Loris folded the missive and sealed it with a bit of wax, then rose and went to the door. "Give this to Fuller and ask him to post it for me, please."

Elen looked at the letter, then cast a smile at her mistress. "Another letter to the master, miss?" she said. "That's the fourth this week."

"Yes, it is," Loris said, "and I shall probably write another tomorrow, though I'm sure that's not any concern of yours. It's a good thing you've decided not to stay in Town, for I doubt any of the households here would put up with your cheek."

"That's because they're all English, miss," said Elen. "They don't have a sense of humor like we Welsh do." Then she curtsied and departed, leaving Loris to wonder at how and why the maid's mood had so greatly improved. Had it been only weeks past that Elen had been complaining about how dull life in Tylluan was?

Five minutes later Loris was descending the grand staircase that led toward the floor where not only the library and her grandfather's study were, but also three parlors, each identified by a different color. There was the blue parlor, which her grandfather preferred for greeting mixed company, the rose parlor, where Loris was expected to entertain ladies—though the only one she'd yet entertained there was Julia—and the green parlor, which was kept for the private use of the family. It was in this parlor that Loris and her grandfather sometimes sat in the evenings before the fire, enjoying each other's company and playing chess. Loris was learning the game and hadn't yet mastered the moves, but Lord Perham was patient and kind and was glad that she showed an interest. Chess was one of his passions.

Fuller opened the parlor door for her, announcing her arrival as she walked into the room. It seemed foolish to Loris that a servant should be required to do such a thing when she could very well open her own doors and announce her own arrival, but her grandfather insisted that a lady of birth and wealth shouldn't be made to do anything for herself. Loris even had a maid to brush her hair out at night. Kian would laugh himself sick when she at last returned to Tylluan and told him of it.

Lord Perham and his guest were sitting in high-back chairs near the fire, one of the earl's several chess tables set between them. Loris could see at once from the position of the pieces that her grandfather had found a far more challenging partner to play with.

The men left off scowling at the board and rose to their feet. Her grandfather stepped toward her, a hand outstretched and a smile on his face.

"Here you are, my dear."

Loris reached up to kiss his cheek. "I hope I didn't keep you waiting, Grandfather. I came as quickly as I could. I see you were well occupied."

"Yes indeed," he said, patting her hand. "You'll remember the particular friend I've told you of, my dear, who spent this past Christmas with me at Perham Hall, and who meets me at the chess club each Thursday when we're both in

Town, and who I've been particularly anxious for you to meet."

"Of course, sir," Loris said. Her grandfather had spoken of the fellow often and always in the most glowing terms. She had the distinct feeling that Lord Perham had hopes that Viscount Brecmont would develop a romantic interest in her.

The earl had become alarmed by the foolish rumors being whispered about Town, saying that Loris already had a secret understanding with one of the Seymour men. She had assured her grandfather that it wasn't so, but though he believed there wasn't any interest on Malachi's behalf, he found the amount of time she spent with and her affection for Dyfed to be rather worrisome. The earl hadn't understood when Loris had tried to explain that Dyfed was like a brother to her, for apparently brothers and sisters among the *ton* weren't given to such frequent or open expressions of affection and rarely spent so much time together day after day and evening after evening.

Added to this was the foolish battle that had arisen between her grandfather and Lord Graymar over who would make important decisions regarding Loris's life.

Loris had never realized just how competitive a man the Earl of Graymar could be, but he was seriously displeased to find Lord Perham attempting to take charge of her Season. Lord Graymar made his will known at every turn, especially at balls and parties, where he and Niclas and Dyfed made a purposeful display of controlling who she danced or conversed with.

There was little that her grandfather could do to counter their behavior in such public places, save to find champions of his own. Viscount Brecmont, Loris believed, was to be the first of these. He was an ideal candidate from what Loris had heard of him, being both young and unmarried and, best of all, an excellent chess player. He was also, her grandfather had said, coming to London with the express purpose of finding a wife this Season. Lord Perham had even been hinting that he wouldn't at all mind having the viscount for a grandson-in-law.

Loris had wondered, amused, whether her grandfather wasn't more interested in bringing a permanent chess partner into the family rather than finding a suitable husband for his granddaughter. But either way, it would be quite a coup to push Loris into an engagement with a man of his own choosing, rather than Lord Graymar's. She understood very well that the earl didn't want her returning to Tylluan or to the bosom of the Seymours.

Viscount Brecmont, Loris discovered as she turned to smile at him in welcome, was an astonishingly handsome young gentleman, just as her grandfather had promised. He wouldn't be looking for a bride long once all the eligible come-outs and their mamas got a good look at him. And he was rich, as well, or so Loris had inferred from her grandfather's description. The viscount was very tall and muscular, with hair as black as a raven's wing and lovely green eyes. His smile, which he gifted her with in return, would slay the hearts of every female in a crowded ballroom within but moments.

"Lord Brecmont has come to London at last," the earl said, "and, more importantly, has arrived to take up the little battle we've been carrying on for the past several years." He smiled at his guest. "We have been tied in matches at the end of each of those seasons, excepting when he was absent from Town two years past, but I have a feeling that this Season I'll come out the winner. Now that my granddaughter has been found, I can fix my mind solely on beating you, Brecmont."

"I will be glad to be beaten if finding Miss McClendon is the cause," Viscount Brecmont countered nobly.

The inflection of his voice caught Loris's attention, and her gaze sharpened. He was Welsh. Though he spoke with the refined accent of the nobility, she had caught the unmistakable musical quality underlying his tone.

"Loris," Lord Perham said, and she had seldom heard such anticipation in his tone, "I make known to you my dear friend Tauron Cadmaran, Viscount Brecmont. Brecmont, this is my granddaughter, Miss McClendon."

Loris had been in the midst of making a proper curtsy, but at the sound of Lord Brecmont's full name her head snapped up and she straightened full-height.

"Cadmaran?" she repeated.

She stared at him wide-eyed. Loris had never met a Cadmaran before, but one of the first things that Ffinian had taught her, which had been drummed into her heart and mind and soul by everyone at Tylluan and all the Seymours, was that Cadmarans were evil. And dangerous. And very powerful. At all costs they were not to be trifled with or ever trusted. And they certainly weren't to be allowed into the homes of good and decent people like her grandfather!

She took a stumbling step backward, almost as if she expected the viscount to suddenly strike her, and the earl grasped her arm, his thick eyebrows snapping together with concern.

"Loris? Are you all right?"

"I'm sorry," she mumbled, striving to collect herself. How foolish! Of course Lord Brecmont wasn't going to attack her in her grandfather's home. Cadmarans were devious, not stupid. The man played chess with her grandfather, for pity's sake. "Forgive me, my lord," she said. "My feet didn't wish to obey me. Lord Brecmont." She made another curtsy— successfully, this time—and rose to find him making her another elegant bow.

When he straightened he smiled again, looking perfectly angelic, though she could see from the slightly amused expression in his gaze that he understood what her thoughts toward him were.

"Miss McClendon," he murmured, "I cannot tell you how pleased I am to make your acquaintance. I had heard rumors of your beauty, and my dear friend Lord Perham assured me they were true when we met at the chess club, but I could scarce believe such a woman exists. I see now that she does."

Loris tried, but failed, to keep from glaring at the man. She didn't wish to embarrass or disappoint her grandfather, but he didn't know who, or rather what, his good friend truly was.

"Thank you, sir," she said icily.

"Loris," her grandfather murmured with a touch of distress, clearly surprised by her manner.

"Please don't be angry by your granddaughter's reaction to being introduced to me, my lord," the viscount said. "I should have warned you beforehand that she has good cause to be distressed by the acquaintance."

Lord Perham looked at him. "How so?"

"Miss McClendon is already very familiar with my cousin the Earl of Llew. His estate lies not far from Tylluan, and he and Lord Tylluan are not, unfortunately, the friendliest of neighbors. I believe you are acquainted with Lord Llew also, are you not, sir?"

"Of course," Lord Perham stated, shocking Loris even further. She gaped at her grandfather, who gave her a rather stern look. "I've known the Earl of Llew for years," he told her. "The Cadmarans are one of the oldest and most respected families in England. Morcar Cadmaran is not only my peer but also a notable gentleman in every regard. As is Viscount Brecmont."

"You are kind, my lord," Viscount Brecmont said, "but, you see, there has not been much love between the Cadmaran and Seymour families for many years. Hundreds of years, in fact. It is an ancient feud between two ancient Welsh clans." He gave a shake of his handsome head. "It would take far too long to explain the whole of it, I fear, but please believe me when I say that your granddaughter, having lived with the Seymours for so many years, has good cause to take every Cadmaran she meets in dislike. I apologize for not having warned you of what her reaction must be."

"Why, that's ridiculous," Lord Perham stated. "Loris wouldn't be so foolish as to treat anyone badly because of some old misunderstanding. And," he added, looking directly at her, "she is neither a Seymour nor living beneath the hands of Seymours any longer. She has no fight with any man, certainly not one who is a particular friend of mine."

"But, Grandfather," she whispered, drawing nearer, "you don't understand. If I could but explain—"

"That's enough, young lady," he said angrily, clearly hurt by what he perceived as her loyalty to the Seymours and by her admittedly uncivil behavior to his guest. "We'll speak of it no more. Beg Lord Brecmont's pardon and then be so good as to ring for tea."

"No apology is necessary, my lord," the viscount said quickly.

Loris knew that her grandfather would insist. If she'd learned anything about Lord Perham in the past few weeks, it was that he was a stickler for the proprieties. But he surprised her by saying, "Very well, Brecmont. If you're quite sure."

"I am," Lord Brecmont said.

Loris looked at him sharply, her eyes narrowing. Cadmarans were almost all greater wizards, which meant that Viscount Brecmont must possess a good deal of magic. She suspected that he'd just used a measure of it on her grandfather. The thought gave her pause. She was a mere mortal and wouldn't be immune to the viscount's powers, either.

"However," Lord Brecmont went on, his tone light and charming, as was the smile he gave them both, "I would like the opportunity to prove to Miss McClendon that we need not be enemies, regardless of the misunderstandings that have taken place between our families—pardon—between my family and her friends. Would you grant me the honor of taking your granddaughter driving this afternoon, my lord? I should be most grateful."

"A splendid idea," Lord Perham said just as Loris replied, firmly, *"No."*

Her grandfather gave her a thunderous look. "My granddaughter will be *pleased*, Brecmont."

Loris shook her head. "Sir, I cannot—"

He ignored her. "She'll be ready at five, sir," he told his guest. "You may come for her then."

And so it was, three hours later, that Loris found herself sitting beside Tauron Cadmaran in an elegant curricle, driving through Hyde Park at the height of the fashionable hour, being stared at by all those who saw them.

She had argued with her grandfather to no avail. He'd countered all her explanations as to why she shouldn't befriend a Cadmaran—any Cadmaran—by saying that they were quite foolish. But that was understandable, Loris was forced to admit. Without being able to tell Lord Perham about the magical powers that both the Seymours and Cadmarans possessed, the lengthy enmity between the two families did seem silly.

Worse than his stubbornness was the fact that Lord Perham had firmly instructed all the servants that they weren't to deliver any of the notes Loris penned to warn Malachi, Dyfed, and Niclas about Tauron Cadmaran's presence in Town. This she had learned from Elen, who had been stopped from leaving the house as well.

Loris had no choice but to do as her grandfather wished and accompany Lord Brecmont through the park. She would be safe enough, she knew, for he could scarce harm her in so public a place. And tonight, at Lord and Lady Hamlin's ball, Loris would be able to tell Malachi what had taken place. He'd make certain that Viscount Brecmont was appropriately dealt with.

"I hope you'll not take it amiss if I compliment you on your appearance, Miss McClendon," Lord Brecmont said politely after they had driven in stony silence for the first half hour. "I realize you had no desire to be in company with me, but I confess myself to be the most fortunate man in London, regardless. I have the distinction, or so I hear, of being the first apart from your grandfather and the Seymours to take the beautiful granddaughter of Lord Perham driving."

"I think I should warn you, sir," Loris said coldly, "that I am not possessed of the manners you're used to finding in society. Which I'm sure you're already well aware of, for if you haven't heard about my lack of refinement from all the gossips in London, then my behavior earlier this afternoon will surely have informed you. Apart from that, I don't have any desire to engage in polite conversation with you. It would be perfectly ridiculous, considering that we both know exactly who the other is. I may not be a Seymour by blood, sir, but Ffinian Seymour has been as much a father to me as if I were, in truth, his own daughter. Tylluan is my home, and I love it as dearly as any Seymour who ever drew breath. The Cadmarans have done everything possible to bring harm and destruction to that home. In my eyes, Lord Brecmont, that puts us very much at odds." She nodded at a passing acquaintance, striving to paste a smile on her lips. "And," she went on, "I'm sure you realize that Malachi will be furious when he realizes that you've used your friendship with my grandfather to be in company with me."

"Yes, I suppose he will be," her companion confessed. "And I do apologize for using my acquaintance with Lord Perham in order to meet you, Miss McClendon. I wished to speak with you, and was quite certain there were topics that you'd rather he not overhear. He's not one of our sympathetics, after all."

"Is that *all* you used?" she asked tautly. "His acquaintance? I had the distinct impression that you were exerting another sort of influence on him this afternoon in order to get your way."

"Magic, do you mean?" Lord Brecmont asked. "I suppose that would be a natural assumption."

"Especially in dealing with a Cadmaran," she said. "What are your powers, precisely? I assume you're a greater wizard, for very few among your clan are born lesser."

"Very true," he admitted. "However, you find yourself in company with one of those few. I am not a greater wizard, Miss McClendon, and possess but one gift, which is neither the gift of persuasion nor of charming mere mortals to do my bidding. You may rest easy regarding my ability to wreak havoc on those you love."

Loris turned her head to look at him for the first time since they'd left her grandfather's town house.

"I don't believe you," she said. "Morcar Cadmaran has done everything possible to rid his family of lesser wizards. If you are one, he would have cast you out by now."

Lord Brecmont's handsome countenance tightened. "He would have done so, save my particular gift is valuable to him. To all the Cadmarans. It is the power of . . . transmutation." He said the word softly, making it sound like a shameful confession.

Loris blinked at him. "I see," she said. "I didn't realize there was such a gift. No one that I know of among the Seymours has ever been capable of turning common metals into gold."

"I wish it were just that," he said, sighing. "Performing mere alchemy would be bad enough, but I have the ability to change almost any simple element into something more complex, and to the reverse, as well."

"Ah." Loris gave a nod of understanding. "Water into wine. Wine into medicine. Or medicine back to water. Like that?"

He nodded. "It sounds wonderful, does it not? And perhaps it would be, in the hands of one of the other families. But mine is an ill-gained power, conceived after centuries of using dark magic. I was unfortunate to be the one cursed with it."

Loris gazed at him curiously. "I should think a Cadmaran would find such tremendous power a wonderful thing."

"Only those who don't possess it would," he said. "I would give my soul to be rid of it. Or to not be a Cadmaran and forced to use it for dark purposes. Wine can just as easily be turned into poison, you see. The crops of your enemies can be changed into weeds, and a harmless hammer into a deadly sword. You'll not believe me when I say this, but I don't enjoy dark magic as other Cadmarans do."

Loris could only imagine how the Earl of Llew had made use of his cousin. No wonder the Cadmarans were so endlessly wealthy, though none of their estates were put to use for either farming or raising cattle.

"I don't know you well enough to believe you," she told him. "But, then, I don't truly know the Cadmarans well, save from what I've heard—none of it good, by the way. You're the first actual Cadmaran I've ever met."

"You've been fortunate, then. What you've heard, what you've been told, is all true."

"You speak so ill of your own family that I can't help but wonder why. Surely they've treated you well, considering what you can do for them."

"You truly don't know the Cadmarans if you can say such a thing," he said bitterly. "Forgive me for speaking to you so bluntly, Miss McClendon."

She smiled. "I prefer it, I assure you, to what you started with. I'm growing full weary of the pretty speeches most noblemen make."

He smiled, too, relaxing a little. "I had heard you were rather out of the ordinary, Miss McClendon, and not merely in the way of beauty. I'm surprised that we've never met before now. I'm acquainted with the Tylluan Seymours. Kian and Dyfed and I used to tumble about together when we were boys, during gatherings of the Families."

Loris knew what it was he spoke of. Every five years the magical Families came together for a full week at one of their large estates to discuss matters of import to their kind and to make agreements and pacts. Even those clans who practiced dark magic attended. She had never gone to those gatherings that had occurred while she'd lived at Tylluan, but Kian had told her they were enormously entertaining affairs, especially for the children, who had the chance of meeting others of their kind who seldom would have crossed their paths otherwise.

"I knew of you, of course," Lord Brecmont went on. "Word spread about Ffinian adopting a ward from London's . . . ah . . ."

"Gutters," she supplied. "Or slums. It's perfectly true, so you may as well use the appropriate word. It's just what I told Lady Springhill when she was having difficulty making herself plain while introducing me to an acquaintance at Almack's."

Loris smiled at the memory. The vicious woman had been trying to insult her in the kindest possible way but had looked near to fainting once Loris corrected her. Malachi, who'd appeared out of nowhere, as he so often did, had been about to make a remark to Lady Springhill himself—probably far more cutting than what Loris said. Instead, he'd been obliged to choke back an unrefined fit of laughter and walk away even without excusing himself. The next day he'd sent Loris a diamond bracelet and a stunning arrangement of flowers with a note thanking her for a most entertaining evening.

"From one of London's less savory neighborhoods," Viscount Brecmont supplied nobly. "But as you never left Tylluan after taking up residence there, and only Seymours visited the estate from among those in the Families, no one knew much about you. And then when I came to London and heard you were here and causing such a stir, I wished to make your acquaintance. Fortunate for me, my friend Lord Perham made the suggestion even before I could make the request."

Lord Brecmont hadn't heard about the supposed *unoliaeth* that existed between Kian and herself or, it seemed, about the effects of the blood curse.

"Why did you wish to speak to me alone?" Loris asked, nodding as yet another acquaintance rode past.

"Perhaps because I was lonely and desired the company of a beautiful woman?" the viscount suggested.

She gave a laugh. "I should think a woman connected to the Seymours would be the last female on earth you'd wish to spend time with."

"But you're not a Seymour," he told her. "And you are one of our sympathetics. The only one, as it happens, that I have yet discovered this Season. I can speak freely with you. Being among mere mortals for weeks on end, having to be so careful of what one says or does, is most wearying. And lonely as well. None of my relatives have come to Town this year—not yet, at least, as they all appear to be waiting for an announcement of great importance from the Earl of Llew."

Loris stiffened. "An announcement?"

"Yes, something that will require as many as can to assemble in London, so it must be in the nature of something celebratory. Perhaps he's found the way to lift the curse that was set upon him, and thus be rid of his blindness. I hope that's so, for although we don't agree on many things, I should think it a terrible thing to be blind."

"Yes," she murmured, thinking of what a dangerous combination London and a large contingent of Cadmarans would be. How was it possible for them to keep mere mortals from discovering about their magic with so many of them about? The other magical Families were always careful to keep large gatherings on their own private estates, away from prying eyes. "I think so, too."

"And so, having been forewarned," he went on, "I decided to come to Town at once to enjoy whatever time I could before a host of Cadmarans take up residence and force me to attend their family assemblies."

At that moment they were hailed by two gentlemen on horseback who were friends of Lord Brecmont's. He politely introduced them to Loris, who endured their flattery with patience. One of them asked if she would be attending the Hamlin ball and, hearing her answer, boldly asked if she would save a dance for him.

"I fear you're too late, Duncan," Lord Brecmont replied before Loris could open her mouth. "Miss McClendon's already been spoken for for the entire evening. Perhaps you'll have better fortune next time."

"Thank you," she murmured as they drove on. "I shouldn't wish to be rude, but between the Seymours and my grandfather, I have few opportunities to dance with others. And even when I do, I must confess that I sometimes find it tiring. I have no conversation, as you've discovered."

"I think your conversation enchanting," Lord Brecmont said, adding, quickly, "and I'm not simply being polite. I mean it truthfully. And my motive in putting off my friends was far more selfish than noble." He glanced at her. "I was hoping you'd save a dance for me."

Loris frowned. "I don't think Malachi or Dyfed or Niclas would be very happy about it."

"But your grandfather would be ecstatic," Lord Brecmont coaxed. "And I would be more than grateful. You're very likely one of the few females in all of London who understand what it's like to be of my kind. I can be at ease with you."

Loris knew what he meant. She felt like a fish out of water, too. And she realized that at some point while they'd been driving, she'd come to believe what he had told her. He wasn't like other Cadmarans.

"Very well," she said. "But you must prepare yourself for the anger of the Seymour men."

He laughed. "I have a lifetime of experience dodging the displeasure of both Cadmarans and Seymours, Miss Mc-Clendon. I've become very adept at it."

Fifteen

The beast was growing stronger. And more dangerous. Desdemona Caslin was finding the *athanc* harder to control, and Kian wasn't able to bring enough animals to the clearing each night to sate the beast's hunger. All of the livestock at Tylluan had been destroyed, and he was obliged to buy sheep from farther and farther away—having already purchased all those that were nearer—and it took more time to herd the animals to the clearing than they had the luxury of.

The *athanc* was wandering across Tylluan's borders now in search of food, ignoring Desdemona's commands until its belly was filled and wreaking havoc on local farms.

The farmers were understandably upset and had come to Kian to make a formal complaint.

"We know the creature has come from here, Lord Tylluan," Edwart Hollis said, angrily jabbing a finger in the air. "And we know that it's you who've been feeding it."

"We don't wish to be rude, sir," put in Ianto Weist, "for we've been glad to have the luck that your kind bring us, especially with the fair folk, and we've always kept quiet to those outside, and happy we've been to do it. But we want a stop to it, my lord, else we've no choice but to bring in the authorities."

"You must understand, m'lord," said Moris ap Pugh, twisting his hat nervously in both hands, "I've lost all my animals, even the young ones. I've nothing for market and nothing to start anew with."

"I understand, of course," Kian assured them. "I'm doing everything I can to rid us of the creature, and when I have I promise you'll be repaid for what's been destroyed. The animals will be replaced and the damaged buildings repaired. I'll make certain that your families don't suffer because of what you've lost."

"That's fine as it is, my lord," Ianto said, "but what if you can't stop the beast? I saw it last night with my own eyes. It's a great, wild monster, sir, and not likely to be stopped even by your magic ways."

"We've heard tell that it's been roaming about for many weeks now, my lord," said Edwart, "and everyone knows you've been buying a great many animals from both near and far. How much longer will it take before you decide there's naught else to be done? It will roam all the way to the border if this goes on."

"It cannot go that far," Kian said. "It's tied to the lake and must return there each night."

Moris stepped forward, his eyes wide. "But then where's it to find food when it's killed all the livestock, my lord? Will it not come for us and our wives and children?"

"No," Kian told them, wishing he believed that himself. "I'll not let it come to that. I promise you—"

"You cannot stop it doing as it pleases even now, my lord," Ianto said. "And I do not think it will know the difference between a man and a beast when hunger drives it. Something must be done *now,* sir."

"Aye, it must," Kian agreed wearily. He had been standing behind the desk in his study when the men were ushered in. Now he sat. "The beast has eaten for the past three days. It will likely eat again tonight and then rest for another three or four. Enough sheep arrived this afternoon so that I can keep the creature at Tylluan tonight. A much larger herd, coming from the south, will have arrived before the nights of rest are done, and I'll have enough to keep the creature sated for two full weeks, at least. We'll gain a few more days when the creature rests again. Give me three weeks to find the answer," he said. "And if I cannot, I'll ask the *Dewin Mawr* to come."

"And if even he cannot stop the creature, my lord?" Edwart asked.

Kian didn't even want to think of that possibility. The truth of the matter was that unless Professor Seabolt found the right enchantment, Malachi would be hard-pressed to do anything that would help—at least anything lasting.

"He's never let us down before now, has he?" Kian asked, striving to give them any comfort he could. And buy himself a little more time.

The men exchanged looks and nodded.

"Three weeks then," Moris said. "And if the great *dewin* can't rid us of the beast after that, we shall call the authorities for help."

The ball at Lord and Lady Hamlin's was a complete success, which meant that it was terribly overcrowded, or a crush, as Julia had explained. Loris had found it to be another of the *ton*'s oddities that for a party to be considered successful it had to be terribly uncomfortable.

But she truly didn't mind so very much. Julia and Niclas were there, standing very close and touching each other constantly, as they almost always did while in public, and looking very happy. Dyfed had arrived at last, dashing and handsome and glowing with the good news that he and Professor Seabolt were getting closer to the answer to Tylluan's troubles, which meant that they might soon be able to go home. Lord Perham, too, was in good spirits, having been very pleased by the state in which Loris and Viscount Brecmont had returned to his town house earlier in the day.

Loris was still amazed to look back upon their drive through the park and remember how pleasant it was. Tauron—for Loris had told him that she found using titles so constantly very tiresome and had given him permission to use her Christian name as well—had told her about the part of Wales where he had been born and raised, and Loris told him of Tylluan. She asked him about the Earl of Llew, confessing a great curiosity about him specifically and about the Cadmarans in general, and Tauron was open and seemingly honest in his replies.

He asked in turn about Kian, Dyfed, and Ffinian, whom he'd not encountered during his last visit to Town, and she told him what she could, leaving out everything about the recent troubles and his own cousin's part in them. Tauron clearly had no idea that anything amiss was taking place in North Wales, nor was he aware of either Desdemona Caslin's or Earl Llew's current machinations. Of course, Loris wasn't precisely aware what they were, either, since no one among the Seymour men believed she had a right to know.

"You look especially lovely tonight, Loris," Dyfed said, admiring the blue gown that had become one of Loris's favorites. It was trimmed in white and silver and made her think of the early evening sky, just beginning to fill with stars. "I wish Kian and Father could see you now."

Loris wished they could, too, but didn't say the words aloud. Instead, she asked, "But where is Lord Graymar? I thought he was promised to come tonight?"

"He was needed elsewhere," Niclas told her. "The family, as always."

Loris nodded her understanding. As the *Dewin Mawr,* Malachi was responsible for overseeing the safety of those who gave him allegiance. Whenever trouble arose, usually related to the danger of mere mortals discovering the powers of magic mortals, he was obliged to go. Quickly. Fortunately, Malachi had the power to travel very quickly indeed. He had arrived at Tylluan on past occasions almost before Ffinian had finished summoning him.

"He hoped to return to Town in time to put in an appearance," Niclas went on, leaning closer to Loris and lowering his voice. "He's determined not to let Lord Perham outdo him in playing chaperone at functions you attend." Niclas glanced at the Earl of Perham, who was standing not far away, conversing with their hosts.

"The devil!" Dyfed suddenly murmured, just as the music for the last dance ended. His gaze was riveted across the room. "Look who's here, Niclas. It's Brecmont."

They all looked, and Loris saw that it was, indeed, the viscount. He was making his way toward them, his progress necessarily slowed by both the crowd and the numerous acquaintances who hailed him. Women all about him turned to watch his tall figure as he passed, and Loris couldn't blame them in the least. He possessed the unnatural beauty that was common to magic mortals. Loris had grown used to being surrounded by such attractive beings but knew that those who hadn't couldn't help but be arrested. Added to that, Tauron was handsomely dressed in evening clothes that suited him perfectly. His coat was dark green, which only made the green of his eyes more pronounced.

"Grand," Niclas muttered. "He's coming this way."

"What's King Midas doing in Town, I wonder?" Dyfed said. "I thought Cadmaran had him locked up in Caerffill after that last incident."

"That was two years past," Niclas told him. "He can't keep the fellow imprisoned forever, can he? He requires the use of his gift too often for that. And Tauron's not made another mistake since then."

"Imprisoned?" Loris repeated, frowning.

"That doesn't mean he's safe enough to be let out in public," Dyfed said.

"He's come to Town to look for a wife," Julia informed them. When Dyfed and her husband looked at her as if she'd uttered something terribly shocking, she smiled and said, "That's the gossip, at least. I keep telling you men that if you want to know what's going on in society, you must spend more time sipping tea in the afternoons with women."

"Cadmarans don't look for their own wives," her husband

said. "They certainly aren't allowed to choose outside their own kind."

Julia shrugged lightly. "I only know what I heard. And all the mamas of available young women are thrilled. Viscount Brecmont will be fortunate to keep from being smothered by all the potential brides who're about to be thrown at him."

"It won't do any good," Niclas insisted. "Morcar will never let his cousin wed outside the Families. Cadmarans don't marry mere mortals, and they don't come to London looking for potential wives or husbands."

Loris was far more interested in the idea that Tauron had been imprisoned . . . and by his own cousin no less. *What had it been for?* she wondered. Perhaps it had something to do with the unhappiness he had toward his own family.

But before she could ask the questions, Tauron had arrived and was making a bow. Dyfed's hand closed over Loris's arm and pulled her back. Both he and Niclas moved to stand in front of her.

"Mrs. Seymour," the viscount greeted, smiling politely at Julia. "A pleasure to see you again, ma'am. And Niclas, Dyfed, I hope I find you well?"

"It's been a while since we've seen you," Dyfed remarked, his voice chilly and unfriendly. "How have you been, Midas? Turned anyone into a statue, lately?"

Loris gaped at Dyfed in surprise. She would expect such sarcasm from Kian, but not his twin. Dyfed was usually the only one in the family who managed to behave in public, no matter what the provocation. But he was gazing at Tauron with grave dislike, and Tauron, she saw, had flushed angrily at the name he'd been called.

"Dyfed," Niclas said in a warning tone before giving his attention to the viscount. "We are well, as you see, Brecmont. Are you in Town for very long this Season?"

"For the remainder." Tauron met Loris's gaze as she stood on her toes to look over the combined shoulders blocking her way. "I intend to enjoy myself as greatly as possible before the rest of my family arrive. Hopefully that will be many weeks away."

"The *rest* of your family?" Niclas repeated faintly.

Tauron nodded. "Yes, all of them, from what I hear. A special gathering for some purpose of Morcar's. I'm sure Malachi will be pleased to know of it. Ah, good evening, my lord." He bowed as Lord Perham joined them.

"Brecmont," the earl said with pleasure. "You're looking well. You've come to collect my granddaughter for the promised dance, have you? I'm sure she's been looking forward to it."

At that moment, the music for the next dance—a waltz—began drifting through the ballroom, and pairs of dancers were taking their places on the floor.

Tauron glanced to where Loris stood, still blocked by the two men.

"I've been looking forward to it as well, my lord," he said, and reached out a gloved hand in Loris's direction. Both Niclas and Dyfed scowled at it, and Loris had to push mightily at each of them to move forward. Straightening her gown, she set her hand in Tauron's and let him lead her toward the floor.

"Why didn't you tell me you'd met a Cadmaran?" Dyfed demanded furiously. "Why didn't you tell me your grandfather is friends—*good* friends—with a Cadmaran?"

They were standing on a garden terrace outside Lord and Lady Hamlin's ballroom, to which Dyfed had dragged Loris the moment her dance with Viscount Brecmont had come to an end.

"I didn't know he was until this afternoon," she said. "I was going to tell you and Niclas when we had a more private moment. Didn't it occur to you that other people were watching your encounter with Tauron? And overhearing what you said?"

"*Tauron*?" Dyfed's expression tightened. "You've only just met him and you're calling him by his Christian name?"

She made a sound of exasperation. "Don't change the subject. You know very well I have difficulty 'lording' and 'ladying' everyone in Town. It may come easily enough to someone born to such nonsense, but on the docks we weren't bothered by the social niceties and, I might remind you, we weren't bothered by them at Tylluan very much, either."

"I don't want you near him," Dyfed stated flatly. "I don't want you spending time with him or dancing with him *or* calling him by his Christian name. I promised Kian I'd keep you safe."

"Then you'd do well to watch your own tongue," she shot back. "Do you even recall what you said? In front of mere mortals, no less? Asking him if he'd turned anyone into a statue of late and calling him Midas. Not only was it dangerous; it was terribly unkind. He's not like Morcar Cadmaran. Indeed, he's not anything at all like any of the Cadmarans you've told me about."

She'd never seen Dyfed look so angry, not even when he was fighting with Kian, and certainly never with her.

"You don't know anything about him," Dyfed said, his voice tight. "I know Tauron far better than you do, Loris. Since we were boys. He can be a fine fellow, I grant you that. And more sufferable than the rest of his relatives, for I actually think he has a conscience. He's always been their black sheep that way, strange as that may sound. But he's still a Cadmaran." He bent nearer and looked directly into her eyes. "His powers are dark powers. You don't know what he's capable of doing, or what he has done."

"What has he done, then, that's so very awful?" she demanded. "Why is he treated so ill by both his family and yours?"

"I believe he's referring to the deaths I've caused. Or murders, as his brother once called them."

Both Loris and Dyfed turned to see Viscount Brecmont standing not far away, listening.

He closed the French doors he'd so silently exited through, then moved forward. Loris was surprised that they'd not heard his arrival, but the music was loud here—Dyfed had probably chosen it for that very reason, so that they could speak without fear of being heard. But neither of them realized just how loudly they'd been arguing; Tauron had clearly had no trouble hearing them at all.

"Kian apologized for that," Dyfed said. "Everyone knows you couldn't be blamed. They were accidents."

"They didn't feel like accidents," Tauron replied. "Not to me. Your brother had the right of it. Others died because of my power and, whether I intended those deaths or not, that feels very much like murder."

"If they had been," Dyfed said, scowling at Tauron as he came nearer, "you'd have been cursed. Blood cursed. The Guardians understood that you were too young to control your powers."

"And what of two years ago?" Tauron asked, coming to a stop directly in front of Loris. He looked at her, his gaze solemn. "When I was a child I didn't understand my gift. When I was just an infant I turned a household pet—a little dog that my mother adored—into stone. I was too little to know how to turn it back in time to keep it from dying. That was but the first of several 'accidents,' but assuredly not the worst. One of my nursemaids soon followed the same fate."

"Oh no," Loris murmured, horrified.

Tauron glanced at Dyfed. "I wasn't allowed to touch anyone after that—neither of my parents, none of my relatives—until I grew older and could begin to learn control. But even then I made mistakes, if I was distracted or ill or overly weary. I could almost always reverse the change in time. But not always. And sometimes it was too late, regardless. One of my schoolmates at Eton was mysteriously found dead one morning. He'd made the mistake of playing a jest on me in the middle of the night, and caught me unawares and half-awake. I turned him back as quickly as I could, but he seemed to have suffered some kind of heart failure. Probably from shock and terror. I don't know. Morcar removed me from school the next day and sent me home to Caerffill.

By the time I was old enough for university, fortunately, I had learned how to avoid making such mistakes, and was allowed to attend Oxford. There were no further incidents."

"Until two years ago," Dyfed said.

"Aye," Tauron agreed, looking at Loris as if he wanted her to understand. "It was at a family gathering at Llew. Some of my younger cousins—just foolish lads—thought it would be amusing to lace my wine with something rather stronger, not understanding that I choose to avoid more powerful spirits for a purpose. They understood quickly enough when one of them ended up a statue." He paused. When he next spoke it was with greater difficulty. "I was too drunk to change him back."

"Oh, Tauron," Loris said, lifting a hand to touch his sleeve. Dyfed's own hand shot out to stop her before she could make contact.

"His parents were devastated," Tauron went on. "Of course they would be. And Morcar was angered to have lost a greater wizard. But the rest of my relatives . . ." His eyes were haunted, filled with pain. "They almost seemed amused. Even the other boys. That's"—he stopped, looked away for a silent moment before turning back to her—"that's what Dyfed means when he warns you to be careful of me, Loris. Of any Cadmaran. Because that's what we are. Evil."

"But you're not," she told him. "No matter what you've done. If it weren't so, the Guardians would have punished you by now with the hope of teaching you otherwise."

"He's a *Cadmaran,* Loris," Dyfed told her. "He knows what he's speaking of." When she looked at him sharply he said, "I don't blame him for what's happened. I never have. Kian is a harsher judge, but you know that better than I do. But he's not alone. Even the Earl of Llew forced Tauron to remain within the confines of his home in Caerffill until he felt it safe to cut him loose. I'd wager anything that's why he came to Town."

"Wouldn't you?" Loris demanded, pulling free of Dyfed's grip. All she could think of was how desperately lonely and sad Tauron had been. Just as she was lonely. As she knew Kian was. "*And* you called him King Midas," she added hotly.

Dyfed made a sound of impatience. "Very well, I was wrong and insulting. I apologize." He shot a look toward Tauron. "But he's a Cadmaran, and if you'll recall, Tylluan is suffering just now because of a Cadmaran—"

At this, Tauron stiffened. "It is?" he asked, looking at Loris. "You said nothing of this earlier, when we spoke of your home." To Dyfed, he said, "And though it's no business of yours, I was in Town last year for the Season. That you never saw me is no fault of mine. Morcar knew that I was safe in public. He had no reason to force me into isolation even for one year."

"I don't care about your past visits to Town," Dyfed countered tautly. "I don't care why you've come to Town this year. The only thing I do care about is your staying away from Loris. She's not on your list of potential brides."

"Dyfed Oliver Arnallt Seymour," she said angrily, "I will not be told who I can and cannot see. If I wish to maintain an acquaintance with Tauron—with *anyone*—I will."

The sound of music died away in the house beyond, signaling the end of another dance.

"No, Loris, you'll not," Dyfed stated firmly. "And I don't care that he's a friend of Lord Perham's. You're not to speak with him after tonight. You're not to dance with him, go driving with him, be in company with him at your grandfather's home, or acknowledge him at all."

"Dyfed," Tauron said reasonably as Loris made a sound of fury. "I certainly don't mean Miss McClendon any harm. My only desire is—"

Dyfed sprang at him with unexpected speed, gripping the taller—and much larger—man by the collar and dragging him near.

"I *know* what your desire is, Brecmont. I'm neither blind, as your cousin is, nor a fool. You're looking for a wife, and what better wife than one of our sympathetics? Especially one like Loris, who is both beautiful and completely at ease with our kind?"

The French doors opened once more, but those on the terrace paid no mind to the number of interested individuals who were seeking fresh air while there was a break in the music.

"Dyfed!" Loris said sharply, grabbing one arm with both hands to make him let Tauron go.

"He doesn't deny it, do you, Brecmont? Your goal is to seek a wife, and Loris is the ideal candidate. You even claim a friendship with her grandfather—how very fortunate—so that you can more easily gain privileges that other men could only dream of. Taking her driving in the park, for example, as I understand you did today."

"Dyfed, stop!" Loris demanded, tugging harder. "You're making a fool of yourself."

Dyfed ignored her. "He doesn't deny it, does he?"

"He can't speak," she told Dyfed. "He can scarce breathe, you idiot!" She shook him so hard that she thought the material of his coat would tear. "Let him go! Let . . . him . . . *go!*"

"Deny it, then," Dyfed demanded, releasing his captive.

Tauron smoothed his hands over his coat and strove to collect himself. It was plain to Loris that he could have readily pounded Dyfed into dust if he'd wished, he was so much taller and bigger, but had purposefully allowed himself to be held.

"I don't deny it," he said. "It would be an insult to Miss McClendon to do otherwise. I came to London seeking a wife, as all the world seems to know, and she was among the first candidates suggested to me by friends. But this will be no surprise to you, for there are any number of men in Town who have hopes where she's concerned."

"Truly?" Loris asked. She'd heard this from Julia previously but thought it ridiculously silly.

"Of course," he went on, "I'd heard of her and knew who she was, and that her grandfather is my friend only made the connection more desirable. And she was not unaware that he approved a potential union. But I'm not a fool, either, though you think me one. I understand the difficulties such a match would encounter between our families."

"You'll never have to worry over that," Dyfed told him hotly. "Loris is already spoken for. By a Seymour. She's one of *us,* and always will be. You can cross her off your list. Permanently."

"Dyfed," Loris said, touching his arm.

He ignored her.

"Do you understand me, Brecmont? Because if you don't, I'll be happy to find another way to explain it."

"Dyfed," Loris said again, and he seemed to hear the warning in her tone.

He looked up—Viscount Brecmont looked, too—to find that they had a large gathering of interested listeners. Niclas was there, and Lord Perham as well. And, standing beside them, the Earl of Graymar, looking thunderously angry.

The scene that took place later that evening in her grandfather's study wasn't merely unpleasant, but painfully so.

Loris sat in the far corner of the room, exhausted and furious, wishing that society wasn't so ridiculously foolish as to make so much of what had been a private disagreement— well, perhaps not so private, as they had been on Lord and Lady Hamlin's terrace. Still, why should everyone care so much about what the *ton* thought? Loris didn't care, and it was her reputation they were discussing, after all. Dyfed, who looked somewhere between regretful and insulted, sat next to her. They had both fallen silent almost immediately after arriving in the room, having been told numerous times by Niclas, Malachi, and Lord Perham to keep quiet.

"I insist upon satisfaction, sir," her grandfather told Malachi, his voice rising a fraction louder than usual. "That young man has made a spectacle of my granddaughter and destroyed the reputation that has already been so precariously balanced."

"He's done no such thing," Malachi stated, his own voice

quite calm, if rather weary. "He made a fact public. What of it? Do you mean to say you have some objection to your granddaughter marrying a Seymour?"

"I object to the manner in which you seem to think you can direct Loris's life, sir," said Lord Perham. "I am not insensible to the debt of gratitude I owe you—the entire Seymour family—for rescuing my granddaughter from a life of poverty and misery, but she is my granddaughter, and *not* a Seymour. I will decide what's best for Loris."

"Lord Perham," Niclas said reasonably, "surely we can come to an understanding without making Loris out to be an object of ownership. She has been a member of our family for ten years. The Seymours have every right to an interest in her welfare, as you do."

"They do not, sir!" Lord Perham thundered. "If I must I shall bring the law into the matter, and you know as well as I that the tie of blood will decide who has the right to determine Loris's affairs."

Malachi rubbed the bridge of his nose. He looked, to Loris, not simply tired but irritable and impatient. The Earl of Graymar had reached the end of his tether and was quickly growing weary of having to deal with the troubles of others.

"What do you propose, my lord?" he asked. "What is it that you desire? Apart from the fact that you wish all Seymours to the devil."

The Earl of Perham drew himself up and considered the matter. Then, more calmly, he said, "I shall take Loris home to Cumberland for the remainder of the Season following her come-out ball. Any further word of an understanding between her and anyone else is to be denied."

"No!" Loris said loudly, standing.

"Silence, young lady," Lord Perham demanded. "You've done enough this night."

"I'll not be silent," she said, striding forward. "I have a right to decide where I wish to go and in what manner."

Malachi dropped his hand and looked at her. "And what is it that you want, Loris?"

Lord Perham looked as if he'd been struck by lightning. "This is *precisely* why she should have nothing to do with the Seymours," he said furiously. "You have no appreciation for the fact that she doesn't understand society and the ways of—"

Malachi lifted a hand and Lord Perham froze midsentence. He froze in every way. Even his scolding expression was fixed in place.

"Oh," Loris said, instantly distressed. "Oh, Malachi, how *could* you? To my grandfather?"

The Earl of Graymar looked at her with thin patience. "Easily," he said. "I've spent the past two days dealing with my cousin Steffan. You know him well, do you not?"

She nodded. Steffan Seymour was a redheaded Seymour, and redheaded Seymours, like Niclas's infant daughter, tended to be mystics. Steffan was exceptionally gifted; he was also quite troublesome and insisted upon making his living as a highwayman, robbing travelers with the help of his band of wild men. They lived, Loris had been told, in a cluster of caves just inside Wales's border.

"He and his men were arrested in Herefordshire and I was made to contend with the local squire—who also serves as sheriff—who proved to be a mere mortal of fantastic proportions. And I do *not* mean in the physical sense. I vow I have never in my life encountered such an astonishing combination of obstinacy and abstractedness. I could write a comedy about the experience and *no one* would believe it to be anything but complete farce."

He moved closer, rubbing at the space between his eyes again.

"I am not in the pleasantest of moods. I'm very weary and not terribly happy with Lord Perham. He seems determined to wrest you from us in any manner that he can, and my dear young cousin's execrable behavior"—he looked at Dyfed, who glared back defiantly—"has only given him further ammunition for doing so."

"He wants to marry her off to a *Cadmaran*, Malachi,"

Dyfed said furiously. "Only think of it—our Loris an accursed Cadmaran."

"Be quiet, Dyfed," Niclas said. "You know very well that Loris is free to marry as she pleases. The *unoliaeth* doesn't force her to wed Kian. Or even to love him, for that matter."

"But *not* a Cadmaran!" Dyfed exclaimed.

"Aye, even a Cadmaran," Malachi stated with finality. "And I find it strange that you should be the one to protest so much, Dyfed, considering that you're so eager to take a dark sorceress as your mate." Malachi speared his younger relative with such a heated look that Dyfed sat down and fumed in silence.

"However," Lord Graymar added, turning back to Loris, "I confess that I should do everything in my power to prevent such a thing happening. And so would Morcar. Tauron's not a bad fellow, for a Cadmaran, but I can't think Loris would be happy wed to him."

"Would you all please stop speaking such nonsense?" she begged. "I have no intention of marrying a man I only just met, no matter how well my grandfather—or anyone—thinks of him."

"Of course we know that," Niclas said calmly. "But Dyfed informed half the *ton* that you're spoken for, and your grandfather is determined to deflect gossip by either making the statement true or taking you away."

"What you have to decide, my dear," said Malachi, "is what *you* want to do."

She shook her head. "I don't know why there should even be anything to speak of. I thought you all believed in the *unoliaeth* between Kian and me."

Malachi looked at her closely. "We do. But what we believe scarce matters now. What do you believe, Loris? You've been absent from Kian long enough to have some idea of what your feelings are, whether you miss him, or not, and whether you want to be near him again . . . or not. Whatever you decide, we must find a way to soothe your grandfather, else he's going to make all our lives wretched."

They were looking at her. Watching. Waiting for her to say something.

The entire matter seemed so ridiculously foolish. Why couldn't they just pretend that nothing had happened at the Hamlins' ball and go on with their lives? The gossip would all blow over in a few days. If she'd learned anything about London, it was that the most recent bit of news drowned out everything that had come previously, and surely someone would do something soon to make people forget the scene on the terrace.

But society, she knew, wasn't truly the problem. It was her grandfather and his feud with the Seymours. He was a powerful man with great influence. Loris already found it nearly impossible to naysay him. On the other side of the coin was the Earl of Graymar, who didn't like being thwarted by anyone, certainly not a mere mortal. Their constant determination to outdo each other was not only unpleasant but also dangerous. Proof was that her grandfather stood in the midst of the room, frozen in place, beneath a spell that the *Dewin Mawr* had felt not the least compunction casting upon him. And Malachi was only a little weary and irate at the moment. What would happen if Lord Perham truly made him angry?

What did she want? Malachi had asked her. What did she believe?

"What if—" Loris cleared her throat and began again. "What if what I want is to go home to Tylluan? Tomorrow?"

The men exchanged glances.

"You want to return to Tylluan?" Malachi asked. "Are you quite sure that's what you wish? For surely you understand that would be upsetting to your grandfather. He would very likely come after you. And the present time is not precisely a good one for a mere mortal to be visiting."

"Oh yes, of course," she said, lowering her gaze to hide how deep her disappointment was. She'd hoped for a moment . . . but it wasn't to be.

"I don't believe that simply going to Tylluan is what Loris truly wants," Niclas said gently. "Why don't you say it in another way, my dear? Malachi's being rather dense to-night. Probably because he's so tired." Niclas cast a teasing look at his cousin, who frowned at him.

Loris looked at Niclas, realizing that he had sensed her emotions. Had she not made herself clear, then?

"I want to see Kian," she said. "To speak to him. Alone. And then I'll know what's best to do. But if I can't go to Tyl-luan, then I don't see how—"

Malachi's expression filled with sudden understanding. He also looked very pleased.

"Ah," he said. "That's different, then."

Loris didn't see how. "It is?" she asked.

"I shall take care of it," he said. "Be patient, and trust me. The matter is settled. Leave us to deal with your grandfather, my dear, and all will be well."

Malachi lifted a hand and made a quick movement, and her grandfather instantly came out of his frozen state.

"—deflecting gossip," he said, just as angry as he'd earlier been. "You'd let her become a laughingstock if it were left to you. Loris, go to your room, dear." He pointed toward the door. "I'll let you know in the morning what we've decided."

"Yes, my lord." He looked surprised by her sudden obe-dience, and she was relieved to be sent away. She walked about the room and kissed each of the Seymours good-bye and ended with her grandfather, who stood in stony silence while she saluted his cheek. "Please don't let yourself be distressed any further, Grandfather," she murmured. "I'm sure that everything will be all right."

Bidding them all good night, she left the room.

Sixteen

$\mathcal{K}$ian came awake to find himself staring into the guileless blue eyes of the Earl of Graymar. And since that wasn't likely, Kian told himself that either he was dreaming or that a mischievous spirit had sneaked into the castle and was playing tricks by taking on the form of the *Dewin Mawr*. Thus satisfied, he closed his eyes once more and attempted to go back to sleep.

"Do you often sleep in your study, Cousin?" Lord Graymar asked. "I should think your bed a more desirable location."

It wasn't a dream. Or a mischievous spirit. Kian sighed and dragged his eyes open again and peered at his relative.

"This couch is more comfortable than it may appear," he said, yawning and stretching before slowly sitting up. "I've been sleeping here a great deal since Loris and Dyfed left. I find it easier to think in this room, and if I need a certain book to answer some question or other I don't have to jog downstairs to find it. I would be grateful, however, if you'd say nothing to Loris about it. She tends to fret."

"Aye, that she does," his cousin agreed.

Kian noticed that Lord Graymar had made himself comfortable. He was sitting in a chair nearby, legs crossed and a glass of whiskey in his hands. How long had he been there and Kian not known? He must have been sleeping deeply indeed to have missed sensing the presence and power of the *Dewin Mawr*.

"How is she?" Kian asked, running both hands through his disheveled hair. "Have you seen her lately? Is she well? Happy?"

Lord Graymar gave him no immediate answer. Instead, Malachi leaned forward and regarded Kian more closely. "What the devil are those scratches on your face? It looks as if you've had a disagreement with a pitchfork."

Kian touched the tender lines that ran the length of one cheek. They'd stopped seeping blood sometime during the night, thank heavens. Loris wouldn't be pleased to find bloodstains on the furniture when she came home.

"It's nothing," he said. "Have you ever seen an *athanc*, Malachi?"

"I confess that I have not," Lord Graymar admitted. "Though I heard the same stories as a child that I assume you heard, too. A great dragonlike beast, is it not?"

Kian nodded. "With very sharp claws. For a monster that moves so slowly when not in its fluid form, it can strike with remarkable speed." He fingered the scars. "I found out just how fast last night. Fortunately, it hadn't finished growing full-height, else its claws would have been longer and more deadly."

"You've taken to attempting physical attacks on an enchanted beast?" Malachi asked, clearly astonished by this. "You know, do you not, that it cannot be killed as more normal creatures can?"

Kian stretched once more, his body stiff and aching. "Of course I know," he said, the words distorted by a groan of discomfort as he brought his arms back down. "But until the enchantment that puts it back to sleep can be found, I've got to discover a way to contain it. Seren is willing to take me close enough to the beast so that I can see whether anything at all affects it. Unfortunately, nothing yet has worked."

"Not that you want my advice," Malachi said, "nor have you asked for it, but I'm going to give it, anyway. Stop trying to solve every problem yourself, and wait until Professor Seabolt unearths the solution. It should be quite soon, for he's making rapid progress."

Kian felt a flush of aggravation. "In the meantime, my people are suffering, and the *athanc* is destroying everything in its path. The local farmers and the villagers have laid the blame and the responsibility at my door. I can't just sit by and do nothing. Not because I got a few little scratches."

Malachi eyed the scratches dubiously, clearly not finding them little. "I'll heal them before I go," he stated. "I'm sure you don't want Loris seeing them."

"How is she?" Kian asked again, far more interested in having news of her than in discussing the dratted *athanc*.

"I saw her but a few hours past, as it happens," said His Lordship. "She is well. I do not believe she is entirely happy."

Kian frowned. "What's happened, Malachi?"

The Earl of Graymar proceeded to tell Kian about Lord Perham—painting the gentleman in colors that were far from flattering, although in Kian's opinion Perham sounded to be just as imperious and stubborn as the Earl of Graymar himself—and the appearance of Tauron Cadmaran.

By the time Malachi finished, Kian was up on his feet, pacing before the fire.

"Damn it all," he muttered. "I never should have let her go. I meant it for the best, and God knows that matters at Tylluan have gone from bad to worse, but I thought— hoped—that the experience would be a pleasant one for her."

"I wouldn't say that it's been unpleasant, precisely," Malachi told him. "And she's had the joy of finding her grandfather, and of him finding her, and regardless what I may think of Lord Perham's determination to cut off all ties that Loris has to the Seymours—"

"Which is impossible," Kian muttered.

"—their discovery of each other has been a very pleasant thing indeed. And I might remind you that Lord Perham doesn't know that Loris is permanently bound to the Seymours by a *unoliaeth*. In his opinion severing ties with our family is not only doable but desirable. Unfortunately, Loris is caught in the middle, and finds it all distressing."

"And now this thing with Tauron," Kian said. "Not that I blame the fellow. He doesn't want to marry among his kind, which means he's got to find a candidate among our sympathetics. Loris is not only a sympathetic but beautiful and charming as well. He'll never find another like her, not in England, and he knows it. I can almost feel sorry for him."

Malachi sighed. "Aye. So can I. Finding a suitable mate for those of us not providential enough to be fated at birth is a troubling matter. Niclas was most fortunate, and it appears that Dyfed has been as well, though we might have wished it had been someone other than a dark sorceress. Still, destiny is a mysterious thing. We cannot always understand it."

"I wish Dyfed hadn't made such a scene," Kian said more thoughtfully. "What could have driven him to be so incautious? Surely he realized Loris would never allow herself to be bound to anyone against her will. That's what she's always disliked most about the idea of the *unoliaeth*, you know." He cast a glance at his cousin. "The feeling that she hasn't any say in the matter. That it's been thrust upon her."

"It makes sense," Malachi remarked, lifting the glass in his hand to sip from it. "Mere mortals have so little understanding of the ways and workings of fate, even a sympathetic like Loris, who has lived with us for so long. Our kind, however, is much more resigned to it. And to finding ways to get around it," he added with a smile. "As to Dyfed, the boy has been deeply unhappy from the moment he came to Town. His judgment was impaired by anxiety and lovesickness."

"But now the fashionable world believes that Loris is secretly betrothed to a Seymour. Rumors had already been floating about Town, and Dyfed only confirmed them."

"And Perham wants to find a way to make them think otherwise," Malachi said. "Perham believes his granddaughter's already precarious reputation has been sullied—which is foolish, considering that being married to a Seymour would be perceived by society as a great boon. Still, I concede that something must be done to put an end to the nonsense once and for all. Apart from that, she wants to see you."

For a moment Kian felt as if his heart had stopped beating. His gaze riveted to Malachi's, and he said, "Loris? She said so?"

Malachi inclined his head. "Given the choice to make her wishes known, that was her desire. To see you. I perceive that this would make you glad as well?"

Kian's heart started beating again, but he still felt dizzy. "Yes," he murmured. "But how? It would be dangerous for her to come back to Tylluan, and I certainly can't leave—"

"Can you not?" Malachi asked. "Dyfed told me that the beast rests for several days. Will that period of rest come soon?"

Kian nodded slowly. "Tonight. We'll have peace for three or four days. Then he will hunt again. But I've enough food to keep it safe within Tylluan's borders for some days following that. I have three weeks altogether to find a solution."

Malachi's eyebrows rose. "And then?"

"Then I've promised to call for help."

"Ah." Lord Graymar nodded with understanding. "I see. We must hope Professor Seabolt discovers the enchantment before that becomes necessary. Not that I won't be delighted to bend my efforts to the task. I would have come anytime in the past months if you'd called."

Kian looked away. "I know that."

"Well, then, I'm glad we understand each other." Lord Graymar put his glass aside. "Now, I want you to make preparations for someone else—perhaps the ever capable Horas—to oversee the problems at Tylluan for a few days." He stood.

"I can't, Malachi." Kian gave a solemn shake of his head. "I would give anything to come away with you to London. To see Loris, even for a few moments of time. But I'm the Baron of Tylluan. I cannot go until all is well."

Malachi disregarded the words with a wave of one hand. "A brief rest is precisely what you need just now. It will clear your mind and refresh your senses. And it will be an ideal time for us to gather with Professor Seabolt and discuss all he's discovered. And you want to know about the Caslins, do you not? There's a great deal to say about them, as well, and I haven't the time or inclination to do so now."

"But—"

"You have three weeks," Malachi said. "I only require one, if that, to settle the problem with Lord Perham. It's time to put the rumors to rest and show both him and the *ton* exactly which Seymour our Loris is betrothed to."

"*Betrothed?*" Kian echoed, stunned. "You know how dearly I wish that was true, but Loris's feelings are completely different. I can't force her to pretend a betrothal with me. Things have happened that you know nothing of. She's unhappy, and needs time to—"

Malachi made a sound of impatience. "Time she has had, and more than enough. And so have you. She wants to see you, and she will. I'll return tonight to collect you. In the meantime, Niclas will make the arrangements. He's having your town house opened and aired in expectation of your arrival."

"Arrangements?" Kian didn't like the sound of that. "What arrangements?" He stepped forward as his cousin began to move toward the door. "Malachi, wait. You can't simply decide how everything will be this time—"

"I don't see why not," Lord Graymar said easily, stopping to collect his hat and gloves from a nearby table. "No one else seems to know what they want, except Loris, and she quite wisely wants to see you. *I* know what that means, even if you're too lost in love to do so."

Kian fell still and stared at him. His heart was beating strangely again. "What does it mean?"

Lord Graymar set his hat upon his head and smiled. "I'm sure you'll find out shortly after seeing her. In the meantime, you might want to consider ways to cause Lord Perham to accept your suit. You won't have long to do so. I want the announcement made at Loris's come-out ball, two days from now. That is where you'll make your first appearance together before the *ton* and all the silly rumors will be laid to rest. Don't worry about packing suitable clothing," he added, giving his attention to putting on his gloves. "I'll put my tailor to work the moment I'm back in Town. He took your measurements last year, did he not? I feel quite certain that I recall sending you there for something to wear to your father's wedding. Or was that Dyfed? Well, it scarce matters, for you're close enough in size, and Binkley can always make a few adjustments if necessary."

"Damn it, Malachi, will you stop blathering about tailors? What the devil are you up to? I don't want Loris overset."

"Good," Malachi said. "Then I'm sure you'll use all the skill and charm you possess. Oh, and be certain not to let her know if you're required to use any of your other skills on her grandfather. She can be quite unreasonable about it."

"My God," Kian murmured. "Never tell me you've been putting spells on the Earl of Perham."

"Very well, I won't tell you," His Lordship replied, and the door opened for him without being touched. "I'll come back tonight. Be ready."

Viscount Brecmont arrived at Lord Perham's town house at noon the day following the Hamlin ball to make his apologies, first to Lord Perham, who assured him that the embarrassment Loris had suffered was not his fault and could be laid solely at the feet of the reckless and rascally Seymours. When the viscount asked if he might express regrets to Lord Perham's granddaughter, regardless of this, the earl called for Loris and then, pleased by her gladness at the sight of the other man, left them in the blue parlor to speak alone.

"Oh, I am glad you've come," Loris said, taking Tauron's hand. "I'm terribly sorry for the manner in which Dyfed behaved last night. I don't know what made him act in such a way. He's been unhappy since we've come to Town and I think took that unhappiness out on you."

"Please don't apologize, Miss McClendon—"

"Oh, don't start *Miss McClendoning* me again, please, Tauron," she begged. "Is it as bad as all that?"

"I believe it is," he said unhappily, pulling free of her touch. "I shouldn't even have come today, for I'm sure it will be remarked upon. But I felt that I had to come and speak with you. You said something last night, and I must know the whole of it. I am not in much contact with the rest of my family, as you may have surmised, and know little of their activities. Has my cousin, Lord Llew, been behind some recent ill-doing at Tylluan? He has been in the past, I know, so I'd not be surprised. But from your behavior, and Dyfed's, it seems that this time Morcar has done something especially bad."

Tauron looked pale and miserable, and Loris's heart went out to him. "Sit down and be comfortable," she said, waving a hand toward the couch and chairs. "I'll ring for tea."

She was careful in telling him about the destruction that had been occurring at Tylluan over the past months. Fortunately, she could quite honestly state that she had no idea what, precisely, was causing the actual damage, for she'd not yet been told, though she related that both Kian and Dyfed believed it to be one of the ancient enchanted monsters, brought back to life. She said nothing of Desdemona Caslin.

"Aye, that sounds like something that would appeal to Morcar," Tauron muttered, accepting the cup of tea Loris offered him. "He prefers the old ways to the new, and he's determined to best the Seymours in any way he can. It's an obsession. But I suppose he can't help himself. He was raised from his cradle for the task. His father, the former earl, was equally obsessed, you see."

"From what I've heard, the disagreements go back too far for anyone to even remember what started them," Loris said. "You'd think someone would eventually come along and decide to stop being so foolish."

"It's not so simple a thing to step out of line among my people," he told her. "The Families only have each other for protection. Those who cause dissension risk being shunned, and left without a safe haven from the world of mere mortals. If I dared to depart from the ways of the Cadmarans, I'd find myself alone, and perhaps even in danger. Morcar would find and punish me."

She looked at him closely. "Malachi would help you, if you asked him to."

Tauron uttered a mirthless laugh. "And then Morcar would kill me, or find a way to manage the task without angering the Guardians."

"You must decide for yourself whether the risk is worth it, then," she said. "I learned early in life how valuable it is to be free to make your own choices." She smiled. "Although *valuable* isn't quite the right word. *Essential* would be better. Essential to one's happiness, despite the danger."

He gave a sorrowful shake of his head. "You are not one of us, Loris. You don't know what it is to *be* one of us."

"I know what it's like to be in the complete sway of others," she told him. "Before Ffinian Seymour took me away from London, I had never made a single decision that affected my own life. My parents chose for me, and then, when they were gone, I became a servant in a tavern and the keeper and his wife decided what my life would be. And if Kian Seymour hadn't saved me, I would have been put into the hands of someone far, far worse, who would have chosen quite a different life for me."

"I've heard the story of what Kian Seymour did. But he was cursed for it, was he not?"

"Aye," she murmured. So Tauron had known of that, at least, if not of the *unoliaeth*. "He was. Because of me. But that's not what we should speak of, Tauron, for that's of no purpose to you. I wanted to tell you how I learned how important it is to make your own decisions, and never let another take that power from you."

He put his cup aside. "Tell me," he said.

"After he brought me to Tylluan, I looked to Ffinian to tell me what to do. I had never learned how to make a decision for myself, and I expected him to guide me, to tell me what he wanted of me. If he'd given me a bucket of water and a rag and told me to scrub all the castle floors I would have done it without question. And gladly. I would have done anything for him, for he was so kind and gentle and loving." She smiled as she thought of him and wished, as she had so often wished of late, that he and Lady Alice would come home soon. "And yet I lived in terror of displeasing him as well, for I didn't want him to send me away. If you think it a terrible thing to be dependent on your family, imagine what it's like to have no one at all to care for and shelter you. If Ffinian had thrown me out, I would have had nowhere to go. No one to turn to.

"And then one day," she went on, "he brought me into his study and sat me down. He took my hands and said, 'Why have you been hiding in the hallways and shadows, darling Loris? Don't you like it here? Don't you wish to go out with the lads and enjoy the fine sun? Or into the garden to see the pretty flowers?'

"And of course I told him that I didn't know what to do, but if he wished me to go out with Dyfed and Kian—though I was terrified of Kian, for he was always following me—or out into the garden, I would do so at once. And Ffinian said, 'But what do you *wish* to do, my girl?' " She sighed at the memory. "And that was when I realized that I was free. That he wanted me to be free, and to be happy. I've never loved anyone as I loved Ffinian Seymour in that moment. He can be the most exasperating man on God's earth," she said, looking at Tauron, who, having met Ffinian on several occasions, nodded knowingly, "but to me he is something altogether different."

"What did you choose to do, then?" Tauron pressed.

"Well, I chose to do what made me feel safe, and what I knew would please Ffinian. I got a bucket and rag and began to clean the castle." She laughed at Tauron's horrified expression. "It was wonderful," she insisted, "and I was happier than I'd ever been before. Because it was my choice, and no one else's, and because I was terribly good at it. And, more even than all of that, it made me feel needed. They did need me, those three foolish men, so very much. Their home was falling down about their ears, and they needed someone to stop it from doing so. And in that way, Tylluan became my home, too."

She took a moment to refill their teacups and to make certain that Tauron's plate was filled with a large slice of cake and a few delicate fruit tarts.

"I know you love Tylluan," he said, accepting both plate and cup from her. "I heard it in your voice yesterday, during our ride."

"Very much," she confessed. "But Ffinian gave me far more than simply a home. Don't you understand, Tauron? He gave me a wonderful gift, when he gave me such freedom— one that I've never taken for granted. I would have been a fool to give it up so easily, having waited so long to have it."

He shook his head. "But I'm not free," he said. "I'll never be free."

Loris gazed at him steadily. "Try telling that to those who live where I once did. Try telling a whore or a dockhand or a child living in one of London's filthy rookeries that you have no freedom, no choice. You make a mockery of the freedom you do have by saying such a thing, especially when there are those who would give all that they have to stand in your place. You'd not see them waste such a chance, believe me."

He stared at her.

"You don't have to do what the Cadmarans tell you to do, Tauron," she said. "You could leave England tomorrow, if you chose. You could find a way to keep from being found."

"My gift," he said. "If something happened, there'd be no one to save me. Morcar would never come to my aid."

"Then make very certain you don't misuse it," she advised.

"And what of you, Loris?" he asked. "Your grandfather believes he's going to make all your decisions from now on.

And he's still hoping for a match between you and me. How will you keep from being forced into what you don't desire?"

"Easily," she said, "for I've already made my choice." Then she changed the subject. "You'll be coming to my come-out ball, will you not? I've reserved a dance for you. Please promise me you'll be there."

$\mathcal{S}$*eventeen*

$\mathcal{D}$o you find the soup to your liking, my love?"

Desdemona lifted her head to look down the length of the long table at Morcar Cadmaran—and knew that something was wrong. Lowering her spoon, she said, "Yes. Very much."

His sightless eyes remained fixed in her direction, disturbingly on mark, and one hand restlessly fingered his wineglass until at last he said, "I'm glad."

She bent her head over the bowl again, sipping another mouthful of the savory mushroom soup, and began to consider how she might best protect herself from the powerful wizard before her.

She had to be careful. She had to think. Clearly and carefully. Most of all, she mustn't let him know she was aware that their situation had altered.

There was a change in him, a subtle change, but it was there nonetheless. Desdemona gave herself a mental shake for not realizing it before this moment. Cadmaran was too quiet, not going on endlessly as he usually did in order to hear the sound of his own voice. And the dining chamber itself was too still. There was no one else here, she realized of a sudden, and the pace of her heartbeat quickened. They were alone.

"How do your dealings with the beast go on?" he asked. "You seem to be resting it more often than you used to do."

Was the soup poisoned? she wondered. *Or the wine?* But no. He would realize that she had protections against such simple, earthly creations. And he didn't possess the gift of making potions himself by using the ancient magic, as she had heard the *Dewin Mawr* could do. Apart from that, Cadmaran would not risk the wrath of the Guardians by doing such a thing. They had already done more than enough by making him blind. This game, Desdemona knew—or at least hoped—the Earl of Llew would play by the rules.

"The creature requires rest," she said, the calmness of her tone belying the fear in her heart, "else it will do no harm when it's called out of the lake. I've told you of this before, but perhaps you've forgotten. The *athanc* must be handled with care, my lord, if you wish to use it to the greatest purpose."

"Of course," he murmured. "I'd certainly not wish to weary or damage the beast. You above all others know how important it is to me that Tylluan suffer as greatly as possible."

"Yes, my lord," she said, pushing the soup aside and casting her gaze slowly about the room. It was a large, medieval chamber, with but two doors and a few small windows. The doors were on Cadmaran's end of the room, and the windows were too small to fly out of . . . unless she had enough time to transform herself. But transformations required patience and concentration, and if she made the attempt, Cadmaran would strike long before the change was complete.

"Do you know, my love," he said softly, "I've had reports that perhaps the creature hasn't been performing of late quite to the level we had previously enjoyed."

"Indeed?" she asked, forcing surprise into her voice. "It seems to be as ravenous in its hunger as ever."

He sat forward. "Yes, my sweet, but has it been as vigorous in its violence? I have heard, though I could scarce believe it, that not a single incidence of damage has occurred for several weeks now, though you've taken the beast out quite often." Slowly, he stood. "Can this be so?"

"Of course it isn't," she assured him. "How very odd that you should hear such a false report. The creature has done a great deal of damage, just as you wished. Tylluan has been reeling from the harm the *athanc* has inflicted."

"And yet," said Lord Llew, slowly moving to push aside his chair, "Lord Tylluan has felt so much at ease that he has departed."

Desdemona prepared herself for battle. Cadmaran was powerful, but so was she, and he was blind. The additional powers he gained from the castle itself weren't going to make matters any easier, but she was ready for that.

"Departed?" she repeated as he began to traverse the length of the table, running one hand along the bare, gleaming dark wood to find his way. "Has he?"

Perhaps if she waited until Cadmaran was far enough along before moving she might be able to surprise him sufficiently to gain one of the doors. They would be locked, of course, but unlocking them would be a child's trick. Getting out the door before he cast a spell at her would be far more difficult.

"Aye, he's gone to London, to celebrate a betrothal. His brother's betrothal, from the rumors I've heard, to the Earl of Perham's granddaughter."

The words worked on Desdemona as no spell could have done. The breath caught in her throat, and shock poured over her like ice water.

"Betrothed?" she whispered. *"Dyfed?"*

Cadmaran checked his progress, tilting his head slightly. Too late, Desdemona realized how much she had given away in a single word.

"Ah," the earl murmured. "So that's what it is."

Desdemona pushed at the chair, ready to fly, only to discover that she couldn't rise to her feet.

The chair, she thought with furious realization. He had enchanted the chair to hold her captive. How very clever. Far more clever than she'd given him credit for being. But it didn't matter.

"Release!" she commanded, and the chair obeyed. She leaped to her feet and scuttled around the side of the table opposite him, knocking aside her wineglass and a candlestick in her haste.

A sudden gust of wind rushed through the chamber, putting out both torches and candles, plunging the chamber into darkness. Chairs came flying out from their places at the table, impeding Desdemona's progress.

She stubbed her toe on one and cursed aloud in the darkness and with a furious motion sent a dozen flames into the air to light her way.

Behind her, Cadmaran chuckled, causing a shiver of apprehension to tingle down her spine. She glanced back and saw that he was standing where he'd earlier been, beside the table, quite far away from her now. Except that now he held a large silver candlestick in his hand.

The sight made Desdemona panic. Her father had sworn that he would never tell another living soul about the one great weakness that could fell her, but she knew very well that money meant more to him than honor. If he'd told Cadmaran . . . she didn't want to think of the possibility.

With another quick motion she sent the chairs back into their places, out of her way, and fled toward the door. Assuming it was locked, she had already commanded it to be open before she reached it. The door flung itself wide with such force that it banged on the wall to which it was hinged. A few more steps and she'd be out.

But Cadmaran sent the door slamming shut again, just as Desdemona reached it, and before she could counter the command he had sent the candlestick flying in her direction. She heard it coming, heard him shout, "Bind!" and knew she'd lost their contest.

Turning, she saw the candlestick coming at her, transforming as it flew, thinning into long, slender ropes of silver. Desdemona made a futile motion to evade them, but the ropes hit with amazing speed and accuracy, slapping as they struck her and wrapping tightly about her body, pinning her arms and legs so that she fell onto the ground, irrevocably bound.

She lay, panting, weeping, disbelieving that her father had done such a thing. How could he have revealed to Cadmaran, to anyone, the secret weakness that rendered her powerless?

" 'Silver ropes to bind the witch, to make her scream and howl and twitch,' " Cadmaran said softly as he slowly felt his way toward her. " 'And when we've set her on the fire, we'll dance about the funeral pyre.' That was once part of a children's rhyme, was it not, my love? Quite long ago, admittedly. The use of silver cords is such a rare and ancient enchantment for capturing a sorceress that I had thought it lost to our kind. But, then, you're not ordinary in any regard, are you, my sweet? You're like the *athanc,* only touched by the old, near-forgotten spells."

"Don't pretend to own a wisdom that we both know you don't possess," she told him hotly. "My father told you. Do you intend to hold me captive like this forever?"

Cadmaran knelt on one knee beside her, patting along her prone body to find her face. When she tried to bite him he chuckled with fresh amusement.

"When did you fall in love with Lord Tylluan's brother, Desdemona? It must have been during your wanderings, for he never came to visit us. How foolish you are. Was it his prettiness that charmed you? It could not have been his powers, for he has none. Not that I mind you taking lesser wizards for lovers, darling. You shall find me the most understanding of husbands in that manner, after we've wed. With the exception of any Seymours. But I don't believe we'll have this lack of understanding again in the future, once you've come to your senses. As to Dyfed Seymour, it appears he'll no longer be available to you, if the rumors that I've heard are true."

"Don't speak of him!"

"No?" Cadmaran asked, stroking her hair, ignoring her attempts to avoid his touch. "Because he's to marry another? But surely you didn't think he would ever marry you, pet. Seymours don't bind themselves to those with dark magic. I must have misunderstood. I thought you merely meant to use him for pleasure, but this appears to be something of far deeper feeling. At least on your part. Dyfed has clearly found another that he prefers far more."

"Don't speak of him!"

And then Cadmaran made the mistake of laughing again.

Desdemona had never been good at being at anyone's mercy, though it had happened so seldom in her life, and only because of her father, that she could count the events on one hand. She had been spoiled and cosseted and treated even from childhood as someone both fearsome and dangerous. What was more, she had never been abandoned by anyone she loved, save her father, and had never loved someone as she loved Dyfed. The humiliation of being tied up like an animal was terrible and the fear of knowing that she was helpless against Cadmaran was terrible, but the pain of knowing that she might lose Dyfed to another was unbearable.

The pain welled up and mixed with the fury and fear, and Desdemona opened her mouth and emitted a wrathful sound that would have given an Irish banshee pause. It was an unearthly scream that shook the entire chamber, causing the tapestries to lose their moorings and dangle at odd angles and plates, cups, and candlesticks to clatter about on the table. The crystal glasses out of which they'd been drinking shattered altogether.

She screamed and writhed against her bonds until her body ached and her voice was raw. And all the while Cadmaran's laughter filled her ears, and visions of Dyfed in the arms of another twisted through her heart. The pain became unbearable and she wept, and then, at last, exhausted, she lay still and silent.

Cadmaran petted her hair again and said, "There, now. You've worn yourself out, and need to rest. I've prepared a

special chamber for you to reside in until you've come to
your senses and remembered who you are, and who it is you
belong to. It is a dark and quiet place, my dear, where you
shall be able to reflect upon your deviousness in complete
peace. I feel quite certain that it won't take long for you to
repent your many sins."

"The beast," she whispered. "You can't manage it without me."

"I don't mean to," he told her. "The *athanc* will have free
rein to do as it pleases now, and without a mistress to guide
it"—he smiled widely—"I fully expect that it will."

Eighteen

She was fast asleep, Kian realized as he gazed down at Loris's still form. Deeply, wearily slumbering. He had hoped she might yet be awake, but she'd clearly gotten out of the habit of waiting for someone—for Liw—to come to her at night. And as much as he wanted to, he couldn't bring himself to wake her.

He wasn't even supposed to be here. Malachi had delivered Kian to his town house but an hour past and informed him that they would be coming soon—Dyfed, Niclas, and Malachi himself—to discuss all that they'd discovered. There was so little time to accomplish so very much that sneaking into Lord Perham's grand town house not only was dangerous but also could risk defeating the very reason for Kian's presence in London.

But he'd had to come, despite the small amount of time he had, despite the danger. He'd heard her calling him—her *unoliaeth*—these many nights. Across the distance her heart had reached toward him, until Kian had felt nearly maddened with a matching desire.

The moon, shining through the tall window through which he'd come, cast light across her slumbering form.

She was more beautiful than his memories had told him. Her hair had been cut, but to delightful effect. The gold in her tresses glowed beneath the moonlight, causing the soft mass of curls that fell loose about her shoulders to look like satin. Slowly, silently, he bent and took one gleaming curl between two fingers, rubbing. It was cool and soft and light—so much lighter than it had been at Tylluan. All of her was lighter. She had lost weight in London, he realized with a pang of guilt, and looked so much more delicate than she had only weeks earlier. And fragile.

She'd been unhappy, Malachi had said. And distressed, torn between what the Seymours and her grandfather wanted. Not certain what she wanted. And on top of all that was Kian's deception at Tylluan and the loss of someone who was dear to her. And what they had shared in her bed.

Aye, she needed rest. A few hours of peace and respite without being asked to do anything, for anyone. If Kian woke her he would send all her peace flying away. He'd do everything in his power to hold her, kiss her, even for the few brief moments the curse allowed.

But he wouldn't wake her. Rather, he would give her something to comfort and soothe, to make her slumbers far sweeter. He had done it before, when he had put her to sleep as Liw, though she'd never realized it.

Slowly, Kian lay beside her on the bed and, propping himself upon one elbow, gazed at Loris's face intently. He closed his eyes and concentrated, thinking of what she would wish to do more than anything in the world. Where she would wish to be. With tender care he wove a beautiful dream, and made a gift of it to her.

"Draceous Caslin," the Earl of Graymar said some time later as he settled more comfortably into his chair near the fire, "is the son of Darin Caslin, whom my father told me about some years before his death. We have never been in much communication with any of the Families outside Europe, but my father had had some dealings with Darin Caslin in the way of correspondence regarding a proposed business venture. It seems that Caslin wished to engage our ships for his importing and exporting business."

Here the earl paused to sip from the wine in his glass and look at the others assembled.

"The Caslin family," he went on, "made itself wealthy as traders, starting almost from the moment when the colonies were birthed. You can imagine the success they had in dealing with the natives, using their powers to at once defend themselves as well as to impress any who dared confront them. But that's neither here nor there," he said dismissively, waving his glass about. "The main point is that my father was never able to put aside his displeasure with the colonies for their act of disloyalty in desiring independence, and couldn't bring himself to agree to the bargain, despite the money it would have brought into the Seymour coffers. His brother, our uncle Declan, died at Camden, you know."

"And that was the last communication we know of between the two families," Niclas added. "How it is that Lord Llew came to be in contact with them is a mystery."

"However Cadmaran managed to establish relations," Dyfed put in, looking at his brother, "he was able to lure Caslin to Europe with the promise of a great deal of money. You'll recall that Desdemona told me of it when I spoke with her."

"Which is the part of the tale that I find particularly odd," Malachi said. "When my father was in correspondence with Darin Caslin he was given to understand that they were among the oldest and most prominent families in Boston. Extremely wealthy and seeking to increase that wealth."

"Gaining wealth has never been a problem for our kind," Kian murmured, gazing into the fire. "And neither has losing it. Only think of one of our own families here, the Theriots. Money pours through their fingers like water, and ever has."

They all nodded and murmured and drank from their glasses.

"But how is it that Draceous Caslin knows the ancient enchantment to bring an *athanc* in Wales back to life?" Kian asked. "Can they have such creatures in America?"

"Professor Seabolt says that these beasts wandered unrestrained all about the earth in the long-forgotten times," Dyfed said. "And even when our Families came here during the time of exile, they did not know immediately how to tether them. It took many years of trying different spells before the correct one was at last found. Once the beasts were put into slumber, it was assumed that no one would ever wish to rouse them again, for even the most evil among our forebears were afraid of the creatures and the destruction they wrought."

"So they failed to keep a good record of how to control the monsters," Kian said. "And generations thereafter didn't record the enchantments because the original remedies had been so poorly kept. Which was utterly foolish, considering how spells for other troubles were so carefully guarded."

"'Struth," Niclas agreed. "We've had far greater fortune in finding spells for repairing broken axes and causing arrows to multiply during battle than in getting rid of great beasts. But you mustn't lose heart, Kian. Professor Seabolt feels certain that having at last discovered the remedy for dragons and sea serpents, we're nearing the right manuscript that will give us the answer."

Kian sighed and turned to look out at the dimly lit room, his gaze wandering over the fading paint and shabby furnishings. This was the town home he had inherited from his father, only just fashionable enough to be acceptable for a member of the *ton*, but far, far away from what Loris had experienced at either Niclas and Julia's home or Lord Perham's palatial dwelling. Loris had been here before, ten years earlier, when Malachi and Dyfed had brought her out of the Red Fox, but Kian doubted she remembered it much. She'd been in such a state of fear, then, and everything had happened so quickly. They'd only remained in London long enough for his wounds to heal sufficiently for them to travel back to Wales, and, given Malachi's gifts as a healer, that hadn't been long.

Since that time, as before, it had served well enough as a home for three bachelors making brief visits to Town, but it wasn't anything near being suitable for a new bride. Dyfed hadn't even stayed in the place during this latest visit but had gone to stay with Malachi at Mervaille.

Mervaille would have been a pleasant dwelling to take her once they were wed, and Malachi would have enjoyed having Loris's company after Kian returned to Tylluan. Unfortunately, neither he nor Loris could pass Mervaille's gates, for no one who was cursed could enter the ancient Seymour dwellings. It was forbidden.

He would have to bring Loris here and pray that she might be able to work the same magic upon the place as she had done with Tylluan. She'd certainly have plenty of time to do so, once he'd returned to Wales.

A scratch fell on the door, and the next moment Abercraf, Niclas's own manservant, peered into the room. He and his wife, Jane, had been lent to Kian for the next few days.

"Everything has been made ready, my lord," Abercraf announced. "Shall I lay out your morning attire?"

"Thank you, Abercraf," Kian said. "You and Jane have already been awake far too long, making the house ready on such short notice. I'm deeply grateful. Go and seek your beds, and I shall be content to valet myself."

Abercraf's expression tightened. "That will not be necessary, my lord. You will find me ready to assist you whenever you require it." And then he departed.

Niclas laughed lightly. "Now you've insulted him," he said. "Abercraf has such tender feelings, you know. But you make an excellent observation, Cousin. It is late, or, rather, early, and we should all leave you in peace so that you have at least a few hours' rest before your meeting with Lord Perham."

They rose to depart. Malachi sent Niclas and Dyfed ahead so that he might speak with Kian alone.

"You know that I'll come to Perham's with you, if you wish," he said, his tone serious.

Kian regarded his older cousin closely. "I know, Malachi," he said. "I'm not afraid of the fellow. Loris has always been mine. I don't intend to let anyone take her from me. She alone has the power to bid me yes or no."

"All the same," Lord Graymar said, "speak with care. He's not one of our sympathetics. Yet."

"He will be," Kian said. "It will make Loris happy, and so he must be brought around to it."

"You don't know how stubborn Perham can be," Malachi warned. "You haven't met him yet."

"No, I haven't," Kian confessed, "but he can't be any more frightening than dealing with the Dewin Mawr. If I've been able to survive your fury, Malachi, I can survive anything."

Nineteen

The Earl of Perham received Kian's early morning visit with ill-disguised displeasure. Having been ushered into that man's study, Kian at last had some idea of what it must be like to be the person sitting on the other side of his desk when he was in a foul mood.

"I had thought you to be in Wales, Lord Tylluan," said His Lordship as Kian approached. "We had no warning of your coming. Loris said nothing of it to me, nor any of your kin."

"I scarce knew that I would be coming to London, myself, sir," Kian replied honestly. "The decision was made on very short notice."

"I see," the earl said, his tone filled with disapproval. "I confess to being surprised at your boldness in coming to visit me. You do not intend to see Loris while you're here, I assume."

Kian regarded the other man steadily, trying to see any resemblance between him and Loris. The eyes were the same, but there was precious little else of a physical nature. Still, there was something about the older man's bearing and blunt manner that put Kian in mind of Loris. Especially when she was displeased.

"I'm sorry to disappoint you, my lord, and I don't wish to appear ill-mannered, but I do indeed intend to see her. Whether you allow it—though I hope you will—or not."

Lord Perham looked mildly surprised but recovered quickly.

"I cannot think it wise, sir. Though I know you've been as a brother to her these many years, and despite the gratitude I feel for what your family has done for my granddaughter, I'm sure it's been made known to you that the Seymour connection has had an unfortunate effect on her reputation. A reputation, sir, which cannot bear much more strain."

"Speaking as someone whose reputation has been through the fire more than once and still come out intact, if not enhanced, my lord," said Kian, "I respectfully disagree. But the fact that your granddaughter's standing in society seems, to you, to be rather frail is partly why I've come. Also because I've been given to understand that Loris has been distressed, and I cannot allow that to continue."

Lord Perham's eyebrows snapped downward. "*You* cannot allow—"

"Because I love her," Kian went on. "And have loved her for many years. My twin, Dyfed, has been as Loris's brother. I have not. To be quite honest, I'm not certain what I have been, save a thorn in her side, but we have never been as mere siblings to each other."

Lord Perham frowned at Kian—rather glared—and said, "Then you are the one that your brother meant—before a crowd of onlookers, no less—when he stated that Loris is spoken for."

Kian nodded. "I am, sir."

"But Loris herself has said nothing to me of this. Indeed, she has scarce mentioned you at all, Lord Tylluan."

Kian wasn't surprised. What could she have told her grandfather about him that wouldn't have been alarming? She could scarce tell Perham about the *unoliaeth* or the curse or their constant arguing. Still, the knowledge hurt a little. Perhaps more than a little.

"Although," Lord Perham went on more thoughtfully, "there have been moments when she's made mention of you in passing. Rather oddly, I must say. I have wondered at it."

"Oddly, sir?" Kian repeated. "In what way?"

"Almost as if she's not aware of it," Lord Perham explained. "She said your name when she meant something else and, when asked what she meant, couldn't remember the mistake. One afternoon not long ago she remarked on how beautiful her Kian at Tylluan was. She had meant to say 'garden' and hadn't realized she'd said your name instead. We had a good laugh over the mistake. I didn't tell her of the other times she'd made the same slip. I didn't think it necessary, and put it down to the strain of her first Season, and of being in London again after so many years." Lord Perham shook his head. "I don't know why I'm telling you this. I suppose you'll think it strengthens your case, but I have no intention of letting you, or any Seymour, take Loris away from me."

"I understand precisely how you feel, my lord," Kian told him. "For I don't intend to let her be taken from me, either. And because I love her, I've no desire to take her away from anyone. Certainly not a grandfather whom she loves very much. But what we wish is really neither here nor there, is it, my lord? Should we not discover what Loris wants?"

Loris's eyes drifted open to find that daylight was already streaming through the window curtains. The morning, she realized with alarm, must be nearly gone, and her grandfather must have been obliged to take his breakfast without her.

She'd had a wonderful night's sleep, such as she'd not had since coming to London, and the weariness that had shadowed her for so many days was gone. And her dreams . . . she could scarce remember having pleasanter ones. Kian had been with her again, and all the loneliness and longing that she'd suffered since leaving Tylluan had vanished. He'd touched her and there'd been no pain. His arms had come about her and his lips had caressed her own, and there had been no stinging or burning. Only blissful pleasure, as she'd shared with him once before. Loris sighed happily just thinking of it.

And then she turned her head and saw the flower lying on the pillow beside her.

"What's this?" she murmured, pushing onto one elbow and picking the flower up. It was a rose, from one of the bushes in her grandfather's gardens. And—she looked at it more closely—there were a few long, light blond strands of hair clinging to it.

The bedchamber door opened and Elen entered, carefully balancing a large tray.

"Oh, miss, you're awake at last!" the girl said excitedly, and set the tray on a nearby table. "I've brought you some breakfast, for I knew you'd wish to get dressed right away and make yourself ready."

Loris pushed into a sitting position. "What's happened, Elen?"

The servant's face was glowing with pleasure as she neared the bed. "He's *come*, Miss Loris. The master. He's below, talking with His Lordship, the earl."

Loris felt as if all the breath had been forced out of her body by a mighty blow. "Kian?" she whispered faintly. "He's come? He's here?"

Elen nodded. "Yes! And looking so fine, miss, dressed like a real gentleman. Just like Lord Graymar."

Loris wasn't paying attention. She had just remembered what the girl had said.

"He's with my grandfather, Elen?" she asked. "Alone?"

Again, Elen nodded.

"Oh dear," Loris said, and threw the bedcovers aside. "I'll forgo breakfast this morning, Elen. Help me get dressed. We have to hurry."

"What *Loris* wants?" Lord Perham repeated. "This is the second time in as many days that a Seymour has proposed letting a young female of birth and fortune decide what she wants. What the devil is the matter with you people? Have you no sense at all?"

Kian settled back in his chair more comfortably. "I often wonder the same thing," he said. "But surely you've realized that Loris isn't like other young women of the *ton*. She will strive mightily to please you, because she loves you, but if you try to force her to your will you may lose her altogether. Because she knows that Tylluan belongs to her and that its doors are open to her at any time. And that if she calls to me, I'll come to her. You could try to control her by locking her away on one of your vast estates, but it would do no good, my lord. I would be able to find and free her, and take her home." He tented the tips of his fingers together and gazed at the other man directly. "What you must decide, my lord, is whether you wish to lose your granddaughter just as you lost your daughter."

Lord Perham winced as if Kian had struck him, and Kian sat forward.

"I apologize, sir," he said, "but I shouldn't speak in so bold a manner if the matter wasn't so urgent. You will not be able to hold Loris by keeping her from me. She will only become desperately unhappy, more as each day passes. We must be together."

Lord Perham shook his head. "I've only just found my granddaughter after years of searching. I can't let her go so soon."

Kian sighed and wondered how he could possibly reassure the older man. His fears were understandable, of course, but at the same time irrational. He was willing to promote a marriage between Loris and Tauron, perhaps assuming that he could control the chess-loving viscount more fully. It was the same need that Loris had for controlling her own life. Perhaps, Kian thought with a touch of aggravation, it ran in their blood.

"I'm not going to take her away forever," he said at last. "Only home, to Tylluan. We will visit at Cumberland as often as you will have us. Tylluan's doors will always be opened to you. I shall give you your own gate key, if you like."

Lord Perham continued to look wretched. Kian cast his mind about, considering what would make an elderly man who'd lost almost everyone who mattered to him feel better about giving his only grandchild away in marriage.

"We will . . . ahem . . . name our firstborn son after you," Kian offered.

Lord Perham lifted his head.

"And let you name our second-born."

The earl looked at him.

Kian smiled. "And the third-born?" He had no idea whether he and Loris would ever have children. The curse might never be lifted to allow them to make the attempt. But the other man was looking curiously intrigued by the offer.

The study door flew open, and both of them turned. Kian was on his feet before Loris started toward him.

"Loris, I—" The rest of the words were knocked out of him as she leaped onto him.

Kian staggered back, his arms folding about her. Her own arms circled his neck, hugging him tight, and her face pressed into his skin.

"Why didn't you wake me last night?" she asked. He felt something wet against his cheek and knew she was crying.

"You were so weary," he murmured, smiling into the softness of her hair. "I didn't want to wake you."

"Last night?" Lord Perham repeated. "What's this?"

Neither Loris nor Kian heard him.

"But I told Malachi I wanted to see you," Loris said. Pulling back, she lifted her face to look at him. Her cheeks were damp. "That I had to speak with you."

"That's why I've come," he said, his gaze moving over her lovely countenance. He had been starved for the sight of her, the sound and feel of her. He knew he shouldn't kiss her in front of her grandfather, but did anyway, and Loris kissed him in turn. But only briefly and then, aware that the burning would start soon, Kian let her go. "I wanted to speak with your grandfather first."

"Lord Tylluan," Perham said more sternly. "Did you see my granddaughter last night?"

Kian glanced at him. "Only for a few minutes, my lord. Nothing happened."

"The dream was wonderful," she told Kian, smiling, though her eyes were still wet with tears. "And I saw the flower. Thank you."

"You're welcome," he murmured. "I hoped you'd be pleased."

"I was," she said. "I am. Is everything all right at Tylluan? Have you made any progress with the troubles? I've been so worried."

"Everything is fine," he promised. "The servants miss you terribly, of course. I've kept your garden in good order. I think you'll be happy when you come home."

"Oh, good," she whispered, and looked as if she truly might begin to cry in earnest. From gladness, he hoped. "I can't wait to see it. And everyone there."

He lifted a hand to stoke a bit of moisture from beneath her eyes. "Don't cry, my love. Everything will be well."

"You stole into my home?" Lord Perham said angrily. "You dared to enter my granddaughter's bedroom—while she was asleep?"

"It's all right, Grandfather," Loris said, still looking at Kian. "He used to come to me in the night often at Tylluan. And I loved him. That's part of what I wanted you to know, Kian. I don't think of Liw so much any longer. When I do remember, it's your face I see, not his."

"Loris, what the devil are you talking about?" her grandfather thundered.

"Please, sir," she said, looking at him at last. "Please let me finish saying what I've come to say. I meant to do it privately, but I think perhaps this is even better, for I hope it will help you to understand. You see, I was very angry with Kian when I left Tylluan, because he had deceived me for many years."

"*Deceived* you?" Lord Perham repeated in an icy tone.

Kian glanced at him. "Yes, I did. Because I was unutterably selfish."

"But that's not so," Loris countered. "Or not entirely. Kian, you gave me something wonderful during those years. A confidant, and a friend. I've asked myself, as I've considered all that we shared, whether you ever once took advantage of my trust or used my confidences against me. It's true that there were times when you argued your own case to me as Liw, but there were just as many nights when you took my side over Kian's—over yours." She moved nearer, gazing into his eyes. "If you gave me the choice of going back, of taking Liw out of my life or having him stay, exactly as he was, knowing that it was you all the time . . . I wouldn't change anything. I'm glad you deceived me, strange as that sounds. I'm so very glad that I know that part of you that was Liw. When I get lonely for him, if I ever do, I'll know where to find him."

Kian searched her dark eyes and saw that nothing was hidden. His heart squeezed painfully in his chest at what he did see. Reaching down, he took both her hands and lifted them to his lips, kissing each gently, one after the other.

"Thank you," he murmured. "It's far more than I deserve."

"You were right about something else, Kian," she told him. "I haven't been happy apart from you. I haven't felt whole almost from the moment I left Tylluan. I don't know if I've come yet to believe in the *unoliaeth*. I don't even know if I truly love you. I don't understand my feelings at all, save that I don't wish to live my life apart from you. I thought, at first, that I'd simply come back to Tylluan and we would go on as we were before, and all would be well." She smiled up at him and shook her head. "But that isn't possible now, is it?"

"No," he said gently. "Not now."

"No, of course not, because my grandfather would be terribly unhappy. Would you not, my lord?" She looked fondly at Lord Perham.

The older man's expression softened beneath her appeal. "I'm afraid that's so, my dear."

"And society would gossip terribly," Loris went on. "I suppose both our reputations would be ruined, for it's one thing if a nobody from London's docks serves as house-keeper to a nobleman, but something altogether different if she's the granddaughter of an earl. I've learned a great deal about the ways of the *ton* since coming to London."

"Clearly," Kian agreed, the pace of his heart growing quickly as each moment passed. He hoped he knew where she was leading with her conversation. It could only be destiny—as the *unoliaeth* was—if they had both come to this room with the same purpose in mind.

"And the thing is," she said, "that I know we shall always argue, Kian, and exasperate each other beyond words. I don't suppose we could ever change ourselves enough to alter that. But"—she looked at him hopefully—"you've told me that you love me—"

"I do love you," he said quickly.

"—and I know you *do* believe in the *unoliaeth*—"

"Yes. Always."

"—and despite the curse, which surely we can find a way to undo, if we both put our minds to it—"

"Very likely."

"—I thought, perhaps, that you might consider marrying me. Because my grandfather would like it," she pressed on nervously before Kian could so much as react, "for he's been trying to find an appropriate young gentleman in the hope that I would consider him, and of course he'd not want me returning to Tylluan to live with you unless we were wed. And I believe Malachi and the Seymours would like it. And if you think that you would like it, then it is what I wish above all things."

She fell silent then and watched Kian with wide eyes, looking terrified. His eyes began to fill, and he blinked to clear them. He bit his lip, hard, to gain control of his voice. He held out a hand, and Loris set her own in it.

"If you would be my wife, Loris McClendon," he said rather unsteadily, "I would count myself the most fortunate man on earth. It has been my dream from the moment I set sight on you." He swallowed and cleared his throat, then looked at Lord Perham. "In truth, Loris, that was my very purpose in first speaking with your grandfather. I had hoped to gain his consent, so that I might ask you to honor me with your hand in marriage." Turning back to her, he squeezed her hand and smiled. "But you did it far better and more sweetly than I ever could have done."

Loris let out the breath she'd clearly been holding. She squeezed his hand, too, and said, "Thank goodness, then. It's settled."

Kian wished he might kiss her; instead, as the seconds ticked away, he knew that the touch of their hands must come to an end.

He released her, and she moved away to hug her grandfather, who was standing as stiff as a rod of implacable iron.

"Is it not the best possible outcome, Grandfather?" she asked, pressing against him. "I shall be safely wed and my reputation restored. You'll not have to worry over it any longer. And you'll come to Tylluan and stay with us for as long as you please, and I'll take such wonderful care of you. We'll play chess every evening before the fire in the great hall, and Kian will show you the best places for fishing and hunting. Our cook will learn how to prepare all your favorite dishes, and Kian keeps a very good cellar of wines and spirits. Our life at Tylluan isn't as grand as what you're used to," she said, pulling away to look up at him, "but you'll come to love it as dearly as I do, I'm certain."

Lord Perham didn't look pleased, Kian thought, watching the man. Not by any stretch of the imagination. But he gazed into Loris's face for a long, silent moment and then looked at Kian.

"I'm sure I shall, my dear," Perham said. "It appears that being Lady Tylluan will suit you very well, and so, of course, I shall be pleased. The announcement will be made tomorrow night, at your come-out ball. I assume that meets with your approval, Lord Tylluan?"

Kian nodded in assent.

"There are certain matters which I should appreciate having explained, however," said Lord Perham, setting Loris away from him and moving to sit in his chair once more, looking imperious and imposing. "Just what is a *unoliaeth*? And what's all this about a curse?"

Kian and Loris exchanged glances.

"He should know before we marry," she said. "It's only fair that he know about the people he'll soon be related to. And when the curse is lifted and we have children . . ."

Kian understood what she meant. Their offspring might inherit unnerving magical powers, especially as their father would one day be *Dewin Mawr*. Lord Perham should be forewarned that his future namesakes would require a great deal of understanding.

Kian took note, as well, that Loris had said "when" the curse was lifted, not "if." The knowledge warmed him considerably, so much that he was willing to undertake the daunting task of explaining everything to His Lordship. Kian could always erase the earl's memory of the conversation if it didn't go well, but doubted it would come to that. Loris had clearly learned how to handle the gentleman, and her grandfather's love for her would open the door to his becoming one of their sympathetics.

Kian pulled up a chair for Loris and placed her in it, then sat in the chair beside her. "I realize it's quite early in the morning, sir," he began, "but if you happen to have something rather strong at hand to fortify you, it might not be a bad idea to have Loris fetch you a glass of it."

Twenty

The wedding, made possible by the special license Lord Perham easily procured, took place two days after Loris's come-out ball. It came off very well, despite having such a short time to buy proper wedding clothes and make arrangements, and was just what both Loris and Kian liked: The ceremony was sensible, brief, and to the point. Best of all, in Kian's opinion, at least, it was binding. For better or worse and whether she liked it or not, Loris was his. She was bound to him now not merely by the *unoliaeth* but also by the laws of England.

His wife. He'd waited too many years to be able to call her that. He said the word repeatedly in their private carriage as they made their way to Lord Perham's home to celebrate a wedding breakfast, saying such things as, "Are you comfortable, Wife?" and, "Shall I open the window a bit, Wife?" until Loris looked ready to strangle him.

Directly after the ceremony she was obliged to comfort her grandfather. Lord Perham had been shaken by the revelations that Kian and Loris, and later Malachi, Dyfed, and Niclas, when they had been urgently summoned to the earl's town house, had made. It had taken hours of Malachi's more detailed explanations, along with Niclas's comforting and consoling manner, for His Lordship to at last accept who and what the Seymours were and to understand the grave responsibility of that knowledge. Especially for his granddaughter, once she had wed into the Seymour clan, and for his future grandchildren. He had given them his vow of silence.

Still, the man had been far from pleased. But if Lord Perham had retained any doubts following the wedding, Loris's serene assurances had wiped them away completely. She knew who she belonged to, and that was sufficient for Lord Perham.

The *ton* seemed to have accepted the news of the union with more ease than anyone expected, as well. Not that there hadn't been tremendous surprise when the announcement of the betrothal and imminent wedding had been made at Loris's ball. But, all in all, the gossip that passed about Town the following day was positive and pleased. Kian supposed there were those who would watch to either see or hear whether the new Lady Tylluan had a child within nine months' time, but there was little they could do about that, save wait for the months to pass and the truth to make itself evident.

It was late afternoon by the time they were able to escape the well-wishers at the wedding breakfast. When they finally arrived at their town house, Kian escorted a weary Loris into the parlor to pour her a glass of sherry.

"I apologize for the state of the place," he said as she fell into a chair with a sigh of relief. "Niclas was kind enough to have it opened and cleaned, and to lend us the services of some of his servants while we're here. You shall have free rein to do what you please with it during what remains of the Season. There are funds enough. Spend what you like setting everything to rights. Make a proper showplace of it. I daresay we'll spend several weeks a year in London, now that you've grown used to it."

She accepted the glass he handed her and didn't blink an eye when, with the flick of a hand, he set the fireplace alight.

"I shall be glad to do as you ask," she told him, looking about at the shabby room. "I confess the house looks just as

I remember it from so many years ago—perhaps a bit more tired. But I fear it will take more than a few days to make any great change, apart from a thorough cleaning, and we'll be going home soon. Won't we?"

He cast a smile at her as he poured himself a glass of whiskey and lied, "Quite soon. Yes."

"Tomorrow?" she asked hopefully. "I shall have to make certain that everything is packed this evening, then."

"Not tomorrow," he said. "Tomorrow we will parade ourselves about Town. I shall take you shopping and buy you some pretty things, and in the evening we'll attend the theater, so that the *ton* can have a good, long look at us."

"The day after, then?"

"Perhaps."

She gazed at him steadily, waiting until he had settled himself in an opposite chair, before saying, "You gave me your promise, Kian, that you'd not keep me from returning to Tylluan."

He fashioned his expression into one of innocence. "I gave you that promise before the Guardians, did I not? Do you think I would risk making a false vow before such witnesses? I'm pleased that you like the bracelet I brought from Tylluan. It looked very well with your dress today."

A circle of gleaming rubies adorned Loris's wrist, and Kian was pleased to see her gaze at them with affection. She looked especially lovely in her wedding dress, composed of pale green satin with delicate gold trim on the sleeves and bodice.

"I do love the bracelet, Kian," she said. "Have I thanked you for the gift of it yet? I believe I forgot to do so at the ball. But we were terribly distracted that night with the announcement."

"Indeed we were," he agreed. "And there is no need to thank me. The jewels are yours, as are the rest of what belonged to my mother, apart from those that she set aside for Dyfed. I suppose Desdemona Caslin will be wearing those particular pieces soon." He sighed aloud and took a long drink. "I'm glad this day is over."

She was silent, and he looked at her.

"What are you thinking, Loris?"

"Of the curse," she said ruefully. "It's been ten years, Kian. We may spend another ten trying to find the way to lift it. It isn't a pleasant thought on one's wedding night." She looked away, raising her glass to sip from it.

No, it wasn't, Kian agreed silently. Despite the fact that they were wed, their relationship wouldn't change in any remarkable way, certainly not physically. They'd no longer have the time they had once enjoyed when he'd come to her as Liw.

"We'll find the solution, Loris," he said. "Once the troubles have been dealt with I'll devote myself to nothing else. And when the curse is gone, I vow upon my life that I shall love you as no other woman has ever been loved. I'll do everything possible to make you happy."

"I know you will," she whispered, gazing into the fire. "There's always been something inside me . . ." She stopped, her brows drawing together slightly in thought. "Since that night at the Red Fox. In the alley. And later, when you gambled for me against Gregor Foss. It seems rather foolish now. Perhaps it was magic, or the *unoliaeth*. But there was a feeling that grew up in me as you spoke, though I thought you quite mad. A hopefulness. For the first time since my father had died. And it's never left me. Despite everything, over all these years, and all that's happened between us." She lifted a hand to lightly touch the place over her breast where her heart lay. The gleaming band of Welsh gold that he'd placed upon her finger hours earlier shone in the firelight at the movement. "It's still here," she said, and looked at him. "Do you think, Kian, that it might be love?"

He clenched his free hand to keep it from shaking. "Don't you know, Loris?" he asked, his voice not quite as steady as he might wish it to be.

She shook her head. "It's not like any other feeling I've had for anyone else," she told him. "I can't identify it. I loved my parents and Ffinian in one way, and Dyfed in another. I always told myself that what I felt for you was only aggravation or anger or even fury. But I don't know what this other emotion is, save that it's grown much stronger since I left Tylluan. When I saw you standing in my grandfather's study, I knew a joy so strong that I couldn't help but weep with happiness. I felt whole again, and I knew everything would be all right, because you would make it so." She looked at him once more. "But is that love?"

He had to swallow before his voice would work. "I hope so."

"Is it what you feel for me?" she asked.

"What I feel for you," he said, setting his glass aside and rising to his feet, "is a madness that often threatens to overwhelm me. Every moment when you were gone from Tylluan I felt the loss. It was empty, all of it. I longed for you to come home," he said, holding a hand out to her. Loris put her own glass down and set her fingers into his open palm. His hand closed and gently tugged her upward, to stand before him. "If you had suddenly walked into the room where I was and railed at me, I would have been content. But I have always been glad of your fury, for it has had beneath it the passion that I dream of hearing in your voice when your heart has at last become mine." Slowly, he drew her nearer. "And there's something more that you bring to life in me," he said.

"What?"

"Frustration," he replied, and lifted one hand to cradle her cheek. "Because I can't do more than this"—he kissed her tenderly but briefly—"without giving you pain. And because I don't know when the day, or night, will come when I can touch you and impart only pleasure."

She held his gaze and then, very slowly, lifted her hand and stroked his cheek with her fingertips. It was the simplest of caresses, and yet it sent a shiver of delight coursing through Kian's entire body.

"Perhaps we'll find another path to pleasure," she murmured, pulling him down to meet her kiss. "One to keep us sane until the curse is gone."

The cook whom Niclas had lent Kian prepared a special dinner in honor of the newly married couple's first night together as man and wife. Malachi had earlier sent over several bottles of the best wine in Mervaille's cellars, including some French champagne that Kian and Loris drank as they lingered over the excellent meal. All in all, it was a pleasant end to an eventful day.

Kian escorted Loris to her bedchamber afterward with the intention of doing nothing more, regretfully, than kissing her and bidding her a good night's slumber. He didn't dare cross the room's threshold, lest he do something that might unintentionally cause her pain. Still, he thought as they neared the door, it was a damnable way to end their wedding night.

But Loris turned to him when they came to a stop and, before Kian could open his mouth, set her hands upon his chest and said, "I took the liberty of laying something special out on your bed before we went down for dinner. Give me a few minutes to change, as well, before you join me." Then she went up on her toes and kissed him lightly and disappeared inside her door.

Kian stood where he was for a long moment, staring at the closed door and wondering whether Loris wasn't laboring under the false idea that marriage had somehow changed the way the curse worked. But no. She knew that far more than a mere ceremony must take place before the Guardians lifted the blight that kept them from physically coming together. Still, she had anticipated him coming to her for some purpose, and Kian, both intrigued and pleased, moved toward his bedchamber door to fulfill her bidding.

Twenty-one

The delicate gown and robe that Julia had presented Loris with that morning before the wedding fit perfectly. Or, at least, she believed it did. Elen, who had helped Loris to don the thin, lacy garment, assured her that there was no other way to put it on, and Loris decided she must be right. If she tried to put the cream-colored satin on the other way, most of the front of her would be entirely exposed, and the gown was already revealing enough as it was.

When will he come? she wondered, looking toward the closed door that connected their chambers. Elen had departed immediately after helping Loris don the fragile outfit and relieve her hair from the tight arrangement it had been put in for the wedding. It had been brushed out and left undone, and then the grinning servant girl had gone.

Loris looked about the room to make certain all was ready. Earlier she had dimmed the oil lamps, leaving the room lit only by the fire and a few flickering candles. The bedcovers had been turned down and the pillows fluffed in anticipation. She cast a glance toward the large bed, wondering if perhaps it looked more obvious than inviting. Kian would probably laugh at her, but perhaps, she thought, that wouldn't be such a bad thing. A dose of his teasing just now might be the very best remedy for putting her foolish nerves in order.

A soft knock came on the adjoining door, and Loris stiffened. Turning, she watched as it opened to reveal Kian standing on the other side, garbed in the men's royal blue silk robe that Julia had also given Loris, explaining that it was a gift for Kian that would be far better given by his wife than a female cousin-in-law. There was a matching pair of silk trousers, which Kian had donned, and slippers, which he had not. Kian stood barefoot, his hair loose and falling about his shoulders, gazing down at himself with plain amusement.

"I feel like some kind of Eastern potentate," he said. "Where the devil did you get these?"

Loris flushed with embarrassment. "They're supposed to be all the rage," she said. "At least, that's what I've been told. Are they not comfortable? They look wonderful on you." Which was true, for she thought he looked marvelously handsome and fine in such a half-dressed state. His chest, partly revealed by the robe, was bare, showing smooth, golden skin. Loris pressed her hands together and strove to swallow down her nerves.

It didn't help, for he was looking at her now.

"Loris," he murmured, moving a few steps toward her. "You're . . . beautiful. I . . ." He shut his eyes briefly and gave a slight shake of his head. "I shouldn't come in. You know that we can't—"

Loris hurried across the room and shut the adjoining door, closing him in.

"I've been looking at this room more carefully," she said quickly, her voice a touch too high-pitched. "It's not so awful as you made it sound earlier. Some new paint and curtains will make it look very well. The carpet is still good, and the furniture can easily be repaired. Do you recall how long I labored to sew all the little tears in the upholstery at Tylluan?"

"Loris—"

"Do you truly like what I'm wearing?" she asked, taking his arm and pulling him farther into the room. "Julia gave it to me as a wedding gift. I confess," she said, coming to a stop and looking down at herself, "that it seemed rather naughty at first, but then it occurred to me that you've seen me in far less." She swallowed again, her face heating, unable to so much as look at him. "At least once."

"Loris," he said again, setting his hands on her arms and drawing her closer. "You not only look beautiful, but very alluring. If I could stay with you the night, I'd be the happiest man alive, just to be able to remove this delightful outfit ribbon by ribbon. I'm going to dream of doing so until the curse is lifted, I imagine."

She lifted her gaze to look at him. "I dream, too," she whispered. "Of that night. Of that one time we had together. Every night since, I've dreamed of it."

"As have I," he murmured. "But until the curse is lifted, dreaming is all we can do. You can feel the pain of my touch already, can you not?" He pulled his hands away.

Loris lifted her own and very deliberately pushed away the edges of the silk robe Kian wore. She placed both palms flat against the bare skin of his chest and gazed into his eyes. "Your touch gives me pain, that's true," she said. "But one thing we've never considered, never asked, is whether mine gives pain to you. You've never complained of the burning, even when I have."

He stared at her for a moment, then lowered his gaze to her hands.

"Does it?" she asked.

He lifted his head, shaking it. When their eyes met, she could see that his were beginning to fill with understanding.

"I've never touched you very much or for long," she said. "But it seems to me that the curse doesn't work both ways. You're not feeling anything yet, are you?" She moved her hands over him in a purposeful caress that made Kian suck in a sudden breath. "A tingling pain? A burning?"

"No." His voice was strained. "It just feels . . . very good."

She smiled. "You've always been the one to do all the touching. Now, I think, it's my turn."

Kian's breathing was unsteady now. "It sounds delightful," he managed. "But it's hardly fair to you."

Her answer was to slide her hands up to the shoulders of the robe and slowly slip it down his arms.

"You touched me that night," she said. "I scarce had a chance to do the same. But that was because I felt so uncertain when I thought you were Liw." Her gaze was fixed on his bare chest. She had seen him like this before, at Tylluan, when he'd removed his shirt while undertaking difficult labor. Loris had always thought him beautiful to gaze upon, but never more so than this moment. She ran her hands lightly over the smooth, muscled skin. He was warm and silky beneath her touch, and the groan of pleasure he bit back only increased the sense of delight she felt. "I'm not uncertain with you, Kian," she murmured. "I want to touch you. Everywhere. Just as you touched me."

Leaning forward, she set her lips to his bare flesh. Kian shivered and groaned again, which only encouraged her to continue. Her hands kept moving over him, caressing his shoulders and arms, his waist and stomach, and her tongue explored the hollows of his neck. His breathing had grown so harsh that it made her feel wonderfully powerful.

"No, you can't touch me," she said when his hands came to rest on her waist. "Remember?" Loris pulled away. "This is my night to do all the touching. Come and lie down."

Kian didn't resist as she led him to the bed or when she bade him to lie down in the middle. He did talk to himself as Loris divested herself of both her robe and gown, saying, "I'm dreaming. I know I am. But if I wake up now I'll bash my head against the wall."

"Does this feel like a dream?" she asked, crawling up onto the bed beside him. She set a hand against his cheek and slowly brought her mouth down to kiss his. Against his lips she whispered, "We're husband and wife now. We can do as we please. Isn't that so?"

"Anything," he agreed huskily. "Everything." He gazed longingly at her naked figure, and his hands curled into fists. "But I'm not sure whether this is pleasure . . . or torture."

She chuckled. "Both."

Rising to her knees, she moved lower and ran her hands boldly over the silk trousers that he still wore. He shuddered when her fingers slid lightly—so lightly—over his swollen manhood, and his hips arched upward, off the mattress. Loris smiled and set her fingers to the ties, then to ridding him of the garment altogether.

"Oh, Kian," she said, gazing down at him, seeing him completely for the very first time. "You're so beautiful." Her hand touched his bare thigh, and he sucked in a taut breath. "So very beautiful."

Kian found the words, and the expression on her lovely face, to be more than a little heartening. He had lain naked with countless women in his youth and had always felt sure of his own charms. But he had never before truly cared what women thought of him before or wished to please one so greatly. Loris was his wife, for now and forever. That she should find him pleasing, even beautiful, was deeply reassuring.

She kissed him again, touching his lips with her tongue until they parted to let her have her way. He moaned beneath the sensual onslaught and was obliged to grab fistfuls of the bedcovers to keep from reaching for her. Then Loris drew away, and her lips slid to one of his ears, the movement sending her hair sliding in a silken caress across his face. It seemed impossible, suddenly, for him to draw in enough breath.

"The thing you don't know about me," she murmured against the sensitive skin of his ear, causing him to shiver with pleasure, "is that I'm not quite so ignorant about the ways of men and women as you may think." Her tongue touched the tip of his lobe, teasing, and then moved upward to follow the line of curves in the shell and, finally, dipped lightly into the ear itself. The sensation wrought a sound from him that Kian had never heard before. He'd always been the master of his sexual experiences before now, save perhaps for his first youthful encounter. Loris made him feel as helpless as a callow youth.

"You see," she said, pushing up to look down at him, "during those years when I lived at the Red Fox, I was often obliged to fetch and carry for the upstairs girls. Especially when the serving girls were busy." She moved lower, rubbing herself against him as she went. "And especially when the upstairs girls were too busy with customers to do for themselves."

Her lips traversed the soft skin of his neck, then moved lower so that her tongue could trace a line over each of his nipples before licking down the length of his stomach. She kissed his belly before looking up at him again.

"I was the one who took up the trays of wine and ale and food. And other things that they needed, as well." Her hand slid lower, and her fingers closed gently about his manhood, squeezing gently. "I saw all kinds of things. Learned all kinds of things."

Kian bit back a moan and shook his head, wondering if he was going to survive until daylight. This was definitely the closest thing to torture that he'd ever undergone.

Her fingers slid up and down, though not, he was aware enough to note, with any kind of familiarity. As pleasurable as her touch was, it was unskilled—which only made it more delightful, for she touched everywhere, seeking, learning the length and feel of him.

"You're trembling," she murmured, sounding fascinated by what she was doing to him. "Your whole body is tense. That's just how I felt, too, when you touched me. Completely beneath your power, but it was so wonderful."

She slid lower, until her lips hovered just over his hardened member. He could feel her breath on him and shut his eyes tightly. He was going to die of pleasure in another moment. He knew it.

"*Loris.*" The word came out as a plea.

"Yes, love," she murmured, and moved even closer. He could almost feel her lips on him. Her tongue. The loud groan he'd been trying to hold back escaped, and he clenched his teeth in a vain attempt to silence it.

Her lips brushed against his skin, once, twice, and the pleasure exploded. He shouted out, unable to stop himself, while his body helplessly writhed and shuddered in ecstasy. Loris had moved to press herself against him, holding tightly. Afterward, when he lay still, save for the harsh breathing that still wracked his body, she kissed him, his face and lips, and murmured words of love.

Several long minutes passed before Kian came to himself, before his eyes focused to find Loris gazing down at him—smiling—and looking very pleased with herself. In fact, it seemed very much as if she'd like to try doing it all over again. Kian understood the feeling. Next to the pleasure of sexual release itself was knowing that one had the power to impart that pleasure—especially to someone one loved. He'd experienced it, too, when he'd given Loris the same gift months ago. But another such episode just now would surely kill him off for good, Kian thought. It had also been the single most exceptional physical experience of his life; he wanted a little time to savor it.

"Thank you," he said, though the words sounded woefully foolish to his ears. Still, Loris smiled a little more widely. "I love you." He reached up a hand to touch her face. "I wish that I might—"

She stopped him with a kiss. "There's no need to say it," she murmured. "I understand. I know the curse will be lifted soon, Kian. Until then, we shall have to share what pleasure we can."

He frowned. "It isn't fair to you that I should receive all the pleasure, and you none."

"I suppose you'll have to find ways to make it up to me, then," she told him. "By being an exemplary husband in every way. For example"—she ran a finger in a lazy circle over a small area of his chest—"you might promise to take me home to Tylluan the day after tomorrow."

"Loris—"

"Or," she continued, "you might tell me the truth about the troubles there. The full truth, whether you believe it will needlessly worry me or not."

He didn't want to do either, for if she knew the truth about the troubles she'd be even unhappier when she found herself left behind in London. But considering the gift she'd just given him, it seemed impossible to Kian not to give something back in turn.

And so, first having tucked her comfortably and warmly beneath the sheets, and having taken a moment to clean both himself and the bed, Kian lay beside her, careful not to touch, and told her about the *athanc*.

Twenty-two

$\mathscr{I}$ really don't think you should, Kian," Loris murmured, though not very convincingly. "I'm sure it's terribly expensive."

"That's no concern of yours," Kian replied. "I would have bought you jewelry as a wedding present, but you appear to be drowning in a wealth of it already. Besides," he added, watching her carefully, "you like it."

Which was stating the matter lightly, he thought with a small measure of amusement. Loris's cinnamon gaze was fixed on the delicate music box as if it was the most wonderful, glorious object she'd ever beheld. She was entranced by the music and the tiny figures that either waltzed in pairs across a shining ballroom floor or sat as a group of musicians, playing upon miniature instruments.

He wasn't surprised by her childlike wonder; she had never had toys as a young girl and had owned so few pretty things in her life—certainly not at Tylluan, where their lives had been ruled far more by function than form—that even the simplest objects filled her with delight.

Kian was going to make certain, starting now, that the feeling never dimmed.

With a nod at the shopkeeper the music box was gently

closed and whisked away, boxed and wrapped and presented to Loris with an elegant bow. She held it in an awestruck silence until Kian pried her fingers free and handed it to the footman to hold, along with the other parcels they'd collected during the afternoon.

Kian had never realized how entertaining buying things for one's wife could be, but Loris was terribly easy to please. She might have grown used to being showered with jewels and fancy gowns and the various other necessities that a lady of fashion required, but none of Kian's relatives had thought to give her the simple items that a young woman who'd never had a childhood desired.

He'd taken her into a toy shop—the first she'd ever seen in her life—and let her wander for as long as she pleased. They'd left with a china doll made and clothed in the image of Catherine the Great and a miniature version of Noah's ark, complete with several pairs of brightly painted animals. These, Loris told him, weren't really for her but for any future children they might one day have. Kian pretended agreement but privately imagined Loris putting a pond into the garden so that she could play with her new toy.

Then he'd taken her to a bookshop, for she loved to read, particularly poetry, and had already gone through all the volumes in the library at Tylluan. She had actually kissed him upon leaving the store, bubbling over with happiness at possessing the latest works by Shelley and Keats.

They had proceeded onward, purchasing a pretty new lamp for her bedchamber at Tylluan, a handsome tea service painted with a delicate pattern of red and yellow roses to replace the chipped and mismatched set at the castle, and a bottle of French perfume that smelled of honeysuckle.

The music box had been the last purchase of the long day, and he had purposefully saved it for last. Loris had protested spending money on the other items they'd bought, regardless of how pleased she'd been when the buying had been done, but her protests regarding the music box were so weak that he knew how much she wanted it.

"Thank you," she said as he settled beside her in the carriage, and took his hand in both of hers to squeeze it. "I shall cherish it forever. It's so very beautiful. Everything—all that you bought for me today—is wonderful."

"I'm glad if I've pleased you."

"But now," she went on, "this must be the end of it. We cannot continue spending funds that are sorely needed at Tylluan. I feel terribly guilty, already, thinking of the sheep that must be replaced, and the repairs to the estate."

"It's all right, Loris," he assured her, turning his fingers to twine them with hers. "We will only be wed this once, and God alone knows when I shall next get you to London. I want the occasion to be memorable."

She smiled in a way that made his heart turn over. "I shall never forget this day, Kian, or your generosity. And the theater tonight—and then home to Tylluan before week's end. Nothing could mar my happiness."

Her contented mood continued throughout the day and evening, and later, at the theater, when they were the object of a great deal of attention from the other theatergoers. So many men who had admired Loris before her abrupt marriage came by the Seymours' box to offer their congratulations and kiss her hand that Kian began to grow irate.

"How can you bear it?" he asked Niclas, who stood at the back of the box during the intermission, watching the parade of men courting attendance on both of their wives. "Look at the way that fellow's gazing at Julia. I should think you'd want to bash his brains out."

Niclas sighed aloud. "You have not been wed long, Cousin, and haven't yet learned that there is nothing so charming and alluring as a beautiful woman who is married. Only wait until the first ball that you and Lady Tylluan attend and you can scarce manage to get a dance with your own wife. This is nothing by comparison."

"Devil take it, I don't want anyone else dancing with Loris. Certainly none of these fops. And I don't want them slobbering all over her hand, either. I'm going to—"

A hand came out from between the heavy velvet curtains at the back of the box to clamp down on Kian's arm, holding him back. The next moment a body emerged to join the hand, perfectly attired and groomed.

"Ah, there you are, *cfender*," Lord Graymar said pleasantly. "Have I managed to stop a murder in the nick of time?"

"Several," Kian told him. "Look at those vultures, slavering over Loris and Julia."

"Quite understandable," the earl replied. "A man must count himself a fool if he could not admire your lovely wives. Good evening, Niclas. I see that your head is a good deal more level than our young cousin's."

"He's but newly married," Niclas replied. "I believe we must forbear with him until he realizes that threatening to relieve his wife's many admirers of their manhood won't particularly endear him to her."

"True," Malachi said sagely. "Very true. The ladies do love to be admired, and a jealous husband spoils the pleasure. Apart from that, I fear Kian won't have the time to fulfill his current desires, understandable as they may be. I must speak with you both. Urgently."

The curtains parted once more, and Tauron Cadmaran appeared. His expression was tense and impatient.

"You've found them," he said. "Good. I was beginning to worry."

Kian felt the muscles along the back of his shoulder tighten. "What are you doing here? If you think you're going to join that pack of mongrels drooling on my wife's hand you can think again."

"Dear heavens," said Malachi, "must you insist upon using such descriptive phrases regarding your wife's hand? It conjures up the most repulsive pictures, and she appears to be perfectly content and, what's more, quite dry. Now, come out into the hall and we shall find a place more private for discussion."

"I'm not leaving Loris alone with these . . . these . . ."

"I'll stay," Niclas promised, relaxing against the wall and folding his arms across his chest. "I perceive that this has something more to do with Kian than with me. You go with Malachi and Brecmont"—he nodded Kian toward the curtains—"and find out what's amiss, and tell me afterward. I promise that no harm will come to Lady Tylluan."

Kian cast a glance back to where Loris was laughing at something that one of her admirers had said to her.

"But—"

"The first man who crosses the line goes over the balcony," Niclas promised, and Kian comforted himself with the fact that his muscular cousin wouldn't have any difficulty performing such a task.

"Over the balcony," Kian repeated firmly.

"Straight over," Niclas vowed.

"Very well then." Kian tugged at the ends of his sleeves and, casting a last worried glance back at Loris, followed Lord Graymar through the curtains.

When Loris awoke the following afternoon, having slept through the morning, it was to find a folded letter lying on the pillow beside her head, with a single rose atop.

She smiled, supposing it to be a love letter from Kian, and gently fingered the flower's aromatic pink petals. What a wonderful day, and night, yesterday had been. She had enjoyed shopping before, but Kian made it far more pleasant, and the theater—she'd spent so much time talking with all the guests who made their way into the Seymours' box that she could scarce remember what had been performed on the stage.

And then afterward, in the early morning hours, when Kian had brought her home and escorted her up the stairs to her bedchamber . . . She smiled, thinking of it. He had sent Elen to bed and acted as Loris's maid, slowly undressing her, bit by bit, careful not to touch too long, but long enough to leave her skin tingling with pleasure. He had kissed her as well, more deeply, a bit longer, always withdrawing before the pain could start. Then he'd let her undress him and they had taken turns touching. Loris hadn't reached that same mindless pleasure that he had taken her to once before, that she took him to again, but it had been far more than she had hoped they would be able to share, at least until the curse was gone.

And then Kian had lain beside Loris, as he had done the night before, and watched until she'd fallen to sleep. She had tried to remain awake, too, but the activities of the long day and night had left her too weary to compete with a man who appeared not to be tired at all. The last thing she remembered was the feeling of his lips upon the top of her head, against her hair, and his voice, low and murmuring, telling her that he loved her. Loris had slid into contented and pleasant dreams and slept.

A knock came at the door and Jane's capped head peeked in. "Ah, you're awake, my lady," she said pleasantly, pushing her way into the room. "I have a tray for you, fresh from the kitchen, with a nice hot cup of chocolate and some warm tarts. I hope you had a pleasant sleep?" She set the tray on the bed as Loris sat upright.

"I did, thank you." Loris pushed her unbraided hair out of her face before picking up the rose and letter and setting them on the tray. "Is Lord Tylluan yet abed?" She nodded toward the adjoining door.

Jane's expression dimmed slightly, and she gave her attention to arranging the small plates on the tray. "Oh no, my lady. His Lordship has already left. He was on his way quite early this morning."

"Was he?" Loris tilted her head questioningly. "That's odd. I know he must have been weary from such a late evening. Did he say where he was going?" She imagined he had made arrangements to meet Niclas or Dyfed or even Lord Graymar for a ride in the park.

"I'm afraid I can't say, my lady," Jane replied, and a look of unease crossed her features.

Loris looked at the maid more closely. "Can't say because you don't know," Loris queried, "or because you've been told not to?"

Jane looked up at Loris at last, and she knew the answer without having to hear it.

"Where has he gone, Jane?"

The other woman straightened and took a step away from the bed. She shook her head regretfully.

"I'm sorry, Lady Tylluan. I'm not to say. Shall I come back in a few minutes to help you dress?"

Loris calmed herself. It wouldn't be right to make Jane uncomfortable simply for fulfilling Kian's instructions.

"Yes. Take this tray away and then come back to me at once. I wish to dress as soon as possible."

She snatched up the missive Kian had left for her as Jane moved to do her bidding, and was reading it before the maid closed the chamber door.

Darling Loris, it began, *I know that you'll be very angry when you know that I've returned to Tylluan—*

"Tylluan!"

She stared at the letter in disbelief, her heart pounding painfully in her chest. He'd gone home without her?

—but I want you to know as well that I've not broken my promise to you. I said that I would not stop you from returning to Tylluan, and I'll not. Yet I cannot bring you back with me, for the danger is greater than before. It seems that Desdemona Caslin no longer controls the creature, which leads me to believe that Cadmaran has discovered her defection. I fear greatly for her safety, even for her life. Without her help the athanc has been left to run wild. An express arrived from Horas, detailing the damage that has been done in my absence. The beast has attacked with greater ferocity, and some of the villagers were fortunate to get away with their lives. Many have been wounded. I must leave at once to stop our troubles once and for all.

But there is more. Tauron Cadmaran ran into Dyfed some hours following our wedding and, in an attempt to congratulate him upon his brother's marriage, made the foolish error of relating Lord Llew's intention to wed, a fact he had only just discovered, himself, having had word from Lord Llew about the impending nuptials. Dyfed asked to whom—

"Oh no," she murmured. "Oh, Dyfed."

—and Tauron unwittingly told him that it was Miss Caslin. Dyfed flew into a rage and left for Tylluan at once, vowing that he would get her away from Lord Llew by force, if he must. Of course, he must be stopped and brought to his senses. I'll be fortunate if I manage to arrive only shortly before he does, even with the use of quick traveling. I imagine Dyfed's ridden without stopping since leaving the day before yesterday, save to change horses, and I fear that he may head straight for Llew.

"He'll be tired," Loris said, thinking with dismay of what Morcar Cadmaran might do to Dyfed, who would be defenseless against so powerful a wizard. "And out of his senses over that woman. You've got to find a way to stop him."

Malachi goes with me, and is bringing Tauron along as well. Brecmont has offered to help us thwart his cousin in the matter of the athanc, *also to help us get Miss Caslin out of Castle Llew, if Malachi will in turn help him to escape England and the Cadmarans. I have my doubts about Tauron's trustworthiness, for it's rare that our kind will betray a family member, but Malachi believes him and I'm too pressed just now to argue the matter. I confess it will be far easier for Brecmont to gain access to Llew, and to garner Morcar's trust.*

"You're going to be surprised by Tauron," Loris told him, despite his inability to hear the words. "He's not like his cousin."

Stay in London, Loris. If you find a way to come to Tylluan, I'll not turn you away. I told you that it belongs to you, that you have the right to come and go as you please, and that is even more true now than when I said the words. But don't come. I cannot worry about the beast and you all at once. I'll return for you as soon as the athanc *has been dealt with.*

Stay in London and enjoy what's left of the Season. Redecorate the town house and make a home of it. Niclas and Julia and your grandfather remain to take care of you and to lend you company. I'll come as soon as I can.

She lowered the letter to her lap and gazed at the fire across the room.

Now what should she do? He had asked her, again, and in a manner that she found difficult to ignore, to stay in London and let him deal with the troubles alone. An obedient wife would . . . well, obey. But Loris wasn't particularly obedient, and her heart told her that she should be at Tylluan. Kian *needed* her.

She was still pondering the problem when Jane returned to help her dress and afterward as she paced in the study, letter in hand. She had reread it several times through, at turns worried and irate.

How could Kian have left without telling her, without even waking her to explain himself and say good-bye? She recalled Malachi and Tauron appearing unexpectedly at the theater and realized that Kian must have known well before they returned home that he would be sneaking out. He hadn't wanted her to argue, of course, or to talk him into taking her with him. So he'd been a coward and left a letter and departed before dawn to make certain she'd be fully asleep.

Stay in London . . . I cannot worry about the beast and you all at once.

"Drat the man," she murmured. "Why must he make the appeal so difficult to counter? I feel guilty even thinking of going."

She heard raised voices in the entryway and stopped pacing. Abercraf's voice was easily recognizable, but the other one—quite loud and excited—was only vaguely familiar. Moving to open the door, she found Abercraf in the hallway, engaged in a heated conversation with a somewhat portly, older gentleman.

"I must speak to Lord Tylluan at once," the gentleman insisted. "At once!"

"Professor Seabolt." Loris moved into the hall. "Sir, what can be the matter?"

"Lady Tylluan!" Professor Seabolt said with relief, removing his hat and shoving it into Abercraf's hands. "My lady, forgive this unexpected visit, but I must speak with your husband. Please tell me if he's at home or, if not, where he's gone to."

"I'm sorry, Professor," she said. "Kian has returned to Tylluan. His brother and Lord Graymar have gone as well."

She did not know Professor Seabolt well, having only met him twice, once at her come-out ball and once at her wedding breakfast, but she recognized his complete despair all the same.

"Please come in"—she motioned toward the study's open doorway—"and Abercraf will bring some tea. Perhaps there's something I can do to help?"

"No, no." He shook his head. "I have to get word to them, somehow. And as quickly as possible. It is a matter most urgent, my lady."

Loris took a step nearer and looked at him very closely.

"You've found the enchantment for the *athanc,* have you not, sir?"

"Yes, at last!" he said eagerly. "But how am I to get it to them if they've all gone?" He paused a moment, then said, "Niclas Seymour! He's not gone away, has he?"

"I do not know," she said, and when the professor turned about to take his hat from Abercraf, who was hovering in the background, she set a hand on his arm and held him fast. "But I'll not let you try to find him until you've given me the remedy, first."

Professor Seabolt looked at her with impatience. "But it cannot wait, Lady Tylluan. I must make certain the news is on its way at once."

"It will be," she vowed. "Come into the study," she said firmly, getting a good grip on him and guiding him inside

the room. "Abercraf, please arrange for a hack and ask Jane
to fetch my cloak and gloves. And send a message to your
master, asking him to be so good as to forbear going out for
the afternoon. Pray God he hasn't already done so."

She pushed the professor into the room and stood in the
doorway to keep him from getting back out.

"And if he has gone out," she went on, glancing at Abercraf, who stood ready to spring away at once, "tell Julia that
he must be fetched back at all costs, and as quickly as possible. Professor Seabolt and I will be leaving for Cousin
Niclas's town house in but a few minutes."

Twenty-three

$\mathcal{N}$iclas Seymour stared at his excited guests, who were both speaking to him at the same time, for a patient moment, then raised his hands to silence them.

"Sit down," he instructed, pointing to the chairs in his study. "And calm yourselves. Your emotions are both shouting at me so loudly that I can't hear a word either of you is saying above the tumult. Sit. Now."

His tone invited no discussion. Loris and Professor Seabolt sat.

"Professor Seabolt has found the solution, Cousin Niclas," Loris said before the professor could catch his breath. "The enchantment that will take care of the *athanc*. We must find a way to get it to Kian as quickly as possible."

Niclas's eyebrows rose and he settled into a chair opposite them.

"Tell me, then," he said.

The professor explained, with many interjections by Loris, and when they had finished Niclas nodded and said, very calmly, "You're right, of course. This information must be gotten to Kian right away." He considered the matter for a moment in silence, holding his hands up again when Loris and Professor Seabolt tried to speak.

"What we need is a mystic," Niclas said at last. "One of our kind who can communicate immediately through the spirits with Malachi, who can then pass the information to Kian. Unfortunately, the only mystic within a hundred miles happens to be my infant daughter, who is far too young to be of any help. It's odd, is it not?" he asked. "Mystics are such bewildering souls. Always underfoot and wreaking havoc when you don't need them, but never around when you do." He sighed.

"Niclas," Loris began, to be silenced once more.

"I understand that you wish to go to Tylluan, my dear, but I cannot allow it. I promised Kian, upon my honor, that I'd neither take you nor lend you my aid. I cannot go back on my word."

The words stunned her. "He made you promise not to help me?" Loris repeated, feeling as if all the breath had just been knocked out of her. "Not even to simply *help* me?"

"It makes perfectly good sense," Niclas said. "Tylluan is terribly unsafe just now. I don't want you to be there, either."

Loris knew that well enough, but for Kian to have asked his relatives not to lend her their aid felt as if he'd somehow not been playing fair. As if he'd cheated on the promise he'd given her. Especially after she'd told him that it was precisely what she feared—being dependent on others, because she wouldn't know how to return to Tylluan on her own.

"But I can help," she argued. "You need a woman for the enchantment to work."

By his expression Loris could tell that she had managed to take Niclas by surprise, which was quite an achievement, considering his particular gift.

"My dear girl," he said, astonishment written on his features, "do you truly believe that Kian would ever allow you to be the one to aid in this task? That *any* of us would allow it?"

"Yes," she said, "I do. Because I would insist upon it."

"Which is precisely why you're not returning to Tylluan until the *athanc* is gone. Now," he said, rising, "you must forgive me for sending you out of the room. Julia is waiting to visit with you, and I must speak privately with the professor. I want to make certain that everything is written down in detail before I leave."

"I shall go with you," the professor said, "if you'll have me. I should love nothing better than seeing one of the ancient creatures."

"Excellent," Niclas replied. "Go home and pack, then. I'll make arrangements and arrive there as quickly as possible. With any luck we'll be out of London well before nightfall. We'll have to ride almost straight through to Tylluan, stopping only long enough to change horses and take the merest rest and sustenance that is absolutely required. I apologize that I don't have the gift of quick traveling, but, as you know, it is limited strictly to those among us who are extraordinary wizards."

"It wouldn't be necessary," said the professor. "I am more than ready for the undertaking, sir."

Loris had had enough. She stood and flung her hands out.

"And what of me?" she demanded. "I'm simply to sit here and wait and do nothing?"

Niclas gave her a level look. "I perceive by your emotions that you intend to find a way to journey to Tylluan on your own," he said, stating the matter quite correctly. "I cannot stop you from pursuing so fruitless a course, but I can try to discourage you. You will not be able to find anyone who will take you to Wales, Loris. None of the servants I've lent you will escort you without my permission, and I'm sure you appreciate how embarrassing it would be to put any of your new acquaintances among the *ton* to the trouble of having to politely decline such a request."

"My grandfather—"

"Has been informed of the dangers at Tylluan," Niclas said curtly, "and is in complete agreement that you must be kept safely away. Now, come," Niclas said more gently, and reached to take her hands in his. "Be reasonable, Loris. Go and stay with your grandfather until Kian comes for you. Or come and stay with Julia. She's missed having you here with us, and would be more than happy to have your company again. It won't be for very long, now that Professor Seabolt has found the remedy. Kian will come to fetch you the very moment the *athanc* is gone. A week or so, no longer than that."

Loris pulled her hands free and glared at him. "You can divine what my feelings are, Cousin Niclas, so I'll not alarm Professor Seabolt by expressing them aloud. I shall find a way to get to Wales. I *will*," she insisted when Niclas smiled as if to humor her. "You may think me as childish or foolish or strong-willed as you please, but I know—despite not being of your kind—I know that I *must* be the one to help Kian."

Niclas looked at Professor Seabolt. "Is there a provision in the enchantment requiring that the woman involved be a loved one? Or a family member?"

The professor shook his head, casting a regretful glance at Loris. "No."

"But I must be there, nonetheless," she insisted. "I'm quite serious, Niclas. I shall find a way to get to Tylluan. Indeed, I might very well even beat you there."

It was a foolish challenge to make, and Loris regretted it the moment she made her good-byes to Julia and the children and left the house. Not that Loris hadn't meant what she'd told Niclas about getting to Wales, but she knew very well it would take her rather longer than it would him and the professor.

But she would get there, she thought firmly as she climbed into the hack and waited for Elen to join her. Even if it meant facing her worst fears.

But she had better do it now, before she lost courage. Or before her anger cooled and her wiser senses came to life.

Drawing in a breath, she steeled herself and tapped on the roof of the hired vehicle. The trap opened and the driver looked in, and Loris gave him the direction she wished to take. She was obliged to repeat it twice and then to tell him, quite firmly, that yes, she did indeed wish to be taken there. He looked at her as if she were mad and muttered something about women in general and the quality in particular, then nodded and closed the trap and changed course.

The Red Fox hadn't really changed much in ten years, but it still seemed very different to Loris. It was smaller, somehow. Less overwhelming. Or perhaps it only seemed thus because it was daylight or because Loris herself was taller and stronger and far more sure of herself.

She stood beside the hackney, staring at the tavern's dirty windows and heavy doors and at the worn sign swinging slowly back and forth in the breeze, and waited for the old fear to rise. It had always lived in her, since the day Ffinian had taken her out of London, but she'd been able to keep it pressed down, out of her daily thoughts. It only came to her when she remembered or if she considered what it would be like to go back—though she'd certainly prayed she never would.

But the fear wasn't inside her any longer. She tested herself, trying to see if it would rise, but it had gone away. Completely.

"We're not going to go in there, my lady," Elen whispered, her voice trembling almost as fiercely as her slender body. "Are we?"

"It's still too early for there to be many customers," Loris said. "If any. I shouldn't be surprised if everyone is yet asleep. You stay here with the carriage, Elen, and don't let the driver leave. I shall want to depart the moment I've finished my business here."

It was safe enough on the docks while it was daylight, especially early daylight. The dockworkers and sailors who passed might look curiously at the odd spectacle of a finely dressed lady standing in front of a disreputable tavern, but they left her in peace and went about their business. And those rougher individuals who would normally be of concern wouldn't come out until the sun had disappeared.

More important, she wasn't going to be here long enough for any trouble to occur. This business was going to be conducted quite quickly.

"I'll be back in fifteen minutes," she told the driver. "Wait here for me and keep an eye on my servant and I'll pay you three times your fare."

He gave her that look again—the one that said, clearly, that she was out of her senses—but nodded.

The front door would be locked. Loris went around the alleyway, to the kitchen, picking her way carefully through the filth in the gutters, and discovered that she was in luck. Not only was the kitchen door open, but there was steam coming out of it as well.

Peering into the darkness and blinking against the heat and moisture, she called, "Hello? Is anyone within?"

"We're not yet open," said a deep, grumbling voice. "Is it work you're looking for?"

Loris knew who that was, and what she felt was still far from the fear she'd expected. Anger, rage, fury. They all welled up at once and pushed her further on.

"I've not come for work, Mr. Goodbody," she said firmly, clearly, "but for something far different."

Her footsteps were loud on the dirty wooden floor as she made her way. He was sitting by the stove, upon which a pot sat boiling over a fire, and was clad in a filthy pair of pants and an equally filthy half-opened shirt that revealed far more of his hairy chest than Loris wished to see. His hair was all askew and his chin unshaved, and he was smoking a pipe and drinking from a tankard of ale. He blinked as Loris approached, and rose from the chair in which he'd been sitting, reading one of the gossip rags that were so frequently published in London.

"Do you not know me, Mr. Goodbody?" she asked. He was so much shorter than she had remembered. Loris towered over him now. But otherwise, he hadn't changed so very much in ten years. Perhaps his stomach was a bit bigger and his hair a bit thinner, but his hands looked just as capable of dealing blows as they had then.

His gaze moved over her slowly, taking in the elegant morning dress that Jane had helped Loris don, lingering on the reticule she held and her fine gloves and hat.

"No, miss, I'm afraid I don't—" He peered at her face more closely and at the color of her hair. "Loris?" he said slowly. "Is it you, girl?"

"You met my grandfather recently," she told him. "And sent me a number of letters informing me of the fact."

"Aye, and had no thanks for it," he muttered. "Well, well. Look at you, then. You've done well for yourself, I see. A lady, are you? 'Tis no wonder that you were so ill a serving girl, always sassing and talking back."

Her brows knit. "I was a mouse," she told him. "I was so terrified of you and Mrs. Goodbody that I scarce said a word. To anyone."

"If not for us you'd not have been reunited with that lord who came looking for you," he countered angrily. "Never a word did we say to give the old fellow a disgust of you. Not a word about those lads who took you off, wanting to keep you to themselves. And what did we get for our trouble?" he asked. "Nothing."

"One of those lads, as you say, is now my husband," she replied evenly. "And he is a baron. A nobleman. He and his brother and father treated me with nothing less than respect and kindness."

"And that would make you a baroness, eh? You, who have me and the missus to thank for your very life. We could have left you in the streets after your father died," he said, and threw up a hand dismissively. "And what do I get for it? Still nothing." He glared at her. "You wouldn't even be standing here if it weren't for us. You would have died out there. Or worse."

Loris gazed at him and knew that it was true. She hadn't liked being forced to live and serve at the Red Fox, but remembered vividly that the one thing she'd feared above any other was being sent away to fend for herself. Alone.

"Thank you, then," she said, "for giving me my life. But the price you asked for it was high. I don't forget that you made a slave of me, and treated me as such. After but a week here I lost count of the number of times you and Mrs. Goodbody struck me, and the hours I labored for you for a few mouthfuls of food and a blanket under the stairs. If we are to compare what each of us gained, sir, during the years that I lived beneath your hand, I believe the most we can say is that we are even."

He grumbled and turned away to stir the foul-smelling contents in the pot, sending even more steam into the already thick air.

"What is you want, then?" he asked. "I've a good deal to do before we open tonight, and 'tis clear you didn't come to exchange pleasantries."

"I need your help," she said simply. "I have to get to North Wales as quickly as possible, and I know that you can arrange that for me."

He laughed and cast a glance back at her. "Why don't you ask your fine nobleman to take you? Or is there some reason why you'd rather he not know? Going to meet a lover, are you?"

"I'm going to meet him," she said. "And my reasons for going are no business of yours. I want to get there in three days' time, or sooner, if possible. I don't mind about comfort or stopping for rest. I simply wish to get there alive and in one piece. Can it be done? Can you help me?"

"You'd need a proper carriage, unless you mean to ride a horse all the way—"

"Is that faster?" she asked.

He glanced at her again. "Might be," he said. "But I doubt you'd get far. Folks wouldn't like it, a woman riding such a distance that way. No, it won't do. You'll need the carriage, and a good man to drive it. Boys to change the horses, and a few reliable fellows for protection." Turning from the pot, he wiped his hands on a cloth and looked her up and down again. "Do you have money?"

"No," she said. "You'll need to arrange for that as well."

He laughed again, fully amused. "Then you'd best find someone else to lend you aid, my fine lady. I'm not footing the bill for your silly wanderings, baroness or no."

"Don't be a fool," she said irately. "You want to be paid for all your troubles, past and present, don't you? This is the only opportunity you'll have. Here." Reaching up, Loris took off her hat and pulled one of the diamond-encrusted combs from her hair, ignoring the curls that fell to her shoulder. She held the comb out to him. "You were always able to pawn goods faster than any man on the docks. This should bring in enough to get you started. Hire whatever and whoever you need, but I want to get started before nightfall, and I don't want to be disappointed in the men, the horses, or the equipage. Spend what you must," she said. "I'll bring more jewels when I return to make it worth your while. And if I arrive at Tylluan within three days or less, you'll be richly rewarded. I give you my word of honor that you'll not be disappointed."

Twenty-four

$\mathcal{A}$ meeting, you say? That's interesting." The Earl of Llew nodded thoughtfully. "Quite interesting. But why has Lord Graymar sent you to deliver this invitation to me, Cousin? I should think he would have found another messenger. And how the devil did you come to be in company with the man? I thought you were in London, enjoying the pleasures of the Season."

Tauron Cadmaran fingered the wineglass set before him on the table at which he and Lord Llew sat. "We met by accident in Shrewsbury," he said, artfully repeating the lie that he and the Earl of Graymar had crafted earlier. "We were lodging at the same inn. I was heading north in order to fetch our aunt Margad, so that she might be present in London with all the family—as you requested—when you bring your future bride to Town. You know how greatly she dislikes leaving Bradford, and she cannot abide journeying even a short distance without company. But no family gathering could be complete without Aunt Margad."

"I see," Lord Llew said. "That was good of you, Brecmont, but I had already made arrangements for our elderly aunt's travel. I'm fully aware of how greatly she hates to journey alone. Our cousin Morlan was to bring her."

Tauron did his best to look abashed. "I should have consulted you first, then. I had hoped to surprise her by my visit." He sighed. "But then I crossed paths with Graymar, and when he told me his reason for coming to Wales, I assured him that I should be glad to change the course of my travels and present his request to you myself. I knew you'd far rather that I come and deliver his message than be made to endure an encounter with one of the Seymours."

"Very true," Lord Llew agreed coolly. "That was well considered, Brecmont."

"We parted ways two days ago," Tauron continued, not letting his cousin's approval affect him. He couldn't risk relaxing in the presence of so powerful and cunning a wizard. "He should be at Tylluan by now."

"Yes," Lord Llew murmured. "I felt his power coming so near to Llew yesterday, and wondered at it. But now that you've come, I understand all."

"But surely you don't mean to actually meet with him," Tauron said, picking up a nearby decanter and reaching to refill his cousin's glass. "From what you've told me, the creature you've set loose is doing exactly as you wish. If Graymar must meet with you, then he must believe he hasn't the means to stop the beast, and it scarce makes sense for you to lend him your aid."

Lord Llew laughed and, with seeking fingers, found his glass and lifted it. "Nay, but it was for this very purpose that I set the creature free. I wanted to draw the lord of the Seymours here, where I might confront him face-to-face, and force him to challenge me. I knew that Lord Tylluan wouldn't be able to manage alone, and would in time have to call for his *Dewin Mawr*'s help." The earl drank deeply, then sighed with satisfaction. "And now he's here at last, and I have my chance to settle matters that should have been tended to long ago."

"Lord Graymar will not come to Llew," Tauron said. "He's not that foolish, to meet you where your powers will be multiplied."

"And he knows that I'll not meet him at Tylluan, a Seymour stronghold," the earl murmured. "But I believe he'll agree to a place neutral to us both, so that our powers will be equal—until the moment he challenges me. Which he will, once he realizes there's no other way to be rid of the *athanc*. There's a mountain not far from here that may suffice. Bryn Chwilen, it's called. It lies between the two properties, and will lend neither of us an advantage."

"Beetle Mountain, eh?" Tauron remarked.

Lord Llew sat forward. "I want you to act as my emissary, Brecmont, just as you've been his. I'm sorry to ask it of you, for I know you dislike the thought of being in company with Seymours any longer than you must, but I fear I must ask you to do this thing for me. You must journey to Tylluan first thing in the morn and offer the compromise to Lord Graymar."

"I shall be glad to do so," Tauron said. "It's an honor to perform any duty that you ask, my lord."

"You will be repaid tenfold for such loyalty, Cousin," Cadmaran vowed.

"There is no need," Tauron told him. "It is an honor, just as I've said. But if you would repay me, then perhaps you'd grant me the privilege of being acquainted with the future Countess of Llew. You've said nothing of her since I arrived, and I expected to be introduced to her at once."

"I should like nothing better than to make my darling Desdemona known to you," Lord Llew said, all politeness. "But I have vowed that no one will set sight on her beauty until I've brought her to London. You'd not wish to make the rest of the family jealous by being granted the boon of knowing her before they do, I'm sure."

"Of course not," Tauron acquiesced with a nod. "Though I confess to every anticipation. Desdemona," he repeated, as if trying the word on his tongue for the first time. "It's an unusual name, is it not? I don't know that I've ever heard it before."

Lord Llew fingered his glass, his smile inscrutable. "It means 'devil's daughter,'" he murmured. "I believe her father gave her the name with every good reason." The earl laughed lightly. "If not, she has certainly lived up to it. She is in truth the devil's own daughter," he said, his tone filled with pleasure, "and will make the Cadmarans very proud indeed."

"But we can't wait until tomorrow!" Dyfed shouted furiously. "Desdemona needs to be rescued at once. She told me that she's been locked away in darkness for over a week, and we cannot ask her to remain there longer." He ran both hands through his hair and gazed at the assembled with exasperation. "I promised her that I would have her safe away from Llew by now."

"We'll get her out, Dyfed," Kian said. "But we won't have a chance of doing so unless Cadmaran is far from Llew—far enough so that he'll not sense a trick. Miss Caslin will understand that better than you think. She's lived long enough with the man to know what his powers are within his own domain."

Dyfed sat down in the nearest chair and buried his face in his hands. "How shall I tell her?" he asked miserably. "What can I possibly say?"

"Kian's right," Malachi said, lounging comfortably in the chair opposite. "The girl will realize that it's best to wait until we can draw Cadmaran away. As unpleasant as spending another day in confinement and darkness must be, it would be far worse to risk being bested by Lord Llew. The one we must worry for is Brecmont." He nodded toward that man, who stood gazing into the fire. "He's going to be in grave danger when the Earl of Llew realizes what he's done."

"I don't care," Tauron murmured. "If not for me, Dyfed wouldn't have learned about Llew's plan to wed Miss Caslin, and nearly risked his life trying to save her without help. But we Cadmarans always seem to be making trouble, even when we don't realize it." He sighed.

"Now, now, don't fall into despair," Malachi said. "I shall send you abroad, just as I promised, and you'll have a new start far away from your unpleasant family. Somewhere on the Continent, perhaps, or even America. Now that the war is long over and matters are more amiably settled with the colonies, I hear that it's actually becoming somewhat civilized."

"And what of you, Malachi?" Kian asked. "Are you certain you'll be ready for whatever the Earl of Llew has planned? He's been trying to achieve a meeting with you for years, and I feel quite certain he doesn't wish to merely converse."

"Llew is a fool," Lord Graymar said. "And always has been. He knows what his powers are and assumes he can somehow force me to issue a challenge, simply because he himself would be so quick to do the same. But you may trust that I'm in no hurry to please the man. I should far rather lend you my aid in getting rid of the *athanc*."

Kian shook his head. "You came to help me find Dyfed and stop him from doing anything foolish, and to allow us a chance to set Desdemona Caslin free. Those are the only reasons you're here, *cfender*."

Malachi looked meaningfully at the long, deep scratches that covered Kian's hands and part of his face and remarked, "After last night's adventure, I should think you'd reconsider. I shall have to take the time to heal those marks before I return to London."

"Scars would be a small price to pay for what I learned last night," Kian said. "I was able to get closer than ever before, to grapple with it physically and hold it in my power for a few moments before it managed to break free. And I discovered something vitally important about the beast in the doing—it cannot change forms while it's held captive. The moment it got free it altered itself into liquid and slid beneath the ground, where I couldn't reach it. But it couldn't do so while I had my hands on it."

Dyfed lifted his head from his hands. "But it's ten times bigger than you, Kian, when it's full-grown," he said. "Or more. How is it that you were able to touch even a part of it without being killed?"

"Seren rode close enough so that I could leap at the beast," Kian said. "I got hold of one of its legs and cast a paralyzing spell which I hoped would affect the entire body. Unfortunately, only the leg and one arm were made useless. I confess I wish I had Cousin Niclas's superior strength, for then I might have held the monster long enough to cast the spell again."

"It's odd that you should say such a thing," Malachi remarked, idly rocking the glass he held so that the contents within swirled. "He'll be here soon. Tomorrow afternoon at the latest, I should think, if his horses can clear the mountain roads in good time. I do hope we're finished with all our various duties by then so that we can greet him properly."

They all stared at him in amazement and Malachi, feeling their questioning gazes, looked up from his contemplation of the tiny whirlpool he held. "I apologize. I should have told you before now, but we have been rather busy making plans to rescue Miss Caslin. I perceived Niclas's presence in Wales just two hours past. He seems to have been riding without rest, else he'd not have been able to cover such a distance in so little time."

"Niclas," Kian said with surprise. "Coming here? But that means he must have set out almost immediately after we did." He made a slow circle about the room, considering, and then his eyes widened as a new thought occurred to him. "He's bringing Loris," he said, panic rising. "But no." He gave himself a firm inward shake. "He gave me his word he'd not do so, and Niclas is as honorable as any man alive."

"That he is," Malachi agreed.

"Then why is he coming?" Tauron asked. "Is he alone?"

"I cannot tell if he has a mere mortal in company," Lord Graymar replied, "for I can only sense the movement of my own kind within the border of Wales. I also don't possess the power to divine his purpose in coming to Tylluan in such haste. But never fear," he said easily, smiling at each of them in turn. "We should find out soon enough. In the meantime, Dyfed had best use his gift to communicate with his lady love in order to inform her of the delay and reassure her of rescue, and Brecmont must hurry back to Llew with my answer before his cousin becomes suspicious."

Twenty-five

*A*re you sure he can't perceive us?" Dyfed asked, his voice so clipped it revealed his nerves. "What about the horses? He might feel their presence, even if he doesn't feel ours. If he knows we're here he'll have a perfectly good reason to take us captive—or worse. The Guardians don't look lightly on interlopers."

"They can't look very lightly on what Cadmaran's been doing to Miss Caslin, either," Kiam replied. "They cast their gazes upon all the exiled Families, not just those in Europe. She's one of us, and he's used her very ill. Apart from that, if Desdemona Caslin is your *unoliaeth,* you have every right to claim her. We aren't going to be punished for freeing her. I'm certain of it."

"But what about Llew?" Dyfed asked again. "He can't know we're here, else he might harm Desdemona. Or use her as a shield. Are you quite certain this enchantment of Malachi's is powerful enough to fool a wizard like Morcar Cadmaran?"

"Malachi's enchantments never fail," Kian said reassuringly. "Llew doesn't know we're here, else he'd already have sent his men out to secure us. Or come himself, more likely.

We need only wait until he's left, and then we can easily enter the castle and find your lady."

"We'll never get into the castle if you're wrong about his servants living beneath a spell," Dyfed argued. The horse he sat astride felt his rider's impatience and moved restlessly beneath him.

"I'm not wrong about the servants," Kian said. "Now be still, Dyfed. You know she's all right. She's told you so."

"She wants *out*."

"She will be," Kian murmured, steadying Seren in the trees among which they hid. "Llew should be leaving soon. Brecmont's been gone only a quarter of an hour, if that. It will take the earl a bit longer to make himself ready."

They were obliged to wait another hour, and then, as three o'clock neared, they saw him depart. The Earl of Llew rode out of his castle flanked by six of his men, three on either side, in a grand manner with banners flying, like a medieval lord heading out to battle.

"He'll have to leave his men at the foot of the mountain," Kian said, "and use the rapid traveling to meet Malachi in time. I should love to be there to see what transpires. We'll have just above an hour at best to get Miss Caslin out and as far away as possible."

"Then we'd better hurry," Dyfed said, and they dismounted.

Kian had no difficulty in dealing with either the guards or the gatekeepers—he simply put them to sleep. Without the Earl of Llew present to lend his power to the enchantment his people lived under, they were helpless in the face of another powerful wizard.

The eerie silence that Kian had experienced on his previous visit astonished Dyfed; he hadn't quite believed that it was as strange as his brother had told him.

"She's not in the castle proper," he said as they made their way through the inner bailey and toward the castle doors. "He's put her in the family crypt."

"Oh, my God," Kian uttered, horrified. "Why didn't you tell me this before?"

Dyfed cast him a curious look. "Would it have made a difference?"

"No, but—a crypt." Kian shuddered. "It makes sense, because she's a sorceress and he knew that she would be left powerless while confined with the dead. I just didn't realize that Cadmaran was quite that heartless. Where do we go?"

"It's behind the chapel," Dyfed said, then paused, in both motion and speech, listening. "Desdemona says there are dogs guarding it. We must be careful. She says these dogs are made of stone."

"Stone, are they?" Kian muttered, and fingered the side of his face that had so recently been scarred by the beast. "After dealing with the *athanc* these many weeks, stone dogs will be like taking a nap."

Several minutes later, having made their way through the gardens to the back of the bailey—with Kian having to stop to put several servants to sleep along the way—they found what appeared to be the crypt, a small stone building secured by ornate iron gates through which they could see a series of steps leading downward. On either side of the gates a giant stone dog stood sentry, with teeth bared and enormous fangs protruding from both the top and bottom of its jaw. They were far bigger than any real dogs might be, slightly taller than Kian and Dyfed, and covered in sculpted muscles rippling convincingly over their stone bodies.

"Miss Caslin clearly has a gift for understatement," Kian muttered.

"She did say to be careful," Dyfed reminded him. "Can you handle them?"

"We'll soon find out," Kian said, and drew in a long breath. "You'll have to go in alone to find her while I manage these brutes. As their purpose is to keep the tomb from being robbed, and as I don't know the enchantment to safely enter without being attacked, they'll likely come to life about the moment the gates are touched, which means you'll have to make a run for it. I'll place a spell of protection on you and have the gates already opened by the time you reach them."

"I'll be as quick as I can in getting her out," Dyfed promised.

"An excellent idea," Kian told him. "I believe they may be good practice for the *athanc*, after all."

It happened just as Kian predicted. Dyfed took off running, but as the gates unlocked and began to swing wide, the stone dogs quickly came to life—and leaped at him. They were just as quickly deflected, one after the other, so that they went tumbling away, but by the time Dyfed was over the threshold they had picked themselves up to charge at him again. Fortunately, the gates had already closed, and the beasts crashed against them with such force that Dyfed, who had nearly tumbled headlong down the stairs in the sudden darkness, almost thought they might give way. Turning, he saw the dogs' great, massive jaws chewing at the bars in order to get at him. Beyond them, standing in the sunlight, Kian met Dyfed's gaze and shouted, "Go!"

The giant dogs turned about at the sound of the new voice and threw themselves violently in Kian's direction. Dyfed had only a glimpse of his brother's determined face and of Kian's hands rising to cast some powerful spell before he turned and made his way down the stairs and into the darkness below.

The passage was narrow and the stairs made for much smaller feet; Dyfed was forced to place both hands against the cold stone walls on either side of him to steady himself. Outside he could hear the furious commotion the dogs made, growling and barking and lunging. The little building shook mightily and he knew that Kian had sent one of the brutes hard against the stones.

Desdemona, Dyfed called silently, and heard her reply, aloud, not far away: "I'm here, Dyfed! At the bottom."

He paused only long enough to reach into his pocket and remove a small white stone, which put forth a dim light, enough so that he could see his way.

"Here!" she cried, nearer now. "Hurry, please! I can't bear it!"

"I'm here, love," he said. He neared the bottom, and before his foot was upon the last step he saw her, lying upon a stone bench, bound in silver cords. Her pale, taut face was turned toward him, and the distress he saw written there sent rage flowing through his veins.

"My God, Desdemona." He was kneeling beside her in a moment.

It was icily cold in the depths of the crypt, and he knew firsthand how dark it had been before he'd come. She had been down here for days now, with only brief visits by Cadmaran and some of his servants to tend to her most basic needs. The Earl of Llew meant to keep her confined in this foul prison until she was ready to beg for his forgiveness and make an oath of obedience to him before the Guardians. Such an oath would be binding; Desdemona would become Lord Llew's slave.

Her cheek was cold when Dyfed set his hand to it.

"How do I get you out of these bonds?"

"You can't," she said, shaking her head. "Only an extraordinary wizard can break them. You must take me to your brother."

The building above shook again, and the sounds of snarling and barking became even more frenzied.

"I'll fetch Kian," Dyfed said. "He can perform the enchantment safely in here."

"No!" she said before Dyfed could rise. "Look about you, Dyfed. The dead are buried here. His magic will be useless. Even Cadmaran couldn't undo the bonds unless I was carried out."

"Grand," Dyfed muttered, casting a glance up to where the furious battle raged. "This is going to be interesting."

He stood, scooping her slight frame into his arms, and headed for the stairs.

Bryn Chwilen wasn't a very tall mountain, compared to those surrounding it. It was more of a large hill but at its topmost portion provided an excellent view of the valley beyond.

Malachi stood beside one of the few trees on the hill and gazed out at Glen Aur, the fine estate belonging to his uncle Ffinian's new wife, Lady Alice. To Malachi's right was Tylluan, rising up into the tall mountains where the castle lay, and to his left was the valley where, some miles farther on, Llew was situated. He could see neither Tylluan proper nor anything at all of Llew, and so he satisfied himself with looking at peaceful, serene Glen Aur and contemplated whether his wild and rascally uncle would be content there. Malachi supposed that Ffinian would be, because of Lady Alice. A man could always be content when he was with the woman he loved.

But Lord Graymar didn't have the luxury of thinking on such things now or of pining for what he had never known and never expected to know. Being the *Dewin Mawr* was a pressing, demanding duty. Kian was fortunate to have been fated for Loris almost from the moment of his birth: he might never have had the time to find a suitable wife otherwise.

Malachi sensed, rather than heard, when Morcar Cadmaran was approaching; like all extraordinary wizards, they both possessed the gift of moving with complete silence.

Malachi turned to greet his adversary, thinking back to the days when they had been boys. They hadn't precisely been friends, but they had at least been friendly on those few occasions when they met. The long feud that had continued between the Seymour and Cadmaran clans made it impossible for anything more to develop between them, and they had both known that they would one day assume the leading roles among their families. But Malachi could still recall long hours of merely being boys together, of caring far more about fishing and collecting insects and playing tricks on unsuspecting girls than about carrying on ancient insults.

"You've come," he said as the other man neared. "I'm glad. I hope you've been well."

The Earl of Llew smiled grimly. "Do you mean apart from the blindness, Malachi? Aye, other than that, I've been very well. And how is the great *Dewin Mawr*? Was your journey from London quite pleasant?"

Cadmaran had come alone, leaving his men at the foot of the hill. They were mere mortals, all of them, and useless in a fight against an extraordinary wizard. The Earl of Llew never employed magic mortals as servants, Malachi remembered, for he believed that mere mortals, being inferior, were more properly suited to be in service to those who were magic.

"It was very brief," Malachi replied honestly, struck anew by the other man's greater height and physical power. Unlike Seymours, the Cadmaran family had inherited the blood of giants, rather than elves, with the result that they tended to be quite large and daunting. And rather stupid as well. "I was obliged to make the journey in something of a hurry."

Cadmaran tilted his head. "Indeed? I can guess as to the reason. You've come about the *athanc,* have you not? At last."

"Not entirely," Malachi confessed. "I fear my cousin is yet too stubborn to accept my help. He's of the mind, you see, that he must face this challenge on his own, and prove that he is worthy to one day be *Dewin Mawr.*"

"Ah," Lord Llew uttered with clear satisfaction. "But you are far wiser than he, are you not, Malachi? You know that there will be no stopping the beast without my help."

"Kian is a capable wizard, Morcar," Lord Graymar replied coolly. "He may yet find the way on his own."

"He is certainly welcome to try," Cadmaran said, and with the staff he held felt for something to sit upon. His black hair had been left to grow long and, unbound, fluttered about his starkly handsome face. "The beast will continue to ravage the land and feed itself as best it can all the while."

Malachi had promised Kian an hour, at least, to get Desdemona Caslin safely out of Llew. Which meant that he must keep Lord Llew not only occupied but also unsuspicious. Fortunately, Cadmaran was as vain as he was powerful and loved to hear the sound of his own voice praising his own

cleverness and cunning. It had certainly been thus when
they'd been boys, and though they'd met but a few times
since becoming adults, Malachi was fairly certain that hadn't
changed.

"How is it that an American came to know about the ancient creatures of Europe?" he asked. "And, of far greater
importance, how did you discover he knew, and lure him
here to Wales to release the beast from its slumber?"

Lord Llew had settled himself comfortably on a large rock
and, looking very pleased with the questions, said, "I shall
tell you a little, if you wish to hear it. But it will not put off
forever the matter that we have come to discuss, Malachi,
though you may desire it. The *athanc* must be stopped, and
there is only one way that you can achieve that goal."

"Tell me about Draceous Caslin first," Malachi said. "And
about his daughter, Desdemona, who controls the creature."

"I should have thought your cousin, who believes himself
to be in love with my betrothed, would have already told you
a great deal about her," Morcar said, laughing lightly. "But I
shall gladly tell you all, for she is a wondrous female and an
admirable sorceress. Sit and be comfortable, Malachi, and I
will answer your questions before we come to an understanding. Or to something rather different."

It wasn't so much that the stone dogs were large and fero-
cious and determined to tear Kian into tiny bits that had
him sweating. It was the innumerable fighting men who insistently appeared from among the various garden path-
ways to attack him while he was already busy tossing the
dogs, by turns, into the air or against the building or up into
the trees. The Earl of Llew clearly had a large army at his
disposal, all mere mortals, fortunately, else Kian would
have found it far more difficult to make them insensible.
Between them and the dogs, however, his hands were sufficiently full, and Dyfed's voice in Kian's head telling him
that he must also somehow find a spare moment to free

Miss Caslin—from enchanted silver cords, no less— wasn't precisely welcome.

She knows the spell Cadmaran uses for turning the dogs back into stone, Dyfed told Kian in his silent speech. *Just get her unbound and she'll deal with the creatures and you can get back to the men.*

"That won't be quite as simple as you make it sound, *fy gefell*," Kian shouted back, loud enough so that Dyfed could hear him, using one hand to cast a spell on the latest wave of fighting men and the other to toss the dog nearest him as far into the garden as possible. Then he turned immediately to tend to its twin, which was actually ripping up chunks of earth in its frenzy to get at him. Kian used both hands to send it flying away, but the other dog had already recovered and was tearing its way through what remained of the shrubs with teeth bared.

Did he even *know* the spell for loosing silver cords? he wondered. It was another ancient enchantment that he'd heard of but never come across before. Cadmaran certainly seemed to prefer the odd, old ways to the new.

"I'm going to toss the dogs," Kian said, shouting again, "and take a moment to put up a shield that will stop them and the men. It won't last long—Llew is far too well protected against such enchantments. We'll have but seconds before they're through again." He paused to put more of Cadmaran's men to sleep—there was getting to be quite a pile of them—then to toss the dogs again. "Wait for me to tell you when," Kian instructed, "and then lay her down before me as quickly as you can."

It took a full minute of dealing with both the men and the dogs before the chance came for Kian to put up the shield; then, *"Come!"* he shouted, and readied himself to free Desdemona Caslin.

Dyfed threw the gates open and sprinted across the small clearing, laying the young woman on the ground as gently but quickly as he could.

The dogs were already throwing themselves against the shield, while half a dozen men armed with pistols appeared.

"Datod!" Kian shouted, and, *"Difetha!"*

Neither worked, and the shield was beginning to give way. One of the dogs had nearly pushed through and would quickly be upon them.

Lifting his hands again, he tried once more, *"Rhyddhau!"* and the silver cords slid away.

Desdemona Caslin came to her feet with a fury of sound and motion, unleashing all her anger and power just as the shield gave way. A sound came out of her—neither Kian nor Dyfed had ever heard anything like it—that was sufficient to put the fear of God into man and beast alike. With a flash of her hands she sent the dogs up into the air—not flinging them away but high up—and kept them there, twisting and growling and clawing helplessly.

"Carreg!" she shouted in that still-unearthly voice that shook the very ground, and the dogs immediately became stone once more, frozen into their twisted positions.

And then she dropped her hands—no, Kian thought as he watched in amazement, it wasn't merely dropping, it was more like slashing. The stone figures were hurled into the garden beyond, crashing to the ground and exploding into hundreds of tiny pieces. The force threw Kian and Dyfed and all of Cadmaran's men flat onto their backs, but Desdemona Caslin stood unaffected, her dark demeanor and scowling expression like that of a demon creature come out of the pit to vent her fury on any who dared cross her path.

Kian rose to his feet first and moved to help his brother.

"Hell hath no fury," Kian muttered, wiping bits of rubble from his sleeve. He would have done the same for Dyfed, but he had already pushed past his brother to gather Desdemona Caslin into his arms. Kian spent a brief moment staring at the clinging couple and wondered what his brother had gotten himself into, wishing to take such a woman as wife. But there wasn't more time to ponder the matter; Cadmaran's men were coming to their senses, too.

"We've got to get out of here," Kian said. "And across the border into Tylluan, where Llew can't touch Miss Caslin."

"I welcome a meeting with him," Desdemona said in a manner that made Kian's skin tingle. Dyfed, however, only gazed at the frightening female with adoration.

"Do you have the gift of levitation?" she asked, and in unison with Kian swept her hand toward the men advancing upon them, sending them insensible to the ground.

"I know quick traveling," he told her, "but we can't leave the horses."

"Only tell me where they are," she said, reaching out to grasp the front of Kian's tunic, "and hold on to me tightly. I can carry you both outside the castle walls, and we may be done with Llew forever."

It was amazing how long the man could talk, Malachi thought as he shifted uncomfortably on the rock upon which he'd been sitting for a full half hour or more, his chin resting in one hand. He'd been hard-pressed several times not to nod off and was put in mind of his school days, when his teacher's dull lectures had tempted him to play tricks with the clocks. Malachi's father, the former Earl of Graymar, had put a stop to such nonsense in the manner commonly employed by mere mortals—a thorough whipping—which had proved to be astonishingly successful in keeping Malachi from using magic so casually again in public settings.

Not that he hadn't gleaned valuable information regarding the Caslin family from Morcar's droning tale. Quite the opposite. He must certainly send Brecmont to America with some of this interesting knowledge to lend him aid. But for the current problem, it added nothing in the way of help.

"Well, that's most intriguing," Malachi said when the Earl of Llew stopped long enough to take a breath. Malachi stood and tugged at the lapels of his perfectly tailored coat, straightening the edges. "Thank you for relating the tale, and also your knowledge and experience of the Caslin family. It was vastly entertaining."

Lord Llew tilted his head curiously. "Entertaining?" he repeated, a touch of confusion in his tone.

"Very," said Malachi. "I'm so glad that we were able to come together and have this meeting, brief as it must necessarily be. I'm afraid I must be going now, however, for I assured Lord Tylluan that I'd be back well before sunset."

The Earl of Llew frowned and slowly rose to his feet. "You cannot leave. We've not yet discussed the *athanc*."

"Perhaps another time," Lord Graymar said. "I must return in plenty of time to help my cousin plan for the beast's wanderings tonight. He received some dreadful scratches last night. Lord Tylluan, not the *athanc,* of course. Clearly, he needs a better plan, and as advice is the only help he'll accept from me, I must make certain to be there to give it."

"But—"

"No, no," Malachi protested, "I can't stay longer, though I wish I could. Perhaps we might meet again before I depart for London and reminisce about old times. But for now, I must bid you good day."

"Malachi—"

"There is one final thing that I must say to you before I go, however, Morcar," Lord Graymar said. "And I hope that you'll think on it well and calmly throughout the coming days, though I have no doubt you'll be in no condition to do so right away."

A wary expression possessed Cadmaran's dark features. "What is that?"

"I will pay you for the girl—for Miss Caslin," Malachi said, "to make up for the loss of her. Tenfold, if necessary."

Cadmaran shook his head in confusion. "She is to be my wife soon. I have no intention of selling her. Certainly not to a Seymour."

"You don't have any choice in the matter," Malachi informed him. "I believe that a *unoliaeth* exists between her and Dyfed, and, if that is so, to keep them apart would only bring down the wrath of the Guardians. Considering that they've already placed a blood curse on you," he said more gently, "I should think that's the one thing you'd want to avoid above any other."

And then, not waiting to see how long it took for the Earl of Llew to comprehend him, Malachi prepared himself for the odd sensation of rapid traveling, closed his eyes, and departed.

Twenty~six

$\mathcal{N}$iclas and Professor Seabolt arrived at Tylluan shortly after Kian and Dyfed returned with Desdemona Caslin, well in time for Kian to give orders for the evening meal to be served in the castle's medieval great hall, as was the custom at Tylluan when guests were present, with all the castle folk in attendance.

Having heard the news that Professor Seabolt had at last found the long-sought enchantment, and being assured by Niclas that Loris was still safely, if not happily, in London, and being successful in their rescue of Miss Caslin from Morcar Cadmaran's clutches, there was a good deal to celebrate.

The *athanc* was going to be finished off tonight. Miss Caslin would help to control the beast, and Kian would perform the enchantment to put it back into slumber. All he had to find was a woman who was willing to play the most important part in the spell, which might, he admitted, be rather difficult, considering how dangerous that part was going to be. But surely one of the maidens at Tylluan would be willing to risk her life for the good of her family and friends. His people were all brave, even the females.

Dyfed and Miss Caslin had retired abovestairs as quickly as they could, waiting only long enough to hear what Malachi had to report about his meeting with Cadmaran and to properly greet Niclas and to rejoice over the news that Professor Seabolt had brought.

They'd been gone for three hours now, ostensibly so that Miss Caslin could have a hot bath and a change of clothes and a little nap before the celebration at dinner. Kian had his own notions as to what his brother and Miss Caslin were actually doing—they'd been unable to keep either their eyes or their hands off each other since being reunited—and though they didn't say so, he knew that Malachi and Niclas and Professor Seabolt had the same thought.

Malachi commented that he would have to approach the elders among the Families as soon as he possibly could in order to gain their approval for Dyfed's marriage, and Niclas said something about first needing to contact Draceous Caslin in the States and obtain his agreement regarding a change of husbands for his daughter.

"I believe I have just the man for that particular task," Malachi murmured thoughtfully. "Though I'm not certain that Dyfed and his beloved will be able to wait long enough for Brecmont to achieve Boston and send word back to us."

Kian, having already had to wait for what seemed like an eternity to be united with his *unoliaeth*, didn't think it so terrible a thing for his brother to have to wait a few months. Apart from that, neither Dyfed nor Miss Caslin appeared to be suffering all that much from the lack of being legally wed.

The celebration dinner was a great success. Despite the short notice, Cook managed to produce a meal that would have made Loris proud.

Before the fine meal was done, some of those who could play and had brought their instruments struck up a tune. Singing and dancing commenced, and, shortly thereafter, Kian and some of those who had the ability to levitate objects had taken up one of their favorite games—sending small objects flying in an attempt to strike various chosen spots about the room. It was rather like hitting the bull's-eye in archery, and whoever struck closest to the mark was deemed the winner. Spoons were the favorite projectiles, doing little harm as they hit candlesticks and vases and tapestries, but when they'd all been spent, the players were left with only forks and knives to continue on with. Unfortunately, these tended to do more damage and break more objects, but as the evening progressed and the wine flowed and the musicians played even more cheerful tunes, those caught up in the game really didn't care.

The contest had come down to a tie between Kian and Malachi. They had long since given up on eating utensils as missiles and were using small unshelled walnuts. The objects they were trying to shatter were several teacups—all mismatched, as they were what had survived of Tylluan's various tea services throughout the years—which Malachi had enchanted to fly about the room in any and every direction. Kian and Malachi took turns sending a walnut flying; whichever of them broke the most teacups would be the winner.

They were encouraged in their efforts by a great deal of shouting and clapping and, of course, by continuing music and boisterous singing.

Loris heard the noise even before the carriage door opened and, stepping out into the darkness, recognized with an inward groan the familiar sounds of dishes being broken.

"Oh, m'lady," Elen said as she gained her feet. "It's one of *those* nights. The ones Master Ffinian liked best." She sounded very happy.

"What the devil's going on here?" Mr. Goodbody, coming out behind Elen, asked. "Sounds like we're back at the Red Fox."

"Yes, it does," Loris said. She glanced at the men Mr. Goodbody had hired, some on horseback, some dismounted, two on top of the carriage. "Two of the boys from the stable are coming," she told them. "Follow them and unload the carriage and then you may all present yourselves to the kitchen. I'll make sure Cook has plenty of food and ale set out to greet you."

This met with murmurs of approval, which wasn't surprising, as they had all labored hard, with little rest or sustenance, in order to arrive at Tylluan with such speed.

"Mr. Goodbody," Loris said, and lifted her skirt to climb the stairs. "Welcome to my home."

"Ha!" Kian shouted with a laugh. "Another hit! Now we're even."

"Not for long, *cfender*," Malachi said. "I shall hit the next one with both eyes closed."

"God save us," a new, masculine voice said loudly enough to be heard over all the noise, "it's *worse* than the Red Fox."

Although the majority of those in the hall cared nothing for the words, they had a profound effect on certain individuals present. Kian's head whipped about so quickly toward the great hall's entry that his neck made a snapping sound. The next moment he was on his feet.

"Loris," he said, with enough surprise and amazement that it caught the attention of all those around him, and the room, by degrees, grew silent.

The lady of Tylluan was a sight to behold, bedraggled from the long journey, with her hair partly undone and her dress muddied and torn. Her face was pale and drawn, clearly showing her exhaustion, and yet Kian had never found her more beautiful. His heart leaped to see her so near, and he could only wonder that he'd not felt her presence the moment she'd crossed Tylluan's borders.

He could certainly feel her now. Her anger was a palpable thing, especially in the stark silence. He knew that his people were glad to see her, for everyone at Tylluan had missed the mistress of the castle greatly, but he was also aware that they feared her wrath. If Loris had been here, matters never would have gotten so out of hand.

Almost more shocking than her presence was that of Mr. Goodbody. Kian hadn't seen him for ten years but remembered the man vividly. He had changed little with time, save that he was perhaps a bit more portly and a tad more bald.

And then Kian realized, suddenly, why the man was there and couldn't help but admire his wife for her bravery and cleverness. None of them—not even Malachi or Niclas—had considered that she would turn to those from her former life for help. They thought they had boxed Loris in neatly, leaving her without a way to get to Tylluan, but she had outdone all their plotting.

"Well," said Malachi. "I confess I am thoroughly taken aback. What an excessively odd feeling."

"She said she would beat me here," Niclas murmured, shaking his head. "She came close enough. I'm all admiration. I must congratulate you on your wife, Kian," he said. "She is a rare treasure."

"Aye," Kian said, his gaze fixed on her, his heart pounding frantically in his chest. "She is indeed."

Loris cast her gaze about the hall, lingering for a long, significant moment on Kian before moving on to take in all the broken pottery on the floor.

"The last of the teacups," she said with dismay, walking slowly forward to bend and pick up a shard. "After what I've told you all about not breaking the few fine things we have left with your games," she murmured, gazing at it as she rose full-height. "When you *know* that these are the last we have." She shook her head, and Kian saw all the castle folk in the hall lowering their heads in shame, as only Loris could make them do. "And despite that," she said in a pained tone, "you use the last of the teacups in order to amuse yourselves."

It was very well done, he thought, and worked upon the vast majority of her listeners exactly as she wished. Of course she failed to mention the lovely new tea set Kian had just bought for her in London, but that wouldn't have been to the purpose. Though she certainly enjoyed celebratory dinners, Loris didn't like them getting out of hand and knew how to trim that fact down to a fine, sharp point that would nettle the people of Tylluan for a good fortnight.

They had broken Her Ladyship's few remaining teacups on the very night—having at last become Lady Tylluan—when she should have come home to a far better welcome. It would be all that the servants, fighting men, tenants, and villagers would talk about for weeks to come.

The silence was complete. Loris looked at the assembled once more, gave Kian a particularly hot gaze, and said, "I'm going to my chamber now but will return to the hall within the hour. I hope, by then, that I shall find it clean enough to welcome the king himself."

The shard she held dropped to the floor, and Loris turned and walked out, Mr. Goodbody and a grinning Elen at her heels.

Kian was waiting in her bedchamber by the time Loris opened the door. He had lit the fire and poured her a glass of wine and was sitting in a chair, one leg crossed over the other, relaxed and composed.

Loris wasn't either of those things just now. Quite the opposite. Her heart had reacted so painfully to the sight of him in the hall that she'd had to cover her fear with foolish anger. Now, seeing him at an even closer distance, it was worse.

He'd been attacked. Successfully attacked. The beast had managed to strike him—his beautiful face and his hands and arms, possibly even the rest of his body. He was attired in formal dress as the lord of Tylluan, with a cuffed, high-collared shirt and a waistcoat and jacket. But she could see the deep scars that ran upward from his hands and downward from his face and chin until they disappeared into cloth. Malachi was a powerful healer, and she knew that the scars would not be permanent. But that didn't ease the fear in her heart or dim her determination to help Kian be rid of the beast.

She longed to go to him, to both fret and rail all at once, but knew better than to do either. The fact that he'd been harmed did little to further the argument she was about to

lay before Kian, and if he didn't agree, he would only go out
and fail with the *athanc* and very likely be hurt again.

"I had to stop in the kitchen first," she told him, pulling off
her gloves. "It was necessary to provide sustenance for the
men who brought me here. And Elen was hungry as well."

"And what of you, Loris?" he asked. "When was the last
time you ate? Or rested?"

"I don't remember," she replied honestly. "But it scarce
matters, for I'm not hungry and I don't intend to rest. Until
later."

"Will you at least take some wine?" He motioned to the
glass he'd filled for her.

She unbuttoned her pelisse and tossed it onto the nearest
chair. "I will, thank you."

As she crossed the room, he rose, picked up the wineglass, and offered it to her.

Loris shook her head. "Not yet," she said, and turned her
back to him. "Unbutton me. Please."

She heard his hesitation and the surprise in his voice as
he set the wineglass aside. "Very well. If you wish."

She could scarce wait to get out of the dress she'd been
wearing for nearly three full days now. There had been no
time to change clothes on the journey, and she was desperate
to be in something clean.

"Thank heavens," she murmured, pulling her arms free of
the sleeves as soon as he had the first few buttons done.

"Hold on," he said, bending nearer to work on the tiny fastenings. "You'll tear it. If I'd known you were this eager to
see me I would have carried you up the stairs the moment I
set sight on you. But that was what I wanted to do even knowing how angry you were." He took a moment to kiss the top
of her neck.

She shivered beneath the soft caress. "I have every right
to be angry. How could you do such a thing to me, sneaking
off in the middle of the night and leaving a letter to explain?"

"It was cowardly," he admitted, "but I didn't want you
coming along, and time was of the essence. If I'd told you,

you would have talked me into letting you return to Tylluan. I find it very hard to resist you, you see." Another soft kiss saluted her shoulder.

Loris turned about to face him, pulling the remainder of the dress away and stepping out of the muddy skirt. She tossed the garment aside and began to untie her petticoats.

"You didn't think I'd be able to get here," she said. "You thought I would be trapped in London because no one would help me."

"No one among our friends and relatives, leastwise," he said, sitting down again to watch with obvious interest as Loris continued to wrestle with her clothes. The petticoats followed the dress, and she sat down in the chair opposite to begin unlacing her boots. Kian moved to kneel before her. "Let me help you with these as well. I'm becoming quite adept at being a lady's maid, as you well know."

She was too weary to argue and leaned back, resting her head and closing her eyes.

"I never thought you would turn to the Goodbodys," he told her, sliding the first boot off and setting it aside. His thumbs ran over the top of her stockinged foot, rubbing away the ache of three days of journeying. Loris murmured with pleasure. "I'm astonished," he went on, "and very proud, that you faced your unpleasant past. And not simply faced it, but used it to your advantage."

"I was surprised, too," she said. "It wasn't at all what I expected. Saving that Mr. Goodbody was willing to do what I wished for a sufficient amount of money. That's why he decided to come along. To make certain he got the rest of what I promised. And also, I think, to keep an eye on the men he'd hired. I'm not certain he trusted them to deliver me safely."

"And if you didn't arrive safely," Kian said, removing the other shoe, "he wouldn't get paid. It appears his greed has its virtues, for he did get you here safe and well, and very quickly. Niclas and Professor Seabolt only managed to best you by a few hours, and they weren't encumbered by a carriage and longer horse changes."

"He was surprisingly good company," Loris told Kian, biting her lip to hold back a moan when he rubbed her other foot. "Mr. Goodbody, I mean. We spent a great deal of time arguing at first about who had wronged the other more—he still feels quite strongly about not receiving any recompense for setting my grandfather in the right path to finding me—and I thought poor Elen was going to leap out of the carriage just to gain some peace. But when we got past that he proved to be quite amiable and a good storyteller. You can imagine how many interesting tales a tavern keeper has to tell. Oh, Kian, that feels too good. You must stop."

His strong fingers had slid up to her calves and were gently kneading the aching muscles there.

"You need to sleep, Loris," he murmured. "Let me put you to bed. We'll talk more of all this in the morning."

"No, I'm not going to sleep," she said, opening her eyes. "I've ordered a hot bath, and afterward, I'm going out with you to meet the *athanc*. But when that's done with," she said with a long, weary sigh, "I vow I'll sleep for a week."

His hands fell still, and he said, clearly and slowly, "No, you're not."

Loris had understood well before she'd started her journey that Kian wasn't going to accept her decision either readily or with good grace. She was prepared for all his arguments.

"Was that Desdemona Caslin sitting beside Dyfed in the great hall?" Loris asked, pushing into a higher sitting position so that she could look at him.

Kian frowned and slowly rose to his feet. "It was. We rescued her from Llew this afternoon. But she has nothing to do with you becoming involved in the matter. Because you'll not be. Get the notion out of your head completely."

"But she is going to help you, is she not?" Loris asked. "Just as she's been doing since Dyfed and I left for London."

"She will," he said, "but it's entirely different."

"Because she's a sorceress?"

He nodded curtly. "Aye."

"But you need a virgin to work your enchantment," Loris said. "The *athanc* can only be held in its solid form long enough to be captured if it lays its head upon the lap of a maiden." Reaching to pick up her wineglass, she looked at him from beneath her lashes and asked, "Do you happen to know of any sorceress within fifty miles of here who is also a maiden?"

He scowled darkly. "You know very well that I don't. But that still doesn't—"

"I'm yet a maiden," Loris reminded him. "Which you know better than anyone else. And as the lady of Tylluan, it is my right to be the one to help with the enchantment."

Kian's expression grew fierce. "There are any number of maidens at Tylluan who would make such a sacrifice for their home."

"I know that," Loris said quietly, sitting forward and holding his gaze. "But you would not ask another to take your place in this task, and I'll not let another take mine, either."

He stared at her in silence and then at last turned away and moved to stand by the fire.

She stood to follow him. "I'm sorry if it makes you unhappy."

"It doesn't make me merely unhappy," he told her as she stood in front of him. Lifting a hand, he cradled her cheek. "It terrifies me. I can't lose you, Loris. Not when we've only just begun to find each other after so many years."

She smiled and set a hand over his. "I don't intend to be lost," she murmured. "I certainly don't wish to be. But I know that I *must* be the one allowed to do this for Tylluan."

"How do you know?" he whispered.

"I'm not certain," she said. "It's almost as if someone told me that the venture will only be successful if I am the one to lure the *athanc* into submission. I'm not merely saying this to convince you, Kian. It's true."

He still looked doubtful, and deeply troubled.

"Do you remember," she said, "when the curse was first laid upon you? Upon both of us?"

"I can never forget it," he murmured. "Why do you ask?"

She moved away a little, trying to find the words to tell him what was in her mind. "I've been thinking upon it as I journeyed from London. Mr. Goodbody reminded me of something that I hadn't thought upon very much."

"What?"

"That you wouldn't wait for help to come before taking on Gregor Foss. He overheard Dyfed pleading with you to wait until help could be fetched, and you refused." She looked at him.

Kian nodded. "It was foolish of me. But this is different, Loris. I've already told you why I must do this alone."

"No," she said, shaking her head. "You've told me why you can't ask Malachi for help. I am but a mere mortal, and you must have a maiden to aid you in the enchantment. This time, Kian, you should accept the help that is offered to you, and not be so stubborn and prideful as you were ten years ago."

His eyes filled with despair, and he said, again, "I can't lose you."

"You'll not," she vowed, moving to stand before him. "You must let me be the one, Kian. If Desdemona Caslin can be allowed to help because she happens to love your brother, then I must certainly be allowed to help the man I love as well."

Twenty-seven

There was nothing more that he could argue after that, though Kian desperately wished he could. But the word *love* had tumbled from her lips, filled with truth and honor, and he couldn't throw it back at her as if it had no meaning.

And so he had agreed and left her to bathe and change into clean and more comfortable clothes. His last glance at her had shown Loris pulling out the remaining combs and pins from her hair, letting it fall loose and free. She was home now and could be herself again. He didn't need to ask to know how intensely happy she was.

When she came back down the stairs her mood was completely changed, much to the joy of the servants, who had quickly cleared and cleaned the mess in the great hall. It looked, now, as if a meal had never taken place that night, and their lady's pleasure and smiling praise for their efforts left them all looking deeply relieved.

Introductions had been made after that. Loris and Desdemona exchanged nods and pleasantries, and Desdemona stated that she was glad to meet a woman of Loris's admirable powers. When Dyfed told her that Loris didn't possess magic, Desdemona merely smiled.

Mr. Goodbody, much the better for some food and ale, took the introductions and reintroductions cheerfully. He remembered Niclas especially well, having been so recently terrified into submission by that powerful gentleman, and, of course, could never forget Kian and Dyfed or the Earl of Graymar. Whatever displeasure Mr. Goodbody once held for the Seymour clan seemed to have disappeared completely, probably, Kian thought, because of the fortune in jeweled hair combs that Loris had given him for his help.

As Kian had expected, Malachi, Niclas, and Dyfed reacted with vociferous displeasure when told of what Loris intended to do. But their arguments fell on deaf ears. She politely insisted upon her chosen course, even when they brought up how deeply displeased her grandfather was going to be, and as she had already gained Kian's acquiescence, there was nothing more to be said or done.

They set out for the lake after that, with the exception of Niclas and Malachi, who agreed, not very happily, to remain in the castle, and Mr. Goodbody, who had expressed no desire to become involved in any unnatural doings.

It was a somber procession, with the exception of Loris and Desdemona, who rode side by side, conversing as if they were long-lost friends. Dyfed and Kian, riding farther behind, looked on gloomily, well aware of the dangers that lay ahead for the women they loved. Professor Seabolt, who wished to see the *athanc* for himself, also to be present in case his expertise was needed, rode alongside Horas, discussing matters both magical and historical, while Kian's entire contingent of men, fighting and otherwise, brought up the rear, pulling along a cart filled with heavy chains that Kian had enchanted earlier.

"This is going to be the end of it, Kian," Dyfed said. "Tomorrow the land will be whole again."

Kian released a taut breath. "I pray it is so, *fy gefell*."

It was unlikely that the *athanc* would come tonight unless it was called. It had roamed and fed for the past four nights and done an enormous amount of damage without

Desdemona Caslin to control it. The village had suffered the most, with well over half the buildings destroyed. It would be years before it could be completely rebuilt and far longer before any of those at Tylluan would forget these past few months.

The lake was calm and quiet when they arrived, with no sign of the beast. Kian brought them all to a stop well within the trees, and he and the men worked quickly to lay out the chains in the place where Kian would be able to make the fastest use of them.

The trap was prepared long before Kian had thought it would be, and the time had come. The night was foggy but not so heavy that the light of the moon couldn't be seen. It was a dim, cold glow, but enough for the business at hand.

"Are you sure you understand exactly what to do?" Kian asked as he and Loris walked out of the trees and toward the shoreline. "You must sit perfectly still. Say nothing to the beast. Don't touch it."

"Professor Seabolt explained everything," she told Kian. "And I must touch the beast if it begins to rise. I must keep its head upon my lap until you've bound it securely, else it might change back into liquid form and escape."

A tremor of panic ran the length of Kian's body, and he brought Loris to a halt. "Don't touch it," he said, the words tumbling out in a hoarse, shaking voice. "I know firsthand how powerful the creature is. Its claws are as sharp as knives. Let it lay its head upon your lap, but if it moves or rises, don't draw attention to yourself. Let me worry about binding it."

She reached up to caress his face. The softness of the gloves she wore warmed his cold skin.

"I won't do anything foolish, Kian. You mustn't think of me, but of the *athanc*. This will likely be the only chance we'll have to be rid of it. Concentrate on the beast."

He gave a shake of his head. "You're asking the impossible of me. You'll not be out of my thoughts for a moment, Loris."

"I know," she whispered. "You won't be out of mine, either. Please be careful." Her fingers traced the line of scars on his cheek. "I would rather not go home with you bearing more of these."

The stark reality of what they were about to undertake, of the danger she was going to put herself in, made Kian suddenly short of breath. He clasped Loris to him tightly and kissed her, hard, with desperation and fear, before letting her go.

They took their places. Kian and Dyfed and the other men hid in the woods. Loris sat down upon a log near the water, where the chains had been laid out close by. She set her feet side by side, striving to keep her knees from knocking together, and smoothed her skirts down. She had worn one of her old, unfashionable dresses and a heavy woolen cloak that she clutched tightly in a vain effort to keep warm.

Desdemona Caslin stood beside Loris, gazing at her in a calm, level manner. She was a fascinating female, Loris thought with a measure of envy, and clearly unafraid of what was to come.

"I shall call the beast from that side of the lake," Miss Caslin told her, "and will direct it toward you. It has a very keen sense of smell, and will likely catch the scent of warm flesh almost at once. Don't let that alarm you, for it moves but slowly, being so large a creature. The professor assures us that it will not kill you if you speak the incantation, and it has not yet killed a human that I know of. But it is a stupid creature, and easily enraged. Take every care, Lady Tylluan."

"Thank you, Miss Caslin," Loris said, her lips trembling as she tried to smile in what she hoped was a reassuring manner. "I'm ready, if you are."

Desdemona Caslin nodded, held Loris's gaze for a long, solemn moment, then turned, black cape whirling, and strode away. The sound of her booted feet crunching on the rocky ground faded far too quickly, and Loris was left alone in the silent darkness. But not really silent, she told herself. The water in the lake sloshed and slapped as it moved back and forth, and behind her, in the trees, she could hear the nervous whinnying of horses. She wished Dyfed would say something to her in his silent speech, but she supposed he was busy communicating with Miss Caslin.

The fog had thickened and the air grown colder. A slight breeze picked up the scent of the water, teasing Loris's senses with the fresh, familiar smell. Everything here smelled wonderful to her, after having been in London. Loris supposed if she was going to die, she could not have chosen a finer place, here in the mountains that she loved so well, helping the man she loved and his people. Their people, she corrected.

Desdemona Caslin came to a stop a good distance away. Loris could scarce make the dark figure out in the fog, but enough so that she saw when the other woman lifted her hands.

The water in the middle of the lake began to swirl, though Loris heard rather than saw it. The sound grew louder, bubbling, and the waves near the shore began to move more violently.

The creature began to rise, parting the fog as it did, slender at first, but growing larger in the way that a sponge grew larger when taking in water.

It was an enormous beast, fearsome and dragonlike, covered in dark, wet scales and as tall as a tree. It began to move toward Desdemona Caslin, but at her command, turned and came toward Loris.

She thought, for one awful moment, that she was going to faint. Her body had forgotten how to take in air, and a wave of terrified confusion made her senses swim dizzily. If her legs hadn't been trembling so badly, she might have gotten up and run, but they wouldn't obey and shook with embarrassing vigor.

Steady, she heard Dyfed say. *The incantation, Loris. Say it now.*

"Ades dum," Loris uttered in a faint whisper, her voice shaking harder than her legs. "Mellesco ferinus. Dormio."

Again, Dyfed said. *Louder. You must draw it to you.*

"Ades dum," she said again, her voice rising to a higher pitch. She was obliged to ball her hands into fists to control their trembling. "Mellesco ferinus. Dormio."

The beast's head turned toward her, and it fell still, its gaze fixed upon Loris. It looked a little like one of the dogs at Tylluan, wondering whether it was being lured forward for a treat or something far less pleasant.

She repeated the words once more, a bit louder, and lowered one shaking hand to touch her lap.

The *athanc* came closer, its scaly legs swirling up great mounds of water as it moved. Its hands were webbed and clawed, with long, sharp points that grew from the ends of what looked more like sinewy tendrils than fingers. At this closer distance Loris could see the beast better and wondered how its huge head would ever fit upon her lap.

"Ades dum. Mellesco ferinus. Dormio."

Come, gentle beast. Sleep.

Loris didn't possess any magic, but the words clearly did. The creature drew even nearer, its black eyes fixed on Loris's face, as if it were beneath a spell. At last it was before her, and, as Loris continued to repeat the words, it knelt and slowly, so very slowly, bent to place its forehead—all of it that fit—upon her shaking knees.

The touch of it, wet and icy and prickly because of its scales, sent jolts of shock skittering through Loris's body. Water drained off the *athanc,* soaking her clothes and shoes.

Her breath came in great, painful gasps, and yet somehow she managed to keep repeating the incantation. She only had to keep the creature there for a few moments longer, and Kian would be able to chain it in its bodily form. Once chained, it wouldn't be able to transform, and then Kian could perform the enchantment to put it back into eternal slumber.

He's coming now, Loris, she heard Dyfed say. *Hold on.*

The moment the *athanc* set its head upon Loris's lap, Kian sprang forward, having already cast the spell to make his movements silent. But he was still obliged to move with care, lest the rocks beneath his feet cause the beast to rise before he could get the chains about it.

It was going to have to be done quickly, but Kian had no worry on that account. Fear for Loris strengthened his powers tenfold. When he lifted his arms to send the chains flying, his muscles were taut with increased potency.

"Adligar attinere!"

The chains flew from the ground and struck the creature full force, almost knocking both it and Loris to the ground.

The creature reacted just as they had expected and recovered from the surprise attack quickly. Before the final chains could take its arms captive, it had wrenched one of the clawed hands free and swung it wildly. With a roar of fury, it also tried to lift its head from Loris's lap.

Kian saw her lifting her arms, heard her shouting the incantation over the beast's wrathful noise, and before he could tell her to stop, she placed her hands on the creature's head and held it down.

Everything happened then in a blur of motion. Kian heard Dyfed and his men rushing out of the trees with thunderous shouts. The beast's claw rose high in the air and began its descent. And Loris shut her eyes against the impending strike, still saying the incantation, still holding the *athanc* down with all the strength she possessed.

"Castrere conficio!" Kian shouted, running toward the beast at full speed. The chains pulled tight, one slid up to clasp the wayward arm, but it was too late. The claw came down, striking Loris across her face and chest, before the chain caught and trapped it.

Kian hit the beast with such force that its enormous body tumbled over onto the ground. It writhed and emitted a howling screech that deafened everyone present, but the chains held fast, and it could no longer transform and slip away. The *athanc* had been captured, because of Loris. She had given

Kian the precious extra seconds he needed to completely confine the beast.

Kian rolled to his feet to finish the enchantment, shouting, *"Vorago aevum!"*

The *athanc*'s yowling came to a halt almost at once, and its frantic struggles began to lessen. Kian's men surrounded the beast and watched as it grew silent and still and as its dark, reptilian eyes began to close.

Kian didn't care to watch as the creature fell into the deep rest that he hoped would last an eternity this time. He went to Loris.

Dyfed and Desdemona were already there, kneeling on the ground where Loris lay. They stood and moved back as Kian approached.

"Oh, God. My God." The words spilled from Kian's lips in a terrified whisper. "Loris."

She had been torn open, with long, deep stripes of red running from the top of her head down her neck and across her breasts. Her throat had been badly cut and her clothes shredded into tatters. She was no longer breathing.

"Loris." He knelt and gathered her into his arms. "Don't," he pleaded. "You can't leave. We cannot be parted."

Tears slid unbidden down his cheeks, and he buried his face in the softness of her unbound hair. Pain, hot and sharp, knifed through him, and he wept.

He had never felt anything like this before—a grief so profound that he knew, as clearly as he had ever known anything, that he would not survive it. Voices and sounds faded around him. All other sensations—the coldness of the air, the darkness of the night, the hard discomfort of the rocky ground—faded. All he knew was Loris, her body physically in his arms but her spirit leaving him to an aloneness that could not be borne.

And it was in that moment, as everything else dimmed, that Kian discovered an entirely new dimension to magic. He closed his eyes and let it happen, discovering the gift as it came upon him, and knew, somehow, that this was from the

Guardians. They had been watching, as they always were, and knew that he couldn't live without his *unoliaeth*. And so they had given him the ability to bring her back.

There were only the two of them, he and Loris, pressed together. Closer, and closer yet, until everything that separated them melted away and they were one.

His heart beat and hers took up the rhythm. His breathing slowed and became even, and Loris breathed as one with him. The blood that flowed through his veins was hers, and when he opened his eyes he saw what she saw. Stars, and the moon and planets, and them, being one, spinning in the midst.

He could hear her voice as if it were his own, asking questions that he asked, too. Where were they? What had become of their bodies, or of the earth, for that matter?

The answers didn't matter, because they were together, as they would have been if not for the curse. They were *unoliaeth* and were floating, as one soul, out of all time and physical restraint. He gave his life to her, and she gave it back in turn.

And then it began to change, as Kian knew it must, and he felt them separating, becoming two again, except that he held on to Loris even more tightly, keeping her with him as they went back.

Physical sensation returned, along with sound and smell. It was like waking from a deep and powerful slumber, such as the one that the *athanc* had so recently been called from. Kian was kneeling on the hard, cold ground, and a tumult went on all about him. Dyfed and Desdemona and Professor Seabolt were all trying to get Kian's attention, and the men were standing about, murmuring. The many horses they'd brought were pawing the ground and whinnying. Kian could even hear the sounds of the water in the lake as it waved to and fro in time with the earth's rotation.

All these things he could hear and envision, but he cared for none of it. Loris was in his arms. She had opened her eyes and was smiling at him, and her wounds had all been healed, leaving behind only the bloodied, tattered gown as proof that she'd ever been harmed.

"Kian," she murmured, reaching up a hand to touch his face. "It's gone."

"Yes, love."

With her other hand she touched her breast, over her heart, and gazed at him with wonder.

"I can feel it here, as if a heavy shadow has been lifted away. It's gone, Kian."

It was odd, Kian thought, that fresh tears should begin to fill his eyes. He had never been happier in his life, but he was weeping like a child.

But she was weeping, too, because she knew, as he did, that the blood curse had at last been lifted.

Twenty~eight

$\mathscr{P}$erhaps it wasn't precisely noble of Kian, but after ten years of impatient celibacy and waiting for the woman he loved to love him in return—and having almost lost that same woman to a fatal blow—the last thing he wanted to do was spend another minute at the lake dealing with the *athanc*.

But it had to be dealt with, and so, ignoring the great interest in the now slumbering beast, especially by Professor Seabolt, who was actually jotting down notes and sketches in a journal with the small help of the nearly fog-shrouded moonlight, Kian floated the creature up into the air until it was directly over the deepest part of the lake and then lowered it into the water.

"Write the enchantment down in as many journals as you possibly can, Professor," Kian advised. "I don't want a future Baron of Tylluan being obliged to wait so long in order to deal with the brute, should it ever be raised to life again, may God forbid it."

As to the other magic that had occurred, bringing Loris back to life and breaking the curse, Kian had no explanations. The new magic that the Guardians had gifted him with was something he would have to ponder for a long while and discuss with Malachi at length in order to understand it. As to the curse, Kian was truly baffled. He'd done nothing that deserved such a boon; indeed, he'd nearly lost Loris forever.

"It wasn't you having to do some great deed," Desdemona Caslin said, casting a patient glance at him. "It was you putting your foolish man's pride away and letting her make a sacrifice for you. Because of love," she clarified when those around her merely looked mystified.

"I believe she must be right, Kian," Professor Seabolt said. "All these years, we assumed you would have to perform some great task, but perhaps the Guardians were simply waiting for you to prove that you learned a lesson about needing someone—your own *unoliaeth,* for instance."

"Of course Desdemona's right," Dyfed said, beaming at his beloved with adoration. "She knows a great deal about how much those who love need each other."

It was nearly dawn by the time they arrived at the castle, though the fog made the sky as dark as before. Kian had sent the men away to their homes, promising that another celebration—much larger this time—would be held that evening. Everyone who lived within Tylluan's borders was to come to give thanks for the victory over the *athanc* and to give the new Lady Tylluan a proper welcome home.

Kian held the reins to Loris's horse as the others made to dismount. When Dyfed looked at him inquiringly, Kian said, "Malachi and Niclas will be waiting for explanations. Do me the favor of making them for me."

Dyfed smiled and nodded.

Kian guided his and Loris's horses through the bailey and to the back of the castle. Outside the gate that led to the gardens, he dismounted and moved to lift her from her saddle. Standing with his hands on her waist, he gazed into Loris's upturned face. For the very first time since they'd met at the Red Fox, so many years before, he saw love, for him, in her eyes. Unvarnished and unhidden.

"Are we going to spend the night in the gardens?" she asked.

"No," he said. "We're going to have one last visit from the spirit of Liw Nos, and then we're going to fondly bid him good-bye."

He sent the horses back to the stable and then picked Loris up in his arms and carried her into the garden, coming to a stop just below her balcony.

They looked up, and Loris said, "I always thought Liw could fly, because he was one of the faerie folk. But I didn't know you could do the same."

"I can't," Kian told her. "And neither could he. Hold tightly, love. I pray this is the last time I shall ever have to come to you in such a manner."

The climb took some doing; Loris was no frail and delicate female, and her long limbs and skirts made it difficult for Kian to both hold her and keep a grip on the brick wall. They laughed, despite the danger, and Loris remarked that if he had not been a baron, he could have made a wonderful living as a thief.

The sound of her voice spurred him upward; there was so much pleasure and joy in her tone and the same relief that he could hear in his voice as well. Tonight their lives would begin anew. Everything in their upended world had been set right, at last, and all the shadows that had once haunted them had been banished.

He set her on the balcony before climbing over the half wall, then pointed at the locked balcony doors and said, "Aperio." The bolt slid silently open.

"Now I know," Loris murmured.

Kian took her hand and led her inside. He bolted the doors again and started the fire, and then, impatient, drew her into his arms.

She came willingly, rising up to meet his kiss. They drew apart after a moment, arms holding each other tight, and waited. A full minute passed in silence, and then another.

"Anything?" Kian asked, sliding his hands purposefully over her back and waist.

Her slow smile told him that it was all right. "There's no pain," she whispered. "Your touch only feels . . . wonderful."

That was all he needed to hear. He picked her up and set her on the bed, kneeling before her to perform the same duties he had done shortly after she'd arrived. Her boots came off, then her stockings, though his hands shook so badly that he almost couldn't undo the fastenings. Her dress, in tatters from the *athanc,* fell off almost without assistance, and when her undergarments refused to cooperate he uttered a low curse and tore the fastenings with impatient fingers.

Loris laughed and reached up to take his face in her hands. She brought her lips to his, murmuring, "There's no hurry now. We have the rest of our lives."

Kian tossed her petticoats to the other side of the room. "I've been waiting for ten years," he said. "And dying for want of you. I apologize." He kissed her, hard, then set her away to start ripping off the remnants of her chemise. "I intend to be the most romantic of husbands in all the years to come, but for the moment, I'm not going to survive another ten minutes unless I'm inside of you."

She laughed again, then gasped as his warm fingers found her bare breasts. "Oh," she said, and arched against him. His lips followed his hands, caressing her face, her throat, and lower to her shoulders as the rest of her garments slid to the floor.

"Oh, my God," Kian murmured, his hands stroking over the soft skin of her back and hips. His fingers tested the swell of her buttocks, the curves of her waist, at last grasping her hips and pulling her tightly against his arousal.

Loris's hands moved over him, as well, and her mouth met his with equal passion. When he teased her lips with his tongue she eagerly opened to him. Her fingers slid over his shoulders, pulling his coat down. Not breaking their kiss, Kian struggled out of it, and Loris set her fingers to his waistcoat and shirt, murmuring with delight as the garments gave way and she could splay her hands over his warm, silky skin. The bold caress made Kian groan with pleasure, but when her hands slid lower, stroking his buttocks, then sliding forward to touch his manhood over the cloth of his trousers, his sanity gave way.

Somewhere in the dim recess of his mind he had a fleeting thought about taking his boots off, but the notion disappeared before he could make any sense of it. He undid the front of his trousers with shaking fingers, tearing the buttons, and then pushed Loris onto the bed.

She opened to him completely, putting her arms about him as he came over her and pulling him down. She said his name, and he heard his own rough voice giving reply, and then he was pushing inside of her, hard and urgent, unable to school himself to gentleness.

It hurt her. He knew it, for he could both feel her untried tightness and hear her gasp of surprise. Regret forced him to stillness, but the pleasure of her, of being inside her, made his voice unnaturally strained.

"I'm sorry." He rested his forehead against hers and opened his eyes. "I didn't mean to . . . I've lost my senses."

"It's all right," she whispered. "It feels . . . it feels good." She drew in a shaking breath and said, wonderingly, "You're inside of me, Kian. We're one now."

Aye, he thought as he began to move in her more slowly, more deeply. They were one, and the pleasure of it was going to kill them both.

"I love you," he murmured, and felt her relaxing beneath him. Pleasure took the place of pain in her eyes, and she began to move in union with him. She said his name and then, as the pleasure grew more intense, murmured, "Oh!"

It was the most erotic thing he'd ever heard and sent Kian over the edge. Pleasure exploded through him just as it washed over Loris, and his last coherent thought as they fell into sensation was that waiting ten years for this moment had been more than worthwhile.

They slept for an hour, cocooned together beneath the blankets. Kian had been too exhausted to even take off his boots

or pants. When they woke, he finished undressing, took a
few moments to help Loris wash the blood from her thighs,
and then made love to her again, far more slowly and gently
and sanely. They slept again, through the morning and into
the afternoon, and when he woke it was to find Loris gently
stroking his fully aroused member. He pulled her to sit
astride him and showed her how to take him into herself,
how to ride him to her own pleasure and then to his. Life, as
far as Kian was concerned, could go on exactly in this manner for the remainder of their days.

But the world had other ideas.

Elen meekly scratched at the door just as they were about
to sleep again, and when bade to enter, refused to come any
farther into the room.

Loris slid from the bed and took up her wrapper, cover-
ing herself and padding barefoot across the carpeted floor to
speak to the girl.

A few minutes later Loris returned to the bed to find Kian
propped up on the pillows, his hands beneath his blond head
and his magnificent body exposed from the waist up. The
smile on his face told her exactly what he wanted to do and
she would have liked nothing better than to throw the wrapper aside and acquiesce, but it would have to wait.

"I never realized how very handsome you are before
now," she told him, climbing up to kneel beside him on the
mattress. With one finger she traced the line of one of his recent scars. "I could do without these, however, though I
daresay if you kept them, women would swoon at the sight
of your battle wounds."

"And then I'd have to make up a tale of having served in
a very different sort of war," he said, drawing one of his
hands out from beneath his head to toy with the edge of her
wrapper. "I hope you asked Elen to have a nice, hot bath
brought up for us. And food."

"A bath?" Loris asked, her eyebrows rising. "For both of
us? Is that possible?"

He pushed up to his elbow, coming near enough to kiss her. His hand stole inside her wrapper to caress her naked breast.

"Entirely," he murmured against her lips, and his clever fingers stroked lightly over her sensitive nipple. "Especially with lots of soap and warm, scented water. I shall enjoy bathing every single part of you."

His lips tasted hers and his tongue teased the corner of her mouth, and Loris very nearly forgot what Elen had just told her.

It took an effort to pull away, especially with visions of bathing with Kian dancing through her brain, but she did, saying, "Cadmaran's coming."

Kian fell still. His hand came out of her wrapper. "What?"

"Malachi sent Elen to wake us," Loris said. "Lord Llew will be here within the hour. He sent word. He wants to meet with you, and with Dyfed."

Kian sat up, staring at her. "He's going to issue a challenge," he said. "To Dyfed."

"To Dyfed?" she said as he tossed the covers aside and stood. "Because of Desdemona Caslin? But I thought they were fated. Lord Llew surely can't challenge Dyfed for something that the Guardians decided."

Kian was searching the room for his clothes. "He shouldn't be allowed to," he said distractedly. "But that's never stopped the man before. I've got to find a way to avoid it. He'll kill Dyfed in a contest."

"Perhaps Malachi should be the one," she said, sliding off the bed to help Kian with his shirt and waistcoat. His long hair was in complete disarray, and she reached up to smooth it back from his face while he busily dealt with his trousers. "He is the *Dewin Mawr,* after all."

Kian shook his head. "That's just what Cadmaran wants. He'll be furious that he wasn't able to engage Malachi during their meeting yesterday. And Dyfed is my brother. I'm the one who must do it. Devil take it," he muttered. "I've ruined these trousers. Half the buttons are missing."

Loris's heart felt as if it had stopped. *"No,"* she said flatly. "No, Kian. Let Malachi take care of this. You dealt with the *athanc* and I understood that, but I'll not lose you because Lord Llew insists upon being a fool."

Kian took her by the shoulders and kissed her into silence. "In the words of a very wise, brave woman," he said, "I don't intend to be lost. Hurry and dress, Loris. I've learned the Guardians' lesson well, and I want you with me when Cadmaran arrives."

Twenty-nine

$\mathcal{B}$y the time the Earl of Llew arrived at Castle Tylluan, Kian had composed himself and prepared for what was to come. He, Malachi, Dyfed, Niclas, and Professor Seabolt had shut themselves in Kian's study for almost the entire hour before the earl's arrival and argued, often at the top of their lungs—excepting Professor Seabolt, who rarely had a chance to say anything at all—over what was to be done.

Dyfed insisted that he must be allowed to fight for his woman, Niclas told him to stop being a fool, and Malachi and Kian sounded as if they were about to come to blows over who had the greater right to deal with Cadmaran.

Desdemona, sitting with Loris in a chamber that had once served as a sewing room for medieval damsels, but now acted as a drawing room of sorts, found the loud ruckus, easily heard throughout most of the castle, all rather amusing. Loris found it grating and not in the least productive. She was moments away from going into the study and bashing their foolish masculine heads together.

She glanced at Desdemona and wondered at how she could be so calm.

"Aren't you worried about what Lord Llew will do to Dyfed?" she asked, pacing nervously in a circle before the fire. "He is a powerful wizard, after all."

Desdemona looked up from the book she'd been perusing. "There is nothing to worry about," she said. "My powers are no longer dimmed by the magic of Castle Llew. If Cadmaran so much as looks oddly at my beloved, I shall kill him. It's a pity that you mere mortals must suffer so for the lack of powers." She smiled and turned her attention back to the book.

Loris knew that she should find the other woman's coldbloodedness alarming, but the truth was that she was comforted. The Earl of Llew was outnumbered by wizards at Tylluan. Powerful, extraordinary wizards. And a dark sorceress who had the ability to give even Malachi pause.

Loris was thankful that Mr. Goodbody and his men had already taken their leave, so as not to witness any potentially alarming scenes. Niclas and Malachi had dealt with them: Niclas had taken care of paying them for bringing Loris to Tylluan, and Malachi had erased all memory of magic from their thoughts. By the time they rode away, they were all convinced that the job they'd done had not only put a great deal of gold in their pockets but given them quite a nice holiday as well. If none of them could precisely recall, some miles later, why they'd come to Tylluan or whom they'd brought, they didn't dwell on the fact too long.

As soon as the shouting died down, Loris and Desdemona rose to join the men in the study. The Earl of Llew was announced a few minutes later.

He came in slowly, blindly, feeling his way with the staff that he carried. Loris, who had never seen the man before, was struck by how handsome he was, despite the blindness. She had been used to thinking of him as evil and therefore as physically unattractive as his nature, but she had been far wrong. Lord Llew put her very much in mind of Tauron, with his black hair and eyes and tall, muscular frame. He was also much younger than she had supposed, perhaps in his midthirties, but certainly not above.

"Ah, Malachi," said Lord Llew. "You're still here, I perceive, along with Lord Tylluan. And Miss Caslin. Hello, my dear." He nodded toward the chair where she sat and took a few steps farther into the room. "I sense other Seymours present in the room, as well, but they must be of the lesser variety, for I do not feel any great powers in them."

"My wife, Lady Tylluan, is present," Kian said. "And also my brother, Dyfed Seymour, as well as my cousin Niclas Seymour. Professor Harris Seabolt is here also, though you cannot sense him."

"Niclas Seymour," Cadmaran repeated with a smile. His strong fingers tightened their grip on the staff. "It's been a long while since you and I have been in company together. How is darling Julia? As beautiful as ever, I should imagine. I often comfort myself with memories of her. She was the last woman I saw before the blindness, you know."

Fury possessed Niclas's features at the casually spoken words, and he took a step forward, hands fisted. Malachi set an arm across his shoulder to hold him back.

"Be careful, *cfender*," Lord Graymar murmured. "Don't let him goad you with his nonsense. Mrs. Seymour is very well, Morcar," he said. "But you would do well not to speak of her in so familiar a manner again. Fighting with my cousin has already caused the loss of your sight. You don't want him taking anything else from you."

The Earl of Llew laughed, and the dark, unearthly sound sent a shiver running down Loris's spine. Kian's arm, which was about her waist, tightened.

"Have the Seymours not already taken enough, then?" Cadmaran asked. "I can only wonder at when you'll be satisfied."

"Desdemona is not yours," Dyfed informed him hotly. "She's not going back with you."

"I have not come to insist that she do so," the Earl of Llew replied, shocking them all.

"Then why have you come?" Kian demanded.

"First," he said, "to admit defeat in the matter of the *athanc,* and to offer my congratulations upon finishing with the beast."

Loris felt Kian straighten slightly, his stance wary.

"Do you jest, my lord?" he asked.

"Not at all," Lord Llew replied calmly. "You have come out the victor in the contest that I forced upon you, and it would be churlish of me to deny the fact. I offer my sincerest congratulations."

"A promise to never again raise one of the ancient creatures would be more welcome," Kian told him.

"I agree completely," Lord Llew said, all civility. "I give you that promise, on my honor."

"Don't trust him," Desdemona Caslin said, sitting forward in her chair. Dyfed, standing behind her, set a hand upon her shoulder. "He's lying."

"Before the Guardians, then," Lord Llew said. "And in their hearing. I give my vow that I shall never again make war upon Tylluan by raising one of the ancient creatures."

"What are you up to, Morcar?" Malachi asked. "This is not like you."

"What of Desdemona?" Dyfed asked. "Are you willing to let her go?"

"Ah, yes," the Earl of Llew said, nodding again toward where Desdemona sat, clearly able to feel the power that emanated from her. "The little matter of Miss Caslin, whose hand as my future bride I obtained in good faith from her father, and for whom I paid a great deal of money. By the laws of England, I could have you arrested and punished for kidnapping my betrothed. But we do not live by the laws of England," he said, "or, rather, I do not."

"The money will be repaid," Kian said. "We accept your disappointment in the matter, but the *unoliaeth* cannot be denied, even if we should wish it."

Lord Llew tilted his head. "I don't believe you understand what you're saying when you speak of repayment," he said.

"It would bankrupt Tylluan to part with such funds. I paid a very large sum for my intended bride."

"You will be repaid," Malachi said. "Just as I told you yesterday."

"Malachi," Kian said angrily.

"Tenfold, I believe you said," Cadmaran remarked. "I confess such a fortune might help to soothe the pain of my loss, but I believe it is the one who gains my bride who is supposed to make repayment. Is that not so, according to our laws?"

"I shall gladly pay," Dyfed said. "It may take time, but I'll find a way to do so."

"There is no need," Lord Llew said. His mocking smile died away, and his expression grew solemn. "I make a gift of her to you, Dyfed Seymour."

A stunned silence followed the words. They stared at the man who stood in the middle of the room, all of them unable to speak.

"I see that I have taken you by surprise," Cadmaran said. "But I assure you that I mean what I say. I release all claims that I may have had upon Desdemona Caslin, and give her freely and without demand for repayment to Dyfed Seymour. What is more, I wish you both happiness in your coming marriage, and give my solemn oath to never cause you either dismay or worry. I give this promise and make this gift, asking the Guardians to once more stand as my judges and witnesses. And that," he said, "is the end of what I have come to say. Good day."

He made a courteous bow, then turned about and, using the staff, found his way out of the room. The doors opened for him and closed behind him after he departed.

Kian and Loris exchanged glances, as did the others in the room.

"Is he in earnest?" Kian asked.

"I don't know," Malachi said. "He seems to be."

"He said it before the Guardians," Dyfed said, his tone filled with wonder. "It must be so."

Desdemona Caslin shook her head. "Something's wrong."

Professor Seabolt, who had been sitting silently in the farthest corner, lost in thought, suddenly rose to his feet. "It's the blood curse," he said, looking at Malachi for agreement. "The blood curse. Don't you understand?"

Malachi was on his way out the door before Professor Seabolt stopped speaking, with Kian at his heels. Morcar Cadmaran was still in the courtyard when they burst from the front doors. He was surrounded by several of his men, already mounted on their horses.

But Cadmaran wasn't paying attention to the horse that was being held for him or to anyone around him. He was standing with his hands held before him, the staff he had clutched only moments earlier fallen upon the ground.

"The devil," Malachi muttered. "He couldn't have known it would be enough."

"What is it?" Loris asked, coming to stand beside Kian. She saw what they were all looking at and found that she, too, was arrested by the sight.

Morcar Cadmaran was gazing at his hands.

He could see.

Slowly, the Earl of Llew turned and looked at the audience assembled on the steps of Castle Tylluan. His eyes moved knowingly over each face, coming to rest at last on Lord Graymar.

"I didn't know," Cadmaran murmured, his tone filled with the same amazement that Loris knew they all felt. "You put the thought in my head yesterday, on Bryn Chwilen, when you mentioned the *unoliaeth* and the blood curse. I only guessed that it would be enough to make recompense for my wrongs. And it *worked*." A wide smile grew upon his handsome face. "I can see. The curse has been lifted. Now, at last, Malachi," he said, "we are equals again."

"You'll *never* be his equal," Kian said curtly. "Sighted or not. You never were."

"I shall be," Cadmaran vowed. "Losing Desdemona was but a small price to pay to regain my sight. You will have to decide, in the future, whether it was worth gaining her for all the loss that you shall suffer. It is a war between us now, Malachi," he said, his black eyes filled with an intense hatred that Loris found frightening. "The Guardians may hear me as they please, but they cannot take my sight away again. They never lay the same curse upon one of our kind twice, and having lived in a hell of darkness these past three years, I fear nothing else."

"Put this foolishness behind you, Morcar," Malachi advised. "I don't wish to live in enmity with you."

"But I do," Lord Llew said. "And I will."

He mounted his horse and took the reins, controlling the massive beast with ease.

"I shall see you again soon, Lord Graymar. Good-bye, Desdemona, my pet," Lord Llew added. "I hope you'll be happy with your powerless husband. If he should begin to bore you, I would be glad to consider taking you back. You need only ask, my dear."

Desdemona's reply was to look at his fallen staff, which still lay upon the ground. Beneath her gaze the object exploded into thousands of tiny shards, causing the horses to whinny and shy away.

Cadmaran laughed with intense amusement and, calling for his men to follow, rode away.

The events of the day cast something of a pall on the night's celebration, but not for the people of Tylluan, who were glad to be rid of the *athanc* and tremendously pleased that their lord had taken Loris as his wife.

Cook grumbled about having to labor to create two festive meals in as many nights, but with Loris back in charge of the servants and preparations, the work went quickly.

The great hall was filled to overflowing with all the people of Tylluan, dining upon dilled salmon, roasted lamb, and beef stew, along with a fine leek soup and plenty of bread and cheese. There was wine to drink and good ale as well and all the music and laughter and singing and dancing that accompanied such celebrations. This time, the celebrants were careful not to break any dishes, and the only games that were played were those that involved the children.

Kian found it impossible to care about either the food or the celebration. A bathtub had been set up in his bedchamber, ready with soaps and lotions and soft towels. Water was being kept hot on the fire, and a bottle of French champagne had been brought up from the wine cellar and was waiting to be opened. He had instructed Cook to leave a basket filled with goods that required little preparation—breads, cheeses, some sweets and fruit—along with plates and utensils. He and Loris hadn't truly had a proper wedding night, a lack that Kian intended to remedy just as soon as they could possibly make a graceful exit.

As soon as the remains of the meal had been cleared, Kian took Loris's hand and stood. He opened his mouth to begin his speech of thanks and departure and then stopped.

"Someone's coming," he said.

Loris looked at him curiously. "Who? Surely Cadmaran wouldn't—"

"It isn't Cadmaran," Kian said quickly, aware of Malachi's intent gaze. "It's a mere mortal. Several mere mortals, in fact. They've crossed Tylluan's borders and are coming to the castle. Very quickly." He looked at his cousin, saying, wonderingly, "I can sense the presence of strangers within Tylluan, and know where they are. I've not been able to do so with any great accuracy before."

"Your powers have increased," Malachi said over the din in the hall. "You may have many such happy discoveries in the days to come."

"My grandfather," Loris murmured. "It must be my grandfather coming. Oh dear. I'm afraid he's going to be very angry. And all of this"—she motioned toward the merry dancing and singing taking place—"is going to seem very wild to him. I so wanted him to have a wonderful first impression of Tylluan."

"He will have, I promise you," Malachi said reassuringly. He rose from his chair and neared them. "Go and rest. Dyfed and Desdemona have already done so, and quite rightly, considering the events of the night and day. Your cousin Niclas and I will greet Lord Perham and keep him company. He will be quite content and pleased with all that he hears and sees."

"But, Malachi," Loris said, "I can't think it right to let you enchant my grandfather."

Lord Graymar smiled. "Can you not?" he asked, looking from one to the other. "Consider it a wedding gift."

"But—"

"You can speak with your grandfather first thing in the morning."

Kian cleared his throat, and Malachi quickly amended, "I mean to say, in the afternoon. Now go on with you both. I'll take care of everything."

Some hours later, as they lay together, comfortable and re-plete against the soft sheets of Kian's bed, Loris said sleep-ily, "I hope my grandfather is all right."

Kian kissed her hair, still damp from their leisurely bath. "If anyone can keep him happy, it's Malachi. I had the dis-tinct feeling when we left him in the great hall that he was looking forward to playing lord of the manor. The great Earl of Graymar in his element."

"He does it very well," Loris said. "I wonder why Malachi has never married. He's very popular with women—all the females that I met in London are half in love with him. Even the married ones."

"I don't know," Kian murmured. "I think perhaps he's never had the time. Being the *Dewin Mawr*, as well as the Earl of Graymar, must be very demanding. It's probably like already being married."

"But that's precisely why he needs a wife," Loris said. "We are so very useful to a husband."

Kian smiled and pulled her against him more closely. "That you are. Very, very useful."

"In many ways," she told him. "You must admit that your life would be far more difficult if I didn't manage the castle and arrange matters to make your days easier."

"You did that long before you became my wife," he said.

"But then I wasn't very, very useful."

"You were," he said, his warm hand pressing against her hip. "But not in the same way."

"And that's why Malachi needs a wife."

"I believe he already has a mistress who has proved quite useful."

Loris turned toward him, lying on her back as he leaned over her. "No, for the other reason."

"To be helpful and make his days easy?"

"To love him," she said, reaching up to caress his cheek. "To take care of him."

"Ah, I see," he murmured. "I can think of another reason for him to get a wife. Several others, actually."

"What are they?"

"To bring him joy with a simple glance," he said, softly kissing her lips. "To give him pleasure with a smile." He kissed her again. "To make him feel strong and whole with but a word. To make him want to rise in the morning just so that he can see her. Hear her voice."

"I'm not sure such a woman exists," she murmured.

"Aye, she does. But Malachi will have to find his own. I spent ten long years waiting for mine," he said, bringing his mouth to hers once more, "and I'm never going to lose her again."

Read on for an excerpt from

TOUCH OF DESIRE

Coming soon from St. Martin's Paperbacks

"GLAIN TARRAN, PEMBROKESHIRE, WALES
"APRIL 4, 1821, PAST MIDNIGHT
"CEREMONIAL GROUNDS

"The site is all that I could have hoped for, and far more. There are twenty enormous monoliths, paired together in a manner similar to those at Stonehenge, all of Welsh blue-stone. I can only guess at the site's date of origin, though it is classically Druidic in arrangement. The stones create a single, complete, perfect circle. Unlike other such sites, no stones have yet fallen.

"The main question"—at this point the wind began to blow so heartily that Sarah had to tether the edges of the page with her forearm—*"is why this fantastic remnant of our historical past has been kept so secret from the government of England and the people at large. Why do the Seymour family and local villagers so vigilantly hide it?"*

The wind apparently had had enough. Somehow, her glasses had slipped far enough down her irritatingly small nose to be snatched off by the wind. Flinging her knapsack aside, she grasped at the air, then went down on hands and knees to frantically search the ground.

"That is the outside of enough!" she informed the element hotly. "I *must* have my spectacles."

And that was how Malachi, the Earl of Graymar, came upon Miss Sarah Tamony.

To say that he was shocked would have been apt.

He had no notion of why she'd come or how she'd ended up in the most sacred and secret place in Glain Tarran, but he did know that he had to get rid of her as soon as possible.

By the time she'd finally circled his way and seen him, he'd decided upon a course halfway between terror and kindness. Extending one palm, he brought forth a small flame, only enough light to help the moon illuminate his face. Making his expression as foreboding as he dared, he said, over the wind, in a darkly stern tone, "What are you doing here?"

She pressed up to her knees and squinted at him, setting one hand over her wind-blown hair to hold it back from her forehead.

"Well, at present," she shouted over the elements, "I'm trying to find my spectacles."

The flame floating over Malachi's palm died away, and he felt himself gaping.

"What the devil are *you* doing on my lands!"

"I'm presently trying to find my spectacles. I don't suppose you might make it stop a moment"—she motioned toward the wind with a wave of one hand—"so that I might discover where they've gone?"

"Be silent!" Malachi told her angrily, then turned his attention back to the wind. *"Dwyn!"*

The wind began to blow along the ground, tumbling leaves and branches and, finally, a pair of battered spectacles, which landed near his feet.

Bending, Malachi picked the spectacles up and examined them in the moonlight.

"They're bent," he said curtly, holding them out to his visitor."

She didn't answer him directly, but spent a long time rubbing them clean with a bit of her skirt, before putting them on.

"Ah, that's better," she declared happily, gazing up at him, her face illuminated by the pale moonlight. "Do you remember me now, my lord?"

Malachi gazed back at her steadily, into a face that he knew well from description, but couldn't recall from memory. She was a beauty. An auburn beauty, with large blue eyes and fine, aristocratic features. A rare, intelligent beauty who knew how to talk her way into getting almost anything she wanted.

Miss Sarah Tamony was a dangerous female.